June

June

A NOVEL

MIRANDA BEVERLY-
WHITTEMORE

CROWN
NEW YORK

Copyright © 2016 by Miranda Beverly-Whittemore
All rights reserved.
Published in the United States by Crown, an imprint of the Crown Publishing Group, a division of Penguin Random House LLC, New York.
crownpublishing.com

CROWN and the Crown colophon are registered trademarks of Penguin Random House LLC.

Library of Congress Cataloging-in-Publication Data is available upon request.

ISBN 978-0-553-44768-2
Ebook ISBN 978-0-553-44769-9

Printed in the United States of America

Book design by Lauren Dong
Title page photograph © Genevieve Naylor/Corbis
Jacket design by Elena Giavaldi
Jacket photograph by Justin Carrasquillo

10 9 8 7 6 5 4 3 2 1

First Edition

For Grander,
who shared so many tales of her childhood a century ago,
and told me of the real Lemon Gray Neely

And for her daughter, my Mama,
who is always up for an adventure, even if—especially if—it's a
wild-goose chase off the beaten path

June

June 2015

CHAPTER ONE

———

OUSES DON'T ALWAYS DREAM. IN FACT, MOST DON'T. BUT once again, Two Oaks was dreaming of the girls—the one called June, who looked like a woman, and the one called Lindie, who looked like a boy. In the dream, June and Lindie lay together in what was, in that era, June's bedroom, just off the stairs.

It was dreaming that rescued Two Oaks out of its present state—from its third-floor ballroom wheeling with bats, down its dusty master staircase, into the foyer piled with mail addressed to the dead, and then back up the ruddy pine of the servant stairs—almost fooling the mansion into believing itself still on the precipice of adventure. The old house summoned the whispers swirling off the girls' tongues, the secrets scuttling inside their quick minds, the push of June's will and the pull of Lindie's desire.

Houses that dream are built for the ages (one or two perhaps, in every small American town). Once revered as grand homes, they are now merely called "buildings." They're the columned fortresses stranded on the back streets you pass on the way to visit elderly aunties; sights to whistle at while snapping a cell phone picture, before motoring on. Constructed by ambitious dreamers (in the case of Two Oaks, an oilman named Lemon Gray Neely, who broke ground on the lot in the heart of St. Jude, Ohio, in 1895), such grand estates spend their infancies priding under the touch of skilled craftsmen, certain they'll provide shelter to everyone who steps across their oak thresholds for centuries to come.

But after decades of relative emptiness, save the occasional mail carrier or handyman, after feeling the sun rake across their sooty floorboards on thousands of mornings, of enduring the undignified encroachment of ivy up their outsides, not to mention the mice nibbling the wainscoting, these houses finally accept the sad truth: they have been forgotten for good. Their foundations grow heavy with the memories of the great men who once burnished the banisters with their warm palms; of the diligent women who baked yeasty swaths of bread in their ovens; of the whistling boys who delivered light blue dairy through the milk doors; and the wild girls who clambered up the Corinthian columns to the second floor under the full moon, hoping for a glimpse of something new. Accepting their decline, these houses slip into their reveries and lose track of their place in the world. They slump their proverbial shoulders, nod to the side, and forget to notice when someone steps in from the snow with a suitcase and a pile of heavy boxes, and opens the chenille bedspread over the most comfortable mattress, and burns a can of Chef Boyardee on the only burner that still works.

But if Two Oaks was lonely, it was also lucky. Unlike other houses, at least it knew what it felt like to be full. At least it had gotten to have a Lindie and a June. Like an old retriever who, abandoned by his human family, lays his head upon the floor and sinks into the sweet fancies of the life he once knew—an exuberant towheaded toddler, a favorite shoe, the smoky waft of bacon—a house falling into decrepitude will luster to life remembering all that came before, which, in the case of Two Oaks, included the dark, terrifying night Lindie bashed in the man's head, his hot brains quivering on her fingertips, yes; but also the open, shimmering promise of the movie stars; the silky noose of the blackmail around everything the girls had come to love; the soft, open moans of the stolen kisses; and the baby.

CASSIE KNEW NOTHING of houses dreaming; she'd have balked. She only knew that since coming to St. Jude, Ohio, the previous December, sheltering in what she still thought of as her grandmother's house—she could not bring herself to call it the snobby-sounding "Two Oaks" with a straight face, or to think of it as her own—she'd had the most elaborate, vivid dreams. Cassie, twenty-five, was going through "a quarter-life crisis," and the house—where she'd never lived before, where even her grandmother hadn't lived very much since moving to Columbus to raise her—had, at first, provided a practical (if frigid) solution: a landing pad just before Christmas, when it became obvious Cassie needed to clear out of Jim's Williamsburg loft, specifically, and New York, in general.

The basement's rusty furnace was broken (as were the roof and the stove and who knew what else); the grizzled handyman she called the next morning jerry-rigged a temporary solution to keep the pipes from freezing, loaned her a space heater, and urged her to call the repair service for an estimate. But now it was June; Cassie still hadn't called. To be fair, the pipes hadn't frozen, but she knew that was pure luck, and she was a fool to think that luck would hold. The roof was, well, soggy in parts, if she was being honest, especially in one of the closets off the ballroom—and keeping the door closed probably wasn't the most mature solution to the problem. Nor was it a great sign that you could stand in the cellar and detect daylight through a chink in the foundation. Cassie didn't know much about houses, but she did know that was bad.

Every day, Cassie woke intending to call the repairmen. All she had to do was pick up the handset of the old-fashioned rotary phone in the round office at the front of the house, spiral the numbers with her pointer finger, adopt a casual, firm tone, and solicit the services of a handful of experts. Every day, she watched herself not do it. Perhaps it was because she couldn't afford it, but the truth was, she didn't really know if she couldn't, because, since November, when she'd inherited the fourteen thousand dollars left in her grandma's account—shockingly less than she'd assumed she'd find there—and set up automated payments via her now neglected e-mail account, she had just, well, kind of ignored every bill, letter, and phone call that had come her way.

She didn't like this particular aspect of her character, nor did she want to spend the winter in a freezing house. In fact, on a daily basis, Cassie forced herself to remember the discomfort of awakening to iced nostrils and a raw throat. She spent a significant portion of her daylight hours wracked with anxiety about the squishy ceiling in the closet directly above her bed. But nothing could get her to call. Maybe she was drawn toward the notion that the freezing of pipes and the risk of roof collapse were exactly the punishing strife she deserved after leaving a good man like Jim, not to mention breaking her grandmother's heart and being too proud and foolish to see that the old woman was dying.

The vibrant dreams that Two Oaks offered made it possible to ignore human needs like heat and shelter. Cassie didn't know the dreams' origins—she believed, as most of us do, that they were born of her own subconscious—but she did know, without exploring why, that these nighttime dramas were much better than anything her waking life offered in that chilly house on those dark, wintry days. Come April, when the tangle of flora out the windows started to turn a hundred shades of emerald, Cassie was sleeping fourteen, sixteen hours a night.

The house nestled further into its thick, auburn slumber, gathering Cassie under its drowsy wing. On the few occasions a sneeze or shattered plate forced it to notice the human in its midst, it brushed aside her potential, considering her presence a temporary state, like the grackles nesting under the eaves, or the family of possums who liked that spot under the milk door. The girl was sure to pass with the seasons too.

THE DREAM OF June and Lindie, which Two Oaks and Cassie shared, went, as it always did, like this:

They were about to enter the month of June. Houses don't care much about time—like many inanimate objects (except for clocks), they don't really understand it—but that particular June of that particular year marked a clear Before and After in Two Oaks's journey from habitation to emptiness, and so the red-numbered calendar hanging above Apatha's cast-iron stove was duly noted: 1955.

Lindie and June lay on June's bed together, in the gilded light cast by June's ballerina lamp, on the night that served as bridge between May and June. Lindie watched June giggle at the notion of being someone named June inside the month of June, a bounty Lindie had been planning to point out all day, since long before she'd clambered up what Uncle Lemon insisted she call the "porte cochere"—the overhang above the drive. Lindie's skin still clung with the damp, warm night sawing with cricket song. First she'd climbed into June's window, then into her bed.

The girls were surrounded by what Lindie had, over the past three years (since June's arrival at Two Oaks), come to think of as her best friend's most essential possessions: the watercolors and jewel-toned hair ribbons sashaying when the cool hush of the fan raked them; a round china box painted with rosettes; the dainty shoes lined up by the door.

A plate of Apatha's oatmeal cookies, of which June had eaten one (and which Lindie, having already downed four, was planning to finish), waited on the side table.

June sat up to examine her face in the mirror. She began to hum a Chopin piano concerto. Lindie swiped another cookie and added the melody to the list of details locked inside her mind, noting June's slightly sharp pitch on the higher notes; another, lonelier night, Lindie would be able to close her eyes in her small, drab bedroom just across the street and conjure up the pleasurable ache she felt here, and imagine herself still inside June's universe.

Lindie opened one of the brightly colored movie magazines she'd splayed across June's bed. *Screen Stars, Photoplay, Silver Screen, Picture-goer;* she'd tied them together with a piece of rough twine for the climb up, and was wondering if she could get away with pinching one of June's ribbons—the emerald one, maybe, which June never wore—for the trip down. From out across the flat, sultry midwestern night floated the faint putter of an old engine, the mewling of a cat, and always, ever, the crickets. School was out. In June's case, it was out for good; she was eighteen to Lindie's fourteen, and she was going to be a bride.

Of late, June's mind swelled with white chiffon and boutonnieres, with chicken cordon bleu and a tall, tiered cake covered in rosettes. The fact that her fiancé, Artie, had been gone from St. Jude for seven months, not to mention that she could count the conversations she'd had with this future husband on one hand, had receded behind the promise of the grand affair her mother, Cheryl Ann, and Artie's brother, Clyde, had been planning since that October day Artie had slipped a simple gold band onto June's finger and promised her a diamond within the year.

June had excelled at geometry; she liked rules. The wedding would fix all that had come undone: her father Marvin's death in Korea; the loss of the family home up on the grand "Golden Block" in Lima upon the discovery of Marvin's gambling debts; and June and Cheryl Ann's subsequent tumble from Lima's high society onto the sawdust floor of small-town St. Jude. A tangential, distant relative had taken them in: Lemon Gray Neely, June's great-uncle by marriage. He'd housed them in Two Oaks's corner bedrooms.

June wondered if Uncle Lem (as her mother insisted she call him) had chosen to build his home with yellow bricks because they matched his name. Rumor had it he'd always been an eccentric, even before the apoplexy that all but silenced him. June was grateful for his charity; of course she was. But Two Oaks was the only mansion in St. Jude, and so, where June had once been one of many girls who inhabited grand homes, in her new life, she was an oddity. She'd started at Memorial High part of the way through sophomore year, when everyone already had friends, and, anyway, she wasn't rich anymore, just living in the shadow of someone else's money, although her mother seemed to forget the difference all the time.

"Wear this one," June said, spreading out the cotton dress covered in strawberries that her bust had outgrown the year before. June was grateful for Lindie too, for the younger girl's devotion, even if managing her felt, at times, like batting at a doggedly optimistic mosquito. June had chosen Lindie as her bridesmaid; she was hoping to wrestle the increasingly feral child into the seafoam chiffon number she'd picked for the July 3 wedding. A bridesmaid had to wear a dress, and though June hadn't seen Lindie in one in more than a year, she wasn't going to let that discourage her. A simple cotton frock in honor of all the excitement tomorrow seemed like a reasonable first step. They'd have to stuff the front, maybe pin up the skirt, but anything was better than Lindie's current state, which summoned to mind a Victorian chimney sweep.

Lindie moved her filthy feet aside to accommodate the strawberry dress. June gestured at the other girl's matted bob and stained dungarees and said, "You're so pretty, Lindie. Why do you want to hide it?" Lindie really was pretty, under there somewhere. She had high cheekbones and forest green eyes with specks of gold that lit up like fire when she laughed. June smiled indulgently as she pressed Lindie's weak spot: "Just try it on. You know as well as I do that the *Erie Canal* people won't cast you if you show up like this."

Lindie frowned; June was right. She rubbed the fine cotton between her fingers. She told herself that the matter of the dress was a mere blemish on what would otherwise be a month of gorgeous possibility. For where June treasured the notion of her upcoming wedding, Lindie desired nothing more than to be cast as an extra in *Erie Canal,* the most extraordinary thing that had ever happened in St. Jude: Hollywood was coming, and tomorrow at that.

Trucks of equipment had already rumbled into town. All day, covered garment carts had rattled into Memorial High, and notices had gone up on the trees of Center Square, asking for volunteers to appear in costume in the background—"extras," they were called, as if they were the cherries on top of the ice cream sodas served down at Schillinger's Drug. But even though the night before, Lindie had overheard her father and his friends discussing the imminent arrival of the film crew, she would only truly believe it when she saw it. Something so good seemed just plain impossible.

"I'll put the dress on first thing tomorrow," she said. A dress wasn't just a dress anymore. It stood for the lives she saw laid out before both June and herself, on the far side of the Hollywood fantasy. Quiet, adult lady lives marked by sanitary belts held on by metal clasps under rubber underwear, of regular bridge parties and dinner clubs, of loose face powder that smelled like old people. She flopped back onto the bed.

"What if you try it now?" June asked brightly, turning back to the wardrobe, riffling again through the other options, although she knew the rest had too many adornments for Lindie's taste, not to mention too much room in the bustline. "We could do your hair. I'll put some rouge on your cheeks. Just to make sure it all fits together."

But Lindie wasn't budging.

"We'll get up extra early, then," June said, in a tone she liked to imagine she'd someday use to address her children. Lindie smiled, relieved, and June thought to ask how Lindie wanted to do her hair, but instead she just smoothed Lindie's temple, which sent the other girl's heart aflutter, then settled down beside her.

"What do you think they're like?" Lindie asked in a romantic daze, eyeing Jack Montgomery on the magazine cover that lay at June's elbow. Before Lindie'd heard of *Erie Canal,* Jack Montgomery was far down her list of favorite movie stars, well below Cary Grant and Bogie, and she'd have sniffed at the mention of Diane DeSoto—a studio actress who'd never been, until now, in a leading role. But Jack Montgomery and Diane DeSoto were (knock on wood) coming to St. Jude, which meant they were a hundred times better than every other movie star in the world.

"Do you think Diane DeSoto really washes her face in milk? How tall is Jack Montgomery? Do you think they're really in love? Will you audition too? You'll try for it, won't you, June? I know for sure I'd get cast if I looked like you."

"Hush." June wouldn't pretend she wanted to be cast. Nor would she tolerate the idea of Lindie crushed by rejection, when all she had to do was dress like a proper girl who washed her face every now and then; how could she be so blind to the advantage of those small improvements? June considered whether she was strong enough to wrestle Lindie into the dress herself, but she knew the other girl would beat her out of sheer cussedness.

"I heard there might be speaking parts," Lindie pressed, even though she'd made that up. "I bet you could get one."

"I can't audition." June rose from the bed and checked her face in the mirror again, an annoying habit she'd been exhibiting in recent months, along with rinsing her hair with apple cider vinegar to give it shine.

"You absolutely can."

"No, Lindie." June's voice was firm. "I'm getting married. It's not appropriate."

Lindie sat up. "You are not getting married." June's sharp look in the mirror told her to adjust her tone. "I only mean you can't get married without a groom, June." Arthur Danvers had been gone for months—since October—and who knew where? Supposedly, he was overseeing his brother's business interests in the South, but Lindie wasn't so sure. "And even if he was here, do you really want to spend your whole life looking up at that pasty face?"

June's mouth tightened. But now all Lindie could think of was the stiff way Artie Danvers had taken June's arm back in October before their fateful turn around Center Square. He was a thirty-five-year-old bachelor funded by his older brother. As far as Lindie was concerned, the only way he'd snagged a girl like June was because she had a greedy mother desperate to sell her daughter off to the highest bidder. "Artie Danvers is a nothing! He's a straight line. He's a cold bath." Her arms stuttered in the space between them, hands pulling for the words that would finally make June see sense. "He's—"

"Stop."

Was that June's mother's step in the upstairs hall, just on the other side of the door? The girls froze, straining to hear above the purr of the fan blades, waiting for a knock, for the scent of Pond's cold cream, for Cheryl Ann to discover June had locked herself in, and insist she open the door right this instant, young lady. But no knock came, and, after a good long exhalation, June's shoulders relaxed. She eased herself onto the bed again, brown hair haloing her face on the pillow.

Lindie put herself down carefully beside June. "My point is, you can't marry someone you don't love."

"And how do you know I don't love him?"

"Because I know."

June smiled again, a weary smile, as if Lindie's affection was something to be endured. "You're sweet to me."

Lindie gentled her voice. "We can leave right now. On my bicycle. We'll pedal over to Idlewyld and hide out until we come up with our next step." As the name of that place slipped off her tongue, Lindie felt the memory of a frog quivering in her hands, out on the edge of that lake five miles away, on the night she'd had June all to herself and allowed herself to dream it could always be just them.

"Little Bear." June tucked Lindie's bob behind her ear and fingered her earlobe. She rubbed it once, twice, as if for good luck, as if, like Lindie, she was memorizing the moment.

Lindie thought, hoped, there would be more. But June turned and nestled into sleep.

Imagine them then, two girls curled in a corner bedroom of Two Oaks, breathing in the metal fan's whir. The floorboards shift and moan. The pocket doors hiccup. Lindie lays her arm across June's warm hip. She keeps her eyes propped open as long as she is able, fancying herself on a still night aboard the *Pequod,* her shipmates at rest, the great white whale fathoms below. Her mind trades the tush-tush-tush of the Ohio crickets for the thrash of a wild ocean she's yet to hear. Her eyelids succumb to the darkness. Only then does sleep steal her.

CHAPTER TWO

———

ASSIE WAS ALREADY HALFWAY TO THE BEDROOM DOOR when she properly awoke. The world was shrieking. She knew the horrible sound wasn't coming from inside her head, but it was already doing damage in there, clawing at the quiet she'd stored up. She could guess what would come next: an anxious headache, a churning stomach, maybe even the sharp urge of diarrhea, tingling palms, the light too bright even with the blinds and curtains closed, with the eye mask on, with a pillow over her head. Until only moments before, she'd been so sweetly nestled in the palm of that dream of those two girls, which she realized had taken place in the very same bed she now called her own, although the room had been full in the dream, of ribbons and watercolors, and also of a succulent devotion that made her ache now that it was out of reach.

The modern world clawed in. The house howled a dreadful, screeching protest. Cassie couldn't bear it. She grasped at the floor for clothes, coming up with a dish towel. She realized she didn't have her glasses on—of course, that was the first problem, she was awake enough now to realize that she was blind—and grappled at the side table and cursed aloud when she heard her glasses crash to the floor. All that time the vicious noise continued. She understood, once she found her glasses and the room crisped into view, that the sound was one only a place as old as Two Oaks could make, as though it were clearing its throat of ancient, thick phlegm, coughing and groaning in the process. But that didn't mean she knew what it meant, why it had begun, or that she liked it.

Then, for a fleeting moment, the clamor ended. Cassie experienced a blessed instant in which the house was just as it was supposed to be—not exactly silent (the dog barking down the street, the rattle of the windows atop the porch line as a breeze scuttled west), but contained. Her eardrums buzzed against the silence. She looked around the bright corner bedroom—the chenille bedspread she'd kicked aside in her sleep, the dust-filled lace valances framing her view like fancy sideways parentheses, the glass of water she had managed not to push off the scratched side table—and remembered herself: she was naked, but not insane. She could resist her body's desire to break at the threat of the world.

But then the sound came back, eight million times worse than fingernails on a chalkboard, and infinitely louder. Cassie wrapped the bedspread around her body and blinked her way out her door and into the upstairs hall. Out here, the clang rattled her jaw. She could feel the sweet residue of the dream sifting off her. She momentarily considered going back into the bedroom to try to grasp the last golden bits of it— two girls, was it? Two girls, both churning with their future prospects— but already she knew it was futile, that the dream was lost. The air on her twenty-five-year-old skin let her know she was all the way back into herself. Released. And if she stood here much longer, she felt certain she would lose her sense of hearing.

She stepped down the stairs, sun refracting through the stained-glass window and casting a green patch onto her right pinkie toe. The house blared on. In the same moment she realized that it was the doorbell she was hearing, it occurred to her that it might be someone from the bank who was ringing it. Anxiety swooped over her as she thought of all that mail she'd watched the blue-suited mailman stuff through the slot in the front door day after day: past-due notices, letters from the bank, from the legal firm that had handled the transfer of the estate. She marveled at her own irresponsibility. The broken furnace, the leaky roof, the cracked foundation. To be the person who lost, or destroyed, the family home after more than a hundred years seemed inevitable and tragic. But then, she was an orphan, her grandmother was dead, and she had no siblings; could she really be faulted for being a screwup if everyone had abandoned her?

Cassie's ankles were briefly patchworked in a rosy bit of light from the stained glass as she stepped down toward her fate. The bank, the bank. Fourteen thousand dollars had sounded like enough money back in November, when she'd gotten the check and the deed, but she hadn't opened any of the cellophane-paned notices, and the phone had been ringing off the hook since yesterday. Shit. It had to be the bank.

By the time Cassie descended the stately home's quarter-hewn oak staircase, slippery from a century of floor wax despite the grime, the bell—it was laughable to call it a bell, really, but there was no such word as *doorblast*—had shut up. Wrapped in the old bedspread she'd pulled from the bottom of the four-poster, Cassie squinted down the ample foyer—dark no matter how sunny the day—and out the front door. She saw movement, but it was far away, and hard to make sense of through the lace curtain that sat against the thick, leaded glass. In between her and the door lay a great heap of envelopes, delivered in manageable daily bits by the whistling mailman, whose face she'd never managed to see; she usually spied on him from the second-story window.

She hesitated for a moment. Thought of going back to bed. But then the phone started up, relentless and desperate as it had been since yesterday morning. The touch of outside—first the doorbell, then the phone—unsettled her in the way little had since she'd moved to St. Jude. Maybe they were repossessing the house. Maybe she hadn't paid enough taxes. Maybe maybe maybe, and as Cassie's mind swirled with the day she feared she'd be having—sweaty palms, dry mouth, pulse scurrying away from her—the anxiety charged up and changed, like quicksilver, into bold anger. Cassie strode through the foyer, kicking the tangle of envelopes out of her way. Screw the bank. Screw whatever they, or anyone else, thought they could take from her. Her grandmother had left this house to Cassie and Cassie alone, and Cassie was allowed to do whatever she wanted here, even sleep until noon in order to spend more time with imaginary people.

Cassie's footsteps sent the crystal chandelier rattling above her. The framed watercolor still lifes quaked as she strode to the heavy oak door. She threw it open.

Summer buzzed.

It hit her like a hammer, a day like this, too much light and color, too many wild roses with too many insects drinking from their hearts. Jogging away from her, down the front walk, was a man in a gray suit, smartphone to his ear. The faint dulling of wind chimes, a tractor roaring up the road, wisps of clouds across the sky like lace netting over a blue dress. Her first impulse, even after six months, was to reach for her camera, to think aperture and focus and light, which way to shoot, what to place at the center of the frame. Her palms itched, her mouth watered; it would be a good picture, or at least the chance to make one. But no; she pushed that desire away. She didn't do that, didn't believe in it, anymore.

To distract herself, she focused on the stranger moving away from her. He was compact. His shoulder blades stretched against the slate gabardine, as though advertising how a jacket was supposed to fit a man. He was nearly to the sidewalk.

"What?" she yelled after him. She regretted the word the instant it slipped from her mouth. She was naked, after all, and wrapped, like a toddler, in a bedspread. Cassandra Danvers was no prophet, but, as the man turned, she instantly understood that she'd just taken the first step to dismantling her hard-won solitude. It was the direct way he looked at her, as though they already shared some kind of binding contract, one from which she would not easily escape.

CHAPTER THREE

———

E SPRINTED BACK UP THE PATH LIKE SHE WAS SAVING HIS
life. Even though she'd essentially become a hermit, Cassie could
still read people like a book. This man coming toward her with a
furrowed brow was stressed out. And much closer to her age—couldn't
have been a day over thirty—than she'd guessed when she spotted his
professional-looking shoulders from behind.

He mounted the groaning wooden steps. Her name trembled out of
his mouth with a question at the end. He pocketed the smartphone and
rushed across the porch. The phone inside the office stopped ringing;
the grackles nesting to the left of the front door squawked to fill the
silence.

Sunlight ricocheted off the tiles that still remained on the Two Oaks
porch. They were gray now, and wiggled in their settings, like diamonds
in an inherited wedding band. Still, even more than a hundred years
old, they were lustrous enough to reflect the sun's beams and make this
man approaching appear to glow. Cassie lifted her hand to block the
glare. He'd been the one calling since yesterday, she understood in a
wave of mistrustfulness; the house phone had stopped ringing the moment he pressed end on his cell.

"I'm Nick Emmons."

His hand was out for a shake, but his eyes darted everywhere but her,
assessing. She followed his gaze up to the dry rot along the crossbeams of
the roof, then to the chipping column at the porch's western corner. She
felt as she had in the hospital, holding her grandmother's wilted hand,
wanting to shout, "This isn't her! You don't even know her!" to the well-
intentioned nurses, with their charts and machines. All he saw here was
a wreck. She narrowed her eyes at this stranger, imagined his foot breaking through one of the ancient floorboards that lined the porch's tile.
He'd be trapped waist-high, out of reach of the doorbell. She'd steal his

smartphone and go back to bed and blame the whole thing on a house with a mind of its own.

But now a breeze carried the scent of him, which was a bit like woodsmoke and a bit like Speed Stick, the green kind, the kind Cassie's first crush, the high school student who'd mowed the lawn in Columbus, had worn. Here stood a good-smelling, impeccably dressed man, washed in the scent of Cassie's early erotic fantasies, the corners of his mouth now pulling up at the sight of her; she couldn't pretend she didn't like the way the hushed blue of his tie played off the gray of the suit, or how a cowlick detoured a sprig of hair off his forehead.

"This place is amazing," he said, and she found herself delighted by surprise.

But it was best to rip off the Band-Aid. "You from the bank?" she asked, pulling the bedspread tight, enjoying the nubble of chenille under her fingertips.

"Eighteen ninety-five? 'Ninety-six?" He sized up the semicircle of yellow brick that framed the front door. "Was this the original entrance? Never seen anything like it."

"Uh," Cassie said, then repeated her question about the bank, which he patently refused to answer. He tapped his foot against the slackened tiles, then turned to take in the view from the front door; she guessed that was his Ford Fiesta out front. A pickup pulled by, the only glimpse of the driver a tattooed arm out the open window accompanied by the twang of the country station. Nick surveyed the roof of the porch again before turning back and asking about the landline. Did she ever pick up? Why didn't she have an answering machine? Did she have a cell? E-mail? She was incredibly hard to get in touch with, did she know that? Cassie watched this Nick Emmons unconsciously pull his cell out twice, both times punching in his secret code, opening up e-mail and text, before switching it off and slipping it back into its home, the pocket over his heart. He was a man who would not hold still.

Cassie thought—and told herself not to think—of Jim. Jim, with his oft-disconnected landline, depending on how tight on funds he was that month. Jim, who, when everyone else went wireless, and Cassie mocked and cajoled him to join the modern age, had been resolute. Jim, who never shaved, and was close enough to fifty that she'd never dared

ask how many years he had on her, who didn't own a suit, and show-
ered only when absolutely necessary. Cassie didn't exactly miss him, and
she knew that ending things had been the right, if painful choice. But
with the arrival of this well-dressed, good-smelling, nosy, busy man, she
found her mind retreating to that unmade bed on the floor of Jim's studio, his paint-stained fingertips playing scales up her spine.

"What do you want?" she asked bluntly, trying to push through this
strange fog that seemed to have dulled her sensibility.

"Oh." Nick's smile faltered. "Right." He cleared his throat and lost
his charge. "Could I come in for a bit?"

They both saw at once that this would not be nearly enough to earn
him entry. He tried again. "I'm here about your—an—inheritance."

So he was from the bank after all. Cassie felt her jaw clench. She
wished she had some clothes on for this fight, but if the time to have it
was now, so be it. "That money is mine fair and square. She left it to me.
I know the house needs a lot of help, but she owned it outright, which
means I own it outright now, and I may not look like I know much
about money and houses and that kind of thing, but I do know you
can't just take it from me until I've had sufficient time to—"

He waved his hand to stop her right there. "I don't know anything
about that. I'm here about money you've just, well, as of yesterday,
you've inherited from someone—a relative?"—he seemed to be having
a wrestling match with his own words, as if every one he uttered was
up for debate—"someone"—he settled for that safe word, nodding dili-
gently over it—"someone I'm not sure you've met . . ." He peered over
her shoulder, into the darkness of the foyer, then tilted his head as he
met her eyes again. He looked surprised when their gazes matched, as
if she'd scalded him. "I'd really love to come in." He cleared his throat.
"To fill you in." He gained confidence, rivering his fingers over the
brass filigree that lay around the doorbell, then looking back at her with
unbridled enthusiasm. "I had no idea you live in such a treasure. This
should be on the register." She frowned. He reined himself in. "Can
I . . . can I come in? It's important."

No, she thought, no, you can't, I'll be the one who decides what's important. But maybe the house wanted him, because, before Cassie said
yes, she knew she was going to say it. When a gentleman came calling,

you learned his business over a pitcher of lemonade served in the front parlor; that had been her grandmother's way.

"I don't have anything on," Cassie said. A quick blush touched Nick's cheeks, just as Cassie caught the scent of him again. A third note, something like juniper, hit high in her nasal passages, where it would linger. She clutched the bedspread. She felt her face grow hot, unexpectedly hot. She'd meant to say, or should have meant to say, something appropriate, like "Fine; just give me a minute." She turned abruptly in to the house. Blind in the dark foyer, she waded through the snowdrift of mail, cringing at the crinkle of paper under the soles of her feet. The pile of correspondence had reached an untenable state; she could see this clearly now that Nick Emmons had followed her inside.

She reached for the banister just as her eyes adjusted. An inheritance, from a relative? But it didn't have to do with Two Oaks? What could that mean? A mistake, most likely; she didn't have any relatives to speak of. Or maybe it was some kind of scam. Maybe Nick Emmons was a stalker, someone who smelled just like Aaron Wilson-Myers precisely because he knew Cassie would go weak in the knees for a man who smelled like Aaron Wilson-Myers, and he was soundlessly slipping up the stairs behind her. At the landing now, she glanced back in alarm, but no, there Nick was, just where she'd left him, turning in wonder at the vast foyer above him, at the curved pocket doors of the round office, at the brass lion's head on the front doorplate, as though he'd never been anywhere so beautiful, and Cassie felt unexpectedly flattered and undeniably proud.

CHAPTER FOUR

———

CASSIE DRESSED FROM THE DIRTY PILE THAT HAD BEEN growing like mold around the outskirts of her bedroom. Once decent, she pushed the weeks' worth of unwashed detritus into the wardrobe, and the rest of it to the far side of her bed, just in case Nick happened to peek in. She laughed at her strange logic. Why would he ever just peek in? Then she made the bed. Why was she making the bed? Why did she feel the need to sniff her armpit and dab on Secret? She was not going to sleep with Nick Emmons, a man she did not know, a man with a message about some mysterious inheritance. She went to the mirror and pulled her hair into a greasy ponytail.

Instead of heading back down the master staircase, Cassie padded across the open upstairs hall, lit by the three fleur-de-lised stained-glass windows in yellow, grass, and rose. She passed three of the home's ample bedrooms, then turned in to the tight, dark passageway that led, to the left, toward the servant hall and stairs, and, straight ahead, into the fourth, underfurnished bedroom.

Into the ruddy servant hall she went. The red pine that lined the walls reminded her, uncomfortably, of a coffin, especially as she glanced into the maid's room and wondered what it must have been like to sleep every night in that tight box above the kitchen.

There'd been a black maid at Two Oaks once, if Cassie was remembering right. Cassie had seen a picture in one of her grandmother's albums. The woman was very old, older looking than Cassie's grandmother had been when she died, hunched and gnarled and skinny but dressed in an apron. To think of making an old lady cook and clean for you. "It was different then," her grandmother had explained primly when Cassie asked. "She'd been at Two Oaks for years. Where would you have her go?" And Cassie had bitten her lip about rich, male racists; one never questioned her grandmother's precious uncle Lem, even though he was sixty years gone.

At the lip of the stairs, Cassie leaned forward and listened for Nick. Nothing. She checked the window; the side street was empty, as it always was this time of day, just porches and lawns, everyone either at their jobs down at the plant or crocheting blankets in front of their morning shows. She wondered if anyone had taken notice of her gentleman caller. She supposed they couldn't think any worse of her, the wayward granddaughter of St. Jude's most upstanding citizen. Everyone knew that she hadn't made it back in time to do much except sit by the old woman's bedside. In the grocery store, or as they eyed her from their front porch swings, she resisted the urge to cry out that it wasn't her fault; her grandmother had kept news of the brain cancer from her. But of course Cassie knew it ran deeper than that, that plenty of things were her fault, and even if she hadn't delivered her grandmother to a painful, lonely death, she'd done plenty to contribute to the disappointing, lonely life that had immediately preceded it.

Cassie stepped down gingerly—the stairs were straight and simple, creaky but secret. She skipped the fourth, noisy step, wondering, as she did so, why she was hiding in her own home.

On the last step, Cassie leaned against the pine wall to listen. She could hear a murmur from the front of the house. That smartphone again. Her stomach snarled. She ducked into the tight hallway and then into the kitchen, thinking to grab herself a bite. But then she heard her grandmother's inconvenient voice at the back of her mind: "Make every guest welcome." Damn those hostess genes.

A jar of green olives stuffed with pimientos—into a white-ridged ramekin. A half-eaten bag of sour cream and onion potato chips that weren't as damp as they might have been—into a cut-glass bowl. She sawed the mold off a hunk of cheddar that had been in the icebox for so long that she couldn't remember buying it. Everything went onto the pressed melamine tray her grandmother had used for TV dinners. Cassie added a carafe of flat 7UP. At least it was cold.

The doorway connecting the kitchen to the rest of the house had always been divided in half all the way down to the doorsill; pine on the service side, oak for company. The tray rattled as Cassie stepped over that line into the foyer, the hollow rib cage at the center of the house, which connected the front door, straight ahead, to both the front and back parlors at Cassie's one and four o'clocks respectively, to the kitchen straight behind her, then the dining room at seven, and, beside that, the master staircase soaring up past the stained-glass windows toward the two floors above. At Cassie's nine o'clock, the foyer tapered out toward a side door that led underneath that overhangy thing where people had once waited for their horse-drawn carriages—her grandmother had called it something fancy she couldn't for the life of her remember—and, finally, tucked beside the front door at her eleven o'clock, stood the architectural wonder of the house, a cylindrical office for which the infamous Uncle Lem had imported a curved mantelpiece and windows. By the time Cassie was in residence, the office's curved doors were wedged halfway open, off their tracks; at least that wasn't her fault.

No sign of Nick as she waded through the pile of mail, hoping not to spill the 7UP. Almost to the front door, starting to believe Nick might, in fact, be there to kill her, Cassie heard him sharply note, "Nick, calling for Max." Then a pause. His voice was coming from the front parlor. "Yes, yes, I know, but he'll have to come through me first." Another pause. "Because that's how she wants it." Cassie turned in to the double-wide doorway just to the right of the front door and found Nick tucked, quite comfortably, into the corner of her grandmother's yellow velvet davenport, the davenport that had moved to Columbus when the old woman came to care for Cassie, and then, once Cassie was off to college in New York, went back to its spot by the wide corner windows of her grandmother's favorite room in the world, fluttering with lace curtains.

"There you are," Cassie said as he begged off—"Have to call you back, Sarah"—drew his phone back from his ear, pressed end, and stood—a bygone, gentlemanly gesture.

"Sit," Cassie commanded as she set the tray down on the busted footstool between them. She'd propped up the broken leg with two two-by-fours nailed together, which worked just fine as long as you didn't move it.

His eyes danced over the ornate plasterwork that connected ceiling to walls. "Lemon Gray Neely," he said, shaking his head with warmth, as if he loved the guy. "What a visionary. Can you imagine what it must have taken to get this neoclassical treasure designed and built in a little town like St. Jude in the nineteenth century?"

"Uh, how do you know about Lemon Gray Neely?"

He tapped his phone proudly. "Googled it. Not a whole lot of information, but at least a couple of hits." Then he rubbed his hand along the dark wood of the doorway, taking in the oak mantelpiece inlaid with red tile and the grandfather clock at the edge of the room, which had clanged and ticked so loudly when Cassie moved in back in December that she'd let the pendulum wind down again.

Cassie allowed herself, for a moment, to see past the crumbling plaster, the spiderwebs spanning the corners, the dust bunnies gathered along the edges of the room. She saw what the place really looked like: shabby, yes, uncared for, sure, but undeniably majestic. She checked Nick again; he seemed genuinely awed.

But she wanted to know about this inheritance. She popped a chip into her mouth. It melted too quickly. She dragged the horribly uncomfortable floral armchair from in front of the fireplace, hoping the action would break Nick out of his reverie. He offered to help, but she waved him off, even though the thing weighed at least fifty pounds, all horsehair and mahogany. It dated from who knew when, and expelled dust when she plopped down in it.

She noticed him eyeing the olives. "Want some?"

"I had a shake on the plane."

"The plane." She lifted one eyebrow mysteriously. "The plane from where?"

He cleared his throat. There it was again—the apprehension she'd first noticed on the porch. "Los Angeles."

"City of Angels!" It came out like an old lady would say it, which she usually didn't care about; she'd accepted her fate. Still, she tried to modulate her voice. "A shake, huh? Like, chocolate, or . . . ?"

"Spinach. Kale. Ginger."

She lifted the olives and shook them in front of him. "Imagine the chemicals."

He took one. Popped it in his mouth.

"So," she said, after watching him eat a chip (small victories), "you mentioned an inheritance."

A tiny frown formed between Nick Emmons's groomed brows. He folded his hands before him, like a child playing businessman. "Do you know who Jack Montgomery is?"

A black-and-white head shot of a movie star from a different era floated to the surface of Cassie's mind. In the picture, the man was leaning toward the camera ever so slightly, hands folded under his chin. He was handsome in an old-fashioned way, with a heavy, dark brow and brooding lips. Where had she seen that picture? It had been taken earlier than the other really famous photo that popped up in her mind's eye: a full-color shot of him chewing at the end of a stalk of wheat, gazing out across an empty, golden field. That particular image was, Cassie knew, a still from that manly movie involving horseback riding, guns, a pretty girl, and plenty of ennui. A pre-Jim boy had taken her to a screening at Film Forum. *Absalom's Ride*? But Jack Montgomery was primarily famous for being famous by the time Cassie was born; he was old, older than her grandmother.

"Jack Montgomery passed away three days ago," Nick said. "Turns out he left everything to you." He said that last sentence casually, but he watched her as he said it. "So I suppose you could say I'm here because of your grandmother. I'm here because of June."

CHAPTER FIVE

———

WHAT FOLLOWED NICK'S MENTION OF THE NAME JUNE
was unprecedented. Yes, the dreams Cassie had been having were all-consuming; yes, they stayed with her during the day; yes, she ruminated on them, sometimes all day long; but they were dreams—just dreams. None of what happened in them actually showed up in her real, waking life. But then Nick said her grandmother's name, and, suddenly, she felt everyone arrive. "Everyone" was the constellation of people in Two Oaks's dreams, a crush of laborers and guests, of those who'd once built the house and maintained it, who'd filled Two Oaks in that party dream Cassie sometimes had, in which a great white tent was pitched over the side lawn and everyone was dressed to the nines.

Two Oaks was stuttering to attention. The mention of those two names together was too much to sleep through. In its excitement, the house ushered forth its crowd of memories, flooding the foyer and the parlors, where Nick and Cassie were discussing Jack and June.

Cassie couldn't see the dream people, not exactly, but she could feel them, gathered around her, gathered around Nick, pressing in from the foyer and peering down from the stairs. Hundreds of people, if she wanted to count, people she'd never even noticed in her dreams but she now understood had been waiting there, on the outer fringes. She could hear them too—voices chattering in gossipy whispers, the thumps of their heartbeats, their swallows, their concern—and smell them—Ivory, menthol Kools, Old Spice, Pepsodent, and, dangling above it all, the heavy waft of a floral perfume. Cassie was surrounded, and, well, it was terrifying.

Cassie had assumed that her active dream life at Two Oaks was a safe—if odd—phenomenon, but this assumption was predicated on her being asleep when the dreams began. Now it was morning. She was certainly awake. She knew this because she pinched herself and she wasn't waking up. It was daylight, there was a man here named Nick, he was saying words to her, but all she could attend to was the house filling with, what, souls? Souls she was starting to think might, alarmingly, be dead. Was that what she was seeing in the night? Ghosts? Were all the dream people really former people, coming to haunt her? Why had they roared to attention at the sound of her grandmother's name?

"June," she said sharply, testing them. Nick thought he was talking to her, and stopped and frowned midsentence. She realized she was sitting at a strange angle, that she had frozen in her chair, her arms tight at her sides, her head lolled back, but she didn't think she could move. And now Nick was onto it too, rising, coming over to her, looking concerned.

They hadn't responded the way Cassie had thought they might. They were just chattering on around her, as though the name meant nothing to them. So why were they here then? Maybe it wasn't June's name after all. Or—Cassie thought back to the moment they'd shown up—maybe it was June's name paired with the name of the movie star.

"June and Jack!" Cassie shouted, and, sure enough, every one of them quieted. The dream people remained around her, but they were noticing her now, leaning in, more interested than they'd been, and the names said together had made that happen. As a little girl, Cassie had loved to feel her pet hamster stilling in her hands, even as its heart throbbed like timpani. That's what it was like now, the house alive but quiet, and the hair on Cassie's arms stood on end.

"June and Jack!" she called out again, and, in the same instant, all the dream people were gone. Cassie and Nick were alone in her house.

At the moment Cassie called out Jack's and June's names, Two Oaks had gone from hardly knowing Cassie was inside it to considering her essential to its survival. Only someone who knew of June and Jack (only someone who knew of the schism and loss and fear and newness born of those two lives entangled), could begin to understand how to mend what had been broken. But Two Oaks could feel it had alarmed the girl, and it wouldn't make that mistake twice. It would calmly observe her from now on, hoping she followed through, feeding her the dreams that would tip her in its favor, but, otherwise, it would keep its dream people at bay, at least during the daylight hours.

Meanwhile, as far as Cassie could tell, everything had gone back to normal. She found herself pressed into her chair, as though centrifugal force had pushed her backward. Gravity was her friend again.

"Are you all right?" Nick was perched over her, a glass of 7UP held above her head, asking her again and again how she was. She couldn't tell whether he was planning to pour the drink on her or offer a sip.

She nodded to quiet Nick's insistent concern, took the 7UP, and gulped it down. He watched her carefully as she came up for air.

"That was . . ."

He nodded. "It looked like you were going to pass out."

She gestured to the empty space, which had, so recently, been jam-packed. "I've never felt it like that before."

His frown deepened. "I'm sure the news comes as a shock. I should have—"

"Wait." Their presence had been so obvious, so apparent, that her incredulity won over discretion. "You didn't feel that?"

"I heard you call out your grandmother's name. And Jack's. And then your eyes kind of rolled back and you went like—" He pushed himself back in a crude imitation of how she'd looked. He winced as he said, "Was that a seizure?"

"I was reacting. To the . . . the way they just—" She clasped her hands together and squeezed until her knuckles turned white. "The"— she almost said "ghosts," then noticed Nick's pursed lips and thought better of it. Talking this openly about the dream people was, like the horrifying pile of mail just a few feet to her left, a sign she'd been spending too much time alone, and she was only just now seeing that. She cleared her throat. "Whatever it was."

His brow furrowed. "Maybe you should lie down."

"I don't need to lie down," she said, her voice rising higher than she wanted. She reached for a handful of chips and shoved them into her mouth. He was still watching her carefully. She uttered a gruff and crumby "Sit." He obeyed. She felt grumpy, ruffled, judged. She'd been wrong to let him linger this long. "So—this inheritance. How much did the movie star leave me?"

He folded his hands in his lap. Back to business. "Thirty-seven million dollars."

At the mention of this sum, Cassie nearly fell out of her chair. Her question had sounded flippant, but only because she'd thought they were playing a flirtatious game. And also because how on earth had an old dead codger of a movie star thought to leave her, Cassandra Danvers, any money at all, let alone money like that? She tried to ask a question about it, but the words wouldn't stick together.

". . . plus a few properties—the home in Malibu, the apartment in Paris, an island in the Caribbean." Apparently, Nick had been talking for a while and, now finished, was awaiting her reply.

"That's . . ." Cassie couldn't even imagine what that amount of money looked like. "That's . . ."

"A lot of money," Nick said, in his patient, gentlemanly way.

Cassie nodded, but she was watching him carefully. It couldn't be this simple, could it? A man bearing $37 million doesn't just show up on your doorstep. "Who do you work for?"

Nick lifted his eyes to meet hers. His irises were a surprising gray, swirled with silver. "Tate Montgomery," he said softly, and the wince was undeniable.

Of course. Tate Montgomery. Jack Montgomery's second daughter, the one who was so famous there was a haircut named after her. Cassie had known Tate was Jack's daughter at some point, back in middle and high school, when she'd pored over fashion magazines. Now the facts flooded back: flat-abbed, perfectly coiffed, ivory-toothed Tate Montgomery had a royal bloodline. The goddess rose up in Cassie's imagination: in her midnight blue bikini holding hands with Max Hall in that famous paparazzi shot from the day they got engaged; locking up her bike in front of the coffee shop on that sitcom she'd starred in for nine years; crying her eyes out on the tarmac in that tearjerker, when Rob Lowe finally went back to his wheelchair-bound wife. Compared to Tate Montgomery, people like Cassie were mere mortals.

"How does Tate feel about her dad's money going to some stranger?" Cassie asked. It felt strange to say only her first name, as if she knew her.

Nick leaned forward awkwardly. "Are you? Just some stranger?"

Cassie laughed, one loud laugh she didn't know she had in her. "Are you asking if I've ever met Jack Montgomery? Uh, no. I barely know who he is."

"So you didn't know anything about this?"

"You're kidding, right?"

He shook his head quite seriously.

"Nick Emmons." Cassie felt positively giddy; this whole thing was absurd. "This is obviously"—she hesitated, relishing how he hung on her words—"an epic mistake." He sat back in his chair, disappointed. She shook her head and shrugged. "Was Mr. Montgomery demented? That strikes me as the most likely scenario. Maybe he, like, picked my name out of a phone book. Maybe he didn't want his children to get his money and a random girl in Ohio seemed like a better choice."

Apparently this was no laughing matter. "Tate is upset," Nick said gravely.

"Understandably."

He cleared his voice. "He left a letter."

"To me?"

"To Tate and her sister."

"The sister's famous too, right?" Cassie remembered that her father had loved the sister. Her name started with an *E*. He'd watched her on TV when he, and this sister, were both young.

Nick frowned at the word *famous*. He was oddly prim, Cassie thought, for a man who worked for a movie star. "Elda Hernandez. Used to be Montgomery. You'd likely know her from *Planet Purple*."

Planet Purple, that was it. A show from the early seventies with low production values, because who needed them when you had barely legal girls flitting around in bikinis, waving ray guns? Cassie could vaguely summon up this bronzed, Amazonian version of Elda with a long ponytail set high atop her head. Cassie had seen the show a few times on sick days; it had played on midday reruns. But these days, Elda Hernandez was three times the size she'd once been. She wore healing crystals over her long linen dresses. She showed up in the tabloids every once in a while, usually for flipping off some paparazzo or saying Hollywood was run by misogynists or making a frank statement about the realities of menopause. There'd been a scandalous memoir, but Cassie had been too young to read it.

"What did the note say?" Cassie asked.

"It said . . . well, it implied that you were Jack's . . . granddaughter."

"Nope," Cassie replied. No, she had a grandpa. Not exactly the fun get-on-the-floor-and-play-with-you type, and dead since she was nine years old, but certainly a decent man, decent enough to urge his wife to move a hundred miles away so as not to disrupt the life of his newly orphaned granddaughter, even though his heart disease was bad enough to kill him within the year. Not to mention that Cassie's grandmother was by far the most straitlaced, morally upright person she'd ever met; it was impossible to imagine her having an affair with anyone. It was impossible to imagine her ever having had sex.

"Arthur was my grandfather," she explained. "June married him the summer she was out of high school. She had my dad exactly nine months later. And, believe me, my grandmother was definitely a virgin when she got married." Nick was looking at her dubiously. "You can't seriously think anyone believes Mr. Montgomery was right? How would June have even met someone like Jack? She was a small-town Ohio girl."

"The thing is . . ." Nick cleared his throat and met her eyes again. She was reminded of the Atlantic on a January day. "The thing is, Cassandra, Jack Montgomery actually filmed a movie in this town sixty years ago this month. Your grandmother would have been eighteen—"

"But that's what I'm telling you," Cassie pressed. "That's when my grandparents got married. There's no way—"

"It's not outside the realm of possibility that Jack fathered June's child." Nick pulled a thick legal document from his bag and handed it to her. It said "Last Will and Testament" across the top, but she didn't want to look at it now, not when Nick could tell her what she needed to know. "Especially because, were he still living, your father, Adelbert Lemon Danvers, would be fifty-nine years old."

She felt that dangerous switch flip inside her chest, the switch that turned her small and afraid.

Nick saw what her father's name did to her, she could tell that by the careful way he watched her. But he went on. "And then there's the matter of your father's first name. According to the Social Security Administration, Adelbert hasn't even been in the top thousand male names since 1932."

"So?"

"So," he said gently, "Adelbert was Jack's real name, before he changed it for Hollywood. Adelbert Michaels."

"What do you want then?" She clenched her jaw. "Obviously you want something." What she wanted was to leave, but this was her house now.

He nodded, as though grateful to have finally gotten to this part of things. "Tate's going to contest her father's will. The good news is she believes, as you do, that Jack Montgomery was not your grandfather."

Somewhere outside, a dog began to bark, sharp and insistent. Had this been any other day, Cassie would have investigated, creeping out onto the porch or leaning her forehead against the front parlor window. Instead, she sat back in her chair and crossed her arms, like a teenager with a bad attitude. "How is that good news?"

His eyes skipped nervously over the parlors again, really just two halves of the same giant room. In the shakiness of his gaze, Cassie noticed the crumbling ceiling, the water-stained wall above the fireplace, the open wiring where there had once been a light switch and from which, only two weeks before, she'd seen sparks shoot. "Well, if you cooperate with Tate, she's prepared to pay you a million dollars."

"Cooperate?"

"We'll fly back to L.A. tonight in her private jet—it's waiting at the airfield. A physician will take your DNA sample. A few swabs of the cheek, and he'll analyze it in his state-of-the-art facility. If you're a match, well then, obviously you'll inherit the thirty-seven million as Jack specified. But if not, you'll fly home a million dollars richer, and Tate will pay all the legal fees to straighten this mess out."

"Why not just swab my cheek and take it to her yourself?"

"We want to do this right." Crossed *t*'s, dotted *i*'s; Cassie supposed she should expect nothing less of Hollywood royalty.

"And if I don't cooperate?" Cassie knew enough about death and what came after it to avoid a whole other family's drama, especially that of the most famous family in the world. But then—$37 million. Not to mention the matter of June's and Jack's names, clasped together. The dream people had certainly expressed an interest in that union, and this fact itched at Cassie, whether it meant she was going crazy or not.

The skin between Nick's eyes wrinkled, giving him a worried frown.

His fingers nervously edged his smartphone. "Your father went by El, right?"

She nodded, wondering what that had to do with anything.

"I like that." He coughed nervously. "El, uh, he had a drinking problem, huh?"

"What?" She was too shocked to say anything else.

"Your art show," he said, as though it was her fault this had come up. "The *Times* mentioned your bravery in their review of your installation piece. The Jack Daniel's bottle on the car floor—they really loved that."

"Are you kidding me?" She felt disgusted, raw, exposed, and incapable of sputtering out anything but utter disbelief at Nick's gall.

He turned red-faced and apologetic in the wake of her reaction. "It's just that his addiction, well, it points to a certain weakness, you understand? I'm sure you can imagine how well connected Tate is. She'll go to the ends of the earth to prove her case if she can't just settle it with a DNA sample from you. Even, you know, even trying to prove that your father, or who knows who else, could have, I don't know, tried to coerce Mr. Montgomery into, well . . ." His hands were open in logical supplication; why wouldn't she just agree? "Cassie, please consider how many resources Tate is willing to devote to this cause." He leaned forward as if offering a helpful tip. "Ask yourself if you're financially prepared if and when she goes after you."

"Goes after me?" Cassie was seeing red.

Nick scrabbled together his things and stood, knee jolting the snack tray and nearly sending the remaining nibbles flying. He swallowed, as if he didn't want to say the words he was about to. "This is a nice house. I'd be sad to see you lose it."

"Okay." A great, roaring power from within pushed Cassie to her feet. "It's time for you to leave." As though she'd asked for this, or had any interest in fighting with rich ladies over some stranger's money. She pointed toward the front door with a shaking hand, imagining what the anger looked like as it licked off of her. "Get out."

Nick was already in the foyer, chandelier chattering with the reverberations of his footsteps.

The heavy door protested as he pulled it open. The front porch groaned under his step. She cursed her earlier daydream of it trapping him out there forever; what she wanted, more than anything, was for this stranger to just be gone.

"If my DNA is so goddamn important to Tate Montgomery, then tell her to come get it herself," she growled. And she slammed the front door in his face, noticing, in the split second before she shut him out, that Nick looked both relieved and appreciative, not at all what she was expecting.

June 1955

CHAPTER SIX

———

THE VIBRANT SCENT OF IVORY FILLED THE ROOM. IT WAS the first day of June; finally, June! Lindie had planned to get to Center Square before breakfast and sniff out the movie shoot. Today she'd finally see if *Erie Canal* was really coming to town. But even for Lindie, it was early; the light filling the room was rosy and low. Already June was primping. Lindie burrowed back into the creamy pillowcase, warming to the idea that June had changed her mind and would, in fact, be coming along to the extras casting. The prospect of putting on that horrible strawberry dress was much more pleasant if June would be by Lindie's side. Together, they'd comb the rats out of her hair, and June would invite Lindie down for breakfast in the grand Two Oaks dining room. The doughy promise of Apatha's biscuits filled the air.

Lindie dozed again, and in that drowse of morning, the big house loved her. It had always loved this little girl who, in turn, loved its creator, Lemon Gray Neely. Before June and her mother moved in, Lindie had spent countless childhood hours helping Apatha wash Uncle Lem's hands with a knit cloth, or skating across the ballroom floor with soft rags tied to her feet. It loved the tangy stain of brass polish on her father's fingertips almost as much as she did.

Lindie was a child who needed Two Oaks; that made her easy to love too. Her mother, Lorraine, had left Lindie and Lindie's father, Eben (and St. Jude entirely), two years after Eben returned from the war, when Lindie was seven. In the ensuing years, Apatha—who kept Two Oaks shipshape, no small feat—had become Lindie's new mother, especially indispensable on those days when Eben needed to balance the books for Uncle Lem's vast business holdings. So sweet were the memories of the little girl gathered onto Apatha's lap in the yeasty kitchen, that though she had grown, and the roost was now ruled by June's mother, Cheryl Ann, Two Oaks still considered Lindie to be its own.

It was in business school in Columbus that Eben had met Lorraine. Eldest son of the original caretakers of Two Oaks—Mr. and Mrs. Loftus Shaw—scrawny little Eben had had a shrewdness with numbers that impressed Uncle Lem. The great man admired the way the boy divided ten cookies evenly among sixteen children, how he estimated the number of apples in a bushel just by looking at the top of the crate. When it came time for a high school graduation gift, Loftus and Ellen were shocked and delighted to receive a large check in Eben's name, accompanied by an enthusiastic acceptance letter to business school in Columbus. The old man had arranged it.

Eben didn't talk much about his parents, but Lindie knew they'd been hardworking folk whose trade was more like Apatha's (sweeping, baking, dusting, waxing) than like his own. Two Oaks remembered its original, lovely caretakers—how they sometimes held hands over the kitchen table, how the sour stink of Ellen's boiled cabbage would fill the whole downstairs, and the awful day when she fell from the ladder while dusting the foyer light fixture. And though the son of these good, simple folk had become a man of numbers, land, and oil, he'd never forgotten where he'd come from. In the days before Cheryl Ann, he and Lindie spent hours on the Two Oaks front porch, tending to the small and necessary tasks Apatha couldn't get to. Sundays, Eben would fiddle with the shrieking doorbell with a Phillips screwdriver, his ledger and fountain pen forgotten on the porch floor, while Apatha read aloud from *Huckleberry Finn*. Beside Uncle Lem on the porch swing, Lindie watched the old man's wrinkled lips putter along with Mark Twain's sentences. Eventually, he would doze off, and, dappled in sweet summer light, Lindie would imagine Jim and Huck on their raft as her father unscrewed a porch bulb atop a ladder, and bumblebees mumbled lazily across the afternoon.

After lunch, little Lindie would help Apatha put up the wash, and the wet, white linens would flap in the sun. In the evenings, Apatha would bring out her darning gourd and repair their socks, or knit cotton dishrags while Lindie lay, chin propped up, in front of the great radio console in the foyer and listened to *The Lone Ranger* followed by *The Grand Ole Opry*. Sometimes at night they'd put an old Strauss waltz onto the Victrola that Lemon and his long-dead wife, Mae, had received as a wedding gift many years before, and the whole house would bloom with the tinny pace of one-two-three one-two-three.

Lindie's drowsy mind mingled with the household's lulling memories of that sweet time, now gone, until she heard a sound that alarmed her. It came from June's side of the room. It was a sound Lindie remembered from Lorraine's days, one she hadn't heard often, but enough to recognize, the sound of a woman getting ready to go out, not to the market or the corner, not to school, as she'd heard June do on plenty of cold winter mornings (the scratch of wool, the slip of buttons), but to impress: the adult swish of ironed cotton as it drops down over a nylon slip.

Lindie sat up. June was standing before the mirror to the left of the window that, in the light of day, now overlooked Lindie's humble bungalow just across the street, where Eben was still snoring, and the dishes remained unwashed. June wore a navy dress that brought out the dark ocean of her eyes. The fabric nipped in at her waist, making her hips seem even curvier than they already were. Her breasts pressed, high and round, against the bodice, as though begging to be set free. Her cheeks were rouged, her lips stained red, her long hair curled and tucked under.

"You can't wear that." Lindie's disapproving tone masked the itchiness of her palms, the shallow lump of her heart as it fluttered far too fast. She wanted to cover June with a blanket. "The movie's set right after the Civil War."

In the mirror, June's face grew solemn. This was the same face she'd made two summers before, the day she'd had to break the news that the robins had flown from their nest and she'd found one of the downy hatchlings with a broken neck just below it. But her voice stayed cheery. "Do me up?" Her dress was open in the back, showing the sweet press of her shoulder blades through her slip. Lindie could just make out the delicate outline of her white brassiere, and ached to lay her palms against those small winged plates, but she sat on her hands. If she didn't fasten the dress, June wouldn't be able to step outside; someone had to save her from flouncing around town looking like some Columbus doctor's wife.

June turned, head tipped to the side, like Lindie was a disobedient child to be indulged. She came to Lindie, sat on the bed, and sighed. "I got a letter. From Artie. He comes back this morning."

"But the mail hasn't come yet."

June held her breath, then let it out. "I got it yesterday."

Lindie flung herself from the bed. They'd wasted a whole day. "You knew he was coming back and you didn't tell me?" That was why June had been so evasive the night before.

Lindie swiped her dirty overalls up from the floor and stepped into them as if donning armor for battle. "We have to do something, June." She hadn't ever truly believed Artie Danvers would be back in time. He'd been gone for months, first in Louisiana, then Texas, then Mississippi—anywhere his brother, Clyde, had a business interest, anywhere but St. Jude. Sure, he'd been sending June postcards, but they were bland and unromantic—"Tried a chicken-fried steak," "Went to a tractor pull"—and June couldn't be serious that she was going to hitch herself to that wagon, not based on a couple of quiet strolls around Center Square before he'd abandoned her for more than half a year.

"You'll have to slip out the window," June said as Lindie untangled herself from the nightdress she'd borrowed. "Mother's up."

The gall, thought Lindie, the gall. Once she'd been welcomed through the Two Oaks front door, but now she had to climb out the window like some common thief, and only because of Cheryl Ann. Cheryl Ann, who had all but banished Eben and Lindie from the house. They weren't even invited to Sunday dinner anymore! It ached Lindie's center to remember what Two Oaks had once offered; she grasped the memory of listening to *Queen for a Day* and *The Romance of Helen Trent* on the parlor floor, poking her small fingers into the honeycombed holes of the radio console's speaker. Well, fat chance she'd ever get to do that again.

It was obvious (to Lindie at least) that Cheryl Ann blamed Eben for her husband Marvin's death. As though just because Marvin and Eben had served together in the war, Eben could be held responsible for Marvin's reenlisting for Korea! Or for getting killed there! Or for secretly losing all his money to gambling! Cheryl Ann certainly didn't blame Clyde Danvers, who'd also served with Eben and Marvin; in fact, she was marrying her daughter off to Clyde's brother. It was no coincidence that the Danverses were the second-richest family in town. Cheryl Ann was a social-climbing snob, but Lindie tried to keep her opinions of June's mother to herself.

She freed her head from the nightgown. She clipped the overalls over her shoulders with a huff, then spat in her hands and rubbed them across her hair, noticing, with deep satisfaction, how hard June tried not to shudder at the sight.

"You're ruining your life, June," she said sharply.

June's face turned red, but, as usual, she didn't take the bait. "The only thing I'm ruining," she said evenly, lifting the empty plate that had held Apatha's cookies, "is breakfast, if I miss it."

Lindie stuck out her tongue. "Fine."

June reached for the doorknob. "Fine." She pulled open the door and headed out into the upstairs hall, where she was reduced to the sharp ticking of her heels down the wide oak stairway. Her sweet scent wafted back through the narrow gap as the door began to close.

Lindie was filled with regret. She suddenly remembered the strawberry dress, the plan for breakfast, the promise of Apatha's biscuits. She rushed to the door brimming with apology. She caught only the briefest glimpse of the nut brown hallway, streaming with the buttery glow the stained-glass windows cast onto the main landing. But then the door fell shut. Lindie thought of June's shoulder blades against the taut slip and kicked the bedpost until the pain in her toe matched what filled the rest of her.

CHAPTER SEVEN

———

EBEN HAD ONCE TOLD LINDIE THAT JUNE'S FATHER, MARVIN, lugged a box of watercolors all over the Pacific islands, taking five minutes here and there to sketch a new leaf or the battered canteen from which he swigged his water. That is, until their C.O. found him painting during mealtime. The man in charge had smashed the paints with the toe of his boot, grinding them into the earth until they were useless. "Real goddamn bastard," Eben had said then, shaking his head. Lindie could count on one hand the number of times she'd heard her soft-spoken father swear.

June's easel was by the window. When June wanted to, she could go on and on about natural light like she was Vermeer, but Lindie didn't mind, because June's whole being got dreamy whenever she felt close to what her father had passed along. Lindie bent to the painting: a still life of Cheryl Ann's favorite blue vase, some kind of red fruit, and six red beads scattered atop a stack of Uncle Lem's leather tomes. Lindie leaned in and made out the script of the only visible binding. The title was sketched out in delicate yellow paint: *A Compendium of Greek Tales*.

Lindie realized with delight that she'd inspired a piece of art. The funny red fruit was meant to be a pomegranate, of course, and the little beads were supposed to be the seeds that grew inside it. A few weeks earlier they'd been talking about Persephone's tale, which June had read for the first time, on Lindie's recommendation. June had remarked how foolish she found the girl in the story; why hadn't she had the self-control to resist eating the food from the underworld? It didn't seem that hard. Lindie, for her part, had confessed that she'd have gobbled up all the seeds, an admission that had set June into knowing giggles.

Lindie didn't know enough about art to tell whether June's painting was any good. She liked it, but she suspected that was mostly because she liked the feeling of knowing she'd helped bring it about. It was clear

that June was never really happy with any of the paintings she made up
here in her bedroom overlooking the wide Two Oaks lawn. June would
nestle each finished piece against the side of her wardrobe as soon as it
was dry; not one of them ever saw the light of day again.

But at least it was something. At least it was hers. Which was another reason Lindie was so opposed to this marriage; because she knew
how easily June would give her paintings up. Lindie could've bet fifty
bucks—if she'd had it—that the day June became Artie's wife, she'd set
down her paintbrushes and never pick them up again. She'd move into
the stark home Artie owned on Center Square and set about sprucing
it up. She'd sew curtains. Tuesday would be tuna casserole night. And
Lindie would be the sucker skulking around June's back porch, waiting
to be given a job—pinning up the laundry, say, or entertaining the baby
that was sure to come—while June darned the man's socks and tutted
over a stain in those stupid curtains.

Then came the scrape of chairs across the dining room floor.
Lindie's cue.

Lindie squinted out at the now-bright morning, checking her own
front porch to make sure Eben wasn't there. Although he likely knew
where she was, they had a tacit agreement that he'd never witness her
sneaky entrances and exits; what he didn't know couldn't hurt him
when it came to Cheryl Ann. But no, good, her father was nowhere in
sight. Best Lindie could do was pray he wasn't looking out the kitchen
window, because the glare made it impossible to tell.

She ran her hand across the windowsill and imagined she could feel
Two Oaks sighing under her touch, like a beloved pet leaning into a
scritch behind the ears. She didn't suppose she'd be coming here much
once June was Mrs. Artie Danvers. Lindie took one last look around the
bedroom, breathing it in, then lowered first one bare foot, then the other,
over the windowsill. She dropped down to a crouch on the shingled roof
and scurried to the overhang, all the while remembering Uncle Lem's
voice from the days before he'd lost it, explaining the entablature at the
top of the house above her—"three layers, Linda Sue: architrave, frieze,
and cornice"; the neoclassical design he loved so well—"Corinthian
columns support both the porches and the classical pediment with the
gabled roof above," and saying of the brass lion head in the plate around

the front door handle, "Well, I suppose I had a great deal of pride in those days."

Lindie loved the flow of the words *porte cochere* almost as much as she hated the indignity of having to climb down the columns that held it up. Her feet found the far side of the smooth column, and her torso and hands followed the downward pull of gravity. She landed atop the three feet of rough stone upon which the column rested, and checked the street for passersby. She was hidden from the dining room, which lay beyond her, where June and her mother and Uncle Lem were already chewing their omelets and potatoes and sausages, pouring milk from crystal pitchers and serving themselves from silver trays, as Apatha listened from the pantry for the buzzer under Cheryl Ann's right toe.

Lindie let her body fall the final drop to the driveway. As she landed, she remembered her movie magazines still strewn across June's bedroom. She'd get them next time, which meant, she realized with delight, that there had to be a next time.

Uncle Lem's yellow brick monument to his fortune lay at the center of the entire city block—the front door sitting on South Street, which would take one right into town. The acres of lush, mown grass were edged with azaleas and rhododendrons. Daffodils and crocuses lined the sidewalks in spring; decorative cabbages did the same in winter; and, for now, the roses were in bloom, sweet in scent and dangerous to the touch. Lindie crouched in the loamy earth, at the foot of the fluorescent pink azaleas that boxed the building. She scrambled toward the front of the house, coming even with the wide, white porch, toes tickled by grass. Then she sprinted out onto the front lawn, alive with bees and butterflies. A robin flushed into the air.

Nearly to the sidewalk, she heard the triumphant sweep of a broom. She froze. She was already caught. Apatha—she knew without even looking. And yes, there the old woman was, standing in the middle of the front walkway, only a few feet away. Apatha took her time scanning the sorry sight—dirty feet, stained overalls, messy hair—finally shaking her head in a fashion that filled even Lindie with disappointment. Above them, a tangle of sparrows battled through the oak, sending down a scattering of new leaves.

It was a sacrilege to trample the Two Oaks lawn. Lindie knew this,

and she played toward it, hoping she could divert the old woman's attention from the real transgression of climbing down the side of the house
in broad daylight. Lindie hung her head and ambled onto the path,
wincing at the slate's heat under her bare soles. Apatha's stare bored into
her. Then she lifted her chin toward the center of town.

"You know," Apatha said carefully, her voice thin but as strong as
steel, "I'll bet if you waltzed up to that movie set, and told them your
father served in the war with that producer, Mr. Shields, you could get
yourself a job."

Lindie had gathered bits about Mr. Shields on her own, through the
vent in her bedroom floor. There'd been many local men who'd served
together—including Eben, Clyde, and Marvin—although it was beyond her how anyone had failed to mention that they'd also fought with
a famous Hollywood producer. Apparently, the movie Mr. Alan Shields
was making with MGM had just lost its location in northern New York,
something about a flood or a drought; in all the excitement, Lindie had
lost the details. What mattered was the movie was called *Erie Canal*.
What mattered was that MGM needed a canal, and pronto. The studio
already had money invested, two movie stars who'd filmed all the interiors and whose calendars had been cleared until the end of June, and
a Hollywood film crew sitting around twiddling their thumbs. What
mattered was that St. Jude had a canal running right through Center
Square.

"Mr. Shields owes your father his life," Apatha said gravely.

"From the war?" Lindie asked, hoping for a gory detail or two. Her
father rarely talked about that time.

"And as far as I can tell," Apatha went on, ignoring Lindie's eagerness, "now that your father found him his location, Mr. Shields owes
your daddy two favors."

Lindie knew Eben didn't see it that way. He was not a man to count
good deeds; she'd heard him say as much through the vent when a few
of his buddies—over for the evening, free to talk and drink and smoke
away from their wives—praised him for bringing all that Hollywood
money to town. He protested that all he'd ever done was sit around a
campfire in the Laruma Valley and tell Alan about the stink of the canal
on hot August days. It was Alan who'd remembered that conversation

all these years later, and, desperate for a location, had flown in with his location scout.

Apatha wore a calico apron over her ironed dress, and smelled of the kitchen, of yeast and cinnamon and butter. Lindie was seized with the desire to fling her arms around the old woman, to lay a kiss upon the dry, sour cheek. But then, Apatha was also the one who'd allowed Cheryl Ann to turn her away; Lindie couldn't soon forget that. She crossed her arms defensively. "What if I don't want a job?"

Apatha's eyes shot up to the corner of the house from which Lindie had just emerged. "Seems to me you've got free time on your hands." She nodded over Lindie's shoulder, where Eben had come out to the rocking chair on his front porch. Lindie ducked her head, thinking of the talking-to she was sure to get from him as well.

Apatha reached her long hand into her right apron pocket. She pulled out a piece of linen. Inside was what Lindie had hoped for since she'd awakened: two hot biscuits. Her mouth watered. She lifted her eyes from the food to Apatha's face, landing on a soft pillow of pity.

"Let her go now," Apatha said softly. "Before it's hard, Linda Sue, just let her go." She pressed the biscuits into Lindie's hands with her cool, knotted fingers. Then cut her eyes away, and walked slowly back toward the mansion's far side, using the broom as a cane. Lindie watched her disappear behind the side of the porch, knowing she'd turn back in through the kitchen door—the only one Cheryl Ann let her use any-more.

CHAPTER EIGHT

———

EBEN GRINNED UP FROM HIS FAVORITE ROCKING CHAIR, wedged in between the front door and the wall that separated his tiny porch from the sidewalk. A book about Chicago lay open in his hand. "You got caught again," he said with glee as, on the other side of the street, Thelma Weadock and Donnagene Lutz scurried toward Center Square.

"It's Chicago now?" Lindie asked coldly. The biscuits had only taken the edge off her spite.

Her father looked down at the book's spine and frowned as if he was only just seeing the city's name. "Who's to say? There's a whole world out there." He shrugged. "I could hang a shingle." He said it brightly, as if the idea of leaving St. Jude was the best one he'd ever had. As if Lindie didn't have her own life here.

"You're going to abandon Lemon?" Lindie was already tired from the day's many fights. Her hand curled into a fist behind her back.

Eben waved his hand dismissively and frowned. "Not until he's gone, Lindie, you know that."

"And what about Apatha?"

Bobby Prange and Walter Eberle rode past, their dirty Keds spinning the pedals of their Schwinns. Sunlight sparkled across the neat edges of their flattop haircuts, the kind Lindie longed to sport herself and, in lieu of that, dreamed of running beneath her palms like newly shorn lawns. "Lindie! Lindie!" they called, without slowing. "They're here! They're making the movie for real!" There was no chance to learn more—already, the boys were gone, zipping toward town and Main Street and the canal in Center Square. These were the boys with whom Lindie had stapled together a grid of Dixie cups across Reverend Crane's front and back porches early one Sunday morning, filling them with water so they were impossible to empty without spilling everywhere; the poor man had had to climb out his window to get to church on time. With June married off, Lindie could already see it would be a summer full of bull-frog catching and hot dog eating contests, of daring each other to steal Chiclets or Beemans Black Jack from Schillinger's Drug. They'd ride out to the Prange alfalfa farm and shoot at tin cans and practice blowing smoke circles, and the boys' mothers would try to tame her with snacks of buttered saltines and Mott's apple juice. But she knew it would be a long time before she slept in a nightgown again, or ran a bristled brush through her hair.

The sound of a motor pulled Eben from his rocking chair and turned Lindie's attention toward the road. It was Clyde Danvers in the duo-tone Chevrolet Bel Air he'd driven home just after Christmas. He was headed to Center Square too. Lindie hadn't gotten used to the sight of Clyde in his new car, which she knew her father didn't think he needed, since Clyde also had a perfectly good four-door Oldsmobile, which did nothing much these days beyond protect his drive from rain.

Clyde pulled up in front of the house. He whistled to her father in their usual way.

"Hello, old man." Eben laughed, saluting from the porch.

"Hey, Uncle Clyde." It was what she'd called him forever, even though he was no relation.

Eben was quick to disparage anyone looking to buy happiness, but Lindie couldn't fault Uncle Clyde for enjoying the finer things in life. She had a soft spot for the man who'd always flipped her the spare change from his pockets and had gotten her her first pellet gun. Sure, he was also funding June's wedding, and helping Cheryl Ann marry June off—to his strange beanpole of a brother, no less—but Lindie knew how single-minded Cheryl Ann could be, so she didn't fault Clyde for that disaster, not by a mile. She just supposed Cheryl Ann had steamrolled him into it, as was her wont.

Clyde reached out the window and knocked the side of his car. "What'd I tell you, old man? First the movies, next the moon."

"Let's not get ahead of ourselves," Eben replied. Lindie looked up at her father's tight jaw. He might appear carefree from the road, but he didn't up close.

Clyde nodded to her. "Will you tell your pops to have a little fun? I swear, it's all figures and sums these days."

Eben put his arm around Lindie's shoulder and squeezed. "I'm not as bad as all that; tell him, kid."

Lindie squirreled away. "I'm going to watch the movie get made too, Uncle Clyde."

Clyde pointed at Lindie like she was something special. "That's my girl." He put his foot on the gas and eased off down the block.

Eben followed Clyde's departure with a solemn gaze. Before Lindie had the chance to follow, he picked up the brown leather shoes that had been sitting on the porch since the weather'd turned warm. "Cat bath first. And a proper shirt." Maybe there was still a chance of getting cast as an extra, even though Lindie knew she'd never look like Thelma Weadock or Donnagene Lutz, with their Breck-bathed locks in those perfect Jesus waves, with their button noses and beribboned ponytails, and skirts giving way to smooth calves.

Ten minutes later, Lindie was clean enough and wearing a pair of her father's boyhood pants and a collared shirt that did an okay job of hiding the bumps growing on her chest. She had shoes on and a glass of milk in her belly. "Do you want to come?" she asked Eben halfheartedly. She couldn't stay mad at him for long; he was so much better than any of the other fathers.

But he tapped his book and shook his head, and Lindie stepped off the porch.

"Oh, Linda Sue," he said, which stopped her cold, because he never called her anything but Lindie, not unless he was talking business, "you might take this and present it to one of the men with the clipboards." In his hand was a sealed envelope.

"What's this?"

"Apatha's idea. One of her best." And he smiled and she scowled as she remembered the job Apatha had mentioned, and stuffed the envelope into her pocket.

BOBBY AND WALTER, little Paul Reveres, had pulled the quiet neighborhood out of its daily rituals and into the electric new. Lindie joined the strange parade toward Center Square. More primping girls tore past her—Gretchen Beck and Ginny Sherman and that preening, stuck-up Darlene Kipp, who stuck her tongue out and pointed her piggy nose up to the clouds as she breezed by. Behind Lindie, Mrs. Freewalt herded along her four little Freewalts. Old Mrs. Bretz and older Mrs. Dowty leaned heavily on their brass-handled canes. Tommy Tinnerman and Chuck Schnarre raced by, dodging a tongue-lashing from one of their mothers. And Mr. Caywood and Mr. Abernathy, in their wool suits, had decided to take the long way to Main Street in order to see all the excitement for themselves.

Center Square was St. Jude's oasis, six square acres of emerald lawn sliced through by the old canal. A refurbished canal boat floated in the trough of water that cut along the park's northern edge, where a tunnel then took the canal out under Main Street and into the country, north toward Lima. Small towns in the rest of the country had paved over their old-fashioned trolley tracks and filled in their locks, but the St. Judians clung hard to their unfilled, mucky mile of the Miami & Erie Canal. In 1861, it had been the most efficient way to move commerce in the nearly landlocked state. Now it did little more than let off a stink in the summer and provide a skating track on the coldest Ohio days. But the St. Judians didn't mind. That Hollywood had come to town only confirmed their good sense to keep things as they were.

Above Center Square, at its north side, Main Street was easily reached by climbing any number of sets of stairs, which led up to Illy's (the town's single restaurant), or Schillinger's Drug (where the soda fountain was), or the Dry Goods or the county clerk's or the Majestic Theater, where Lindie would sometimes stay for six hours at a time, watching the cowboy movies loop.

The western side of the square, where she stood now on Front Street, usually offered a view of the high schoolers flirting in the band shell, of children playing tag below the clock tower as it rang out the hour, and older couples strolling together below the elm groves that peppered the far reaches of the green. But standing there on the first day of *Erie Canal*'s shoot, Lindie was half-convinced she'd traveled back in time. To her right, on the southern edge of Center Square, Memorial High was ground zero for the costume department; already, her classmates were emerging from the main door dressed like their grandmothers, in jewel-toned dresses with long sleeves and high necks. Some wore wigs, some little hats high up upon their foreheads, and they giggled to each other, oblivious to Lindie as she made her way through them. A young man with a clipboard and a megaphone directed the costumed hordes to the eastern end of Center Square.

Lindie took advantage of a break in the man's announcement and asked where she'd find the extras casting. He looked her over for a moment. "You're a girl?" he asked, drolly.

Lindie was seized with panic and regret—she should have worn the strawberry dress. She knew she was blushing—she could feel herself turning red as a tomato—and stammered a frustrated "Yes sir."

He cleared his throat. He was trying to figure out how to put this delicately.

Embarrassed as she was, she knew all at once that he was right. She'd look stupid with a wig pinned onto her head and a blue gown flouncing around her. She'd trip and fall after even one step in those girlish shoes. But she couldn't walk away, not now. Of anyone in this town, she deserved to help make this movie. She needed it so much more than the Darlene Kipps of the world.

Lindie pulled the envelope from her pocket and shoved it at the man. "And what's this?"

"I'm fast, sir," she said. "I can run. I know every back alley of this town and the name of every person who owns a business. And the name of his son and his dog and his wife, for that matter."

He lifted the megaphone to his lips and called out to Mr. and Mrs. Fishpaw, the old couple who were always reading the newspaper together on their porch on the corner of Maple and Pine. "That way," he said, waving his clipboard toward Chestnut. "Please make your way to the town hall." They obeyed. He looked back down at his clipboard, then up at Lindie, startling as if seeing her for the first time. "And what do you want from me?"

"I want you to read it," she replied, still holding out the envelope.

He considered her request, then decided to open the letter. It was backward to Lindie's eye, but she could see it had been written in a steady hand. He held it to the light and examined it carefully. "You're a friend of Mr. Shields?" he asked dubiously.

"My father fought with him in the South Pacific."

He pursed his lips. "He speaks highly of you here." Then he folded the letter up and handed it back. She wondered what Alan Shields—whom she'd never met—could have written, but she wasn't about to question it when the man cocked his head toward the set behind him, where men were lifting lights onto scaffolding and a crowd of extras was gathering. "Tell Casey you're a P.A."

"What's a P.A.?" Lindie asked, already pushing past him into the heart of things.

He laughed drily, as though he pitied both her ignorance and her fate. "You'll see."

CHAPTER NINE

———

UNE BOWED HER HEAD IN PRAYER. THE DINING ROOM WAS
a large, dark rectangle at the back corner of the house, designed,
she sometimes thought, to make one feel as though one lived inside
a jewelry box. The walls were brown tapestry, the mahogany table designed to seat twenty, the sideboard a floor-to-ceiling triumph of curved
tiger maple and paneled glass. Under her mother's watch, the thick
chocolate curtains stayed closed against the daylight, so the chandelier
burned above; the leaded-glass window which led out to the small back
porch was the only indication that the sun had come out to greet the
new month.

Every few minutes, Apatha would come through the pantry door
bearing a pitcher of juice or a new dish of butter; it was all June could
do not to get up to help the dear old woman. But not today; today she
would obey. June could feel her mother's eyes scrutinizing every square
inch of her body: the open collar, the thin blue belt. She folded her
hands in her lap, ready for the verdict. But, as the quiet moment neared
its end, she smiled to herself. No tongue had been clucked her direction.
She had done well.

"You must excuse us earlier than usual this morning, Uncle," Cheryl
Ann began, deciding that grace was finished. "It's a special day for June.
She's engaged to one of the Danvers boys—you recall?—and today he
returns from his travels."

June was certain Lemon had no idea about, or interest in, her affairs,
but, for her mother's sake, she accepted a hearty spoonful of eggs and
replied, "The nine o'clock bus, is it?" Uncle Lem gaped and sputtered,
more than half of his eggs already on the bib Apatha had sewn from
oilcloth. June wished she could feed him. But she wouldn't try it, not
today.

"The nine o'clock from Columbus," Cheryl Ann repeated. This information had been relayed nearly a dozen times in the day before, a pleasing fact plucked from the simple, folded letter which now sat beside Cheryl Ann's grapefruit spoon.

June could vaguely remember a time when Cheryl Ann had been beautiful; it might not have even been that long ago. But since Marvin's death and the loss of everything she held dear, the woman's lustrous hair had grown thin and her face had been swallowed by a conspiracy of chins. Her back hurt and she made sure June knew it. She often passed wind and rarely excused herself. June didn't begrudge her mother the genuine heartache she'd endured, but it was the way Cheryl Ann kissed her disappointments full on the mouth that appalled June, though she'd never have admitted as much to even Lindie.

June watched her mother shove a sausage into her mouth while she prattled on about changing the floral arrangement in the front hall especially for Artie's return. She asked, without really asking, what recipe June thought Apatha should use to make the roast on Sunday: "I'd prefer her to use Mother's recipe, but not if she ruins it again. What gives her the idea she knows best?" June knew Apatha could hear through the pantry door. Cheryl Ann knocked on the mahogany tabletop, pleased with her intolerance. "She'd be sitting right beside me if she had her way."

Most of Lemon's eggs had made their way to the floor. But Cheryl Ann dished up another pile for him as though it hadn't been torture to watch him wrestle with the last batch. "I'll confirm the church with Reverend Crane, and ask Clyde again about the reception hall. We have plenty to do, now that we know the date is firm and the rooster has come home to roost—what do we have, thirty-some-odd days? Hmm? June? June! Stop mooning."

"Yes, Mother, thirty-three days." June watched her mother crest the next speculative wave, fluttering through seating charts and the menu and what flowers they might use and having June fitted again with Mrs. Jamison, because June had gotten nice and fat in her happy engagement, hadn't she?

June pushed her eggs around her plate. The wedding, she reminded herself—the wedding would be wonderful. Artie's big brother, Clyde, was paying, and he'd promised she could have any kind of cake she wanted. No expense spared! Clyde was a rich and handsome bachelor.

June supposed he must feel protective of her and Cheryl Ann, must believe that marrying them into his own family would be a way to help out the family of his wayward war buddy, like saving the two women left on a sinking ship. Not to mention that Clyde obviously loved his younger brother, Artie, because why else would he be going to all this trouble? Clyde Danvers was the man who got things done; June supposed she liked the feeling of being a necessary aspect of one of those things. She hadn't felt necessary in so long. And so what if the prospect of the wedding filled her with pleasure, and thinking of Artie himself made her feel, well, a hollow unknowingness? She believed that her simply taking the leap of faith that she could be a good wife to tall, quiet Artie Danvers might be enough to get them both through the first year or so, and by then she'd probably love him anyway, because that was how it worked.

The grandfather clock chimed the half hour. Cheryl Ann jumped, her hand fluttering over her heart. She frowned at June's full plate and shook her head, wiping her mouth with the cloth napkin. "Time to go, time to go."

"But the bus isn't until nine," June objected, then, wondering why on earth she was complaining about getting free of her mother early, stood. "No, you're right, I should leave extra."

June watched Cheryl Ann ring for Apatha, remembering what her father had told her before he'd redeployed, when she'd come in to his carpentry workshop and begged him not to leave, not again. "When something seems impossible, find a part deep down inside yourself that's strong," he'd said, wrapping his large hand around June's, then tightening his grip. "Clench it, like a fist." It had hurt, to feel him squeezing her fist so tightly inside his own. But she had understood.

CHAPTER TEN

———

THE MOVIE PEOPLE WERE STRANGERS, BUT LINDIE DIDN'T need to know their names. They fit together like gears; it was plain to see that if any of the pieces of the mechanism malfunctioned, it could be replaced with a die-cut replica. The camera operator operated the camera, and the costume department sewed the ladies into their long, bustled dresses, and the cinematographer was the man with the small telescopey thing in front of his right eye. The studio had even brought along a fellow whose sole job was to wrangle the ogling crowd; most St. Judians between the ages of one and a hundred had come to watch the show. Lindie had never taken crowd control to be a skill until she watched this man handing out flyers that called for more extras in the days ahead; then, just as a wave of excited whispers threatened to crest over the relative quiet, he hushed the onlookers with one Svengali-like look, and she understood he was a master of his profession.

There were plenty of job-related nicknames—Scripty or the "script girl" was not a girl at all but a bookish-looking woman who noted every alteration to the script with the pencil that was otherwise tucked behind her petite ear, Crafty was where the crew got their meals, and P.A. stood for production assistant, which was a glorified name for the person who could, and would, be asked, at a moment's notice, to count two thousand silk buttons out for a seamstress, or move ten crates of apples a half dozen times until the director and the production designer agreed on their placement in the background, or make sure the flowers for the leading lady's dressing room were delivered at 10:00 a.m. on the dot. In short, a P.A.'s work was exhausting, thankless, and underpaid, and Lindie loved every second.

Casey was in charge of the P.A.'s. That first day there were four of them, and Lindie was the only child, only local, and only girl. She certainly hadn't appreciated how influential that letter from Alan Shields had been; once she handed Mr. Shields's letter over to Casey, he'd reluctantly told her to go tell the horse and wagon that it needed to move to the other side of the square in order to be in the shot. Casey was youngish—couldn't have been but a few years beyond June—but just as mirthless. He wore brassy wire-rim glasses and a grave expression, and, if he didn't see you running, he was glad to remind you how replaceable you were.

Lindie was happy to ask how high when Casey said jump. In her first hour on set, she ran two messages to the lighting crew, took a note from craft services up to Illy's restaurant indicating they'd be in need of a case of Coca-Cola come noon, discovered she didn't have authority to deliver that letter, went back to Illy's to tell them to forget it, returned to set to discover that Crafty did, in fact, need a case of Coca-Cola after all, and could she also ask Illy's for some 7UP, and went back to Illy's to reconfirm that she'd be back at 11:30 to somehow shoulder two cases of glass-bottled soda back to set on her ninety-pound frame. Then she jogged down to the Memorial High gymnasium before anyone asked for Dr Pepper.

The vast room with the shiny wood floors was just as hot and loud as it was in the winter months, when it was jammed with the sweaty basketball team and the hollering cheerleaders. Dresses, shoes, racks of hats, and a dozen members of the costume department, pincushions tied to their wrists, filled the floor. Someone had dragged the lunch tables into the long space; on one, hundreds of men's shirts waited to be ironed; on another, shawls were sorted by color. On the bleachers waited a thrilled scrum of St. Judians, eager to be transformed. Lindie ignored the jealous pit in her stomach when she saw that mean-hearted Darlene Kipp was one of the lucky ones.

Lindie presented herself at one of the lunch tables, where a man with a pin between his lips crouched at the feet of pretty, young Mrs. Sudman, already transformed into a vision of the last century in a cerulean gown. Without lifting an eye, the man, named Ricky, shoved a tomato pincushion at Lindie and told her to pin up the back of the wide dress. "If they'd sent us here a week ago instead of sitting us on our asses out on the lot," he seethed, as though Lindie knew what he was talking about, "I'd have all these finished by now." On the table above him, scores of taffeta skirts were draped, in deep shades of evergreen, eggplant, and plum. Lindie whispered that she didn't know how to sew.

"I'm not asking you to sew," he said, sounding more like a peeved friend than a punishing father, "I'm telling you to pin."

So pin she did, and though Ricky fussed as he went over her uneven pinning with his needle, he didn't fire her. He was a grown man but funny in the way even Lindie's father wasn't funny. He talked sometimes like women talked—"Oh, sweetheart," and "Honey, if you ask me . . ."—but he was also firm in the way of men, especially when he called up the next girl for her fitting. Lindie stayed by his side as they hemmed four more dresses, and her skills improved.

When Lindie saw that the fifth girl up was Darlene Kipp, she almost announced she had somewhere to be, but Ricky would have balked, and he was the kind of person you wanted to have think the best of you. Darlene teetered up onto the little stool and smirked down. Her legs were swathed in midnight blue taffeta that scratched under Lindie's fingers.

"Why don't you sew this one?" Ricky suggested, handing Lindie a matching spool of thread and a long, sharp needle.

A lump formed in Lindie's throat. "I told you I can't," she said fiercely. She knew she'd ruin the costume; Darlene's costume, at that. She couldn't invite any more abuse from the girl who'd thrown erasers at her head and locked her in the janitor's closet and, worst of all, often called her "manchild."

Darlene remarked loudly, "Yeah, just sew it, Linda Sue."

Lindie felt her face grow scarlet. She told herself she didn't care what horrible Darlene thought of her. And it didn't make sense that she cared about Ricky; she'd only just met him. She mumbled that her father hadn't cared to teach her the things that had brought about her mother's moving out.

Darlene snickered above them. "Raised by a colored woman." Her hand fluttered to her chest in mock concern. "Poor little boy."

Without a second's hesitation, Ricky took a pin from the corner of his mouth and jabbed it straight into Darlene's juicy ankle. She howled in pain, grabbing at the site of the injury. Stumbling off the stool, she seethed like a bull, skirts rustling around her. Through gritted teeth, she

told Ricky she'd have him fired. He calmly stuck the guilty pin back
into his tomato and said, "Be my guest, honey. I'm sure my boss—who
paid to fly me all the way from Los Angeles—will take your word over
mine." He batted his eyelashes, wrapped an arm around Lindie, and
squeezed.

Tears cascaded down Darlene's furious face as she stormed off. Victory soared through Lindie at the sight, and Ricky shook his head as he
watched the girl go. Then he turned to Lindie and took her hands, dark
eyes boring gravely into hers. "My darling little Dorothy Parker, if you
want to get anywhere in this life, we must teach you how to sew."

An hour into the day and Lindie was already in love with all of it.
Her St. Judian existence, which had seemed perfectly enjoyable even the
day before, suddenly revealed itself to be excruciatingly dull. She was a
P.A. now. That was all that mattered. And it was why she didn't consider
the fact that, because of the movie, Artie's 9:00 a.m. bus from Columbus, which June was on her way to meet, wouldn't be stopping at the bus
stop in Center Square. In fact, any thought of June or June's concerns
had flitted straight out of Lindie's head—a first, to be sure, in years.

CHAPTER ELEVEN

———

B Y THE TIME JUNE NEARED FRONT STREET, THEY HAD started shooting, the imperative "Quiet on the set!" reverberating through the crowd. Nearly everyone in town had flocked to the other end of Center Square, where they could get a better view. Hidden as the St. Judians were by the elms, hushed as they were by their handler, and distracted as June was by her imminent reunion, she saw that day only as her mother had planned it. She paced herself on the sidewalk. Scanned down over her body filling out the new dress; she was not a girl in pigtails anymore. She found the part of her that liked that truth, and clenched it.

With fifteen minutes until the bus arrived, June was already at Center Square. She'd take a walk around it once, and keep herself on a slow tread. She crossed Front Street gingerly, hardly noticing the particular emptiness of the sidewalks and brushing aside the occasional bubbling murmur from the far side of the elms. Something was going on down there—a burst pipe maybe, or a fender bender—but it was none of her concern. She had to focus all her goodness on Artie's arrival; she couldn't let anything get in the way of this stroll. She held her head high and pasted a smile across her lips, so everyone in St. Jude would see how happy, how ready, she was to become Mrs. Artie Danvers.

"Ma'am? Ma'am? You'll have to go around." A bespectacled stranger holding a clipboard stood in her path. He was young, but already a man. He scowled.

June stepped to the left and he matched her, blocking her from moving forward. She stepped to the right and there he was again. "Excuse me," she said briskly, pointing toward the end of the green. "I'm on my way to meet my fiancé's bus." She noticed then that Mrs. Dammeyer's lawn down on the end there was filled with neighbors, all jostling for a glimpse of something June didn't understand.

Once again she tried to edge around the man, if you could call him that. Once again, he stopped her. "You're right in the middle of our shot."

The movie—she'd forgotten all about the movie. The memory of Lindie's excitement over those ridiculous magazines flushed June with frustration, and this imperious little man blocking her way made it worse. All she wanted to do was meet Artie's bus.

"Well, you're right in the middle of the bus stop," she said, putting her hands on her hips, "and my fiancé is due to arrive on the nine o'clock bus from Columbus."

He shook his head triumphantly. "The bus has been diverted."

"Where?"

"Hell if I know."

June could see he was actually enjoying this, enjoying swearing at her and making her wait. His colleagues behind him were starting to get restless. They were calling to him, removing the caps from their heads.

June crossed her arms. "Well I'm going nowhere until you say where the bus is stopping, since you're the reason it's not where it's supposed to be." She could feel the eyes of the crowd, the crew, and the extras turning in her direction, noting her haughty air. But she thought she might cry if she couldn't get Artie's arrival over with, once and for all.

Just then, Darlene Kipp emerged, wailing, from Memorial High. She was a sight—tearstained face, hair a-tangle, the overlong skirt of her costume gathered in her fists. She spotted June with the man and re-doubled her sobs, running toward him. He blanched at the sight of her, and June felt momentarily triumphant, until Darlene was upon them and wailing, "They attacked me! They attacked me!"

"Miss, please," the little man said distastefully, "I can't understand a word you're saying."

Darlene shuddered under a forced sob. "That horrible little seamstress-man stabbed me with a pair of scissors, and that awful little friend of yours Linda"—here she turned on June—"was his accomplice."

The man sighed down over his clipboard, shaking his head. "I'll be back soon, ladies." He headed over the bridge and toward the crew, who, along with the rest of the town, was watching June and Darlene with a great deal of interest. The crew formed a huddle around the man, heads shaking, fingers wagging, shoulders raised in consternation.

June turned on Darlene, who had stopped crying the instant the man walked off. Darlene's frown had been replaced by a satisfied smile that June wanted to smack right off her face.

"How do you have room for all that meanness? You're such a scrawny little thing," June said in a low voice.

"I have witnesses"—Darlene sniffed—"so you shut your mouth right now, June Watters. Besides, you know as well as I do that you're only going to make it worse if you try to help that wretched Linda Sue."

"What I know," said June, who'd had it up to her eyeballs with this day, "is if you want to come dance with dumb old Charlie Philips at my wedding, you'll keep your own mouth shut, leave my friend alone, and get off this set at once."

Darlene's hand was on her hip, her lips pursed tight. "If that freaky little friend of yours comes near me one more time I swear I'll gut her like a—"

In an instant, Darlene's eyes went from flashing at June to jumping to something right behind June's head, which, at once, caused her ugly little face to melt into extraordinary softness, as though her true self had flitted out from behind a dark mask she'd been wearing her whole life. A doughy smile brightened her wide mouth.

Confused, June turned to discover a tall, broad man standing just behind her, hand poised to tap her shoulder. She recognized him at once, but she couldn't quite make sense of him. It was as if each part of his face disappeared as she glanced at the next bit of him—nose, eyelashes, ears, smile. She tried to place his name, but her mind churned too slowly. She knew, with certainty, that she'd never seen him in her life. And yet she also had, which was impossible, until she thought of the stack of Lindie's movie magazines now lying on her floor.

Jack Montgomery. Could it be? The man standing before her looked everything and nothing like the Jack Montgomery in Lindie's magazines.

June's limbs were numb, her mouth was dry. She felt suspended in time as she watched the man tip his hat and utter words she couldn't quite comprehend, bending to kiss Darlene's hand and apologizing for any unpleasantness that might have occurred in the costume area.

Darlene waved her hand breezily. "It's no trouble," she gushed.

The movie star suggested Darlene might want to go back for a proper fitting before shooting began for the day; he insisted she push to see Ethel and Ethel alone. "Ethel's the best there is," he said. "Which is why she'll be hard to get. But you, my dear, deserve the very best." He kissed Darlene's hand, winked, and offered a playful bow. Darlene nodded a dreamy assent and practically floated off toward the high school, turning more than once to wave and giggle.

Once Darlene was out of earshot, he turned to June, who had caught up to herself. Jack Montgomery was just a man standing before her, like any other man, handsome, yes, smelling of Brylcreem, but also weathered, real, with a touch of tobacco, and the salty dusting of leftover sweat. His eyes were an extraordinary, odd, violet—the color of the sky just before a summer shower, although his hair was as jet-black in real life as it appeared on screen. It was odd to discover she felt calm, now that he was close to her. That he felt familiar.

"That should get rid of her for a while," he said brightly.

"I beg your pardon?"

He leaned in as if they shared a joke. "There is no Ethel."

"Oh," June managed, wondering how much of her conversation with Darlene he'd overheard. Where had he come from? She felt a little dizzy, a little strange, as if under a spell.

"I liked how you stood up for your friend," he said.

Could it be that Jack Montgomery was just plain nice? Just the kind of person who'd help out someone he didn't know? She was about to ask how he liked St. Jude when he lifted a finger.

"So I heard you want to be in my picture."

She felt herself blush. "No," she said. "I want to know about the bus."

"I can get you a speaking part." Was he teasing her? Or did he mean it? He pointed toward the man with the clipboard, who was watching them, along with a lot of other people, from the other side of the canal. "I know the guys in charge."

June felt the eyes of her neighbors and the movie people darting all over her curve-hugging number. The rouge on her cheeks that had seemed fresh at home now felt brazen. "I'm sorry to trouble you."

"Not very sorry. Not sorry enough to give up."

She blinked back hot, embarrassed tears. "Well, if he'd only told me where to—"

A wary kindness softened Jack's stormy eyes. "Don't let old Danny get to you. He's a sad little fellow with a sad little job." He did his best impression of a gatekeeper, frowning over a clipboard, wagging his finger.

"What's it going to be," he said quietly, intimately, "you in or not? You drive a hard bargain but my final offer is a supporting role."

June felt her embarrassment recede now that Jack's eyes were on her. The world had hushed around them; everyone was waiting to see what he'd do next. And he seemed to be waiting on her.

She shook the cobwebs from her head, forcing herself to think of Artie. "I just want to know about the bus."

"Right," he said, wagging his long, straight finger in recognition. "The fiancé. Someone mentioned a fiancé."

In the same moment, Lindie emerged from the high school, having narrowly avoided Darlene, and spotted June standing just inside Center Square, flirting with someone who looked impossibly like Jack Montgomery. Lindie backed up behind the overgrown hydrangea and whistled. She couldn't have dreamed this up, not in a million years, not the way June and the movie star seemed to match each other, how each curved toward the other, how they already appeared to be keeping each other's secrets.

"Danny!" Jack called, without moving his eyes from June's.

Danny started coming their way. "Yessir, Mr. Montgomery."

Jack held up his hand to tell Danny to stay where he was. "The bus stops where?" he called again, twinkling eyes never leaving June's face. He was putting Danny in his place for June's sake.

"Cherry Street, sir," Danny yelled back. "Cherry and Pine."

"Cherry Street." Soft, and private, as though she hadn't just heard the other man yell it, as though it was just the two of them. "Cherry and Pine." Only a block away, off the green, in front of the library. If she hadn't been so hotheaded, she'd have guessed it herself.

"Well, thank you very kindly," June managed, waiting for him to go back to set. Instead, he stood back and bowed, gesturing to the walkway before him. His violet eyes danced over her. She realized the movie star was planning to watch her walk away.

June's feet took on a life of their own. It was a delicious sensation, walking under the gaze of this man. She felt herself flush, but she couldn't keep her hips from swaying as she stepped away from him.

Lindie had never seen June walk like that. It was more than the walk, though. It was that she no longer looked like she was playing dress-up. She looked like she'd been made for that tight blue dress, with her hair done up and her lipstick brighter than an apple. Lindie's collar felt tight as Charlie Philips, racing by to catch a bit of the movie action, stopped to tip his hat. He turned and stumbled and watched June go, so taken with the sight that he didn't even notice Jack Montgomery standing there beside him. Everyone was watching June. No one had seen a thing like it.

CHAPTER TWELVE

———

I T WAS 9:06 WHEN JUNE FINALLY DASHED AROUND THE CORNER of Cherry and Pine, and 9:07 when Lindie slipped around it and hid behind Mrs. Holcomb's boxwood hedge. The back of June's sharp black heel had started to chafe, forming a blister she knew would punish her for weeks to come. But she pressed through, hiding her limp.

She looked like herself again, a little hesitant, a little careful, and Lindie felt a relief she didn't know how to name. Seeing June so altered by that famous man had made her far less predictable in Lindie's eyes, which was why Lindie couldn't resist following her. She figured as long as she came back to set jogging, Casey wouldn't know she'd been slacking.

They heard the roar of the bus before they saw it. Would Artie Danvers kiss her? Did she want him to? June straightened herself as the bus turned the corner before braking to a sigh at her feet. Would she kiss him back? The doors pushed open. The sun was hitting the windows, so it was hard to make anyone out, but the tall figure fourth in line was sure to be him. First was Mrs. Royce, back from her regular Friday night visit to her daughter's down in Lancaster. Next, a mother and young son who passed June by, noses in the air, as if she didn't exist. So the next person off would be Artie.

But it wasn't. It was the strange, lanky boy who always wore a baseball cap and whom the girls had once seen throw a tin can at a stray dog. After him came a middle-aged woman gathering up her knitting.

June leaned forward after the knitter stepped off the bus. Surely, surely Artie was coming. He had simply let the ladies go out before him. June realized the bus driver was reaching to shut the doors and heard herself shout, "Wait!"

The driver frowned.

"My fiancé's on this bus," June said, realizing how unsure she sounded. "Arthur Danvers? He's tall . . . he's, he's handsome."

The driver smiled wryly. "No one handsome on my bus today." He closed the doors in her face, gunned the engine, and rolled off into the morning, leaving her in a cloud of fumes.

June watched the bus go. Artie had fallen asleep on it. Any moment he'd wake up and yell, "Stop this bus!" and it would come screeching to a halt, and he'd dash off and come running toward her, arms outstretched, like something out of a Jack Montgomery movie. Lindie didn't want June to marry Artie Danvers, but she wanted that grand romantic gesture for June's sake. She couldn't bear to see the way her friend's shoulders slumped, how small she had so quickly become in the large and disappointing world.

The bus drove off.

June stood in front of the library until Mrs. Wilson, who held weekday Bible study in the main reading room—and was apparently of the belief that the St. Judians would rather study Proverbs 31:30 ("Charm is deceitful, and beauty is vain, but a woman who fears the Lord is to be praised") than watch Jack Montgomery film the first scene of *Erie Canal*—unlocked the front door and asked June if she'd like to come inside. June said no—she knew better than to be sucked in by Bible study—but neither could she stomach going home, or back to the movie set, or anywhere else in that godforsaken town, and so she hooked her shoes over her fingertips and headed west, letting her stockings fray along her soles, lifting her eyes at Lindie as she passed without a word.

BY DINNERTIME, LINDIE had learned a very rough whipstitch, and delivered the Cokes without incident, among a dozen other things. The crew had broken for the day, heading back to their housing on the other side of town. But Lindie didn't go home. Eben was a believer in Vienna sausages eaten straight from the can, in anchovies and popcorn and the occasional slab of fried Spam; Lindie preferred to beg by Apatha's kitchen door. Besides, that meant a glimpse of June, although she'd probably still be moping over Artie. Lindie could have walked the block to the far side of Uncle Lem's house, but her cherry-colored Schwinn, with its bright headlight, sharp little bell, and a backseat carrier made of chrome, offered an irresistible swagger. She still couldn't shake the sight of June walking saucily away under Jack Montgomery's gaze.

Apatha opened the Two Oaks kitchen door after Lindie's first knock. "She's not with you?" she asked in a low, worried voice.

Lindie's heart sank. "Artie wasn't on the bus," she explained. "And I was working all day."

Behind Apatha, Lindie noticed a man eating the fried chicken dinner she'd hoped would be hers. His skin was lighter than Apatha's, but it was dark enough that his presence would be noticed in town. He was younger than her father, but old enough to know better than to slouch over his food. He nodded in Lindie's direction, but didn't get up or even say hello.

"My nephew, Thomas," Apatha explained, as if annoyed with them both. Lindie edged into the warm room, which smelled deliciously of hot oil. A single fly buzzed against the ceiling fan. The oven ticked with leftover heat; the linoleum tiles had been freshly mopped and offered up a lemony scent. The door to the foyer stood open, which was unusual; Cheryl Ann preferred to have her food appear on the dining room table without being reminded of the labor required to make it.

"I didn't know you had a nephew," Lindie said. She felt a twinge of jealousy; she'd never seen Apatha with her own blood.

"I didn't know it was any of your business," Apatha replied crisply. Now was when she'd usually open the china cabinet, take out a plate, and pile it with a crispy battered chicken thigh and a pillow of mashed potatoes, which would be followed by her special remedy to cure all that ailed: hot milk steamed with honey and vanilla. Instead she called out "Mrs. Watters?" toward the front of the house. She lifted her chin toward Thomas, who wiped his mouth on the napkin.

"Is that her?" Cheryl Ann called out from the front room.

"It's not my fault," Lindie griped. Apatha sniffed unsympathetically. Thomas stood in advance of Cheryl Ann's entrance.

June's mother marched into the room, fists balled tightly into her doughy hips. "Where is she?" She glowered.

Lindie explained that the younger Mr. Danvers hadn't gotten off the bus. She left out the part about how this only proved her point that he was not a suitable husband.

But she didn't need to speak out of turn to make Cheryl Ann's lips tighten into an angry sphincter. June's mother needed Lindie, and they both knew it, which only made things worse. "So Arthur missed his bus. That doesn't excuse this kind of behavior. She'll come home at once."

As though Lindie was the one to blame. "I'll tell her. If I find her," Lindie added, though there was really only one place June could be.

Cheryl Ann shooed Lindie out the door. "Bring her home. Tell her I won't tolerate this." Lindie noticed Apatha rest her hand, briefly, on Thomas's shoulder, and he sat back down to the half-eaten dinner. The screen door slammed shut. And now Lindie was outside again, empty belly growling. The first mosquito of the season landed on her wrist. She watched Thomas chew his hot meal as she boarded her Schwinn.

LINDIE PEDALED SOUTH, nearly out into the alfalfa fields that bordered that side of St. Jude. But before she reached them, she turned in to the Elm Grove Cemetery, speeding past those gray headboards of eternal rest. Cheryl Ann hadn't been able to pay to bury Marvin in the cemetery in Lima; it was Uncle Lem's charity that had afforded this patch of earth.

By the time Lindie got to her, June had weeded every inch of her daddy's grave. She looked up at Lindie with dry eyes.

The night was hot; Lindie wished she'd brought her canteen. She could have gone for a can or two of Vienna sausages, come to think of it. Instead, she fished a limp Marlboro from her pocket and lit it from a flattened box of matches. Then she slumped down beside June. Their backs pressed up against Marvin Watters's name. Lindie offered a drag. June took the cigarette with her dirty fingers and drew a long inhale. She was already in trouble with Cheryl Ann; might as well get her money's worth.

June handed back the cigarette and ran her arm across her chapped mouth.

"Jack Montgomery," she said. The name was hungry in her mouth.

And Lindie knew June was asking her, telling her, to get him.

June 2015

CHAPTER THIRTEEN

———

I T WASN'T THE DOORBELL THAT AWOKE CASSIE THE NEXT MORN-
ing. She certainly wasn't done dreaming, and she'd definitely had more
than her share of Jack Daniel's the night before. But the voices were
insistent; real, solid voices, not the tendrils of conversation that swirled
through the dream Cassie and Two Oaks were having together—of June
refusing to come home, and Lindie volunteering to rescue her (although
familiar, this young version of June was unrecognizable to Cassie, and
Lindie was a mystery). The kitchen had smelled divine in the dream—
grease, chicken, potatoes; Cassie's stomach ached with soured whiskey.
She pulled her forehead from the pillow, wincing at her headache. Whoever was below her window was loud and logical, a point that Cassie's
hungover, half-asleep self couldn't help but find offensive.

A woman: "I am listening to you, I am, but why we have to hike all
over creation instead of just ringing—"

"I'm saying be nice. Just. Be. Nice." Nick?

"I'm very nice." The woman's voice again. With a smile this time.
Cassie fumbled for her glasses. The crack in the ceiling clicked into
focus. Cassie traced her eyes up and down the thin line, trying to puzzle
out the contradiction of the woman's voice—she had heard it before,
hadn't she?

"You guys, I don't understand why we can't just ring—" (Another
woman, her voice on edge. She sounded like California. Young.)

"Because I said so." Definitely Nick.

Three of them. They circled toward the back of the house. Cassie
groaned. The night had not been what one might call restful; she
couldn't quite hold on to what exactly had happened in the dreams,
but she knew they'd been a tangle of hope—something about a man
coming back after a long time—and, oh yes, had she dreamed about a
movie? Someone—that tomboy, maybe—was excited about a movie?

Could it be the same movie? Jack Montgomery's movie? Silly, but tempting, to think so. And irrelevant to her waking problems. What the hell was Nick doing back here? She thought she'd done a pretty kick-ass job of shutting him down. She should have known it was too easy.

"Slow down, I need your arm." The first woman's voice tickled at Cassie. They were nearly around the back of the house now, if Cassie's ears could be trusted. "Slow down, I need your arm." The sentence played over and over in Cassie's mind. She kept almost knowing who was speaking, and then the realization would scuttle away from her. And then:

What had Cassie said just before shutting Nick out? Something about how if Tate wanted Cassie's DNA she'd have to come get it herself?

Oh shit.

Cassie bolted upright. She ignored the swooning world, the nausea at the pit of her stomach, the throb at her temples. She put her foot to the floor, accidentally sending the empty Jack Daniel's bottle skating across the wide boards. She ignored the clatter as she strained to hear the woman's voice again. The trio had moved all the way behind the house now, so she could make out only occasional laughs, a light touch of conversation lilting in the open window.

Cassie discovered she was already dressed, if you could call the jeans and dirty T-shirt she'd been wearing the day before "dressed," and though she regretted looking even worse than she had when she'd opened the door for Nick yesterday, she needed to find out—desperately, in an embarrassing, gawking, fangirl kind of way—if who she thought was down there was who was really down there.

Cassie crept down the staircase, appreciating the ancient, slippery thrill of her sock-covered soles over each step. Hangovers make every sensation raw and more pronounced, for better or worse. Midlanding, she stopped to lick a smudge of tomato sauce off the corner of her shirt, remembering now that there'd been Bagel Bites. And sleuthing! Yes, now she could remember—she'd searched the closets for a trace of Jack Montgomery. Love notes, mementos, that kind of thing. She'd found letters, but they'd been disappointing. A stack from some girl named Lindie, bearing a Chicago postmark. This particular stash of missives had started in 1956; Cassie had shuffled through, opening ten or so of them, ending with one stamped 1958 and ignoring the rest once it was apparent the chicken scratch was never going to mention Jack Montgomery's name.

But wait! Cassie remembered brightly, suddenly, that she had found something later on, with more whiskey under her belt. Not the letters—something else. Something that glimmered with the possibility of June's connection to Jack. What was it? Maybe that was why she'd ended up drinking even more. Celebration—yes! She'd been jubilant, huddled beside the closet of the fourth bedroom, fingers and knees covered in dust. She'd lifted the bottle and toasted the dream people and her grandmother too, and gulped the tawny elixir, which appealed to her not at all now that morning had come.

The salty tang of Bagel Bites lurched in Cassie's stomach, especially as she tried to think, more reasonably, about the implications of her discovery, of Nick coming back, of the possibility of Jack and June having made her father together. The initial shock had worn off, and in its place had settled sorrow and trepidation and, on the other hand, movie stars and millions of dollars.

The Bagel Bites wanted to come back up. She couldn't hear the voices anymore; she guessed the people were coming around the far corner of the house, turning behind the kitchen, which meant she had a few moments left to pull herself together, but not enough time to empty her stomach and come out on top. Deep breaths. Deep breaths. She gripped the banister and forced down the bile, closing her eyes against the sunny colors the stained glass was insisting on painting her home.

Down the stairs to the foyer and then what? Right to the dining room and kitchen? Straight ahead into the back parlor? Left to the front porch? She strained to listen. The visitors passed the triple windows at the parlor floor. She crouched to spy. One of the three people was certainly Nick; she herded her mind away from the miasma of doubt and excitement and fury and worry that she felt at the sight of him. There was also the question of the young woman with long blond hair, and another woman—petite, lean—but she was wearing a baseball cap and sunglasses, impossible to identify between the overgrown rhododendrons and fluttering curtains and the contrast of the bright day.

Cassie made it to the front door, mentally applauding the Cassie of yesterday, who'd been inspired after slamming the door in Nick's face, if not to go through the pile of mail in the foyer, then at least to push it wholesale into the office. It looked as though she was planning to start a bonfire in there—tempting—but at least it was no longer blocking the front door.

Which she then opened, discovering the light was all funny for morning. Too yellow, too flat. The revelation of afternoon made Cassie's conviction waver; she knew what Nick would think when he saw her: not a grown-up. But why should she care? Did she care? Why did she care? She wished she had time to go back upstairs, change into something better. No, that was caring, wasn't it? Not caring was standing here, wearing whatever she wanted. Wasn't it? Should she disappear back into the house, and let them wait by the front door, let them ring? She wasn't sure she could handle that horrible sound again.

Before she had a chance to decide, the people emerged around the edge of the front porch and looked up at her, one, two, three.

Nick, with a smug smile on his face, as though he'd accomplished something grand.

A lean, blond girl of about Cassie's age, who squinted first and then flashed a winning, white smile.

And Tate Montgomery.

Good god, yes, Tate Montgomery in the flesh, removing her glasses and cap, climbing the steps, getting closer and closer like she had stepped out of some ridiculous Technicolor movie where she was larger than life and a chorus of strings swelled at the sight of her. But this was not a movie at all. It just kept going.

Tate Montgomery's eyes were the color of the Atlantic on a sunny day. She held out her hand. "I'm Tate," she said. Her voice was liquid. Her grip was strong.

CHAPTER FOURTEEN

———

NEW YORK HAD TAUGHT CASSIE TO BE COOL AROUND FA-
mous people. There was Susan Sarandon, that one time in Union
Square, and that opening Cassie'd worked at Alexander Pyke
when the cast of *Girls* showed up to support someone's husband, and
that afternoon Jeff Bridges popped in to buy his wife a painting. Jim,
the Pyke girls, and New Yorkers in general played it cool around famous
people. It was an easy pose to adopt: the hooded, brief glance at someone whose work happened to put them on the big screen and pay them
obscene amounts of money, followed by a feigned disavowal of caring.

But as Cassie clasped Tate Montgomery's baby-soft hand, she heard
herself babbling. "Wow. You're really Tate Montgomery! I'm Cassandra.
Cassie. You should call me Cassie. Hi. Nice to meet you. So nice to meet
you. Hi."

"Can I . . . ?"

Cassie realized what Tate was asking only after she felt herself pulled
into a hug by America's Sweetheart. Cassie's lungs were filled with the
sweet smell of honeysuckle as her eyelids fluttered shut. Cassie's heart
became a hummingbird. She hadn't allowed herself to fully luxuriate in
what it would mean to be a Montgomery until this moment. Her aunt
would be this woman—this perfect, rich, ultrafamous woman. And
Cassie would be rich too, rich beyond any measure—away would float
all her anxieties about keeping the house, about what to do with the rest
of her life. Not to mention she'd be able to buy herself clothing woven
from the fairy fabric with which Tate's white shirt was apparently made,
which was softer and lighter than the white fuzz that spun aloft through
St. Jude yards on summer afternoons.

The movie star pulled back. Her small hands fell upon Cassie's shoulders. Her eyes glistened. Tears? Joy? Up close, her beauty was exquisite,
something Cassie had never noticed on the big screen, where a goddess

apparently passed for a perfect average. The woman's skin glowed with either a flawless tan or the illusion of it. Not a golden strand of long hair was out of place. And the parts of her that Cassie had always seen as round on-screen were actually angular. She was muscular, lean, and didn't stand over five foot five; Cassie felt like a towering beast above her in her size ten jeans and large T-shirt.

Tate turned to Nick. That smile had graced a million photographs. "You didn't tell me she was so pretty."

Nick flashed Cassie a careful look. "Good afternoon."

"I see you're back," Cassie uttered, trying to ignore the wincing disappointment that he hadn't told Tate she was pretty. No, she thought, no, shut up, you don't care.

"I hope we didn't wake you," he said. "We didn't want to . . . ring." A playful, teasing hesitation before the final word.

"Actually," she volleyed, "I've been awake for hours. I heard you circling. I was in the bathroom." From the croak in her voice and the sleep still in her eyes, she was obviously lying. Not to mention she had just invited all of them to imagine her on the toilet. Off to an epic start, Cassie, she thought. But she doubled down under Nick's careful gaze. "I wondered who was trespassing."

Tate's eyes were back on her, her knuckles smoothing Cassie's cheek. "Blame me. For everything. I shouldn't have sent him to do my job. I should have been brave enough to face you myself. Forgive me."

Cassie noticed Nick open his mouth. But then he stopped himself. He took up his phone and was rapidly absorbed; whether his sudden interest was feigned was impossible to tell. The blond girl—she was too skinny and fresh-faced for Cassie to consider her a woman—was texting. So the moment was Tate and Cassie's (Cassie was to come to learn this was how the entourage worked—they were fully opinionated individuals when Tate deemed them necessary, and expected to retreat into invisibility when she decided they were not).

"I want to thank you," Tate purred, putting her warm palms on Cassie's cheeks, her face a symphony of sorrow and joy and compassion. "No, I need to thank you. For giving me a second chance. For inviting me. I'm thrilled to make this moment ours."

"Oh," said Cassie, wondering if, in fact, what she'd done was extend an invitation. Not that she minded—it was just not exactly how she remembered her conversation with Nick going. She snuck a quick glance at him, wondering what kind of game he was really playing. But any cynicism or doubt melted away in the heat of Tate's attention. Tate Montgomery was here in St. Jude and she might be Cassie's aunt. Cassie mumbled, "Thank you so much for coming. It's really nice. I can't believe I'm meeting you, actually. I'm such a huge fan."

Did Nick snort? Cassie glanced at him, but he seemed locked into his little machine. Tate's hands fell from Cassie's skin; the spots where her palms had been now pulsed. The grackle babies squawked greedily as their mother returned with food.

"Hank?" Tate turned toward the blond girl, whose head snapped up from her phone as though she'd been in sleep mode. She stepped forward, beaming a winning grin at Cassie.

"This town is awesome! So old-fashioned! I superlove it!" She climbed the steps and offered an outstretched hand. "I'm Hank, Tate's right-hand gal. I thought Ohio was all strip malls and Burger Kings!" One of those tall, pretty people who could compliment and insult in the same breath, and was, apparently, serious about the fact that her name was Hank.

"Okay," Cassie heard herself say, seeing herself and the moment in a dizzy twirl from above. "Okay. You guys want to come in?"

"You know what, Cassandra?" Tate said, and Hank and Nick and Cassie all looked at her at once, each of them appreciating the empathetic angle of her head. "I'd love that."

CHAPTER FIFTEEN

———

THEY HAD FLOWN FROM LOS ANGELES, BUT TATE ASSURED her it was nothing; they slept on the plane all the time. Cassie assumed she meant the private jet and tried not to squeal with envy and awe. She offered them water (all she had); they politely declined. She was relieved not to have to serve them cloudy glasses filled with the brackish stuff that chugged from the faucet, but she really had no idea what came next, except that, if she didn't line her sour stomach soon, they'd all be sorry. They stood awkwardly in the front parlor because there weren't enough seats. The house felt dark and shabby, especially under Hank's eyes, which scurried over every chunk of missing plaster and the curtains stiff with dust. Cassie's eyes met Nick's briefly, and he offered an encouraging smile.

"Did you know," he began, gesturing around the front parlor as if he was a college tour guide highlighting the institution's most esteemed building, "that this neoclassical treasure—called Two Oaks by the locals—was commissioned by Cassandra's grandmother June's great-uncle Lemon Gray Neely in 1895?"

Cassie couldn't imagine they were remotely interested, but Tate asked what Cassie knew about Lemon—"what a fabulous name!"— and Hank's attitude did a one-eighty as she fingered the lace curtains. Frankly, the extent of Cassie's knowledge about Two Oaks and Lemon Gray Neely ended just about there (and, to be honest, the dates were fuzzy).

But Nick had done his research: "He was the stuff of legend. A handsome, rich wildcatter—that's what they called an oilman who took risks. Six foot tall. Born poor in Titusville, Pennsylvania, where Edwin L. Drake established the very first oil well drill in 1859. Lemon learned at Drake's knee, then made his way here, to Auglaize County, which was booming with black gold by the 1890s—imagine the California Gold

Rush, but with oil instead. Lemon got a loan from Drake to buy up the fertile farmland that lined Lake St. Jude, just a few miles west of here. Lemon and his rivals were the first people to dig offshore wells on American soil. Can you believe it? Offshore oil wells in the middle of Ohio?"

They all shook their heads in awed incredulity, as though they'd been wondering for years where the first American offshore oil wells had been drilled. Cassie felt a grateful shimmer for the binding properties of Nick's nerdy optimism.

"Anyway, he made his fortune, fell in love with a local girl—Mae, I think her name was. Decided to build a house, but not just any house—he wanted it to last for the ages. He acquired these three acres, and decided to set the home's doorway in the natural center of those two large oaks—" He turned and pointed toward them, still there, on either side of the front walk. "Then he had three wooden houses built on a few empty lots across the street to house the workers." He gestured beyond the other side of the house, and Cassie knew exactly the small Victorian bungalows he meant; the one on the corner was where the nosiest neighbor lived, an old woman who obviously thought she was invisible but Cassie had seen peering through the blinds more times than she could count.

"Lemon had a draftsman down from Cleveland, and a bricklaying crew up from Cincinnati. He imported lathers and carvers from Germany, promising fair pay. In exchange for a roof above their heads, these men dovetailed, whittled, and built an estate Neely imagined would survive wars, christenings, cold winters and hot summers. It was a home built for the ages, built for generations."

Here Tate laughed and clapped her hands together. Cassie noticed the large diamond sparkling there, so big it couldn't possibly be real, except, of course, it was. "And here you are! Five generations later, as predicted! What an amazing house to grow up in."

"I didn't actually grow up here," Cassie replied, genuinely sorry to burst Tate's bubble, until she realized that, given Nick's threats, these people probably already knew all about her parents, and more. Her words hardened under this wary realization. "I grew up in Columbus. My parents died when I was eight. This was my grandparents' house"—in light of yesterday's news, every other word now seemed laden with uncomfortable meaning—"but my grandma came down to Columbus and lived with me there. I'd already lost my parents; she didn't want me to lose my friends, my school, you know, everything else." She'd said this speech a thousand times, but it was taking on new meaning in front of this audience. "My grandpa died when I was nine, so there really wasn't much reason to come back here. We spent a few summers in St. Jude, that kind of thing, but then I was a teenager and this was the last place I wanted to be. Really, it was only when I went off to college that my grandma moved back in."

Guilt overcame her as she looked around the shabby room; how had her grandma let this place get to this state? Why hadn't Cassie taken better care of her, especially after all those years when the shoe was on the other foot? She felt a knifing sorrow, which was quickly replaced with a nauseous quaver at the base of her stomach. She needed to eat or else.

"Illy's! We should go to Illy's," she blurted.

Tate glanced at Nick, and Cassie understood that the woman had been instructed to tread carefully. No sudden movements. Cassie felt an oddly intimate desire to throttle Nick for scheming behind her back, although, to be fair, he did work for Tate, and Cassie and he hadn't exactly left things on allied terms.

"It's a restaurant," Cassie clarified. "The only restaurant, actually. Unless you want Buffalo Wild Wings from the Pantry Pride parking lot." Hank balked, which was satisfying.

Nick cleared his throat and gave Cassie a look that belied very bad news. "Good idea. Only—well, Tate isn't 'here,' if you catch my drift. Officially, she's three thousand miles away, and it's best to keep it that way. You can't begin to imagine the circus this town will turn into if word gets out she's here. Paparazzi, neighbors wanting autographs . . ."

Tate glared at Nick, which shut him up. It was the same glare Cassie had used with her grandmother in high school, an "oh my god you are embarrassing me" look intended to shut someone up. Cassie felt a swoon of sympathy. Of course Tate Montgomery couldn't walk into a restaurant and expect to stay incognito; just look at her. Cassie had never imagined looking like that could be an inconvenience.

"What?" Nick bristled under Tate's glare. "This is how Margaret would have handled it. Don't you want me to handle it like Margaret?"

"I wasn't thinking," Cassie apologized. "The bad news is I don't have any food in the house." She added (lest there'd been shakes on the plane), "And I'm going to need something soon."

"Do they do takeout?" Hank chirped. "I'll pick it up! I love a witch hunt!"

"Goose chase," Tate corrected, then turned to Cassie, softening her whole demeanor. "Yes, full bellies for everyone. Illy's sounds divine."

Nick pulled a stack of twenties from his wallet—Cassie realized that, unlike nearly every other woman in the world, Tate wasn't carrying a bag—and Hank left for Illy's with her maps app open. Nick's phone rang, and he took the call into the dining room. Tate asked for a place to powder her nose. Through the front parlor window, Cassie watched Hank turning this way and that on the sidewalk as she tried to get her bearings. Lord only knew what the irascible waitress at Illy's would make of Malibu Hank traipsing in to order egg-white omelets and spinach salad with lemon juice on the side.

Cassie realized with sudden horror that she might not have recycled those tabloids that had been sitting beside the downstairs toilet for months, each with its own Tate Montgomery headline: TATE'S PREGGO FOR SURE!; TATE AND MAX IN PARADISE; HOW TATE STAYS FIT. Her stomach flipped like a Tilt-A-Whirl; she nearly went to the bathroom and knocked, then realized that would only make things more embarrassing.

Nick reemerged from the foyer. He was holding a bottle of Perrier. "From the car," he explained, pulling a small packet of Advil from his pocket.

"I thought I told you to leave me alone forever," she said gently, holding her hand out.

"That's not how I heard it."

"Apparently." She wouldn't trust him, not yet, but she'd enjoy his kindness while it lasted. She rested the medicine on her tongue and sipped the bubbly water, which tasted like the best thing on earth. "I look that bad, huh?"

"No," he said plainly. But he wanted to say something else.

"What then?" she asked.

His weight shifted imperceptibly toward her. "You look—"

"Well then," Tate interrupted, emerging from the bathroom, "shall we have a chat while we wait for sustenance?"

At the sound of Tate's voice, Nick jolted away. He pulled his phone out and strode back into the foyer, past Tate, whose footsteps crisply marked her way to Cassie on the couch. It was clear, then, to Cassie, that, whatever this flirtation meant, it was something Nick didn't want Tate to know about, which felt like a delectable secret, until she remembered what had brought him there in the first place, and then, once again, she tried not to feel like puking.

CHAPTER SIXTEEN

———

ASSIE FELT SHY AND BREATHLESS AS SHE TURNED HER
eyes once again on Tate, sitting just beside her on the yellow
couch. She wondered how many times a famous person could
astound you simply with her presence. Cassie couldn't even tell if the
woman was wearing makeup, that's how good the makeup job was. It
wasn't that her breath didn't smell, it was that it smelled indescribably
good, like actual baby's breath. She looked, every second, as someone
regular might look while glimpsed through a soft-focus lens.

Tate held out her left hand and pulled the giant, sparkling rock off
it. The diamond was so big it should have had a different name, like
superdiamond, or ultrastone. Tate held it up to the light, as if assessing it
for the first time. Slices of Ohio light filled the room as the rock's facets
flashed in the sun.

How odd for Tate to hand it over. "My engagement ring," she said.
Cassie supposed that was her way of explaining she wasn't giving it to
Cassie. It was weighty in Cassie's hand; the precious metal of the band
retained the star's body heat.

Popular opinion in the New York Cassie'd so recently belonged to
had diamonds pegged as politically appalling on two fronts—the blood
of African miners, and the trappings of marriage. For those reasons, and
the fact that she was pretty sure she didn't believe in lifelong monogamy,
she'd never once imagined a big, flashy rock perched on her ring, certainly not a stone of this size. But, just for a moment, Cassie thought
about slipping it onto her finger, this ring which she knew Max Hall
had given Tate in that famous proposal on the beach at Cap Juluca. The
fantasy felt positively velvety.

"Max—my husband—had it reset," Tate said, tilting her head beside
Cassie's as they looked at the rainbows it sent shimmering across the
parlor.

"Yeah," Cassie said, cringing at her heh-heh-heh as she felt her face grow hot, "I know who Max is." Max Hall, lead singer of Aloysius, hot in skintight leather pants, making love to the microphone. Max Hall, voted Sexiest Man Alive two years running, winner of Grammy Awards for Album and Song of the Year and every other best the music business could conjure. Max Hall, a man Cassie had imagined doing all sorts of things to her on more than one occasion, especially in her teenage years, especially under her comforter on Saturday mornings, based on one particular hair toss in the video for Aloysius's hit "Alms," as he cast his eyes down and howled the word *devoooootion*.

If Tate noticed Cassie's lust for her husband, she didn't let on, or maybe it was a Hollywood thing: no jealousy, at least not when it came to what your spouse was selling. Tate gestured to the ring. "This was the stone Daddy proposed to Mommy with, after they wrapped *Erie Canal*." Tate's eyes turned sad as she mentioned her movie star parents, but her smile stayed the same. Cassie could vaguely remember something scandalous about Tate's mother. Drugs? Drinking? She'd died relatively young, that was all Cassie could recall; Cassie supposed the childish term Tate used for her mother belied that. What was the woman's name?

Tate's gaze batted about the room. "I'd always meant to come to St. Jude myself. Mommy and Daddy spent that May shooting all the interiors in L.A., so it's not like they met here. But she always said St. Jude was where she knew Daddy was the one . . ." Tate's sentence trailed off as she was overcome by emotion.

Cassie had seen the woman before her cry too many times to count. Tate's movies had taught Cassie so many things, from how to French kiss to how to be the kind of gal who charmed and impressed men with a combination of self-reliance and fawning attention. Not to mention that Tate had influenced most of Cassie's fashion choices between the ages of fourteen and twenty-two. It followed, then, that Tate had taught Cassie how to cry. Cassie understood this as she watched the event unfold in real life before her: the plunge of the woman's chin, the tears rolling down her cheeks like silver sequins.

Cassie's parents had died when she was a little girl, so the loss had mostly hardened like a ball in her gut, but there were still days when the wet sorrow nearly drowned her, and she could see now that Tate was only just discovering that grief would come and go like a tidal wave. Was it wrong to feel proud of how much more she knew about this particular topic, how much more experienced she was at orphanhood than this ultrafamous superstar who was married to a rock god? Cassie let Tate weep, because it was her experience that it was awful to be made to feel you should stop, especially when you were grieving your dead parents, and she decided to share that tidbit of wisdom at some appropriate point in the future.

When Tate had composed herself, she folded her hands in her lap. "So now you understand," she said, as though she'd just completed a complex math proof.

"Understand?"

"Why I have to know. As soon as possible. I have to know if all that"—it looked as though Tate might cry again, but then grit killed the tears—"if the romance and the proposal and the fairy tale my parents fed me on was a lie. If the only reason Daddy asked Mommy to marry him was because he felt guilty for knocking up some townie."

Tate seemed to have forgotten that that "townie" had raised Cassie. Nick hadn't. He appeared, briefly, in the doorway, catching Cassie's eye, offering a glance of apology.

Tate didn't notice him. "You must help me, Cassandra Danvers. You must." She grasped Cassie's hand again and pulled it to her chest. "Daddy and I were so close at the end. We simply didn't keep secrets anymore. We'd worked so hard on our relationship, especially over the last ten years. I just . . . I can't believe he'd betray me like this. Can you understand that?"

The thing was, Cassie could. She, too, could not conceive of a world in which the woman who'd raised her—moral, kind, careful June—could have done any of the things that a positive DNA test would mean: have an affair, raise a clandestine love child, keep a secret from, yes, any of her family, but especially from Cassie. It hurt Cassie's heart to imagine the burden it would have been to keep such a secret for sixty years. And yet, a part of Cassie itched with the crazy prospect that June might have done just that. June was touchy about secrets. Hadn't that been the whole problem with the art show? What was it she'd said to Cassie in a low, devastated voice, outside the gallery? "What have you done, Cassandra? That was for us. That was our business, and not for the world to know."

Tate grew fervent. "I don't even care about the money—well, I care a bit, naturally, some of it was Mommy's money, and anyway, he was my father, I don't think it's wrong that Elda and I believe we should inherit what we deserve—but truly, what I care about most is getting to the bottom of what happened. I just want to know the truth. And the only way to know is to test your DNA against mine."

"What happens if you find out I'm not related to you?" Cassie asked bluntly.

Tate looked startled that Cassie had any questions at all. "Well," she began carefully, as though the possibility was only just occurring to her, "I'd offer you a compensation package for all your troubles—"

"Yes," Cassie said, impatient with the tiptoeing, because the money wasn't what she'd meant, "a million dollars, Nick said that."

Tate's spine was straight, and Cassie got the impression she was hoping Nick would reappear to help her. "And then we'd . . . leave you be."

"You'd be done with me."

"Oh goodness no, I don't think of it as that! I hope you won't either. I just meant that once the test is administered—just a cheek swab, by the way—I'll take care of all the logistics. You literally will not have to do one thing, pay one penny, in terms of lawyers. I'll settle this whole mess for both of us, and you'll, you know"—Tate's hands shuffled before her—"you'll . . . get back to your life."

It was then that they heard the steps on the porch: manly, rapid. As they approached the front door, it became clear that they were not Hank's. Nick and Tate reacted so quickly, it took Cassie a moment to figure out what was happening: the quick, shared glance toward the entrance, then Nick grabbing an afghan off the edge of the davenport (where it had been for who knew how long), Tate pulling it from him and tossing it over her head, Nick putting his arm around her and shuttling her into the bathroom under the stairs, as though she was a wanted woman. Nick turned to Cassie and mouthed: "Do not open it," and so Cassie stood there in the foyer, frozen, while the man approached the door, supposing this was what they'd meant when they said no one should find out Tate was in town. Did paparazzi really work this fast?

How had they discovered Tate's whereabouts? Cassie's heart pounded as she heard the man reach the door—she nearly ducked at the possibility of the doorbell ringing—and then the mail slipped through the slot.

Nick and Tate, barricaded in the bathroom, reemerged at the sound of Cassie's hooting laughter. She could barely get the words out as she clutched the new batch of past-due notices and tried to explain it was only the mailman. They looked amused, but certainly as delighted as she'd expected them to be, and then Nick asked if he and Tate could have a minute. "Something's come up," he said ominously, then they shut themselves back in the bathroom and Cassie found her way back to the couch.

What would June want Cassie to do about the DNA test? What June had said at the art show kept roaring up; she'd clearly valued privacy. Which meant, Cassie knew, that she'd loathe this, all of it; she'd be especially mortified to know her granddaughter and three strangers were speculating about her sex life, regardless of whether she'd ever even met Jack Montgomery.

There was nothing Cassie could do about that now, but she could be respectful of the old woman's memory from here on out, which meant shutting this down the fastest way possible. If there was a clear way to do so, Cassie supposed she should pick that option, only it was hard to tell what that was. On the surface, taking the DNA test seemed to be it, because there'd be a definitive answer on the other end. But then, if the answer was yes, that would yield the result exactly opposite to what the June in this scenario would have wanted; suddenly the whole world—or, at best, Cassie, Elda, and Tate—would know that Jack and June had slept together.

What did Cassie want? Thirty-seven million dollars was nothing to shake a stick at, and if she did the DNA test and it turned out positive, well, it was as good as winning the lottery. Wasn't it? Only what if she took the test and it said no, he's not your grandfather? Sure, there'd be Tate's million dollars, which she wasn't going to sneeze at. But putting money aside—if she could do that—she wasn't quite sure how to proceed. Jack Montgomery had thought he was her grandfather; now that she knew that, could she ever truly unknow it? Even if he was wrong about her paternal line, something had made him believe he'd fathered her dad. She knew her grandmother liked her secrets kept, but could Cassie bear not to find out if good little June Watters and big-shot Jack Montgomery had shared a bed, or maybe even a romance, if not a son?

Maybe Cassie wouldn't be considering delaying the DNA test if Tate had shown much interest in discovering the ins and outs of their potentially shared history. But it was clear that Tate didn't want to find out why her father had left everything to Cassie; she only wanted to find out if Cassie's father was Jack's son, and Cassie was starting to realize these were two vastly different things. Cassie was pretty sure she was more interested in finding the answer to the first problem than to the second, which was really annoying, because it would be nice to have $37 million, or even "just" a million, as soon as humanly possible. But maybe, more than money, what she wanted was Tate's help, Tate's entourage, Tate's resources. Cassie could already see that the only way to get all that was to make Tate wait for what she wanted.

Tate came back from the bathroom, and Nick headed off to the dining room, leaving behind a cloud of exasperation, which Tate deftly ignored and Cassie wondered at, briefly, before turning back to her own concerns.

"Even if I'm not your niece," Cassie said, her throat feeling suddenly, horribly dry, "because that's what I'd be, isn't it?—there's still a chance . . ." She took Tate's hand in hers while it was still accessible and, gripping it tightly, started again. "Since your father named me in the will, and he mentioned me in that note you got—even if I'm not biologically related, well, there's a chance that he loved my grandmother, right? A chance that she loved him? Even if he didn't get her pregnant."

Tate withdrew her hand.

Nick appeared, magically, in the doorway.

"No offense, Tate," Cassie said, "but I don't think you want to know the truth. What you want to know is whether your father conceived a child with my grandmother. I think I'd like to know more than just that."

Cassie was giddy now, but Tate looked positively alarmed. Cassie hadn't done anything like this in a long time, taken a risk, jumped into the unknown. She'd forgotten how good it made her feel. In fact, her first impulse, as she stood, was to take a picture, because the room had suddenly grown so still, so taut, that all she wanted was to capture it, freeze it, save forever how particular and dangerous this moment felt. She believed herself to be powerful and brave, especially as she remembered exactly what she'd found the night before, the cause for her celebration, and she knew, at last, that she was going to go and get it, and show them, and try to make them see that her DNA wasn't all they should be after.

CHAPTER SEVENTEEN

————

ASSIE CAME DOWN VIA THE MASTER STAIRCASE; IT FELT like the moment to make a grand entrance. When she returned to the front parlor, sneezing from dust, Tate and Nick grimaced at the periodicals in her arms. True, the whole collection looked like any old stack of long-forgotten magazines: *Life, Screen Play, Movie Life.* Cassie wouldn't have thought anything of them at any other point, but discovering them at the back of the closet, under a Montgomery Ward bag after the day she'd had, had given them new meaning.

She flipped the top magazine open, eyes watering from the flaking pages. On page 57, she stopped at a photograph of the man she'd pictured at the mention of Jack's name: that dark brow, those handsome eyes, a devilish grin. He had a little girl on his lap. She was laughing up at him, clutching a teddy bear.

"Jack Montgomery loves his days at home with his beautiful daughter Esmerelda," the caption read.

In the *Screen Play* underneath the *Life,* a seven-picture spread: "Jack Montgomery and Diane DeSoto's Beautiful New Home!" The house was one of those Hollywood fantasies—rolling lawns, tall columns, courtyard fountains; it occurred to Cassie that the architect had been trying to conjure up the kind of vintage charm that Two Oaks possessed without even trying.

A copy of the *Los Angeles Times* from the sixties held a birth announcement: "Jack Montgomery and Diane DeSoto announce the birth of Tate DeSoto Montgomery." Tate took the crumbling newspaper into her hands, cooing at the news of her own birth, and Cassie itched again for her camera; there was something about the urgency in the woman's face that Cassie wanted to secure on paper.

It went on like that, a six-inch-high pile. As far as Cassie could tell, the magazines' only commonality was mention of Tate's father. Cassie watched Tate and Nick as they scrutinized the articles. What would it mean for June to have had a secret love worth $37 million? It would mean June had lied to Cassie and to Cassie's father, El, and to June's husband, Arthur. It would mean Jack had lied to his wife and his girls. It would mean both of them had kept their shared secret to their graves. And if Cassie said no to the DNA test, well, she'd be asking Tate and Nick and Hank to help her squirrel out any evidence of this supposed affair, which was pretty much the opposite of what June—secretive, private June—would want. But then, June was gone, and Jack was gone, and Tate and Cassie were the ones left to make sense of the mess their guardians had left for them. Maybe Cassie needed to stop feeling so guilty.

"Help me," she blurted, as soon as Tate closed the final magazine. "Help me find out what would have led my grandmother to keep these, and I'll give you as much of my DNA as you want."

Tate smiled tightly. She placed a magazine back onto the stack on the table. "My dear"—she was icy now, superior—"many women stockpile celebrity rags."

"My grandmother wasn't just any woman," Cassie said, bristling anew at the "townie" reference. "She was the woman who raised me. A very unsentimental, practical person who didn't keep movie magazines lying around." Now that she'd mentioned it, Cassie crossed into the back parlor and opened the cabinet that held June's VHS movies. She tore through the cardboard covers, black-and-white images with the names of the stars printed across the front. How was it she had never noticed that Jack Montgomery's name was splashed over nearly half of them? She held one up triumphantly. "It can't be a coincidence that a person who appears in every one of those, and on nearly every one of these, a man who was filming in this town sixty years ago, is the same person who just named me as his sole heir." But all that time, she was doubting it too, seeing her grandmother bent over Artie's bedside in his last days, how she'd wept for him, and called him the love of her life. Why shatter that illusion? Why not just let the old bird rest in peace?

"I'm sure your grandmother was quite special"—Tate sniffed—"but my father had millions of fans, girls who collected posters and Playbills and God knows what else." A part of Cassie agreed with this; why was she even arguing the other side?

But Nick cleared his throat. "True, Tate, but it appears he only claimed one of those women's granddaughters as his own."

Both Tate and Cassie gaped at him. He crossed his legs nervously in the floral armchair, then uncrossed them, then crossed them again.

"We'll go through the house," Cassie said, since it seemed Nick wouldn't be of any more use, "and we'll look for other clues. In the meantime, there have to be people we can ask. Did your father keep a diary? Can we go to his accountant?"

Nick turned to Tate. "We do have his private papers."

Tate hummed a deep, yogic exhale.

"So we'll send for your father's private papers," Cassie said, "and comb them for any mention of my grandmother. And then we'll interview anyone who might have known either of them at the time. We can even interview people in St. Jude, people who knew them that summer."

"It might not be the worst thing, Tate," Nick offered, surprising Cassie. "No one knows you're here. You could lie low for a bit." Cassie had the feeling he was speaking in subtext about something beyond her reach, but, regardless, she hated how miserable Tate looked; the woman was, after all, her childhood idol.

Cassie softened her voice and tried to get Tate to meet her eye. "Can't we just try? For them? Don't you want to know if they shared something special, something good? Maybe it means something different from what we think it does."

The front door jangled open. "You'd think I was speaking Mandarin," Hank griped, barging into the front parlor bearing armfuls of plastic bags. "They have no idea what egg whites are, and I guarantee the bacon isn't turkey." Her cute little nose wrinkled.

Nick rushed to relieve her load. Hank caught his expression, then turned to take in Tate's and Cassie's. "Why so glum?"

Tate's hands were placed on her thighs. Centered again, she opened her eyes calmly. Serenity poured out of her as she offered a practiced smile. "Just a change of plans, sweetie. Seems we'll be enjoying Ohio longer than expected."

June 1955

CHAPTER EIGHTEEN

———

TIME MOVES DIFFERENTLY ON A FILM SET; NOT UNLIKE HOW it moves in a hospital waiting room, or at an airport gate with a flight delay. The gathered tribe is united by faith and fear, hoping and believing and wondering if they're asking the impossible, until the good news comes—the scene finally gels, the emotion swells, the assistant director yells the day's last "cut!"—and everyone breathes a sigh of relief and slips back into their own skin. A day of shooting can feel weeks long, which is how, by the Friday afternoon of the first week of *Erie Canal*'s film shoot, after only three days of P.A.'ing in Center Square, Lindie felt she'd spent the most important era of her life on a film set.

By Friday, which was June 3, they'd made a good dent in what the crew was calling the "townspeople scenes," which required a handful of extras to mill about in the background of Center Square while Jack Montgomery and a few of the actors who'd been flown in from Hollywood shared dialogue. The scene had them talking about their characters' service in the Civil War, and in the upcoming election in Monroeville (that was the name the screenwriter had given the Hollywood version of St. Jude). Everyone was sure Jack Montgomery's character, Aloysius "Skip" Branigan, would be elected mayor. When Jack spoke Skip's lines in his careful drawl, the name fit.

The biggest shooting days, the ones that would require two hundred extras, were to come the following week, during the election sequence, when the dastardly incumbent mayor would defeat Skip Branigan. Then Skip's already wounded spirit would plummet into the downward spiral that would ultimately bring about his tragic end on that stormy night out alone on the canal.

Next week was also when Diane DeSoto, who played Jack's love interest—an honest farm girl named Mary who'd awaited his return from the war with only her pioneer spirit to protect her—would join the set in St. Jude. Word had it she was flying in on Sunday, and that she and Jack had been pretty cozy back on the MGM lot when they were filming the interiors. That was certainly the impression Lindie had gotten from her movie magazines, and though, only three days before, she'd believed Jack and Diane were the couple of the year, she now wished, for June's sake, that that was a bunch of rubbish.

Lindie hadn't read the script of *Erie Canal,* but she'd gathered that, although it was supposed to be about the years after the Civil War— when the heroes of the North returned to their old jobs and towns to discover that nothing was quite the same—it was really about men like June's father, who'd gone to Europe and returned home with hearts and minds that didn't work the way they were supposed to anymore. This was the primary reason she was glad June wasn't hanging around set; the topic would surely upset her. But Lindie also liked June's absence for a guiltier reason: for the first time she could remember, she felt unencumbered. Hours passed when she didn't think about June once. When she did, she was scheming about getting June an audience with Jack Montgomery, which felt both grown-up and in deliciously direct disobedience of Cheryl Ann.

That Friday, Lindie loafed around Crafty, waiting for Jack to pass on his way to his trailer when they wrapped for the day. It wouldn't be long; the light was turning golden, the shadows stretching across the green. The thought of June made the envelope in Lindie's pocket burn. The missive had been in her possession since she'd gotten home the night before, when Eben had handed it across the table with a bewildered frown, asking what kind of business she had with Arthur Danvers. In the privacy of her room, she'd ripped the letter open, only to discover it contained a letter within a letter. The part addressed to her read: "Dear Linda Sue, I hope you won't mind me asking you to deliver this. I'm convinced Mrs. Watters is reading June's mail, and I wanted this to get to her without anyone else tangling in it. Could you do that for me? A."

Lindie had read and reread his tight cursive, which was pretty in a womanly way she was happy to scorn. And the presumption! The idea that she'd gladly risk her hide to deliver a note for someone she hardly knew, and certainly didn't like, someone who'd made a promise to be on a bus from Columbus and then didn't even have the courage to tell June he wouldn't be on it—well, Artie Danvers had another think coming if he considered her his ally.

But then, she'd read the note he'd sent to June. Of course she couldn't show it to June now, because June would see how much Lindie had handled it, even if Lindie disposed of that second sealed envelope marked "For June's blue eyes only" (in her state Lindie'd had no qualms about slipping her nail under that envelope's flap to rip it open).

Lindie didn't want June to like Artie. But it was hard to hold this letter against the man:

June, sweet June—

I'm sorry I wasn't on that bus. And I'm sure you'll find it strange when I say here, again, that I care for you. Believe me—it's only because I do that I stayed away. Poor girl—I know you are only marrying me because it's what they've asked of you. And so I'll do my best to keep away until after July 3—maybe forever if I can help it. I want to marry you more than anything in the world. But I can't bear the thought of forcing you into it.

Then again, maybe Artie was like most men, and had only written these persuasive words to look good. June was lucky she had Lindie on her side.

JACK AND THE REST of the cast played the scene a fourth time as the natural light slipped lower, Jack crossing from camera left to camera right, the actor who played the mayor shaking his hand. For the fourth time, they volleyed the quick exchange of dialogue about the dangerous assignment up the canal, and then the director yelled his "Cut!" and the A.D. yelled "Break for the night!" and everyone breathed a sigh of relief that soon they'd be home, eating their Friday night casseroles.

Jack picked his way across the lawn, shaking the hands of a few lingering extras, clapping the director on the back with a hearty laugh. Jack's shadow was long between the shadows of the elms. Lindie straightened her spine and cleared her throat. He stopped in his tracks and beamed her his watty smile. "There you are, Rabbit Legs." She'd earned this nickname after only a few hours on set, although how he'd picked it up, she had no idea. He seemed so focused whenever she saw him, on his lines, his fellow actors, the weak-kneed extras, that she couldn't imagine he'd had the time or energy to learn her nickname.

"You said to talk tomorrow, sir," she said. She'd taken him off guard the day before, before she'd gotten Artie's letters, when she was more sure of what to do, and less apprehensive of the consequences. She'd just stepped into his path and said, "That was my friend June you were talking to about the bus stop. She'd like to meet again." He'd been due in makeup. She'd expected him to laugh her off set. But instead he'd nodded briskly, as though it were a perfectly understandable request, and told her to find him tomorrow. Well, now tomorrow was today.

Today, Jack lowered his baritone voice. He leaned in close, so no one else could hear. He smelled like cedar—safe, damp. His brow furrowed. "Is she sure?"

Lindie wasn't expecting him to ask that. She certainly didn't have a considered answer. On her side of childhood, she wasn't sure of anything; she just leapt in feet first and hoped she survived. Such a query would, indisputably, have sent June for the hills. And then she thought of Artie's letter in her pocket, how quickly it would sway June back to Artie's camp. Lindie wanted so much more for June.

"She's very respectable, Mr. Montgomery." Lindie's throat clamped tight around the truth. "I believe that's what's going to ruin her life. She's going to do all the things she's supposed to do and she's going to be miserable because of it."

He watched her finish, then nodded slowly: once, twice, before parting his prized lips to tell her his plan.

CHAPTER NINETEEN

———

INDIE STOOD BELOW JUNE'S WINDOW. IT WAS PAST TEN
that first Friday of summer. The moon was bright, just shy of full,
and quick-moving clouds acted as curtains before it, first opening,
then closing, the night. In spite of this dance above, St. Jude remained
positively sultry and still. Plenty of mosquitoes. Plenty of sweat. Lindie
fanned herself with Artie's letter. She knew she had to get rid of it, but
she didn't know how.

A large cloud blackened the moon. Under its cover, she shambled
up the column of the porte cochere. She hoped she'd stay shadowed
until she'd clambered up to June's window. Apatha had been direct
when Lindie had brought June back to the house from the cemetery two
nights before: "You let June be." Thomas was gone by then, but Apatha
still hadn't offered Lindie dinner, not even after she'd been the one who
rescued June.

Once on the second story, Lindie was surprised to be met with a
closed window; she'd assumed June would be eagerly waiting. She
rapped on the pane and peered in.

The room was dark, but Lindie could see her friend's form under the
chenille bedspread. The easel, wardrobe, and bed dominated the room;
by comparison, Lindie's rickety bedroom furniture—left over from her
grandparents' days, or maybe even from before that, when the workmen
building Uncle Lem's house had lived there—was already half-broken
by the time she'd inherited it. Her fingertips pattered the cool glass.
June was ignoring her. Lindie tapped again. June finally sat up. She saw
Lindie—of course she saw her. But she didn't move. The night turned
bright again. Lindie ducked out of the window and flattened herself
against the brick wall, praying Apatha wasn't waiting below with that
broom.

That time against the side of the house gave Lindie an opportunity to consider letting June be. She wouldn't show her Artie's letter, but she wouldn't tell her Jack's plan either. Was that the right thing to do?

The night dimmed again. And, without necessarily meaning to, without having fully decided on her next move, Lindie found herself tapping at the window again, tapping and tapping, until June finally came toward her. June cracked the window just wide enough to speak through it. "What?"

June was trying to hide any trace of her tears, but Lindie caught their tracks down those pearly cheeks in the moonlight. "What's wrong?" she asked dumbly. She hadn't realized June was crying.

June shrugged. She looked up at the night. The moon was reflected in her eyes and on her glossy face. Her cheeks were flushed, her lower lip wet. Something twanged inside of Lindie. She wanted, needed, to end any pain June might be enduring. She put her hands under the sash and pushed the window up so they stood inches apart. Perhaps there was a third option—neither Artie nor Jack: simply to mention the passion boiling inside herself. She'd tell June how good she thought she was, how much she wanted to give her happiness, how she'd only ever do right by her. Only how to begin?

But June spoke first. "I know you don't understand why I'd care for a man like Artie Danvers. Sometimes I don't even understand it." She glanced at Lindie, narrowing her eyes. "I know you think it's weak to marry him." Her mouth gripped tightly in on itself, but her bottom lip quivered. "So maybe I'm weak then, Lindie." She shook her head. Lindie couldn't bear to see June wrapped inside this torment.

"I don't know myself, Lindie, not like you. But I do know that I liked how he made me feel. I was looking forward to him coming home. To getting married . . ." And then she was weeping in earnest.

"Don't cry," Lindie mumbled.

June looked at her again, brow furrowed. "Clyde was over here today promising Mumma he was doing everything he could to find Artie. That means Clyde doesn't know where he is, doesn't it?" She seemed to sober then. To age. June's gaze grew flinty as a blade. "I'm a fool. I've been sitting here for months waiting for a man who doesn't even want me."

The letter, fine, the stupid letter. "He does," Lindie said, hanging her head.

"Oh hush," June barked. "Don't pretend you care."

"I don't care," Lindie said, "I know." She reached for Artie's letter in her breast pocket, fingering its edge.

But June's next words stopped her. "You're here to sneak me out?" It was something about the way she sounded: hopeful, encouraging. As though what she wanted, more than anything in the world, was for Lindie to say yes, which was not a common occurrence; Lindie could count on one hand the times Miss Goody Two-Shoes had snuck out her window. Anything would scare June off, even on those nights when she'd promised to come: a stomachache, the sound of distant thunder, a sudden convenient fear of heights.

"You want to sneak out? Even now?" Lindie tried to hide her happy shock.

June sighed. "I might as well start living."

Lindie dropped Artie's letter back into her pocket.

"And he'll be there?" June bit her lip and leaned on the *he'll*. Lindie knew, for sure, that June didn't mean Artie Danvers.

Their eyes met. Lindie felt a flurry in her gut, dizzy and bright and awed. "He arranged it, June."

June's hand fluttered to her throat like a bird flushed out of the undergrowth. It flitted to the back of her neck and tended its tendrils, then found a perch on her cheek. It turned back into a hand then, blotting and wiping any trace of sorrow. She straightened her shoulders toward the night, toward the safe hush of their quiet, sleeping town.

CHAPTER TWENTY

———

N THE SHADOW OF THE GARAGE BEHIND LINDIE'S HOUSE, JUNE clambered onto the back of the Schwinn. She begged Lindie to reveal their destination. She preferred to walk—she always preferred to walk, especially when Lindie was at the handlebars—but Lindie told her it was too far, and that was all she'd say. Then she shushed June. All it took was freezing her finger in the air, as though she'd heard someone approaching; the power Lindie could occasionally wield over June was intoxicating. June wrapped her soft arms around Lindie's narrow torso. Her breath unfurled into the younger girl's ear. Lindie pedaled them onto the gravel alley behind the house, keeping tight to the bushes.

They needn't have feared; they could have ridden straight down the middle of Main Street and no one would have seen them. It was Friday night, nearly eleven; the pious were abed, the drunks were down at the Red Door Tavern, and the few who liked adventure were headed out, incognito, to the eastern side of town. Just in case, Lindie kept to the darkest, emptiest roads.

"I've arranged a whole shebang," Jack had explained with a self-satisfied smile. "Everyone will be there."

Lindie had shaken her head vehemently. "She won't come if it's everyone."

"And if she sneaks off to meet me alone, you don't think they'll talk?" He'd pointed to the old ladies, gathered across the south side of the street, watching him as lions might eye their tamer. "They'll know. They always find out." He'd taken a handful of salted nuts from Crafty and tipped back his head, dropping them all into his mouth at once. "But a girl can come to a party, can't she?" He winked. "What's the harm in that?" And he'd tousled Lindie's hair and, loosening his costume's old-fashioned bow tie, headed to his trailer.

LINDIE PEDALED THEM out past the farms on the two-lane road. The waxing gibbous moon colored the world as though in slate pencil. All the familiars turned strange. Behind them, the spire of the Presbyterian church became a dragon tooth piercing the sky. Above them, the newly leaved trees roiled in a chalky swirl. And the neat, low rows of wheat stretching out toward morning had become endless lines upon which a giant school-age child might practice her delicate hand.

"Where are we going?" June asked again, but politely, because she knew Lindie would reach back and pinch her if she heard one more complaint. Lindie nodded at the saltshaker boxes on the horizon. Since the spring, they had been sprouting, seemingly fully formed from the razed earth. You'd count four on a Tuesday, and by Friday morning there'd be three more.

Of course, Bobby Prange and Walter Eberle had gone exploring early in the spring. They'd returned with a tale of a lunatic war veteran turned security man who roamed the construction site with his shotgun and a pack of wild dogs, and, though Lindie never believed the story, it had been enough to keep the rest of the St. Jude hooligans from making the construction site their regular hangout spot. Still, nearly every adventurer among the under fifteen set had, at one point or another, snuck through Mr. Rohrbach's soybean fields to spy on the bright yellow American forklifts and diggers gobbling up the farmland. Workers came in from Lima and Dayton with hammers and tar paper and white paint. They ate bologna sandwiches and bags of potato chips during their lunch breaks, but Lindie'd only heard reports, because Eben had been strict about giving the builders a wide berth. Lindie suspected that had less to do with her physical safety and more to do with the fact that this particular development was the first stage in what he derisively called "Uncle Clyde's quest to change St. Jude for the bigger," although Eben remained tight-lipped beyond that.

What little Lindie knew about Uncle Clyde's brainchild she'd learned via the vent that lay at the foot of her bed and opened directly down onto the living room. Occasionally, a few of her father's cronies came by for a game of cards and a bottle of whiskey. At Eben's house there was no woman to harangue them for talking till all hours of the night; as long as the floorboards didn't give away Lindie's eavesdropping, her father's friends were happy to forget there was a future woman listening above.

In her darkened room, feeling the weight of her drowsy limbs as she lay upside down in her bed to lean an ear over the vent, Lindie had bought into Uncle Clyde's "master plan" the way children are wont to do; namely, she'd taken it as fact. Clyde and the other men who ran the town were responsible for how it was shaped, for its rules and regulations, for its future. Men deciding was how the Goodyear plant had come to town and given so many fathers jobs, and how Memorial High had gotten a new gymnasium with shiny floors. Men deciding kept St. Jude safe; after all, most of the men deciding had shot the Nazis and their cronies to smithereens, and, as far as Lindie knew, that had turned out quite well for everyone involved.

Clyde's plan was four-pronged. It rested on the cornerstone fact that only two-lane roads could carry anyone out of St. Jude and, for that matter, bring anyone in. These country highways were as straight as if they'd been traced with Apatha's wooden yardstick, and they'd been built for horse carts, not for the great American driving sedans that folks were buying these days. As the crow flew, there were direct routes from St. Jude to anywhere else in the state of Ohio, but one had to follow those little two-lane roads at right angles, making stair steps across the wide-open countryside, since no roads went straight from town to town.

But the U.S. government was deciding to build an interstate system, wide and fast, which would connect not just towns to cities but states to states; they were going to pass a law about it. These roadways, to Clyde's telling at least, would create great commercial booms for the small towns that happened to be along the way. After all, travelers had to stop for gas, food, and lodging. And why couldn't St. Jude be one such place? It already had the lake—a potential tourist draw—and the sweet little town to pull at the heartstrings, not to mention the potential tourism dollars brought in once *Erie Canal* was released and everyone wanted to see "Monroeville" in person.

And, speaking of the interstate, it just so happened that Clyde's buddy, Mr. Frederick Ripvogle of Lima, was on the short list to win the contract for the new interstate that Ohio wanted to build on the western side of the state, from Toledo all the way down to Cincinnati. Ripvogle was friends with the governor; Clyde said he'd had it from Ripvogle's mouth that he was a shoo-in.

Once Ripvogle won the bid, he'd be sure to design the interstate so it came just by the eastern side of St. Jude, near where Clyde's new development was now sprouting. Clyde would fill that side of town—currently just wide-open fields with cows mooing—with all sorts of novelties: perhaps one or two of those new fast-food restaurants, maybe someday a roadside hotel. These niceties would not only improve the lives of the current St. Judians but also be a draw for young families looking for a safe, affordable place to live that combined town with country. And when these families wanted to move in, well, Clyde's brand-new houses would be waiting just for them. Eben and a few of the guys who were "getting in on the ground floor," as Clyde called it, would invest a little of their "nest eggs" and "it would pay them back handsomely." In spite of Eben's doubt, which seeped up to Lindie through the rafters— "Clyde, what if the law doesn't pass? What if Ripvogle doesn't win the bid?"—she felt hope buckle the backs of her knees as she thought of her town, St. Jude, on its way up in the world, and all because of her uncle Clyde's dream.

Since the first of Clyde's houses had gone up, the wagging tongues had had their share of complaints—the walls of those new houses were too thin! With just a poured concrete foundation and no cellar, where were you supposed to store your potatoes? And surely no one would ever give up their Victorian in the heart of town for a flimsy one-story wooden box two miles outside of it, where it smelled of manure more days than not. But, as Lindie pedaled the last quarter mile toward the development, calves aching and forehead dripping with sweat, she surged with pride. She steered them through the newly erected stone wall, which stretched out on either side of the drive, as though signaling the beginning of an ancient ruin.

"This is private property," June hissed as they passed into the first row of houses.

Lindie braked and turned to June, panting. "Feel free to wait here."

June's mouth formed a prim line.

Lindie scanned the night for the rumored rottweilers that should be tearing them to pieces—not a sign. She smirked at the prospect of bragging to the boys about coming out here after dark.

As her breath stilled, she could hear something—a murmur. A pulse. A thrum that brought the night alive in a way they'd never heard before. It was coming from the far end of the development, the houses Clyde had built first.

June's arms found their familiar spot above Lindie's hip bones. They rode on.

THE SMALL, NEW houses were dark, row after row. How many had been built? On treeless street after street, the white houses looked like boxes on a factory belt, waiting for their dolls. The occasional breeze that had felt so exhilarating back in town was wilder out here, less predictable. It danced between the vacant houses, whose picture windows should have framed mothers and fathers on their davenports. The wind whipped across the concrete driveways, which would soon house family station wagons. The moon disappeared again. June gripped Lindie tighter.

Lindie had known the houses were unoccupied; Clyde had wanted them built in advance of Ripvogle's gaining the bid, which was sure to be announced any day now. "Get ahead of the market," that was another phrase she'd heard Clyde use. But Lindie never could have imagined the empty development felt like a ghost town.

The wind flapped June's hair across Lindie's lips. The sound in the distance was becoming music. June pressed herself into Lindie's back. Whether Lindie could imagine June's heart pounding into her or it was really possible to feel that necessary organ through the thin layers of cotton between them, didn't matter. Lindie felt they were one, and so, for that moment, they were.

Nearly at the last row of houses, beyond which lay the central Ohio plains stretching on until morning, the girls heard the crow of a mariachi trumpet. Then the bike shot straight into light and color and sound. Lindie slammed on the brakes. Stretched above was a string of Chinese paper lanterns, the kind Lindie'd only read about in books. Every house blazed. Music, too, music everywhere: "Rock Around the Clock" and Satchmo on his trumpet and "Unchained Melody." Music with a rattling backbone that Lindie didn't even know existed but now could never unknow. And the people! Mostly from the film crew, but no longer automatons. Here they were, laughing, drinking, dancing up against each other in a way Lindie was certain was against the law. June's face was a blaze of wonder as she took in the strange sight, the world lit up as never before. It felt as though they had stumbled upon a group of fairy people from a storybook, the kind who swiped children and were gone by morning.

CHAPTER TWENTY-ONE

——

S O HOW'S THAT FIANCÉ?" JACK ASKED JUNE, MOTIONING TO the collection of booze set out on a card table at the foot of someone's driveway. June shook her head in a polite no. He opened her a Coke. They were in the middle of the road, surrounded by the crew and their guests. Everyone seemed to be moving together, amoeba-like, in the way of such events, which inevitably take on their own heartbeat and disappointments, although the night hadn't gotten to that yet.

To Lindie, Jack said, "Rabbit Legs, I can't, in good conscience, offer you any of this poison. But a Coke?" He pulled another one from the galvanized bucket. Together, they watched June's lower lip curl under the rim of the sweating bottle she held. The cold, wet sugar left a vibrant shimmer on Lindie's tongue. She felt giddy and sick at the sight of Jack's eyes on June, his face an ache of hopeful hunger.

"Let's not talk about my fiancé," June said playfully. The cacophony of the party had changed: "Ain't That a Shame" mingled with the sultry howl of a jazz trumpet, now layered atop Margaret Whiting and Johnny Mercer incongruously declaring it was cold outside. Each piece of music played out a front door of one of the pillbox houses that continued to the end of the road, where civilization once again met country. Lindie admired Clyde's wherewithal to secure these tenants; she wondered if the studio was paying him, or if he supposed he could just tell potential buyers that Jack Montgomery had slept in their master bedroom and that would be enough to make up the difference.

Suzie, the makeup girl, waved to Lindie as she led a young man down the road. Only a few feet away, a grip, Andy Number One, was dancing very close to Luella Caywood, the pretty girl who worked the soda fountain at Schillinger's Drug. Andy's face was at Luella's neck, and her arms were flung around him. He rocked against her in a way

Lindie hadn't quite gotten up the nerve to conjure, even in the privacy of her bedroom.

"These are your friends?" June asked flippantly. Lindie couldn't tell which of them she was addressing. June sounded so nonchalant, and yet neither of them had ever seen anything like this before.

"My colleagues," Jack replied.

"Lindie!"

She turned to find Ricky standing behind her, drink in hand. Beside him was another man, Sam, whom she recognized from Crafty. She turned back to introduce them to Jack and June, only to find that Jack and June were walking toward the house Jack had apparently claimed as his own. Lindie wondered for a shocked minute if they planned to go inside, but they stopped at the lip of the small concrete porch, each leaning against one of the columns that held up the tiny pediment above the entryway.

"That your friend?" Ricky asked, whistling.

Lindie shrugged.

"Lucky girl," Sam said, eyeing Jack.

"I wouldn't be so sure." Ricky was frowning. He leaned closer toward Lindie. "Jack got mighty cozy with Diane DeSoto back in Los Angeles. I don't think DeSoto likes competition."

Lindie cracked up at the thought that June (even her beloved June) could be considered the rival for a goddess who graced movie magazines. "They're just talking," she said.

Ricky held up his hands and backed away. Then he clapped Sam on the shoulder and bid Lindie good-bye. Her eyes followed them as they headed back into the party. Why did it make her so lonely to notice that simple touch on the shoulder, the way Sam smiled at it, the way Ricky's hand lingered there? Sam's eyes danced over Ricky's face, and Lindie felt a surge of hope, crushed, quickly, by the truth of how impossible, unimaginable, her unbridled mind could be.

She turned from them then, forcing herself to look elsewhere. Lindie made her way up the small concrete walkway toward Jack and June until she found herself between them, below them, knees scrunched up under her chin, a kid sister. She listened and let them forget her.

It was chitchat at first, the kind of small talk people have when they find themselves side by side in a railway car. He did a good job of leveling the playing field, speaking, at first, of himself as a regular Joe—how much he liked the burger down at Illy's, how, when he'd been a little boy in Arkansas, he'd loved to catch fireflies on nights like this—did they have fireflies here in St. Jude? Then he told her about his little girl, Esmerelda, who was four years old, and the girl's mother, Conchita, whom he'd met in Las Vegas but was now living in Houston, remarried to a man who owned a car dealership. "She didn't love me, not the way I was made, but I don't regret marrying her, not for a minute. I love our little girl. Best thing that ever happened to me." The way he described it, divorce sounded not only normal but appealing. Lindie smiled, thinking of how horrified Cheryl Ann—and most of the adults in St. Jude, save Eben—would be to hear Jack talk like that.

When Jack asked June about herself, she skipped Artie altogether, quickly turning to her father's death in a way that surprised and wounded Lindie; she'd believed herself to be the only person in which June would ever confide such matters.

"I miss him every day. I try to do right by him. I'd like to believe he'd be proud of me."

"I bet up there in heaven he counts himself a lucky man," Jack said. "To have a smart, beautiful daughter who honors him still—that's a father's dream."

Up and down the road, crew members were kicking back on their front porches. Some were even necking, Lindie realized. She wanted, suddenly, to get away from whatever was blooming between Jack and June, but she also knew she couldn't bear to miss it.

"Oh, we had the best times." June's voice warmed. "He loved to paint. He got me a little box of watercolors for my fifth birthday. We used to hike out to Lake St. Jude and spend hours just putting the world on paper."

"Do you still paint?"

Lindie could almost hear June blushing in the darkness. "I try."

"I'll bet you more than try."

"I'm not much good."

"Hogwash!"

June laughed her delicate laugh, lacy and modest. "I only have my bedroom to paint in now, since Mumma won't let me roam free anymore. I just keep painting the same five things over and over. They're wretched."

"I don't believe that for a minute." This guy was good.

June remembered Lindie then, and nudged her with her foot. "Tell him."

Then both sets of eyes were upon Lindie, as though she was suddenly the most important person in the world. But she didn't know how to answer, whether to insult or lie, so she shrugged, and then they forgot her again.

"Do you have a favorite painter?"

"Papa did. He loved Jackson Pollock. Do you know his work? Papa came home from a trip to Columbus with a *Life* magazine tucked under his arm. I sat with him and he showed me how the man painted. All these photographs of this funny little bald man with these giant canvases covered in lines, splatters, like he'd just let the paint find its own way over the canvas. Really, we'd never seen anything like it—" June had been talking louder and louder, but she pulled her words back suddenly. In their place, her fingers wove and unplaited themselves.

Jack was quiet then too. Lindie looked up at him, wondering if something had distracted him from the conversation. But it was just the opposite: he was looking at June intently, and June, in turn, was gazing back. Jack's voice returned, low and melodic across the warm night: "I'd never given much thought to Jackson Pollock, June. But I'll tell you, you make me want to go out and buy a Jackson Pollock painting tomorrow."

"Well, you can't," she said, starting to giggle. "They're absurdly expensive, and enormous too, you'd need a giant house and bank account to match . . ." Her voice faded as she realized he had both.

"Do you still have that magazine? I'd love to—"

Jack's voice cut off as a honking car, flashing its headlamps, dispersed the crowd on the road. There was laughter and some cursing, and the dance floor remade itself twenty feet down as the car pulled up in front of Jack's. Jack stood upright and frowned. Lindie recognized the car at once: it was Uncle Clyde's, the forest green four-door Oldsmobile he'd replaced with the Bel Air.

June, too, was now standing at attention and watching for who would emerge from her fiancé's brother's car. Lindie had half a mind right then to pull June into the bushes, to squirrel her out through the hedge and around into the backyard. But Uncle Clyde would understand they'd come for the adventure, and, anyway, were they committing any sins? Like Jack had said, a girl could come to a party.

Thomas, Apatha's nephew, popped out from the driver's side. He was dressed in a suit. He jogged around to the passenger door at the curb, opening it to reveal the leg of a lady—heeled, stockinged, and delicate in the ankle. A gloved hand emerged next, and Thomas supported it as the woman attached stepped out onto the newly poured sidewalk. It took Lindie a moment to recognize her; the woman was wrapped in a stole. But then she smiled as though Jack and June and Lindie had all been waiting for her to arrive, and a wave of starstruck reverie overtook Lindie: Diane DeSoto had leapt off the page of a magazine and into Lindie's hometown.

The famous woman wore a black suit. Though the night was dark, it was clear she was ten times more well arranged than any other woman in St. Jude, and probably in Ohio. Her legs went on for miles, her waist spanned mere inches, and her hair was a blond, elegant shock in the moonlight. Once on her feet, she let go of Thomas's hand, and he rushed to the trunk to unload suitcases and hatboxes as Clyde Danvers emerged from the other side of the car, rushing to offer his arm to the movie star. She wore him like he was a foregone conclusion. Clyde and Diane strode toward Jack's house, Diane with a tight smile, Clyde with a broad and knowing grin, as though he'd caught Jack, June, and Lindie with their hands in the cookie jar.

"Throwing a bit of a party, I see." Clyde chuckled when he was halfway up the lawn. To Lindie, he said, "I suppose I shouldn't be too surprised to see you here. But you"—he meant June—and then he whistled. Lindie caught a flash of the silver pistol that was always holstered at his side, and her stomach did a flip she couldn't explain.

Jack stepped off the concrete porch toward Diane, who smiled icily as she passed herself into his arms. She put one gloved hand onto Jack's broad chest and pecked his cheek. "Surprise, darling."

Clyde took Jack's hand and shook it as though they went back decades. "I'm your biggest fan, champ," he declared. He was a broad man, one of the handsomest there was in St. Jude—his square jaw and faint limp a reminder of the war hero he'd once been. But, seeing him there beside Diane DeSoto and Jack Montgomery, Lindie thought him ugly for the first time in her life. She felt as though she was looking at one of those fun-house mirrors she'd seen at the Parish Festival the summer before; the whole world was askew.

"Miss DeSoto was able to fly in early," Clyde, still shaking Jack's hand, explained on Diane's behalf. "But seeing's how we've got no telephone lines out here yet, there was no way to let you all know. So I had good old Thomas drive down to pick her up in Columbus, and then they swung by to get me so I could be sure to bring her out myself."

Diane turned to Thomas and said, "Thank you."

Thomas nodded, but he was clearly as starstruck as Lindie. He busied himself with the woman's things. Lindie wondered how he'd landed the job as driver, and, if it was Apatha, why she was helping him these days, and not her.

Clyde's eyes were back on June. "So what are you doing all the way out here, girlie?" What was it about his tone that set Lindie so on edge? This was her uncle Clyde, the man who'd taught her how to ride a bike. She forced herself to smile at him.

"Lindie's been working on the movie," June blurted, taking Lindie's hand. "She brought me out to meet some of her friends, and then Mr. Montgomery was kind enough to get us Coca-Colas."

"Don't worry, I won't tell Mumma." Clyde winked. To Lindie, he said, "Or grumpy old Pops, for that matter." His grin spread wide as he turned toward Jack. "Important to celebrate. Course, we did have an agreement to keep the local girls out of it." He cleared his throat. "But I suppose the ones already claimed aren't doing any harm." He rubbed his hands together. "Can't wait to see Miss Watters here make an honest man out of my kid brother, Artie."

Diane seemed to have tuned them all out; she was absorbed in removing her gloves, tugging at each of the fingers, one at a time. Once one of her bare hands was available, Clyde took it in his own, kissed it, and offered a sweeping bow. "I'll make sure Thomas sets up your place as per your contract," he told her, and here he tapped the sheaf of papers sticking out of his breast pocket, then stuck his thumb toward the unlit house beside Jack's. "You're right next door." He winked at Jack. To the girls he said, "Want a ride home? That's a long way for two little girlies through the dark night."

"No thank you," Lindie said. "We've got my bike."

"And we were just about to leave," June added, a tremor in her voice.

Clyde watched them for a moment. "Suit yourself," he replied, then made his way back to the car and picked up what Thomas couldn't manage. Then it was just Jack and Diane standing before the girls, like a movie sprung to life. Just like in a movie, they ignored those watching them.

"If you don't mind, darling," Diane said, leaning into Jack, "I'm terribly weary from all that flying." She stuck out her bottom lip in a mock frown. "I need a hot toddy and a good foot rub. And I must hear all the ins and outs of this charming little ville." Her fingers walked up his chest and cupped his chin. "We've got some catching up to do."

Without a backward glance at Lindie or June, Jack led his leading lady and her entourage to her door. The girls didn't stick around long enough to watch them go inside.

June 2015

CHAPTER TWENTY-TWO

———

CASSIE DREAMED OF THE GIRLS AGAIN. ONE STOOD OUT-side the window that lay at the very foot of Cassie's bed. She was bathed in moonlight, perched precariously on the roof. The other girl was already in her nightgown, and she stood inside, at the very lip of the house, looking out at the night. June, inside, was crying (but Cassie didn't know her yet). Lindie, outside, wanted to help June—no, it was more than want, it was need—but all she could do was let her friend weep, let her feel as terrible, as abandoned as she felt. And then June suddenly brightened and hardened, grew strong somehow, stronger than Cassie had given the girl credit for, as though she'd clenched some invisible muscle inside her, and the night grew elastic in its possibility, and Cassie understood that something tremendous was about to happen.

Cassie woke up. She lay in her bed, listening to a creaking sound she'd never heard before, which was coming down through the ceiling above her. She hoped it wasn't an imminent sign of roof collapse.

She got out of bed and went to the window that had been so vital to her dream. She stood where the sad girl had stood, only the world outside was visible now, illumined by daylight. Out across the weedy, unmowed lawn, Cassie could see the small wooden house where the nosy old woman lived, one of the houses Nick said had been built for Lemon Neely's builders. She wondered if the old woman in residence was peering at her right now, and she stuck her tongue out just in case.

Cassie dressed. She listened for signs of life, but all she could hear was that constant, strange lament of the floorboards from the ballroom on the third floor. She hadn't climbed up there since being dive-bombed by a family of bats one drunken night in the early spring. But curiosity had gotten the better of her. Before she went, she lifted her dust-covered camera from the mantelpiece, where she'd set it the very day she moved in. It had film in it, and a few shots left. She tried not to think about what the early part of the roll had captured: Jim, New York, a life that was no longer hers. She loved using film, loved how it limited your eye, made you careful; loved the long process between making a picture and getting to hold it in your hands. Digital was fine if you simply wanted a record of things, but film had been made for something more complicated. She felt an itchy desire to see again through her old eyes. She hoped the dust hadn't caused any damage. She blew the camera off all over, then removed the lens and held it up to the light.

Something funny had happened on a few occasions over the course of the past two days, something Cassie hadn't felt in more than a year: she'd wished she had her camera. She'd witnessed specific moments she wanted to capture on film, and the fact that she'd lost them still clung to her with sticky regret. There was the instant before she'd called Nick's name on the path, and that quick spot of time when Tate rediscovered her birth announcement. Things were definitely over with Jim, but she could see now, with the benefit of distance, that he'd given her the guts to trust her instincts when it came to making pictures. Yes, June's reaction to Cassie's art show had eroded that a bit, but Cassie pushed her mind away from her grandmother's doubt as she looped the camera strap around her neck and headed toward the stairs. Who could this hurt? Everyone was dead.

Cassie clambered up to the third floor, past the landing with its large stained-glass window, complementary to the ones on the landing one story below. The sound got louder and changed, then stopped altogether. Up at the lip of the third floor, she discovered Hank and Tate limberly bent into downward dog. The great, open room unfurled behind them, across the front, back, and western sides of the house; its wide, dark floorboards glowed in the morning light. The women's bodies were lean and muscular, their yoga clothing hugging every glute and ab. Every muscle was flawlessly formed. Cassie resisted the urge to scowl.

She glanced toward the dreaded closet, wondering about the state of the roof in there. She felt a curdle of worry in her gut. She forced herself to turn away, to pretend, for the moment, that the problem wasn't there.

Instead, she lifted the camera to her eye and framed the shot. The light was tremendous up here, ricocheting off the floor. She could have stolen the picture, but she knew, from experience, that that wasn't sustainable if you wanted to gain trust.

"Can I?" she asked in a voice that she knew didn't match their Zen-like state. "The light's great."

Their heads jerked up. Hank wrinkled her nose. Tate said, "Of course."

Cassie didn't miss Hank's apprehensive glance back at Tate, or the way Tate's eyes batted Hank off. Cassie took the shot, messed with the aperture, got another one.

"Obviously I'd ask before I did anything with them," Cassie explained, framing another shot, clicking the button. "But I probably won't. They're for me."

"She's an artist," Tate explained, as though Hank was being overly protective, even though she hadn't said a word. Tate ascended out of downward dog and swiped a towel across her forehead.

"Hope we didn't wake you." Hank stood reluctantly.

"That's fine," Cassie said.

"We made ourselves at home"—Tate shrugged apologetically—"but we should have asked first." She was pretty much the most gorgeous thing Cassie'd ever seen. Cassie felt her insides go gooey.

But then she caught Hank's side eye, and it was impossible not to say something snarky. "I just hope the bats who live up here are actually nocturnal."

Cassie took pleasure in the involuntary twitch of Hank's whole body. "Bats?" she squeaked.

"Okay if we find someone to relocate them?" Tate asked calmly.

Cassie couldn't help but feel benevolent toward Tate. "That'd be great, actually."

"Be sure whoever takes the job won't be disposing of them," Tate instructed. "Bats are vital to the ecosystem. I saw something on Animal Planet." Cassie nodded along, as if she'd read a dozen books about bats.

Hank wrinkled her nose distastefully for a split second, but then a smile bloomed across her face, and she nodded exuberantly and said,

"I'll find someone today!" To Tate, she asked, "Continue?" Her eyes cut a swath across Cassie's disarray. "Do you want to join us?" Cassie had to give her points for sounding genuinely hopeful.

Tate came toward Cassie then. She seemed somehow lit from within, smelling nothing like Cassie's putrid funk after she exercised, although Cassie couldn't quite recall when that had last been. Tate led Cassie down the stairs without a backward glance at Hank, who mumbled, "But we're not even halfway through."

On the landing, they heard Nick's voice. "There you are." He stood below them, at the center of the wide upstairs hall. He had his phone out, of course. Cassie was suddenly aware of the parts of her body exposed to the air: the dip in her V-neck, her bare calves sticking out below her shorts. She took out her camera and snapped a picture of him.

Nick reared up in alarm.

Tate rolled her eyes and put her arm around Cassie. "I said it was fine."

Cassie focused her lens on Nick again. She liked how directly she could look at him, how close she could get, how his eyes glanced up at her, then squirmed away under the camera's eye. She thought of how he'd spoken of her father, of his drinking, of her art show, and felt a triumphant wave of revenge as she clicked another shot.

"Could you please not?" he asked, hand nervously fluttering at his hair.

"Relax." Tate giggled. "This is what an artist does. She takes her environment and makes sense of it by using her god-given talent." Tate continued down to the open hall and handed Nick her sweaty towel and empty water bottle. "I'd like ice water," she said.

He nodded and looked up at Cassie. "We've got to go."

"Do we have an appointment?" she cracked.

He surprised her with a nod. "I didn't want to wake you. But I called the library at nine, and talked to a lovely woman who works there"—his voice was all business as he scrolled through his phone to find her name—"Mrs. Prange. She gave me the names of three St. Judians who were living here back when *Erie Canal* was made. I called around and made a few appointments. Mrs. Weaver is available starting in"—he checked his phone again; it read 10:19—"eleven minutes."

"We're going to ask her if she remembers my grandmother banging Jack Montgomery?" Cassie was showing off now, feeling brassy. Something about Nick's squeamishness made her eager to press him.

"Best, I think, to simply see what they offer, uh, on their own."

Below her, Tate sniffed in amusement. "You can't expect her to go without breakfast, Nick."

He nodded, still frowning. "I'll make you a shake. Or you could grab some raw almonds."

"Raw almonds?" Cassie couldn't mask her incredulity. "Uh, no, I'd like some real food, like, you know, an egg sandwich." Cassie didn't really care what she had for breakfast (well, she wasn't eating what Nick called a shake, or raw almonds), but something about Nick this morning made her want to tousle his proverbial hair.

"Hank!" Tate called up the stairs. "Make an egg sandwich?"

"Oh," Cassie said, wishing she'd kept her mouth shut—she'd rankled Hank enough. "No—I'm happy to make it myself."

But Hank was already barreling past them down the stairs. "I'd love to!" She flashed a smile on her way past.

"And take my towel, Hank," Tate said. "Really, you should be dealing with that."

Hank nodded, chastened, and gamely took the towel from Nick as Tate continued to chide her. Cassie felt embarrassed simply witnessing this interaction, but Tate went on as if it was the most normal thing in the world. "And I need water. Ice water. That means cold." She turned to Cassie. "You thirsty? You want ice water?" Cassie shook her head in a vehement no. But Tate pressed Hank. "Make her ice water. Leave mine just inside the bathroom door while I'm showering, but please, for the millionth time, don't let the steam escape."

"Absolutely," Hank replied brightly, as though her dreams had all come true, and then she disappeared down the stairs.

"Is that an orange shirt?" Tate asked Nick, eyeing him.

Nick looked down at himself. "I thought it was rust."

She shook her head. "You know I can't stand orange."

Nick nodded willingly, as though that was a perfectly reasonable statement. Before he changed it, he just wanted to remind Tate that, while he and Cassie were gone, she should be sure Hank called Jack's lawyer for any suggestions of others to interview. "We're looking for anyone he might have confided in, written to, that kind of thing." He'd arranged for Jack's papers to be delivered sometime that afternoon, and, in the meantime, if it was all right with Cassie, he thought Hank would be best utilized by going through all the closets to turn up anything of interest beyond the stack of magazines.

Tate clicked her heels together and saluted. "And may I shower first, master?"

Nick bobbed his head. Tate blew Cassie a kiss and slipped into the bathroom.

"There are letters too," Cassie volunteered, hoping Nick wasn't really going to change his shirt—he looked good in rust, and it was ridiculous that Tate had suggested he do so. "Letters between June and some girl named Lindie, but I couldn't find anything useful in them."

"In the back closet?" Nick was already tapping this latest development into his phone, into a folder he'd labeled "St. Jude, Ohio," as if he might mistake it for the notes he was keeping on another St. Jude, somewhere else in the world.

"And there was an address—Lindie lived in Chicago—so"—Cassie popped into her room, reemerging with the envelope she'd sealed the night before—"I wrote to her." She felt triumphant as she waved it before him.

"Great." Nick plucked it out of her hands and added the address to his database. "We'll have Hank express it."

"Poor Hank," Cassie whispered, and Nick frowned in surprise. "She's like a slave," she mouthed.

Nick quickly dismissed it. "It's her job. It's her dream job. Trust me—she's in heaven."

"Okay," Cassie said. "But let me mail it." But he already had the envelope by then, and she mumbled, "I know, I know, it's her job," as he went off toward the back bedroom, where he just needed to change his shirt before they took off.

CHAPTER TWENTY-THREE

———

A S THEY PULLED OUT OF THE DRIVEWAY, CASSIE NOTICED
the pair of eyes peeking through the living room blinds of the
Victorian on the corner. Tate's people might be able to make
vehicles magically appear somewhere between the local airfield and Two
Oaks, but they did not know how to take the pulse of a small town; had
they rented a beat-up Ford truck, no one would have looked twice, but
a brand-new Range Rover with tinted windows was bound to get attention.

Nick was dependent on the SUV's GPS. Cassie loathed the machine's
calm, assertive voice, especially because Cassie told Nick at least six times
that she could navigate them to the Three Oaks Estates herself. Three
Oaks—the name leapt out at her. Two Oaks, Three Oaks; was the development linked to the house she now owned? And the town green, where
they were now turning, was named Montgomery Square. She smiled,
wondering if it had been named after Jack, realizing she didn't know as
much about St. Jude as she'd thought. She hadn't even been aware that
a movie had been filmed here, or anything about the building of Two
Oaks. She snuck a glimpse at Nick as they turned right up Main Street
per the GPS's instructions; he looked like a kid on Christmas.

She'd only ever seen the downtown strip as a depressing eyesore, with
its boarded-up windows and the old theater marquee dangling with
consonants—all that remained of its plastic lettering. But with Nick beside her, she could almost imagine the wonder that downtown St. Jude
had once been. He slowed the car and pointed out details she'd never
noticed: the gold numbers someone had gilded on the inside of a glass
door, and the hitching post still attached to the former Dry Goods. The
Majestic Theater marquee hung above a long, glass-enclosed promenade
that had once held notices for upcoming shows and spectacles.

Nick whistled. "What a gorgeous old town."

Cassie checked him again. "You're serious?" She couldn't quite buy that he was this into it.

But he turned to her with an absolutely genuine expression and said, "Of course."

A laugh hiccuped through Cassie.

"What?" He scowled.

"You're a conundrum." They passed the mayor's office, occupied by a lone lady manning the phone.

"You have no idea," he replied. She could detect the trace of a smile.

The next mile was a scattering of industrial buildings, some wooded areas, a few empty fields, and then a single suburban development that included the house where Mrs. Weaver, their interviewee, lived. Nick slowed as they drove through the gates, really just two low stone walls with the name of the development in rusted metal along one side. The houses were different over here: humbler, modern, nothing like the historic fortifications that occupied the center of St. Jude. These were buildings that had obviously been constructed on an assembly line. Cassie pressed her face against the SUV's cool glass and let her eyes skip over the little boxes. Maples towered above each street; they were, she guessed, at least fifty years old.

They found Mrs. Weaver's small white house, neatly surrounded by hedges and a red line of geraniums. There was a white Buick the size of a sailboat parked in the driveway, standard issue for elderly Ohioans. Nick drummed the steering wheel. "I told them we were working on a project about the summer of 'fifty-five. So we won't ask anything direct about June and Jack, okay?"

Did he really not trust her judgment? "Yeah," she said, irritated. "Sure."

He cleared his throat. She could feel his eyes on her. "I don't want her name dragged through the mud," he said quietly. "This is a small town."

A PETITE, ELDERLY woman with a halo of white hair answered the door. She tightened her cardigan as though the warm air they risked trailing in was colder than the frigid air-conditioning she was standing inside.

"Mrs. Weaver?" Nick asked.

The old woman smiled with a secret as she adjusted her pearls. "No, no, I'm Mrs. Albert Deitz."

Nick reached for his phone and frantically started scrolling through it. Panic hunched his shoulders. "I'm so sorry," he said. "I thought our meeting with you wasn't until twelve thirty."

The woman's smile hadn't faltered. "Oh, it was. But, you see, then Janet and I realized you'd called both of us, and I live only one street over, and we thought perhaps it would help to talk to both of us together." Her shoulders rose impishly toward her ears.

Nick's phone found its resting place in his pocket again, and then they were being ushered inside, and Mrs. Weaver was emerging from the kitchen with a tray of Velveeta on Ritz and a pitcher of Hawaiian Punch the color of maraschino cherries, which Cassie couldn't wait to watch Nick choke down. Raw almonds indeed.

Mrs. Weaver was taller than Mrs. Deitz, and slightly less adorable, but her hair had the same cotton-candy quality. Her house was an altar to white carpeting and linoleum and recliners and lazy Susans. A wooden cabinet held dozens of porcelain figurines in various adorable country poses; the top shelf bore a fifteen-piece Hummel crèche, which had been meticulously dusted. Cassie wondered if Nick knew that, as soon as this woman had gotten his call, she'd started cleaning.

"Well then," Mrs. Weaver said once she'd distributed the food and drink and settled into a velvety, mushroom-colored armchair in the immaculate living room. "How we can help?"

"Oh, but first," Mrs. Deitz said, hands clasping beside her face, "do tell us how long you've been married. We love a romantic tale."

"We're not married," Cassie said quickly as Nick choked on the punch.

Mrs. Deitz's face fell. "But he said—"

"I said we were partners," Nick said, turning to Cassie with his hands up.

"Yes, partners," repeated Mrs. Weaver. "That's what my lesbian granddaughter and her . . . partner call themselves."

Nick was nodding frantically. "Yes, yes, of course, I'm sorry, I meant working partners. We're working on a project together." His hand jogged back and forth between him and Cassie, doing his best to indicate strict professionalism.

"Of course," Mrs. Deitz said, bobbing her small head, although Cassie didn't think she really understood.

"Do you mind?" Cassie asked, pulling her camera from her bag. The ladies preened and posed at the sight of it, pleased to be deemed worthy of notice; she already knew, for this reason, that the first picture she took would be dreadful. But if she could gain their trust, earn their respect, she might be able to capture these women not as they wanted to be seen but as they were. She'd be able to break through their carefully built façades and expose a bit of what they loved and feared. She was already thinking of the front porch—it might be just the place. At the end of the interview she would suggest they go out there.

Nick pulled his phone from his pocket and opened his notes app. "We don't want to take up too much of your time"—he said this pointedly, as if Cassie's photography was doing just that—"but we're very interested in the summer of 1955, specifically when they filmed *Erie Canal* here in St. Jude."

"You're June Danvers's granddaughter?" Mrs. Weaver asked.

Nick and Cassie exchanged a quick look in which he tried to convey he hadn't mentioned that. "Yes," Cassie said, because there wasn't any reason to lie.

"Your grandmother was the heartbeat of this town," Mrs. Deitz offered.

"Thank you."

"She means it," Mrs. Weaver insisted, giving the impression that she didn't particularly agree. "June was on every board, at every meeting, and volunteered at every fund-raiser." She sniffed. "That is, until she moved to Columbus to help with you."

Cassie had never much considered what the St. Judians had thought about that.

But Mrs. Deitz smiled to cover up the disapproval lingering in the air. "Since June's family was from Lima"—for Nick's benefit, she added, "that's about thirty miles up the road—we didn't know her when we were children. But she fit right in when they moved here."

"I wouldn't say right in," Mrs. Weaver quipped.

Nick ignored that. "Why did her family move down to St. Jude?" The old women exchanged a look. Mrs. Deitz sent a testing smile out to Cassie, and Cassie realized she was supposed to give the old woman permission to tell her family's business. Only thing was, Cassie had no idea why June's family had moved from Lima to St. Jude, and obviously she was supposed to, so she dipped her eyes as though, despite her reluctance to air dirty laundry, she'd allow it.

"Her father was killed in Korea," Mrs. Deitz said, but Cassie had the feeling that wasn't the half of it.

"He gambled away the family's fortune is what happened," Mrs. Weaver said sharply, as though, simply by being his great-granddaughter, Cassie had carried a dangerous strain into her home. "He lost them everything. And then he went and got himself reenlisted in Korea without even telling his wife. And got himself killed over there. After that, June's mother, Mrs. Watters, had to sell the house, their furniture, even their car. They couldn't show their faces in Lima again. They would have been out on the street if Mr. Neely hadn't taken them in. Or at least that's what my aunt Biddy, who lived in Lima, told my mother."

"And Mr. Neely wasn't even their blood relation." Mrs. Deitz leaned forward now, clutching her pearls, caught up in the thrill of the sixty-year-old gossip.

Mrs. Weaver nodded. "June's father was the nephew of Mr. Neely's first wife, Mae. But she'd been dead for years."

"The influenza epidemic, I heard?" Mrs. Deitz asked.

Mrs. Weaver shrugged and rolled her eyes, as if speculation was beyond her.

"Regardless," Mrs. Deitz said, "once your grandma grew up, it was like she'd never lived in Lima. She just fit right in here, joined the sewing circle, the bridge club, the dinner club. It was too bad, though, because her mama was real sick. But Mr. Neely died real soon after June married your grandfather, and he left the house to her, which meant June and her mama could stay put. Her mama didn't have many more years ahead of her, and there was the baby on the way. Good thing they didn't have to move anywhere else."

Cassie heard her grandmother's accent in these old women's mouths; it flattened words and elongated vowels: "move ee-in," "he died rull soon after." It made Cassie homesick for the woman who'd raised her.

Nick cleared his throat. "Fascinating," he said, in a stilted voice. And then, "So, if we could just get back to 1955 . . ." The old women tittered as he tried to draw their focus to the matter at hand. "Do you remember if there was much interaction between the movie stars and everyone else?"

"Not if you were Diane DeSoto," Mrs. Weaver said. "She was always on her high horse. I know it ended badly for her, and I'm not one to speak ill of the dead, but you could tell just by looking at her that she couldn't stand St. Jude."

"She didn't mingle," Mrs. Deitz explained.

"She stuck to Jack Montgomery like glue."

"*Erie Canal* was the movie they met on, right?" Nick asked, playing dumb well.

Mrs. Weaver nodded, lips tightening. "It was clear they'd already started their . . . affair before they came to Ohio. She wouldn't let him out of her sight. They lived next door to each other, at the far end of this development. Can you believe it? One can only guess what they were up to. Of course we were all completely blind to that kind of thing."

"Well," Mrs. Deitz contributed, "there was a rumor that he was sweet on some girl in town . . ."

"Who was she?" Nick asked, feigning casual interest.

"Oh, I'm sure it wasn't true." She shook her head vehemently. "Jack and Diane were practically engaged. Everyone wants to imagine a movie star would fall in love with you, but it doesn't happen."

"Well, it wouldn't surprise me to find out he'd been carrying on with all kinds of girls. He was a flirt." The lines around Mrs. Weaver's mouth found their disapproving groove.

"You would know," Mrs. Deitz teased.

"He only said he liked my dress." Mrs. Weaver ducked her head in feigned humility, and Cassie could see the awkward gosling she'd once been. "Besides, I was married by then. I did not flirt back." She pointed to Nick's phone. "And you can write that down."

Cassie avoided looking at Nick. "Do you remember anything about my grandmother during that summer? Did she help out with the movie? Did you ever see her with Diane, or . . . Jack?" Nick shifted uncomfortably beside her.

"June had nothing to do with the movie whatsoever," Mrs. Weaver said. "I don't know if she thought she was better than it or what. If you don't mind my saying, she was a bit . . . prissy." Mrs. Deitz made a tutting noise, and Mrs. Weaver said, "I'm sorry, Annette, but they're asking, and I'm going to tell the truth." She sighed, gathered herself, and turned back to Cassie. "June was real pretty, you know." There it was again, that "rull." "But she'd come from a rich family up in Lima, and she held her nose in the air when she first moved to St. Jude. That kind of thing just didn't impress us here. And then, well, she went and got engaged to Arthur Danvers, and she made sure we all knew it. As if we were desperate for Arthur Danvers. Which we were not."

"Your grandfather was a very nice man," Mrs. Deitz interjected, frowning apologetically.

"June became much more bearable after the wedding. It was a simple affair, very small. Not even a reception, if I remember. I think it was good for her to be humbled." Mrs. Weaver mused on her own profundity for a moment, then nodded with definite force. "And then she had the baby—your father—and became just as common as the rest of us."

"And your father!" Mrs. Deitz said, clapping her hands together in delight. "What a nice little boy he was."

Cassie did her best to avoid the bruise that had formed at the center of her chest.

"June's friend Lindie helped with the movie," Mrs. Weaver mentioned, as the thought occurred to her.

"Do you think Lindie was a lesbian?" Mrs. Deitz asked. They'd obviously had many such speculative conversations.

"She did like to dress like a boy."

"If she'd been born nowadays maybe she'd be transgender." Mrs. Deitz was clearly pleased she'd remembered the word.

Mrs. Weaver shrugged dismissively.

Mrs. Deitz went on, nodding at her victory. "I read an article about transgender youth. They're at risk."

"Well, Lindie seemed just fine nosing into everyone's business, that's all I know for sure." Mrs. Weaver leaned forward, pointing to Nick's phone, so he took down what he could. "She moved to Chicago the same summer as *Erie Canal*. With her father. It was just the two of them. Her mother had run out years before. A redhead. There was talk she was a prostitute."

"Janet!" Mrs. Deitz clutched her pearls again. Mrs. Weaver smiled saucily and delicately picked up another Ritz.

"Anything else?" Nick asked.

The old women sighed in unison. They mentioned a few tidbits about the parts they'd played—both had been extras in the election scene, and could recall in impeccable detail the swish of their taffeta dresses—but that was all they had.

"But you're going to talk to Henry Abernathy?" Mrs. Deitz asked as they walked toward the front door.

"Yes," Nick said, checking his phone, "we're going over there this afternoon."

"He'll know much more than we do." Mrs. Deitz reached for the doorknob. "He had bad lungs as a child, so his mother told him history could be his sport. It's been his hobby ever since. He knows every single thing about this town. He's quite something."

"He's quite single," Mrs. Weaver said, and Mrs. Deitz turned the color of strawberry ice cream.

"Ask him if he has any pictures of the party Jack and Diane threw at Two Oaks," Mrs. Deitz said, ushering them onto the front porch.

"They threw a party?" Cassie asked.

"Close to the end of the film production, so it must have been the end of June. It was a big event—everyone in town went. Albert took me. We danced the fox-trot to a live orchestra, set up under a big tent right there on the lawn. Your great-great-great-uncle Lemon was sick by then, and quite old. But when they opened up the house for that one night"— she clapped her hands in delight at the memory—"oh, it was a grand affair indeed."

"I wore emerald chiffon," Mrs. Weaver said, batting her eyelashes, swept up in her friend's romantic description.

Nick shook their hands, and Cassie was about to do the same when Mrs. Deitz gently touched her arm.

"And may I just say"—the small woman looked apprehensive now, and as she hung her head at a familiar angle, Cassie knew exactly what was coming—"I'm so sorry about your parents. We were all just so sad when it happened."

Cassie had learned it was rude to cover your ears when people said such things. She pasted on a sympathetic smile, because that's what people wanted when they brought up your orphanhood. "You were a lucky girl to survive that," the old woman said, as the other nodded along gravely with wide, hungry eyes.

Even a year before, Cassie would have shocked them with a gruesome tidbit—the severed hand, maybe, or the sound of the Jaws of Life gnawing through the twisted wreck above her. Instead she simply said, "Thank you."

"Well, I think June did right, moving down to Columbus so you could stay in your home," Mrs. Deitz said, as though Mrs. Weaver didn't. "I know we all missed her, but it was the best thing not to make you move to St. Jude, where everything would have been new."

"We only wish she'd made an effort once you were off to college, at least on the house," Mrs. Weaver interjected. "We thought she'd stay put in St. Jude once you were off, or at least that's what she told us she had planned. But Two Oaks has fallen into such disrepair. It's an eyesore, is what it is." Her voice dripped with recrimination. Cassie told herself to take deep breaths and bite her tongue.

Mrs. Deitz was incensed. "She took her job as guardian very seriously is all, Janet, and who's to blame her that she cared about her own granddaughter more than some old house?" To Cassie, she said, "You must have loved all those visits she took to New York."

"Visits?" Cassie asked.

"The last few years. All those visits to New York City! Why, she was hardly in St. Jude at all."

"Personally, I can't stand the place," Mrs. Weaver quipped. "There's at least seven reasons I could never live in that city, and three through six are the people."

New York? Loved it? There'd only been that one trip, last summer. The disaster, the last time Cassie had seen June, if you weren't counting the hospital. "I think you must be confused."

Mrs. Weaver and Mrs. Deitz exchanged a quick glance. Then Mrs. Deitz frowned. "Must be our mistake." She snuck a nervous peek at Mrs. Weaver before adding, "Your grandpa Arthur was already sick when your parents passed. Plenty of people think June should have stayed to nurse him through the end. But I think what she did was saintly."

Mrs. Weaver's eye roll made her feelings known on that subject. She squared herself to Cassie and added, "Now you're living there, can we expect you to mow?"

Cassie had a sudden urge to throttle the cream puff.

"You know what?" Nick said, putting his hand on Cassie's lower back and flashing both ladies a smile. "We really must be going. Thank you both so much."

Next thing Cassie knew, Nick was backing them down the driveway. His sleeves were rolled up over his elbows; his hands were sure on the wheel. The old women waved from the front porch, set side by side like a pair of salt and pepper shakers. That should have been Cassie's picture; she could see it now. But she didn't, couldn't, take it. Somehow Nick knew not to say a word for miles.

CHAPTER TWENTY-FOUR

———

THEY STILL HAD AN HOUR AND A HALF BEFORE THEY WERE
due at Henry Abernathy's. Cassie didn't want to go home. Nick
didn't say as much, but she could tell he liked the idea of an hour
out of Tate's purview, so she suggested they stop by the DQ, just up the
road on the other side of St. Jude.

"DQ?"

Cassie laughed, incredulous. "Dairy Queen. Are you human?"

He laughed at himself then too. "I'm from California."

"You don't have Dairy Queen in California?"

"We do," he said, as they passed Hair Priorities, Clancy's Tables N'
Tubs, and Buckeye Storage, "but we don't nickname it."

It was an old-fashioned Dairy Queen, really just a shack, where boys
ditched their bikes, and girls giggled against the counter, and families
jammed themselves around the two red picnic tables that overlooked
the Paris Drycleaners, with the saddest white cutout of the Eiffel Tower
Cassie'd ever seen. Nick wanted to take their burgers and fries to go—
"Wouldn't it be nicer to sit in Montgomery Square?"—but Cassie insisted the only reason to endure the DQ food was to line your stomach
for ice cream. He insisted he didn't want any ice cream, really. She replied that if he tried to eat raw almonds for dessert, she was going to
scream. After they licked the salt from their fingers, she carried their red
tray up to the garbage can and ordered them each a soft serve dipped in
chocolate. The chocolate hardened like a shell within the minute. She
showed him how to eat from the top down, so as not to overcrack the
chocolate—with occasional licks across the sides, of course, to get rid of
any errant drips—and she could tell, from the way his eyes rolled back
in his head as he chewed, that he hadn't tasted something so good in a
long time.

THEY DROVE THE three minutes back to Montgomery Square. Out of the car, Cassie watched Nick's eyes skirt across the library and the fire station, squat brick buildings made for the ages. They strolled toward the old canal. The deep trench was empty, save for the thick sludge at the bottom. Cassie wondered the names of the men who'd first dug it out.

"How do you know so much about history, architecture, that kind of stuff?" she asked, turning to Nick. "You seem really into it."

"My mom," Nick said. "She's a production designer. She, uh, she's the one who's hired to decide how a movie should look."

"Like she's the one who says the curtains should be blue?"

"That the curtains should be just a shade lighter than royal blue, and that the house should be three stories high and have white clapboard siding, and that the ballroom should have chintz wallpaper, and that the winter snow should be two and a half feet deep. Every last detail, that's my mom."

"Wow, that's a cool job."

"Yeah, and it wasn't easy for her to get there, either." He picked up a pebble and chucked it into the canal, where it made a satisfying thwock. "Just about every other production designer at her level is a man. She had to work her way up, let things roll off her back, fight for what she wanted. She started as an art director—that's the person who carries out the production designer's vision. So she spent a lot of years doing what other people wanted. Now she finally gets to be the boss." He looked proud.

"Anyway." He picked up a handful of stones and lobbed them, one by one, into the canal. "It was just her and me, so I spent a lot of time hearing about trompe l'oeil and cathedral ceilings and the Spanish Inquisition and . . . If I hadn't learned to like it, I would have lost my mind."

"And that's how you met Tate?"

"Yeah, my mom was doing a movie a few years back and needed an extra set of hands, so I helped out on set."

"What movie?"

"Agnes." He said it with a soft *g*, like the French did—"An-yes"—and Cassie tried not to melt. It was one of her favorite movies, featuring Tate as an impoverished laundress in postwar Paris. The role had been a bit of a stretch, but Cassie thought Tate had been magnificent, especially in the scene when she learned that one of her three children—all presumed dead—had survived the occupation.

"That's a great movie," she said, trying to sound nonchalant.

"Oh, thanks." He seemed suddenly shy. "I mean, I didn't really have much to do with it. But you should tell Tate—I bet that would mean a lot." They followed the canal diagonally across the square, through the shade and around overflowing garbage cans; this was where the teenagers came to drink on Friday nights. "Anyway, I was looking for work at the time, and Tate's assistant, Margaret, noticed me, said they were looking for someone to join Tate's team."

"So how long have you been working for her?" He bristled under her scrutiny, and Cassie laughed. "Tell me to shut up whenever you want; I'm just curious."

"No, I get it, it's a strange job. Um . . ." He looked up, to the tops of the elm trees above them. "Five years? But I've only been doing this job for a couple of months." He cleared his voice, suddenly uncomfortable. "Since Margaret left."

"You're, like, Tate's head assistant now?"

"Something like that."

"And you like it?"

"Of course. Hundred-and-thirty-hour workweeks, not remembering what time zone you're in, never getting to have a private life—what's not to love?" He was joking, of course, but Cassie wondered if the bravado didn't hide some doubt.

So she pushed. "Do you ever feel like you're living someone else's life for them?" He frowned, but, before he could answer no, she elaborated. "I mean, like the sweaty towel thing—how she just gave it to you—do you ever feel like you're, I don't know, doing someone's dirty work? I don't mean it in a bad way, I'm really asking."

His frown turned thoughtful. "I guess I just don't see it that way. It's like, here's this tremendously famous, successful person. There aren't enough hours in the day for her, on a basic level, to survive; she wouldn't physically be able to eat and cook and read four scripts and exercise and go to a costume fitting, and all the hundreds of other things she's expected to do in a day. She needs someone else to manage the nitty-gritty. She needs me. She needs Hank. She's incredibly humble about it, actually."

"Do you ever want your own life?"

"I like my life." They'd crossed over into something less friendly. Cassie knew she should back off, but she couldn't help it; she had the distinct feeling that it was Nick the assistant, not Nick the man, who'd threatened her with eviction two days before. He'd seemed so uncomfortable, regretful, so out of his element, and she couldn't shake that relieved look he'd given her when she slammed the door in his face.

"And what's the endgame?" she asked. Almost to the old high school, they'd nearly reached the end of the canal. "What do you want to do with your life?"

She saw, then, that she'd pushed too far. He turned toward her, his mouth set in a tight line. "Well, what's your endgame? I mean, this seems like a pretty solid plan, hiding out in the middle of Ohio while your house falls down around you."

She held up her hands in surrender. He kept his eyes on her for a minute, and then, together, they turned back toward the car, walking in silence until he said, in a calmer, kinder tone, "I don't have an endgame."

To which she could honestly reply, "I don't either."

CHAPTER TWENTY-FIVE

———

ENRY ABERNATHY LIVED OUTSIDE OF TOWN, OFF LAKE ST. Jude, on what the old women had referred to as one of the "fingers." Neither Cassie nor Nick had understood what that meant until they found themselves tracing the edge of the water up and around what could only be described as a finger, into a much newer development than where they'd been that morning. The GPS's instructions were measured as they closed in on the house. The brown water slopped restlessly against the rocky banks; the lake had been polluted for as long as Cassie could remember, and, though plenty of boats were moored just along the shore, she'd never seen anyone swim in Lake St. Jude.

The house stuck out on its own little peninsula off of the aforementioned finger, like a hangnail, a wooden structure shaped like a modern interpretation of a whaling ship, tall and compact with too many windows to count. Mr. Abernathy waved his cane down at them and told them to come around the back and up the stairs. Cassie took a picture of him from the driveway, before they climbed to the back porch, which overlooked a wide swath of water.

He was older than the old ladies—maybe even ninety—but just as vibrant. He was wiry and strong, like a Jack Russell, with bright, clear eyes. He was eager, the second they came in the door, to show them his extensive archives, which took up most of the top floor of the house. "Business closes down? I take their bags of receipts. Grandpa dies? I say, 'Give me all those old albums with strangers you don't know in 'em.'" His blue eyes twinkled. "Then I play detective."

On the wall, Cassie noticed a photograph of a dirigible flying over the vast Goodyear plant just outside of town. In what had once been some kind of rec room stood shelves and shelves of identical five-inch navy binders. "My son built these," Mr. Abernathy said proudly, knocking the sturdy pine. Cassie's eyes skimmed the identical typed labels stuck to the outsides of the binders, which, on one side of the room, were grouped chronologically (starting all the way back in 1867) and, on the other, alphabetically by subject ("Goodyear Plant," "Lake St. Jude," Schillinger's Drug Receipts"). Mr. Abernathy had been employed by the county clerk's office, but it was clear this magnificent collection was his true life's work. When Cassie mentioned this, he nodded proudly that he'd been approached by more than one local library and historical society, asking him to donate all his papers. He chuckled. "They won't know who gets what until they read my will." Cassie wondered if all old men were essentially the same—pleased at the thought of heirs scrambling for their legacies.

Nick asked about *Erie Canal,* and Mr. Abernathy hauled down two binders marked with the name of the movie. Inside were dozens of clippings and paraphernalia—a pressed corsage that Diane DeSoto had supposedly worn in the cotillion sequence, a prop election flyer, not to mention the articles (from the *Columbus Dispatch* and the local paper, the *St. Jude Caller*) that sported photographs of Diane and Jack stepping out of limousines and laughing in front of the small brick fire station that still stood on Montgomery Square.

Mr. Abernathy directed them through both binders, tapping his knotty finger on the pages and offering fact after fact—who had written the article, the collection where he'd discovered it, and any identifying details in the photographs ("That's Mr. Hammacher's barbershop, down on Main Street. He had a speaking part in the film but it didn't make the final cut"). But when Cassie pressed for more speculative or personal details about anyone in the photographs, about Diane or Jack or even June, Mr. Abernathy's face would cloud. "Well, I don't know about that," he answered carefully a few times, until Nick shot her a look and she decided to hold her questions until the end.

As soon as they finished looking through the second *Erie Canal* notebook, Mr. Abernathy held up a finger and said, "Nineteen fifty-five! Big year for St. Jude, but could have been bigger." He sat back in his chair and folded his hands over his little hump of a belly. "The movie was only here for a month, and then things went back to normal. I guess if it had been a hit or something it might have made a difference—there would have been tours, that kind of thing. It would have turned St. Jude into a tourist destination. Have you seen it?"

"What, *Erie Canal*?" He'd been talking so long, she was surprised to be asked a question. "No. Have you, Nick?"

Nick shook his head. "It's hard to get your hands on."

Mr. Abernathy mused for a moment, clearly weighing what to say next. He settled on "Well, I'd be curious to see what you think." He paused judiciously. "I'm not one for movies."

But before Cassie could dig for dirt, he went on. "What would have truly changed the game for St. Jude was if the interstate had come just east of town on its way down to Cincinnati." Turned out Mr. Abernathy had a whole notebook devoted to what he called "a little-known bit of St. Judian lore." According to him, a contractor named Mr. Ripvogle, based in Lima, had nearly won a construction bid that would have "transformed this town. Everything seemed to be in place, but the national bill wasn't passed until 1956, and by then Ripvogle was off the project. There was some talk he tried to bribe the governor"—he wagged his finger—"which was a no-no."

It was the first time Cassie'd heard him speculate. Although she wasn't remotely interested in this particular topic, she feigned interest, hoping she'd be able to get him to guess about Jack and June; if he knew anything about an affair, it would be based on rumor and innuendo, not hard facts.

He clapped his hands sharply then, and said, "Oh, how rude! I've forgotten you're descended from Lemon Gray Neely!" He got down another notebook, all about Two Oaks, and asked did she know that Neely's wife, Mae, had died in the great influenza epidemic of 1918 in Two Oaks's master bedroom? And had Cassie seen Neely's mausoleum down at the Elm Grove Cemetery? And did she know how rich Neely had been in his heyday? First the oil, then the land? "And then, when he died—poof! Gone." He leaned forward and said, "Your grandmother should have gotten everything."

Should: another speculative word.

Cassie leaned forward to match him. "But she didn't?"

He grimaced and shook his head, as though Cassie'd been the one to bring it up. "I don't like to gossip."

"Please make an exception for me."

He glanced hesitatingly between her and Nick, then leaned forward in his chair and lowered his voice, as if someone was listening at the door.

"Well, it all comes down to money. That's the trail history leaves, at least. June and her mother, Cheryl Ann, moved into Two Oaks in 1952, and lived with Mr. Neely and his maid, Apatha. They were related to him only tangentially—Neely's wife, Mae, had been the aunt of Cheryl Ann's husband, Marvin—who was also your grandmother's father. But Mae and Marvin were both dead. So it was quite generous of Neely to invite them in." He paused for a moment to let Cassie catch up. "In the meantime, June gets engaged to Arthur Danvers, Clyde Danvers's brother. Now Clyde was a real man about town. He knew everyone; he built that Three Oaks development over there on the other side of town, he owned every building on Main Street—well, the ones that Mr. Neely didn't own. I always wondered if there was some kind of arrangement there. The marriage of a Danvers to Mr. Neely's potential heir would have really been something."

"But it wasn't?"

"That's just the thing. June marries Arthur, becomes a Danvers. Mr. Neely dies, and so does Mr. Danvers—the older one, Clyde, I mean. June and Arthur move, almost at once, back into Two Oaks with Cheryl Ann, and they nurse her through her final illness and June has their child—your father, Adelbert. But here's what's strange: Mr. Neely was a millionaire, many times over. He owned land, ran oil fields, and had plenty of cash. Two Oaks was a grand home, certainly, but the real prize was his money. And I knew June and Arthur, and they didn't live like that. They were always just getting by, making enough to take care of themselves and their son, and do what they could to maintain Two Oaks. But it was hard on them. That place required a lot of upkeep."

"Believe me," Cassie interjected, "I know."

"But they should have had plenty of money!" He was in his own world now, incensed by the injustice of inadequate facts. "If Mr. Neely left everything to June, they should have been living in luxury. So the question remains: where did all that money go?" Mr. Abernathy flipped to a page in the third binder. As far as Cassie could tell, it was a town record covered with figures and acronyms she didn't understand.

A phone rang out, piercing the silence.

Mr. Abernathy looked alarmed. Cassie turned to find the source of the sound. Of course—it was Nick's phone. Nick grabbed the little machine from his pocket. Cassie caught a glimpse of the screen. It said "Tate." Well, she thought, he'd silence it and call Tate back when Mr. Abernathy was done. But, instead, Nick stood and held up a finger. Then he answered. "Yes?"

Cassie glared to get him to hang up. But he was absorbed in the conversation, blind to her, as though everything had evaporated but the sound of Tate's voice. "Well, good, that's progress, but did you tell him I'd call back?" It was clear, from his tone, that this was not an emergency. "No, nothing important. Yes, I can talk." Then he held up his hand in a vague gesture of apology and strode out of the room.

Cassie watched him go in shock, then turned back to Mr. Abernathy and apologized. The old guy looked suddenly exhausted, confused; the call had interrupted his train of thought. Cassie's blood boiled at Nick's selfishness. She pointed to the paper. "What does it mean?"

The ancient man looked down at the paper uneasily. He rubbed one eye like a baby. She knew she should let him off the hook, but now she was thirsty. She'd never known anything about this part of June's life. She tapped at the numbers to redirect him.

He sat as upright as he could, nodding down at the page, translating. "Only a month after Neely dies, and someone is selling off his land. Acres and acres and acres of it. Someone made a lot of money, but that money left this town. I don't know where it went, but it didn't stay here, I'm sure of that." His gaze drifted up and out the window before him.

"So what do you think happened?" Cassie asked. "Who was it? Who got the money?"

His eyes squinted. His voice grew foggy. "It's the historian's job to stick to the facts."

She was impatient at this coyness; he'd been happy to guess at the truth only moments before.

Mr. Abernathy closed the binder and shook his head.

"Please," she pleaded. There was so much she didn't know. So much she hadn't known she didn't know. It seemed necessary, all at once, to understand who had stolen from her hardworking grandparents.

Mr. Abernathy stood with effort, carefully tucking one binder under his arm and leaning on his cane to take it back to the empty spot where it belonged. Cassie gathered up the others and followed him. She could tell he didn't want her to place them in their spots herself, so she passed them to him and waited for him to complete the task alone. Her "please" hung in the air, but she wasn't going to beg again.

Mr. Abernathy brushed off his hands and turned to her, opening them in apology. It would have made a great shot.

"I don't know what happened," he said. "That's the problem. People die and your chance to ask goes with them."

Cassie's heart flipped at his wisdom. It was tragic and cruel and true. She was furious at herself for losing the chance to ask June about Arthur and Jack, to find out what it had been like to lose her only child, Adelbert, in the accident, or how she'd felt about moving down to Columbus to raise her only grandchild. Cassie would never hear from June about losing her father in a foreign war, or watching her mother auction off their things. Or what Two Oaks had been like when June was a girl, or Mr. Neely. All of it was gone.

Cassie had been so bound up in her own life that it had never occurred to her to be interested in June's. And now it was too late.

Mr. Abernathy patted her on the shoulder. "You need anything else, you know where to find me." He was ready for her to go, she could tell, ready to sleep away the afternoon. She felt the urge to lift this old treasure into her arms and carry him to his bed, to read him a story and tuck him in, to watch how quickly sleep would overcome him. But instead she thanked him, apologized again for Nick's departure, and let him escort her unsteadily to the top of the porch stairs. The light was turning orange outside, the afternoon already fading toward evening. She had her camera, but she could tell it would cost him something if she took his picture.

"Oh," she said, turning quickly at the top of the stairs, "Mrs. Deitz mentioned you might have pictures of a party the *Erie Canal* people threw at Two Oaks toward the end of filming? It sounded like quite an event."

"I was there," he said. "Diane DeSoto asked me to hold her gloves. But I've never been much for crowds. I didn't stay long." Mr. Abernathy's small, square shoulders rose up to his ears, then slumped down with his exhale. "People throw out everything. I can't rightly remember who was taking pictures that night, but even if I could, I doubt they're still in existence." He gripped his cane tightly, his ire ignited by people's stupidity, and he looked sad as she descended the stairs.

SHE KEPT HER mouth shut for most of the drive home, until the stupid GPS urged them into the outskirts of St. Jude. They were only moments from Tate and Hank, and Cassie couldn't stop herself. "That was rude."

Nick glanced over at her, then back to the road.

"You should have turned your phone off. And you definitely shouldn't have answered it."

"It was an important call."

Fury uncoiled itself inside of her. "More important than that old man? More important than finding out what happened to my grandmother? I thought you were here to help me."

"I'm here," he said briskly, "because it's my job." His jaw tightened. "Some of us have them, Cassie."

What nerve.

CHAPTER TWENTY-SIX

———

HAT NIGHT, CASSIE'S BACK WAS A DAMP POCKET OF SWEAT against her sheets. Her thirst did battle with her bladder. Two Oaks was restless too, creaking and moaning, rattling and shifting. It liked having a person in every one of its beds, and proper dinners taken at the table, and the sound of laughter rafting through the front windows. But something wasn't right yet—all was not as it was supposed to be. The tall, golden-haired girl, for example—she was good at what she did, goodness knows, Two Oaks was grateful someone had finally thought to mop—but she was perfunctory in her gestures, doing only what must be done. In its heyday, Two Oaks had considered itself the kind of house that inspired its people to greatness, but everyone inside it now seemed to just be getting by.

Cassie flopped and tossed in her hot bed, incensed anew every time she thought of Nick's smug little face, and his dig at her about how "some of us" had jobs. Also, he'd been dead wrong to take that phone call. Did these people truly believe they had more worth than the Mr. Abernathys of the world? That they could waltz into someone's life expecting her to give up her DNA? Two could play at that game. She would make them wait even longer for the test, even though she had to admit that, so far, they'd turned up no evidence of an affair. And how was it any business of Nick's whether she had a job? What if she did have a job? That would teach him. Okay, fine, she didn't, technically. ("Well, what's your endgame?" he'd sniped—she could see him so clearly in her mind's eye, and she sat up in fury.) She savored the fantasy of letting slip that she was a very important, highly paid corporate attorney. Or a doctor! A research doctor. A research doctor with a specialty in infectious diseases. She finally found sleep with the taste of sweet, juicy victory upon her tongue.

Did she dream? Maybe. When she opened her eyes to the bright room, she realized that, for the first time since she'd moved in, she couldn't quite put her finger on where she'd gone in the night. Surely she'd been somewhere inside these four walls, surrounded by strange souls. She squeezed her eyes shut, trying to place herself back inside the dream she must have been having, but her mind was a black, empty drum.

She strained to hear voices. She knew they would already be awake, even though it was murderously early on the West Coast. People who judged you for not having a job invariably woke before the sun. She pressed her feet into the floor, baptized in new wrath at the promise of Nick's expression when he caught her trudging down the stairs still in her pajamas. Being judged in her own home! It would not stand.

SHE FOUND THEM in the kitchen. The women were in their yoga outfits, and Nick, of course, was on his device, one bare elbow—unsheathed from his dark blue button-down—resting on the rickety table. She frowned at it like it was a bad dog.

Tate was reading a Deepak Chopra paperback. Hank was standing on a chair before one of Cassie's kitchen cabinets, scrubbing with a wet rag. The sum total of the food Cassie had possessed before these people arrived—a can of green beans, two cans of tuna fish, and a pickle jar with one perfectly good specimen still floating inside—was in a stack by the recycling bin. She lifted the camera to her eye and took a picture.

"Good morning!" Hank chirped when she heard the click. Nick gave a start, a small wave without eye contact, then scurried into the pantry and then the dining room, all while still on his phone.

Tate closed her book as Cassie crossed to the chair Nick had just occupied, realizing that the linoleum tiles of the kitchen floor were a good ten shades lighter than they had been when she'd turned in. Mopping! Damn Hank and her industry. But the smile Tate offered Cassie actually seemed to warm the room, melting even Cassie's icy mood.

Cassie wondered if this was her new normal—Two Oaks full of successful, busy people who awoke at dawn. The full repercussions of what she had proposed were finally settling in: these people would stay until they found something that would prove or disprove an affair, at which point she'd give them her DNA. She hadn't much considered what that proof would look like. Or why she wanted it. She'd half-expected they'd just steal from her hairbrush and do the test on their own, but that didn't appear to be on the agenda. She should find herself a lawyer. She really should. But, despite Hank cleaning like a maniac only a few feet away, ponytail swinging as the sponge squeaked and scrubbed, unpleasant as the previous evening's interaction with Nick had been, Cassie had to admit that Tate was an oasis, and that, as a whole, the last few days had been, well, better than most of the days in the months preceding them.

"Espresso?" Tate asked, pushing her Prada glasses atop her head.

Cassie noticed the shiny silver espresso maker over Tate's shoulder, on the countertop beside the stove. Where had that come from?

"Hank, make her an espresso?" Tate asked, a command masked as a question.

"Of course!" Hank enthused. She hopped off the chair and snapped off the yellow gloves she'd brought home from the grocery store the day before, slapping them down over the sink. She crossed the kitchen and spooned beans into the grinder, which purred at the press of the button.

Cassie caught a glimpse of Tate's serene face again. It wasn't Tate's fault—or even Hank's—that Nick had been a jerk. "Sleep okay?" she asked, like a hostess was supposed to.

"Like the dead," Tate insisted with a calm smile.

"That mattress is ancient," Cassie said. "And I should have vacuumed."

Tate smiled indulgently.

"My room is so pretty!" Hank had gotten the third bedroom, the one Cassie liked least. It was the darkest of the bunch, and scratching animal sounds filled the walls at night.

Hank crossed back to the sink and filled a shot of water, then poured it into the reservoir at the top of the espresso maker. Her hands worked quickly, next filling and tamping the beans into the brew group. Cassie had pegged her as a former yoga teacher, but maybe she'd been a barista in another life. Once Hank slid the ground beans into place, she pressed another button and placed a small white espresso cup—also new to Cassie—under the spout. Back at the sink, she snapped on her gloves and crouched before the undercounter cabinet. She was like a hummingbird; Cassie wondered how many calories she had to consume to keep this up all day.

"Does every bedroom have a fireplace?" Hank asked. The cabinet under the sink was a time capsule of toxic cleaning products and rags furry with dust, and Hank wrinkled her nose, which Cassie had come to learn was the closest she got to expressing disgust.

"Yeah," Cassie said, resenting that a proper grown-up like Nick probably knew the details about the fireplaces: the kind of tile inlaid around each one, and where the wood in the mantelpiece hailed from. She had no idea.

"What's . . . this . . . ?" Hank asked, pulling an unidentifiable brown wad into the light.

"It's not a rat, is it?" Cassie asked coolly.

Hank shrieked and dropped the wad into the garbage can. Cassie leaned over it and raised an eyebrow. It was a piece of rusted steel wool; she'd known that all along. "Nah, not big enough."

Tate tittered. Hank scowled. Cassie beamed.

The espresso announced its arrival with a tapered tinkle. Hank attended to it, bringing the hot nectar to Cassie's right hand as though there was nothing she'd rather do in the whole wide world. It wasn't the worst thing to have a personal chef / housecleaner / errand girl at your beck and call, even if the food was mostly low-carb and practically vegan, and you risked permanent blindness from the wattage of her overused smile. Cassie thought of last night's dinner—the red peppers stuffed with a mixture of quinoa and spices, the homemade baba ghanoush and hand-ground flaxseed crackers—and she smiled apologetically at Hank.

Hank abruptly clapped her hands together. "Whole Foods delivered at six a.m.!"

"I thought you went to Pantry Pride yesterday," Cassie said, thinking of the many bags Hank had been unloading onto the kitchen table when Cassie and Nick had returned from Mr. Abernathy's. There wasn't a Whole Foods for at least a hundred miles; Cassie wondered about the cost of the delivery alone.

"Pantry Pride is great for basics," Hank said with her signature nose crinkle. "But it just doesn't carry the kind of selection we're used to. We needed specialty items—quinoa flour, baby kale, heritage grains. And of course we mostly eat organic." Her pert little shoulders shuddered in a delighted shiver. "I can't wait to make you my tofu loaf." She practically skipped out to the pantry, and, just like that, Cassie was back to wanting her dead.

Tate returned to the Deepak Chopra, pulling her glasses down to the bridge of her button nose. She looked mussed, morning-like, but nothing like a real person actually looks first thing. Cassie took a sip of the espresso and nearly fainted; she hadn't tasted anything so good in months. She wondered how long her pride would win out over asking Hank to make her breakfast.

Hank reemerged with two Whole Foods bags filled to the brim and disappeared for another load. June would be appalled to see Cassie sipping a hot beverage while Hank worked alone. So Cassie contritely followed Hank through the pantry and into the dining room.

The morning light pressed rainbows through the clear, beveled glass that was set into the dining room's back door. A dozen paper bags lined the mahogany table. Nick had been in there on the phone, but now he was leaving, heading into the foyer, without a glance back. Apparently he was avoiding her today.

Cassie went to lift one of the bags.

"Don't worry about it," Hank said.

"I'm happy to help."

Hank shook her head, trying to take the bag Cassie was lifting. She reminded Cassie of a child grabbing for a toy. "It's my job." These people were obsessed.

Cassie followed Hank back into the kitchen bearing a hard-won bag filled with more kale than she had eaten in the last ten years. She set it on the counter. The kitchen looked as it had before her parents' accident, before the house had gotten lonely; spick-and-span in a country way that Cassie had never been able to achieve on her own. She opened the refrigerator, already, to her eyes, full, save for the bottom left crisper drawer, which held a Ziploc of film cartridges. She held them up and waved them at Hank, back with another load. "I'll get these out of your way."

Just then, Hank tripped, spilling half her bag—plums, avocados, apples—across the kitchen floor. Cassie rushed to help her, but Tate sighed, wiggled her manicured toes in their flip-flops, and waved Cassie away. To Hank, she said, "We'll get out of your hair so you can whip up those blueberry quinoa pancakes you promised."

"Ready in twenty!" Hank called from her hands and knees as they headed into the servant hallway and out to the foyer. Did Cassie imagine a touch of desperation in her voice?

In the hallway, Tate turned to Cassie and rolled her eyes. "She can be so intense." Cassie nodded in annoyed agreement, even though she wondered, Wasn't Tate mostly the reason Hank was like that? The poor girl hadn't meant to spill the produce on the floor. But then, it was Hank's job; Hank herself had been eager to point that out.

In the front parlor, Nick was off the phone. "Well, she said yes." But he didn't look particularly happy about the news.

Tate replied crisply, "Damn right she said yes."

"Who said yes?" Cassie asked.

Nick smiled at her, a brief, perfunctory smile, as though she was a stop sign or a pair of pants, something neutral and inorganic. She decided she was going to walk away from him first, as soon as she found out what they were talking about.

Tate gestured to the couch, but Cassie crossed her arms and held her ground.

"You said you wanted answers . . ." Tate began.

"And Jack's papers will definitely be here today," Nick said, all business to Tate. "They apologized for the delay . . ."

"But the truth is it sounds like you struck out with the older generation. And Hank and I went through the house yesterday and found very little. And the lawyers have already been through Daddy's papers once. I don't imagine we'll find anything new . . ."

"And given"—Nick cleared his throat—"that you've made it clear you refuse to relinquish your DNA until we've turned over every rock, and given that we, each of us, have lives that cannot be permanently put on hold"—everything about Nick that Cassie had found appealing seemed to disappear as he talked in this snippy, businessy voice; she had half a mind to slap his cheeks to try to rouse the real Nick in there, sputtering for breath—"well, I believe it best to cover our bases."

Cassie couldn't bear to look at that smug face a second longer. "Well?" she asked Tate.

Tate sighed. "My sister, Elda, is coming."

Jack's oldest: Elda Montgomery. Except she had a different last name now, Cassie remembered. Elda, whom Cassie's father had crushed on as a young man. Every time Cassie thought of the woman, she felt a softness for her, a softness she was holding because her father couldn't hold it anymore.

"She asked me to send the plane," Nick added.

Tate pursed her lips, then acquiesced as Nick's nostrils flared. "I know, you're right, it's how Margaret would handle it. By all means, send the plane."

Nick smiled genuinely to himself, and then at Cassie. The warmth in his victory warmed her too, in spite of herself. Then she remembered that Elda was only a few years older than her father; she would have been little more than a toddler around the time of Jack and June's supposed dalliance.

"And what does Elda know?" she asked. "Does she remember anything? Did she say something about my grandmother?"

Tate shook her head dismissively. "But she fancies herself the family historian. She did all this research when she wrote her book." She pronounced the words *research* and *book* like they were poison.

"I think she will be helpful," Nick said quietly.

His phone rang. He checked it and visibly blanched. "It's him."

Tate answered—"Max"—and strode from the room and up the master staircase. Cassie went mushy at the thought of *the* Max Hall on the other end of that line. She was surprised at Nick's face; he looked worse than he had the day he'd rung her doorbell.

"I'm not 'refusing to relinquish my DNA,'" she said, air-quoting him back to himself. "Well, I am, but you don't have to say it like that. It sounds mean."

He blinked back at her in surprise. "I'm sorry."

"You should be." The wind was knocked out of her sails by the apology, so before he could walk away from her, she made her way toward the stairs herself, trying to remember what the house had sounded like when no one else was in it.

CHAPTER TWENTY-SEVEN

———

ASSIE ESCAPED TO THE BACKYARD IN A PAIR OF JIM'S paint-splattered overalls. The land was tangled with vines and choked with weeds. What had once been lawn was now a jungle of wildflowers and tasseled grasses, which Cassie personally thought looked okay, although, from the state of her neighbors' lawns, she could tell she was in the minority. More than seventeen years before, when June made the move down to Columbus to care for Cassie, June (and, when he'd been spry, Arthur) must have needed help maintaining such a vast lot—three acres, with the house plopped right in the middle. But if Cassie's memory was any indication, the old woman had done much of the gardening herself. Cassie could clearly recall June's tidy, small canvas gloves gripping a hand rake, and the set of her petite back as she hunched over a flower bed that needed weeding. Under June's watch, the exterior of Two Oaks had always matched the interior: everything in its place.

But it was more than just being diligent and skilled that had made Cassie admire her grandmother's gardening. As a girl, June had supposedly loved to paint—in fact, Cassie believed the fading still lifes now hanging in the foyer had been hers—and it was that word, *love*, not taken lightly, that recalled June to Cassie whenever she spent time in this garden. Cassie could remember the old woman's delight over a new bud, her slender finger gingerly scooping up a beetle to wonder at its coloring. Once, they'd fallen into a fit of giggles over a squirrel's stuffed cheeks; they were in the side yard, and Cassie flopped onto her back and watched June's laughter braid with hers into the summer sky. It was the same rare burst of possibility as when June turned on Chopin piano concertos and they danced around the living room.

In contrast, the garden was now a wild mess. But it took more than one season for a tended plot to grow feral, didn't it? The flower beds sprouted unusual outcroppings, while whole other swaths of the garden seemed to have gone dormant. Cassie wished she'd been paying more attention during what she'd seen as the obligatory biannual trips she'd taken to St. Jude over the past seven years; she'd always just assumed that June's green thumb was keeping the place in shape, but, now that Mrs. Weaver and Mrs. Deitz had implied June wasn't even in St. Jude most of the time, Cassie had been seized by a kind of paranoid guilt. Where on earth had June been? Why hadn't Cassie seen evidence that she was spending time elsewhere? The state of the garden would have been a helpful clue. Instead, Cassie had spent those visits whispering to Jim on her cell phone, or scrolling through Facebook for the latest from New York, where her "real life" was.

She took a deep breath and settled onto the ground. She lifted the camera to her eye. Churning worms. Leaves rotting into the damp earth. The potent tang of manure rising into the nostrils. Azalea bushes the size of bears. She should have hired someone when she moved in. Just as she should have had the roof patched three months ago, when she'd noticed it growing soggy, or dealt with the boiler, or called whomever Hank had surely already called to deal with the bats flitting across the third floor come sundown.

"Refuse to relinquish your DNA"—she'd thought Nick mean to say it that way, but he was right. She was doing just that. And why? Why not just get it over with, find out a clear answer, one way or the other? She could save the house and garden without a second thought, and she'd finally get to be alone again. Maybe she should just let them swab her.

"Hey."

Cassie squinted up into the halo of sun to see Nick standing with two of her grandmother's crystal tumblers. They were tinkling with ice cubes she hadn't made. She took a picture of him squinting down at her, then reached up for the glass.

"What is it?" she asked.

"I wanted to apologize."

She'd meant what kind of drink it was. Nick had suit pants on, but he settled down beside her anyway, ending up closer than he'd probably intended. It took Cassie's eyes a few seconds to adjust from the bright sun to the shade made by their proximity.

She held up the glass—its contents were red. A lemon slice bumped against the rim.

"Hibiscus tea," he said, "sweetened with agave." He took a sip. "Not so bad."

The ice cubes banged against her front teeth. "I could go for a soft serve about now."

He grinned.

She sighed. "Tate's life is so . . ."

He waited for her to go on.

"There's nothing ugly or unpleasant. Not one thing out of place, or uncomfortable, or—"

"You'd be surprised."

She'd been so restrained, so coolly disinterested, but now she wanted to ask him everything—about Tate's sex life and what Tate and Max were like together and what Tate's house looked like and if she really was best friends with Jennifer Aniston and Reese Witherspoon and how much money she made on her last movie and if Tate had told him whether Tom Cruise actually was a good kisser.

But instead, Nick said, "I think all that perfection only makes dealing with reality harder. You should have seen her when she found out Jack had given everything to you."

Cassie fell back onto the ground. She still couldn't get her mind around a movie star leaving his entire fortune to her instead of his daughters. It was so messy, so unkind. How could he have done that to them?

"You're right," Nick said, after a minute. "I get mean. Mean and dismissive. It was rude to pick up the phone at Mr. Abernathy's. I've called him to apologize." He cleared his throat in his nervous habit as his fingers plucked a piece of grass. "And I'm sorry I made that comment about you not working. That was mean too. Not to mention none of my business." He looked out now, across the garden; she followed his gaze. "But it's more than that, I know. I was warned, before I took this job, that it's easy to fool yourself into thinking you're doing the most important work in the world." He laughed. "My mom hates it. She says she hates Tate, but I know that's not it—she hates what working for Tate turns me into."

"So why do it?" Cassie asked.

He picked up his glass from the dirt, drank deeply, then ran the back of his hand across his mouth. Cassie's mouth watered as he lay down on the grass beside her. She became aware of every little blade of grass up against her back. She shaded her eyes to get a look at him. Up close, she could see each individual sprout of stubble on Nick's cheeks and chin, the delicate creases in his plump lips.

"I like helping Tate," Nick said, really considering her question. "She needs me. I don't think there's anything wrong with enjoying feeling needed."

Cassie thought of his downcast expression when Tate had taken Max's call up to her bedroom. How he'd paced Mr. Abernathy's driveway on the call the day before, head cast down, hands gesturing in exasperation. How stressed he'd seemed on the day they met, when he'd been sent all alone to Ohio at Tate's behest. How could she tell him that she wasn't sure he did like it?

As if on cue, his phone rang again. He smiled and tried to ignore it, but she laughed and told him to answer already. He took it from his pocket and silenced it, throwing it onto the grass between them. In a few seconds, a missed call notice came up: Max.

"Something's going on with Tate's marriage, isn't it?" Cassie asked, putting the pieces together just as the question slipped from her mouth. "Something you're supposed to fix."

He looked at her again, carefully, slate eyes meeting hers. "I'm probably not supposed to talk about that," he said slowly. She could feel his eyes on her lips, on her eyes, and back again. It seemed, all at once, that neither of them much cared about the state of Tate and Max's marriage.

Cassie felt a laugh bubble up inside her; it came out nervous, even dismissive. As soon as it escaped her, Nick looked away, and she wished that she could take it back. "Tell me about Jack." She was eager to keep his attention. "What was he like?"

Nick pulled himself up onto one elbow and looked down at her. She tried to ignore the warm sensation pinging through her body as she imagined what it would be like to feel him on top of her.

"I only met him a couple times. He was nice enough, I guess."

"You don't sound convinced."

Nick shrugged, looking out over the yard. "Elda's take is . . . more complicated."

The memoir had been scandalous, but Cassie couldn't remember the details. Nick's phone beeped. Cassie tapped it. "You can call him back, you know. I really don't mind."

But, instead, he sat and rolled up his sleeves. He sank his hands into the brown earth. She'd assumed he'd be fussy about getting dirt under his nails, but he'd done this before. She joined him; they worked side by side for a good bit of time without saying a word.

Cassie felt her awareness expand as she focused on that one little patch of earth. A butterfly alighted on a tuft of grass only a few feet away. Bees bumbled by. And the sound of birdsong was everywhere, chirrups and shrieks and melodies—none of which she knew how to name. She could hear Nick's breath beside her, and, when she held still, she noticed the thump in her right wrist as it pulsed with her heartbeat.

The cool dirt gave pleasingly under her grip. She grabbed a handful hard. "We weren't close at the end." She knew he had no idea what she was talking about. "My grandmother and me."

His hands kept working the soil.

"I mean, we were close in the years right after my parents died, when I was a kid. She was my world. I clung to her, and she gave up everything she had—this house, her marriage, all her friends. Of course I didn't appreciate any of it."

"Be easy on yourself; you were eight."

"Well, I should have appreciated it later on. But all through high school, I treated her . . . I don't know. I just wanted to get out of there."

"You mean you acted like a normal teenager?"

"And then I decided I couldn't stand Ohio anymore," she said, ignoring him. "I had to go to the biggest, best city in the world. Had to get away from my small-town grandmother. I just assumed she'd finally get to move back here, to St. Jude, so she must be happy as a clam, you know? Who cared if she didn't approve of my life? If she hated my art. If she didn't like my boyfriend. It was my prerogative to make my own choices! As far as I could tell, she'd never made any of her own; she'd only ever done what she was told. And now I find out she might have had some secret love affair with a movie star? Maybe even a child with him? That she lied to my father and me, my grandfather, too, about all of it?" She shook her head, tried to ignore the tears blurring her eyes.

"So what exactly are you upset about?" At first, Nick's question sounded accusatory, judgmental, but she looked at his placid face, and realized he was really just asking.

She sighed. "Part of me wants to find out she had this great love with Jack Montgomery. Or even just a hot night, you know? Passion. Something fun. But it also scares me, because if I didn't know this huge important thing about her, which was maybe the most important thing there was to know . . ."

He waited for her to finish, and when she didn't he said, "Then you think you didn't ever really know her?"

The few tears that had ambled down her cheeks had been precursors to the sobs that now wracked her body. "And then we had this huge fight last summer, and apparently she was sick, but she never told me, I didn't find out about her tumor until after she was already in the hospital. I got on the first plane I could, but . . ."

"Lunchtime!" The sound of Hank's voice, accompanied by a clanging bell, ricocheted off the back porch. Cassie wiped her cheeks with her shirt at once and hopped up, accidentally kicking over Nick's tea as he, too, scrambled to his feet. They looked guilty. Meanwhile, the bell clanged maniacally in Hank's hand. "I love this thing!" she called. "I found it in the pantry!"

"What's for lunch?" Nick asked.

"Margaret's cauliflower bisque."

Cassie's stomach rumbled with reluctant enthusiasm as Hank disappeared into the dining room.

Nick looked back at her once Hank was out of sight. "Maybe she kept it a secret to protect you," he said. "Maybe she didn't want you to ever feel this terrible, and she thought that keeping silent was the best way to make that happen."

But Cassie needed this conversation to be over now; she'd dug too deeply, too quickly. She forced a smile. She made her voice light. "Everyone loves Margaret, huh?"

Nick looked briefly panic-stricken. "I don't know anything about that," he said crisply. He turned away from her and charged toward the house. As she crossed the lawn behind him, Cassie watched that tight spot between his shoulders and wondered how it was possible to ache to feel someone's lips one minute and be just as certain that you wanted to punch him in the gut the next.

CHAPTER TWENTY-EIGHT

———

M Y DARLINGS!" ELDA TOOK UP MOST OF THE ENTRANCE OF
Uncle Lem's, arms outstretched, swathed in scarves, reeking of
patchouli. She was larger than life: her voice a little louder than
it needed to be, hands flung wider, smile just a bit too broad. She pulled
Hank and Nick and, yes, even Tate, into a firm hug that looked uncomfortable. "My sweet, sweet darlings." She stuck out her bottom lip. "Less
than a week ago we said good-bye to that wretched, wonderful man . . ."
Tate pulled away, narrowing her eyes as she watched Elda smear Hank's
and Nick's cheeks with greasy kisses. Just when Cassie thought Elda's
grief might go nuclear, Elda caught sight of her and dropped the others
like dirty rags.

"Is this her? Can this beautiful creature possibly be her?" Elda
charged Cassie with an ample smile. Just before impact, Elda stood
back, assessing with a cocked head. "Well, goddamn it, she looks just
like him. Same red aura."

Tate shot a sharp look at Nick.

Cassie stuck out her hand. "Nice to meet you."

"Would you like to get settled?" Nick asked, stepping forward for
Elda's bags.

But it was futile. Elda smacked Cassie's fingers aside and plunged
her into a gut buster, from which she released Cassie only after the girl
gasped.

"This house is epic," Elda said then, her voice booming as she turned
in the foyer to take it all in. "You're sitting on a treasure." She stopped
and caught Cassie's eye. "Haunted, right?" She winked. "I can smell
it. You must have the most tremendous, orgasmic, Neanderthal night-
mares in this place."

Nick interrupted with the suggestion that they discuss sleeping ar-
rangements.

They were going to have to play musical beds because there were only four big bedrooms. Cassie volunteered to sleep on the couch, but everyone balked. Tate claimed to be thrilled with giving up the master bedroom, but they all knew that wasn't happening. Hank ohmygosh-superlovedherroom but was totally into giving it to Elda, except that Hank's bedroom was right beside Tate's, and everyone but Elda knew that Tate wanted Elda as far away as possible. That left Nick's room, the one isolated at the end of the hall, and, since he was the gentleman in the group, he insisted on moving Elda in there, which meant his only options were the couch, or a mattress on the floor in either the maid's tiny room right above the kitchen or the third-floor ballroom, where the bats would be roaming free, at least until the man came to relocate them.

"ARE YOU SURE you'll be okay in here?" Cassie asked an hour later, as she helped Nick clear the floor of the maid's room, restacking her boxes along its edge. Hank would return from Walmart soon with an inflatable mattress to fill the whole space. This room was much bigger than the one Cassie had rented in New York, but it felt positively minuscule in a house this size.

"I can sleep anywhere." Nick grimaced as he gripped a particularly heavy box. "What's in here?"

"My photography stuff," she said, surveying the only belongings she'd brought with her, back when she'd been full of dreams of turning this big house into some kind of art studio. She couldn't forget the doubting way Jim had shaken his head at her, or ignore how right he'd been.

"You should unpack it. You should use it."

She'd been flirting with the idea herself, of seeing if she could turn the pantry into a darkroom, ever since she'd picked up her camera again. She shrugged noncommittally though.

"Why'd you move here?" he asked. "Sounds like you had a good thing going in New York. That *Times* review was something."

She had the whole thing memorized: *Cassandra Danvers's remarkable installation is just the right mix of acidic and angry, to re-create, in its viewer, the acute sensations of the emotionally bereft.* She flinched at the memory. Most days she wanted to forget the whole thing: all those hours of work, the sudden attention, Jim turning green with envy, the phone calls from the collectors, and, yes, even an inquiry from the Whitney Biennial, and then, right when she thought she had everything she wanted, her grandmother's ashen face in the middle of the gallery, the way she'd looked like she might faint on the spot, her quick retreat to the sidewalk, her shocked expression when she said those words to Cassie out on the corner while she tried to hail a cab—"What have you done, Cassandra? That was for us"—and the ensuing weeks of silence, until the call Cassie got from the hospital. After nursing June through her last days into the dark night of her death, Cassie had returned to New York, tried to make it what it had been to her so recently, a place of hope and opportunity. But that had proved impossible, and on a cold December day, she'd put most of her worldly possessions on the curb, tossed her iPhone into the East River, and taken the Greyhound back to Ohio.

But she didn't want to talk about June.

"My boyfriend asked me to marry him," she said instead, because that was also the truth. Poor Jim, who didn't even believe in marriage, desperate enough to keep her in New York that he believed putting a ring on her finger would solve their problems.

Did Nick look hurt? If he did, the glance was fleeting. And why should he care that someone had once wanted to marry her?

"I guess your answer was no."

She held out her hands to refer to the house, and was about to reply with something momentous and heart-pounding and cinematic—"I married this instead" or "What, you haven't seen my husband around here?" (accompanied by a sad smile), or simply, "The answer, my friend, was no"—but before she could muster it, they heard a clattering on the floorboards above them. They both looked up as it intensified. It was coming from the ballroom.

"Animal?" he asked.

She blew the hair off her face and shouldered her box to the side of the room. "Probably one of those bats."

"Shouldn't a bat be asleep?" There it was again, panicked, scuttling. A raccoon? But how would it have gotten up there?

Nick leaned forward with an excited smile. "Let's investigate," he said, and, before she could protest, he left her.

Cassie followed him across the upstairs hall. The door to Tate's bedroom was closed. They could hear murmurs coming from behind it, a good sign, Cassie thought, since it meant Tate and Elda were catching up. Maybe they'd already found something helpful about their father and June; the possibility heartened Cassie as she climbed to the third floor at Nick's heels.

She'd forgotten how warm it got up there during the day. How it smelled of old wax mixed with something like straw or hay. How the heat combined with the scent of mown grass coming through the cracked windows made her want to curl up and sleep. They crouched in the doorway, listening. At first they heard nothing, and she made a crack about getting back to work, but just then the sound came again, a thwack against the window, followed by a panicked flutter. Nick put his hand up to his lips and stepped into the ballroom.

The sound was coming from the wing to their left, which stood above the foyer and, above that, Cassie's bedroom. They rounded the corner with their hands raised; Cassie wished they'd thought to bring tennis rackets, or at least a broom.

They saw the robin at once. It was still, on the floor, and Cassie felt a sick quaver in her gut; she didn't think she could handle a dying animal just now. But, at the sight of them, the robin startled, flying over their heads and battering itself against the line of windows at the back of the house; the bird was perfectly fine.

"It's trapped," she observed.

Nick nodded. "Wonder how it got up here."

"We should call someone." She didn't quite know who, but Hank would, and she started toward the stairs, keeping her eye on the bird the whole time, now hunkered down on the other end of the vast room. But Nick was going to the closet, the one she'd been avoiding, and opening it before she could tell him not to.

"What are you doing?" she whispered as she heard him rustling around in there. She angled herself out of the sight of the closet; she didn't think she was ready to see what it looked like inside.

He emerged with bits of plaster on his head, empty-handed. "There's a hole in your roof," he said calmly, and then he started to unbutton his shirt.

She stared at him, in wonder and confusion—was this really how he was going to seduce her? With a dive-bombing bird in their midst? After confirming her worst home ownership fears? She laughed.

"What? I'm going to help it."

"How?" She tried not to peek at his nakedness as he pulled his arms from the sleeves. His biceps were muscled, his chest smooth, and the smallest trail of hair traced from his navel down into his waistband.

"I was looking for a sheet or something," he said, as if that explained it. He opened the shirt before him and crouched down, then crept toward the far end of the ballroom and the bird.

Cassie thought, for sure, that the robin would fly again, but Nick's movements were calm and deliberate. He was halfway to it when, in a low voice, he said, "Once I've caught it, I'm going to need you to come open a window."

Her pulse was pounding in her ears, her eyes darting back and forth between Nick and the bird as he neared it. The tension was akin to what she felt watching a scary movie; she put her hand to her chest and nearly gasped with each step Nick took. She wanted to take a picture—she knew it would be beautiful—but she was grateful she'd left her camera downstairs. She'd rather just be there, in the strange moment when time seemed to stand still and only a bird seemed to matter. Putting a camera to her eye would have taken her away.

The robin twitched and fluttered its wings, but it did not fly. Nick froze. He waited until the animal stilled. Then he began his slow progression toward it once again.

The bird flapped its wings when Nick was only a few feet away. Cassie would have ducked, but Nick took his chance and flung his shirt wide, hooking it over the robin like a net. The small body thrashed under the fabric, but the shirt did its job. In seconds, Nick had scooped up the whole bundle while Cassie ran to the window just beyond him, flinging it open.

Nick lifted the shirt out into the open air. The robin flew free.

Cassie turned to Nick. He was slick with a dewy layer of sweat. He was smiling. She wanted to kiss him. So she did.

He kissed her back, a slow, long kiss that made her knees go soft. He smelled of that deodorant from the days when lust first stirred in her, but more deeply, he smelled of himself. She realized she had grown to treasure the way he smelled. It was incredible to be kissing him.

He tucked a feather of hair behind her ear, pulled back, and beamed. "I'm glad you said no," he whispered, and she knew he meant Jim, and she was glad too, even though at the time it had been heartbreaking.

Nick leaned in for another kiss. He drew her up against him, and she felt the skins of their arms touch, felt the whole front of her body lean against the bare front of his, and that pressing against each other was right and risky.

He pulled away again and said, "Get your roof fixed." She nodded and silenced him with a soft, long kiss.

"Don't let her hand you your sweaty towels anymore," she said when she came up for air, since it seemed they were swapping advice. She was about to go in for another one, relishing the firm press of his hands as they moved down across her back, when they heard something downstairs, just below them. Not an animal, but just as feral; the desperate tones of a sudden, piercing squabble.

"Shit."

Nick was already halfway across the ballroom, hitching his arms through his sleeves. Cassie was a half step behind him. They dashed down the stairs and discovered the famous sisters on the floor below, on either side of the doorframe to the master bedroom, faces inches apart. It was hard to untangle their voices; each was high-pitched and venomous.

Tate: "You shut up right now, you keep your mouth shut, you will leave this house before I'll hear you talk that way again."

Elda: "Oh, I'm sorry to burst your bubble, little princess, I'm sorry the world isn't all lollipops and blow jobs, but he was a dick, Sis, a D. I. C. K. dick. Does the fact that he gave everything to a stranger not clue you in to that fact?"

It was clear they would have happily gone on like that for hours had Nick not managed to push Tate into the bedroom and shut the door with both of them inside. Cassie was left in the hallway with Elda, whose nostrils flared.

Elda pointed her finger toward her sister's closed door again and again, as if pressing an elevator button. "She is ludicrously stubborn." Inside, Cassie could hear the low rumbling of Nick and Tate's exchange, but she couldn't make out the words. Elda went on. "Why she gives two shits whether he was a good man is beyond me. He was a Hollywood star! Are we surprised he was diddling farm girls? No, we are not!"

On the other side of the thick oak door, Tate raised her voice in response, but Nick shushed her again. Cassie decided not to go after the farm girl comment. "He was her father," she said.

Elda's knowing laugh shook the hall. "He was my father too, and that's precisely why"—she raised her voice again—"I see who he truly was." To Cassie, she said, "She thinks her parents had some kind of great romance." Her voice turned to poisoned sugar. "Jack Montgomery and Diane DeSoto and their adorable daughter, Tate." She buried her finger into her chest. "But I was there. I was witness. I was the one who saw him belittle Diane. Who saw how she berated and threatened and, yes, spat at him. Who saw her snort and drink everything in sight." Her voice lobbed again toward the door. "The truth is, they hated each other. It's no surprise she killed herself."

The door swung open as Tate flung herself into the hallway. Her face was now crimson, her hands murderous. Cassie took a step back as Tate closed in on Elda. "Don't. You. Dare." Tate's voice was no longer shrill; it was icy and filled with power.

Even Elda seemed a touch concerned. She backed toward the stairwell, holding her hands up in supplication. Behind Tate, Nick scratched at his brow. He approached Tate and placed his hand gently on her back just as she reached toward her sister's neck.

"Tate," Nick said, moving his hand to Tate's shoulder.

She shook him off.

"Tate, take a step back."

"Get off me."

Nick flinched, but he wasn't moving; Cassie felt proud of him for holding his ground, and burned at Tate's nasty expression as the woman went at her sister once again.

"You can't do this," Nick said, this time closing his hand around Tate's arm.

She wheeled on him. "What are you, deaf? I told you: Get. Off. Me. Or do you need me to remind you where your checks are coming from?"

Elda cackled. "You going to fire him too? Just like poor Margaret? I guess that's something else Daddy taught you—how to treat people."

"Shut up shut up shut up," Tate cried, putting her hands over her ears. "Your voice is—"

"Enough." Cassie heard herself bellow the word before she knew she had something to say. "This is my house. You are guests in my house and you will stop this now." They all looked appropriately chagrined. She went on. "You." She pointed at Elda. "You have such a good memory? I need to know everything about the summer your father spent in St. Jude."

"I was four," Elda replied, crossing her arms.

"Well, I'm guessing Tate didn't fly you out here on her plane just so you could go at each other."

Tate nodded smugly in agreement, as though her hands were clean. But Cassie jabbed her finger at her. "You want to get out of Ohio as soon as possible?"

Tate's eyes widened at the bald truth. Then she nodded, once.

"Well, stop bullying people for five seconds and actually sit with your father's papers. Not Hank. Not Nick. Not Me. You."

Nick cleared his throat. "What about me?" he asked.

"Go to the library," she boomed, not because she actually had a plan, but because they were all blinking at her as if she did, and she figured that there had to be something useful at the library, and also that maybe she could go along and they could kiss some more in the stacks or something. Nick nodded nervously, and she wanted to smile to reassure him, but then she'd lose her edge.

"Well?" she thundered. "Get to work."

June 1955

CHAPTER TWENTY-NINE

———

INDIE WAS AWOKEN BY THE SCREEN DOOR YAWNING AJAR. IT was rare for Eben's friends to come by on a Sunday night. As her eyes fluttered open, she listened for the usual back claps and hand-shakes and the heavy wallop of bourbon on the table, waited for the sharp tang of cigars rising through the vent at the foot of her bed. There was none of that, though; just her father's gentle voice welcoming in a guest, and a quiet male voice returning the niceties.

Lindie clambered to the bottom of her bed, where she flattened herself and listened.

The other man said something as he came into the room, something that made Eben laugh. She heard two dining chairs graze the floorboards. Whoever this man was, her father did not offer him a drink.

"Well, Eben, you can imagine I'm curious," the other voice said. It was closer now, more distinct, and Lindie knew at once that it belonged to Clyde Danvers. "Thought you might be throwing me a surprise party." He sounded amused at the thought.

"I wanted to discuss a private matter," Eben said. Lindie could imagine her father's hands waving Clyde's concern away. It was the same gesture he employed whenever Lindie objected to the prospect of moving out of St. Jude, or when she awoke from a bad dream about her mother coming back to steal her away. "Just a little something that needs clearing up."

"Do tell." But before Eben could begin to answer, Clyde spoke again. "Did you know Lindie came out to that movie party on Friday night?"

"Far as I know, she was asleep in her bed."

That made Clyde laugh. "I admire you, Eben, I really do, bringing her up on your own. I can't imagine it's easy. We both know she's got a bit of her mother in her."

Eben grunted. The air grew thinner. Lindie ached for Clyde to elaborate; she hadn't been sad to see her mother go—Lorraine was not the type to kiss a wounded knee—but that didn't mean Lindie didn't want to know everything about her.

But instead Clyde returned to the subject of Friday night's festivities. "The party was very grown-up, if you catch my drift, Eben. Men. The crew." He laughed again. "Lord knows I count myself lucky to have dodged daughters and wives. So take my advice with a grain of salt. But while I'm at it—would it hurt you to put her in a dress? She's a growing girl, Eben. She can't be wandering all over creation in overalls anymore."

"I'd like to see you try." Eben's voice sounded tamed, as though he was holding it back with reins, when what it wanted to do was run wild. He sighed. "But you're right. She shouldn't have been out at the development, especially not after dark, especially not with grown strangers. I'll speak with her."

"Don't get her in trouble on my account," Clyde protested. "I just want her safe. You know I love her like she was my own."

Something skittered through the air—something invisible and razor sharp. The night stayed quiet for a bit after that.

"Funny, though, you should bring up the development," Eben said, after a while.

"Why's that?"

"What are you calling it these days?"

"Thinking it might be Two Oaks, actually."

"You can't call it Two Oaks, Clyde." Lindie liked how normal her father's voice sounded again, just perturbed.

"That old bastard might own half the town, but he doesn't own the name. Show me anywhere he's got a copyright on it."

"It's a matter of respect."

"Three Oaks, then. You like that better?"

Eben was silent. When he spoke again, he had made his voice tranquil. "I've been going over Mr. Neely's papers, just like every year. To make sure everything's in place. And, well, I discovered an irregularity."

"Fancy word."

"It seems"—Eben pressed as though he hadn't heard—"that a good eight acres of Three Oaks is actually built on Mr. Neely's land."

"I own that land." Quick as that.

"You own some of that land. You own the land to the east and north, but you don't actually own"—Lindie could hear the scuttle of paper upon the table—"this land." She imagined her father's finger jabbing at a map.

Clyde started laughing. "What a regular Sherlock Holmes you are!"

"Didn't take much sleuthing," Eben said evenly. "Just common sense."

There was a quiet patch then, in which Lindie imagined Clyde was leaning over the map to get to the bottom of the misunderstanding. After a while, he mused, "What an oversight! Can't believe I could have done something so dumb."

"You know what, Clyde? I don't think it was an oversight," Eben said coolly. "Three years ago, you tried to get me to sell you that land and I said no. You thought I forgot, didn't you? The only reason it took me this long to say anything was I couldn't believe you'd actually build houses on land you don't own. I didn't think you were that stupid."

"Now see here," Clyde replied, quick as a snake, "I made an honest mistake, Eben. I'll be the first to call myself a dang fool. But it's water under the bridge now. The houses are built! I'm happy to consider cutting your old pal Lemon in on the profits of the home sales; that seems fair. But you know how I see it? My honest mistake does him a favor. Before I got to it, it was all just empty land out there, waiting to be turned into something worthwhile. Now that land is making us money! Changing our town for the better!"

Eben didn't reply.

"Anyway," Clyde continued, "it doesn't really matter what you think. That'll be my brother's property soon. Good old Artie will put that ring on June's finger, Mr. Neely—God bless him—will pass on to the next life, and all his worldly possessions, and his money, and his land"—he enunciated that final word—"will go to June."

An icy, untamed feeling crept up Lindie's spine: a combination of fear, fury, and righteous indignation. Her stomach soured. Had Uncle Clyde just admitted he wanted June to marry Artie because of what he assumed would be her inheritance?

But Eben kept his head. "Don't count your chickens, Clyde. Even I don't know who Mr. Neely's heir is. The only person who knows is Mr.

Neely's lawyer down in Columbus, and you don't hold any sway there. You're a big fish in a small pond, Clyde. A big fish in a small pond."

"I don't see the point of this," Clyde said, sounding annoyed. "Why bring me over here to rub my face in a mistake? I said I'm sorry."

"You haven't, in fact."

"You want something, Eben?" He sounded plain angry now. "Spit it out."

"What I want," Eben replied, voice just as fierce, "is for you to take those buildings down."

"Take them down?" Clyde cracked up, but it was a dark laugh, not a bit of friendliness about it. "You want I should tear down the hard labor of men? Oh, Eben, you got me good! You must be a damn fool to think this town wants to see progress demolished. You're missing the big picture, old man. The future. This is our chance to get a piece of it. Ripvogle's this close to getting the bid. This close, Eben. You know as well as I do that that interstate will change this town and make it great. I'm giving you a chance to be a part of that greatness. To make something of yourself, something that doesn't belong to some highfalutin old pansy who still treats you like the trash you were born into."

"Time for you to leave," Eben said, sliding his chair back from the table.

"Sure, sure," Clyde replied, sounding wounded. "I'll leave, if that's what you want, just like I came when called. But I'm my own man, Eben. I do what I want. Don't screw this up for me."

Next came their footsteps, followed by the squeal of the screen door. Lindie crept up to the small, cracked window that looked out over the front porch. The night was cloudy, the light from the moon dissipated over the whole world. Lindie could make out the glint of Clyde's pistol at his belt as he shoved his hands in his pockets and stalked off into the night. After that came the sound of the front door closing, and the bolt being laid across it. Then Lindie heard a great, terrible crash from downstairs—glass against wall—but nothing of note after that.

CHAPTER THIRTY

———

INDIE WOKE BEFORE THE SUN AND CREPT DOWNSTAIRS, half expecting to find all the dishware smashed to smithereens. But no trace of unpleasantness lingered from the night before, not even shards in the trash can. The moon had already set. In the safe shadow of the kitchen, she wolfed down a bowl of rice with milk and sugar and chugged a cup of Maxwell House. She left her dirty dishes in the sink, fearing washing them would wake her father.

On her Schwinn, Center Square and Main Street sailed by. She'd been told she'd find the set easily beyond the northern outskirts of town, along the canal, but the world was still dark, and, as buildings gave way to country, an anxious knot formed at her center. Clyde would likely be on set. Lindie didn't know how to be around him today, which was a strange thing, since she'd always known before. Nor did she know if she could trust him, or if it was fair anymore to blame June's engagement on Cheryl Ann alone. She pedaled harder as an unfamiliar glumness overtook her. The set was nowhere in sight.

She saw them eventually—trucks, ladders, trailers pulling into place—at the edge of a cornfield divided by the canal. The sun had started to rise; in the cool light she could make out a few men mowing the edges of the water. The rest of the crew was gathered around Crafty, sipping coffee from their army green thermoses. Lindie nodded a hello to Ricky, and noticed Thomas dressed in a suit, leaning against the front of Clyde's Oldsmobile, smoking. Lindie waved a perfunctory hello; Thomas tipped his hat and offered an equally careful smile. She supposed he'd been hired to drive Diane to set every day. She thought of Jack folding into Diane on his front walk, and felt a wave of hot shame, first on June's behalf, then on her own, for having had the audacity to think a movie star might treat June with the tenderness she deserved.

She resolved to punish him by ignoring him completely, although she was sure he wouldn't notice.

But a bit before lunch, when the temperature had rocketed and Lindie had been holding a shade umbrella over the script girl for so long that she couldn't feel her sunburnt arms anymore, Jack walked by and obviously tried to catch her eye. Lindie lifted her nose into the air until she felt his gaze fall away.

At lunch, Clyde found Lindie at Crafty, which was set up down the canal a few yards, out of sight of the film set. The P.A.'s were supposed to eat last, which translated to grabbing the scraps the rest of the crew didn't want, but Clyde handed her a picnic basket packed with a ham and cheese sandwich, an apple, a bag of potato chips, and a cold Coca-Cola. Underneath the lunch, wrapped in a linen napkin, was a whole coffee cake. They both knew it was Eben's favorite.

"I asked Casey if it was okay," he said, pitching his thumb toward her boss, who offered them a truculent nod. Clyde elbowed her and chuckled. "He doesn't look too thrilled, does he? Eat up, kiddo. You've been working hard."

Lindie's stomach growled. She'd been surviving mostly on pieces of Wonder bread. She settled down on the edge of the canal, feet dangling. After a few bites, Clyde said, "Take that cake home to your pops. I had my girl make it."

Lindie looked up at his familiar face. His mouth didn't quite know how to say what it needed to.

"I'll tell him you're sorry," she offered.

He took his hat off and hit his knee with it, smiling. "You do just that, kid. You do just that." And off he strode, and Lindie warmed with relief.

JACK BECAME PERSISTENT as the day blazed on. If he wasn't on camera, he was lurking nearby, just at the edge of whatever task Lindie had at hand. It was a strange thing, to have the most wanted man in town so desperate for her audience. But Lindie wasn't going to be stupid; it hadn't escaped her notice that Diane was on set too. Dressed in a brown calico costume, with a drab braid weaving her platinum hair—to lend her the illusion of having just barely survived the Civil War—Diane was keeping tabs on Jack. Lindie's loyalty lay with June; of course it did. But there was something beguiling about Diane's devotion to the movie star. Her glance flitted to him again and again, like a butterfly to a colorful bloom. Could Lindie blame her for wanting to have him to herself?

"Lindie."

It was long past noon. After a few more hours on set, Lindie was back at Crafty, where Ricky and a few others from the costume department had set up a makeshift area for quick patches and hems. She was perfecting her whipstitch on a petticoat when she heard her name and turned in to the sharp afternoon sun to find Thomas standing there. He was tall up close, and thin. His eyes darted around the whole world.

"He says it's important." Thomas leaned his weight back on his rear foot; he wanted less to do with this business than she did. Over his shoulder, Lindie made out Jack leaning against an old shade tree even farther down the canal. She checked to make sure Diane was occupied; she was twenty yards in the other direction, quoting the same overwrought speech she'd said six times already. Given how clumsily it tumbled from her tongue, she was likely to be saying it many more times before they broke for the day. Lindie put down her mending.

JACK REMOVED HIS old-fashioned hat and placed it over his heart, as if Lindie was a lady. "Please forgive my rude behavior. I don't like how that shindig ended."

The gentle way he formed his words, the careful dance of his unusual eyes, and his use of the word *shindig* almost made Lindie smile. But she wasn't letting him off that easy. "So Diane's your girl?" She liked calling Diane a "girl," although she'd never have had the guts to say that to Diane's face.

Jack's breath sawed out. "It's complicated."

Lindie pulled a cherry lollipop out of her pocket, one she'd been saving for a special occasion. She licked it, then held it to the sky, reveling in its blood red transparency. "Enlighten me." It was rare she felt any power over anyone, let alone a man, let alone a famous one.

He glanced around set, eyes squinting into two straight lines. The sun was still strong, the clouds a pale fairy floss blowing across that big, midwestern sky. "It's the studio." His voice was a growl as he lit a Lucky Strike. "They've sunk too much money into this movie"—he waved toward set—"and it's going to be a goddamn flop." Lindie opened her mouth to protest, but he cut her off. "They whored me and Diane out to each other to try to save their investment." If he minded saying that word in front of her, he didn't show it. His voice had grown passionate; gone was the sparkling Hollywood charm. "They do this when they're worried. They sell the glossies on a fairy tale. If the public smells romance, that just might fill the theaters, no matter how terrible the film is."

He took a drag and, distracted, offered a cigarette to Lindie, who took the opportunity to swipe two. He raised an eyebrow, pocketed the pack, and went on, furrowing his brow. "Diane's new to this whole thing. In case you haven't noticed, she isn't very good."

Lindie stifled a giggle. It was hard not to notice how many times it took Diane to say even a basic line correctly. The woman missed her cues and marks, even after spending a whole month on set in Los Angeles.

"Poor thing has started to believe the fairy tale," Jack said, his shoulders softening as he took another drag. "I guess she thinks making an honest man out of me would be a better job than Hollywood star." He shook his head. "Well, good luck." Then he sucked on the cigarette hard. "She's stubborn, I'll give her that much. She refuses to believe that pretending I love her is just another acting job."

Lindie felt hope for June, then pity for Diane. And pity for Jack too, for that matter. But then she forced herself to think sensibly; he wanted her to feel sorry for him? He had more money than anyone she knew, his name adorned movie posters, and he was being forced to date the most beautiful woman Lindie'd ever seen. She stuck her lollipop into her cheek and crossed her arms. "A gentleman never speaks ill of a lady."

"She's not a lady, that's what I'm trying to tell you." He threw the cigarette to the ground and stomped it out. "She's mean. She's manipulative. I had to ignore you girls the other night or she would have made your lives miserable."

Lindie sniffed and looked beyond him, as she imagined a wounded lover might. "Doesn't sound like an apology to me."

Jack nodded, ducking his head like a kid. "It's nothing to do with you or June, and I'm sorry. I had no idea Diane was coming early. Please let me make it up to you."

Lindie kicked at a tree root sticking out of the ground. Her saliva pooled around the bright, red taste. She weighed her options. The land was flat as if it had been rolled out by Apatha's wooden rolling pin, the sky an endless arc of blue.

"I'd like to see her again." Jack's voice trembled. Lindie had to look at him to make sure it was real.

"But how can I know you won't do that to her again?" She was really asking; all at once, he seemed old and wise, like a father should be, and she wanted him to have a simple answer, the kind Eben had when she needed to feel safe.

"June is a real good person, Rabbit Legs," Jack answered. "That day I met her? She was defending you to some horrible girl who said the meanest things. And June wasn't mean back, she was just, you know, herself." Lindie did know. She thought no one else ever saw that about June. "I don't meet many good people."

And like that, a plan formed in her mind. Rough around the edges, thin in places, but a plan nonetheless. Once she'd thought it, she couldn't pretend she hadn't.

"I'll tell Thomas where to take you," she said, at last. "Tomorrow night."

Jack smiled to himself, a different smile from the one he used with the world. Lindie was already smoothing over the plan's jagged spots, imagining how she'd offer it to June, how she'd cajole her, how it would feel to answer June's will with her own, and bring June to Jack's side.

CHAPTER THIRTY-ONE

———

B UT IT WAS NEARLY MIDNIGHT, WEDNESDAY THE EIGHTH, before June's breath warmed Lindie's ear again, and her hands gripped Lindie's belly. Together they rode through the cool, chirruping night, which smelled of cut grass and hummed with nocturnal possibility as the waning gibbous moon, still nearly full, glowed above them.

June was reticent, demure, so much so that it had taken two days to convince her. Lindie could understand the tug within June; she wanted to meet Jack, but it would be difficult to trust him. So Lindie had done her best to woo June with tall tales of Jack's regrets and apology, until June shushed her with a beleaguered sigh and agreed to come along.

Now here they were, past the western town line on the two-lane highway that belonged to them. Lights and buildings were a memory out under the open canopy of stars. Lindie pulled over to the side of the road, gulped from her canteen, and checked behind them to make sure no one had trailed their escape from the alleyway behind the garage.

"Want a smoke?" she asked, offering June one of the Lucky Strikes she'd bummed off Jack.

"Where are we meeting?" June asked. She didn't like Lindie smoking except when she wanted one herself. Lindie tucked the cigarette back into the front pocket of her overalls and ignored the question. She knew if she answered before they got there, June would forbid it; Miss Goody Two-Shoes hated trespassing.

Lindie had first heard about Idlewyld as a little girl. Lemon Gray Neely had acquired it in his heyday; legend held that it stood on the first parcel of land he'd sucked dry of oil in the great Auglaize County boom of the 1880s, before the black gold dried up and Uncle Lem and his fellow wildcatters found more reliable, lucrative territories in Texas, Oklahoma, and Louisiana. As a young man, Lem would supposedly sit on the Idlewyld porch with a cigar and watch his rigs drink on the far rim of the lake. But, by 1955, few remembered precisely where the old camp was. Sometimes the football team would drive out, searching for it as a place to party, but there were plenty of fishing and hunting shacks down the access roads, and certainly nothing as grand as the retreat that existed in their fathers' stories. In Lindie's imagining, Idlewyld had a porch twice as long as the one on Two Oaks, and stood three or four stories tall, with broad windows lighting up the night. This imagined lodge had danced upon the wall as her father breathed it to life at bedtime, his voice a ringing promise. Even the name: Idlewyld.

Naturally, Lindie had been beside herself when June had finally offered to take her to Idlewyld the August before. June knew exactly where the place was—apparently Cheryl Ann had found an old map and taken June out there for a Sunday picnic, only to declare it a hazard and forbid June from ever going again. Lindie had begged June to take her for weeks, until the older girl finally caved. The night they'd planned on turned out to be hidden behind layers of rain-heavy clouds; thunder threatened to the west. At the window, eyes darting up to test the sky, June suggested they put off the scheduled trip. But school was starting up again. Artie had been courting June, and Lindie could smell what was coming on the air. She knew they'd never go if June didn't take her right then.

Ten months later, on the night Lindie took June to meet Jack five miles out of town, on the long, flat road that could take them all the way west to Indianapolis if they'd let it, they turned to their left onto a gravel road marked only by a broken white post. They dismounted just a few feet onto the gravel, as soon as the sudden oaks above them cut out the ambient light. The access road down to the lake was straight. The bass chorus of bullfrogs from the swampy waterfront affirmed they were heading in the right direction. June hemmed and hawed as Lindie knew she would, and Lindie, predictably, won her over.

On the night June had brought Lindie to Idlewyld the first time, they'd found the house by wading into the overgrown weeds, their hands the only navigation in the night. They'd cursed and laughed and bumped their shins and almost given up hope until June found a lip of porch and, satisfied they were finally far enough from civilization that no one would see them, dared to switch on the flashlight Lindie hadn't known June was carrying.

On the night they were to meet Jack, Lindie was prepared with her own flashlight. She'd bought it with her emergency fund, which she kept hidden in the coffee can in her father's garage. She felt ennobled by spending her meager savings on June's adventure with Jack. June would never know how selfless she'd been; Lindie liked how this secret sacrifice made her feel.

They neared the end of the gravel road. June was a step ahead. Lindie could almost feel the warmth radiating off June's back, detect the sultry sweat curling in the forbidden forest at the back of her neck. Lindie licked her lips. It occurred to her then, like a shock of static electricity, that what they were actually doing was meeting a strange man in a dark place, without having told a soul. Fear locked itself around her. Perhaps Jack would be unkind, brutal. Maybe June would need someone to defend her—and suddenly that thought produced a second wave, of something else, something powerful, and arousing, that choked the fear.

Then June gasped. Lindie shrieked. She grabbed for June, but instead tripped over June's body as she crumpled to the ground. Lindie landed on top of her, but not in a graceful or gentle way, not as a lover might hope to fall. June yelped and pummeled her fists up against Lindie, telling her to get off and let her breathe.

Lindie fumbled for her flashlight, but, before she could turn it on, he was there. His flashlight cast the world into neat yellow. He bent over them. He untangled their limbs. June whimpered when she put weight on her right ankle. Jack slung her arm over his shoulder and helped her to the porch.

Jack had a kerosene lamp waiting. It flickered in the breeze off the lake, revealing a picnic blanket spread along the front of the porch, with pillows surrounding it and a basket of food. The smell of the kerosene-laden dirt in the smudge pots filled the air and fought off the swarm of mosquitoes hungry for new blood. He'd brought a thermos of hot chocolate and a tin of oatmeal cookies, made by Crafty exactly to his specifications.

They tended to June. Lindie tried to switch her flashlight on, but it wouldn't cooperate, and, anyway, Jack was already at June's knee, palpating to learn the extent of her injuries—a scrape along the ridge of her shin, a slight twist of the ankle. Relieved June was all right, Lindie backed off. June had certainly suffered much worse climbing down from her window, and Lindie'd never heard her complain. But Jack remained bent over June, dabbing at the scrape with a damp handkerchief. He handed June the flashlight, and she shone it out beyond them, the beam losing itself into the vast, watery darkness, as insects rushed into its glow, until she flicked it off and the night fell into a natural play of shadow and fire.

In the dim flicker of the kerosene flame, Jack's fingers gently cupped June's knee. He was dressed in shirtsleeves and slacks, handsome, simple. Lindie listened to their gentle conversation—his words tender, hers grateful. She expected June to brush him off—that's what June would have done with her—but her voice carried sorrow and appreciation, a kind of cooing softness that she never offered Lindie.

"Did you go inside?" Lindie asked Jack abruptly. June had taken her right into Idlewyld that first night, snaking her hand up through a broken pane to turn the handle to the locked front door.

"If you're asking if I broke into someone else's house," Jack answered warmly, "the answer is no." He sounded playful again, self-assured, not at all how he'd sounded when he begged for another chance with June.

June laughed. The joy carried off into the darkness, where Lindie could no longer catch it. Why had Idlewyld been the place she'd decided they should meet? Why hadn't she considered what bringing him here, for June, would take from herself?

"Did anyone see you leave town?" Lindie asked, eager to find fault.

"I told you, Rabbit Legs," he said, letting go of June's leg but still looking down at it, "I've got plenty of experience slipping out of sticky situations."

"I'll bet you do," she muttered.

June cut her eyes at Lindie. Lindie fiddled with the switch of her flashlight again, greedy to blind June, but the dang thing was a lemon. And anyway, all Jack had to say was "I'm a master of disguise," in that voice that was amused and assured at once, and June forgot all about Lindie as she laughed all over again.

Lindie stepped up onto the porch. She stood over them. Neither of them looked the slightest bit interested in a tour. "Let's show him around," she said loudly.

She'd been surprised to learn that Idlewyld was nothing but a shack, nothing like the place in Eben's stories. Once, long before, it might have been called a cabin or a cottage, but Uncle Lem's camp out on Lake St. Jude was as abandoned as the old man's mind. Over time, it had grown true to its name, becoming a half-feral place, growing back to the earth. Weeds poked through the floorboards. A tree had come in through the back window, and the wind gasped through the broken panes that lined the front of the humble building. On the night June had brought Lindie there, they'd found the place in shambles, and had made a little spot for themselves in the center of the shack's only room, dragging a waterlogged mattress out of the way to make their own sitting area on a mildewed wicker couch.

They found it just as they had left it. Lindie noticed the spot where June had dented the sofa cushion after the rain started and they had taken cover. She placed her hand in that empty pool and cursed herself. Idlewyld would no longer be theirs. Already, from the way June took Jack's hand as he led her over a broken board, already, from the way he said, "What an enchantment," she could see that someday, in the not too distant future, they would look back on this very night, and neither would recall that Lindie had been along too.

CHAPTER THIRTY-TWO

———

THE GIRLS MET JACK OUT AT IDLEWYLD NEARLY EVERY night of the next week. It was a foregone conclusion that Lindie would always come along—June needed a chaperone, and a ride who could get her home before first light—but each of the three of them understood, without discussing it, that those nights continued for the sole reason that Jack and June had begun to believe that nothing was as real, as important, as those few hours they possessed in each other's company, in the hush of that decrepit, dark cabin, learning everything they could about the other's world. From Lindie's spot on the mattress in the corner, where she'd pretend to read or nap as they mooned, she realized they reminded her of babies, the way babies only ever wanted their mothers, and treated the rest of the world as a disappointment, nothing in comparison to the promise of being once again in the company of the apples of their eyes.

June slept in daily, nibbling from the tray Apatha was made to leave outside her door at Cheryl Ann's insistence; the poor girl was obviously heartbroken that her beloved Artie was yet to return, so completely heartbroken she simply couldn't get out of bed, and Cheryl Ann, though not a woman who considered herself indulgent of moodiness, couldn't help but encourage June's eagerness to become Artie's wife.

June would have lingered in bed all day had Cheryl Ann let her. All she wanted, during the daylight hours, was to recall the rosy curve of Jack's bottom lip in the lamplight, and the way he'd laughed at her story about getting her baby teeth knocked out in the skating accident, and the gasping way it felt to look at him sometimes, as if he were made of fire and might accidentally burn her up. She wanted this forever—the promise of him, the memory of him, without having to ever make a choice, and she relished poring over their hours together, believing her possibilities were infinite, as infinite as he made her feel. But eventually

Cheryl Ann would open the bedroom door and insist June join the day, and so June would sigh and cast her smile into a sniffle, and agree to spend a few hours on the place cards, and nod her head and accept assurances that Artie would be back soon—Clyde had promised!

It wasn't that, now that June was meeting Jack, she didn't imagine herself being married to Artie anymore; she genuinely enjoyed her scheduled dress fittings and sighed admiringly over the silver being shined for her wedding reception. But it wasn't as if she did imagine it either. Over the course of those ten days, she simply allowed herself not to think beyond the next trip out to Idlewyld. She became a girl who ran her hand over her best dresses, deciding which one to wear that particular evening, who enjoyed the pleasure of drawing the chosen garment over her flesh, and of running a brush through her glossy hair, who endured the crawl of the minutes until midnight, when she would at last be able to step out her window and into the world again, free and ready to enjoy it.

In that same weeklong period, Lindie didn't sleep much. There were late night rides out to Idlewyld and early morning calls for *Erie Canal*. Not to mention that she was working harder than ever before, darting all over town at Casey's behest, and with a smile on her face, which didn't come naturally. In contrast, the nights in Jack and June's company, while electric at first for their novelty, soon ran into each other, not as they did for June—into a swooning fog of delicious possibility—but because nothing, as far as Lindie could tell, was actually happening. To her eyes, what Jack and June did on those nights amounted to a whole lot of polite chitchat. They sat in their assigned spots—June on the wicker couch, Jack on a creaky old kitchen chair—and combed through the minutiae of each other's lives, oohing and aahing over the dumbest details. Every night, June made Lindie swear an oath of secrecy, as if anyone would care about the name of Jack's first puppy, or the cost of the violet gown June had worn to the winter formal.

Into this strange week slipped Diane DeSoto. Lindie didn't suppose she was keeping Diane a secret from June, not exactly, but neither did she recount the surprising development of Diane adopting her as what Ricky called a "set pet." If Jack noticed, he didn't mention it, and Lindie grumpily supposed he simply didn't notice, because he didn't notice anything but June.

It was Thursday the ninth that it began, the morning after the girls first met Jack out at Idlewyld. Lindie was helping Ricky buff black leather boots in that field beside the canal when Casey called her name. She stammered a "yessir," wondering what she'd done wrong, when he pitched his thumb over his shoulder. Turned out Diane had requested a P.A. to stand just off camera to hold her carafe of lemon water, a concoction she swore by to keep her voice in check, and she liked the idea of the P.A. being a girl. Within the day she asked whether Lindie thought her hair should be reset. Even more bizarre, she started taking Lindie's advice, a turn that did not win Lindie any favors in Hair and Makeup until she learned to say she wouldn't change a thing.

Inside Diane's trailer, pink and pillowed, Diane drew bright red Elizabeth Arden lipstick onto Lindie with her cool, sharp fingers, and Lindie found she didn't much mind. It was nice to brush Diane's golden tresses, even though Hair had asked numerous times to leave that to them. Diane missed her poodle, Bernadette, and told Lindie of the dog's adventures in the Hollywood scene; she even had a funny voice for the dog that never failed to make Lindie giggle.

In between scenes, Diane asked Lindie to run lines. Lindie would sit in the makeup chair with Diane's name embroidered on the back, and Diane would drape herself across the pink velvet couch Ricky claimed she'd had brought in all the way from Chicago. It was hard for her to remember her lines; they'd run the scenes twenty times or more, and still she'd be fumbling over sentences that Lindie could recite as if she'd written them herself. "Why can't I seem to remember?" Diane asked once, voice shaking. Lindie assured her she'd get it, even though it seemed like a lie. She came to understand that Diane DeSoto was like cotton candy: light as air, but, if you gripped her tight, she hardened. Lindie wondered how the woman had gotten that way.

Despite their closeness, it made Lindie's stomach churn to see the way Diane looked at Jack. Toward the end of that second week of shooting, Diane and Jack took thirteen takes of a scene in the rotunda erected just for the occasion in the middle of Center Square. In the scene, Diane's beautiful, determined Mary wept and pounded Jack Montgomery's chest, cursing him for leaving her alone in order to take a canal boat up to Albany. In every take, Diane would turn to leave, but then he'd grab her arm and pull her back to him, take her chin into his other hand, and bring her in for a rough kiss. Again and again, thirteen times Lindie watched Jack kiss Diane. In between takes, he unhanded her, but Diane clung close, giddily eyeing him as the makeup girls touched her up or the director gave them notes. That night, as Lindie watched June climb down to meet her, she wanted to tell her friend how Jack had spent his day; it would certainly make the evening more lively. But she knew she wouldn't. She wanted those twenty minutes of June's breath against her cheek. She knew June would shoot the messenger.

That wasn't the only secret Lindie was keeping from June; she still had Artie's letter. She wanted to be rid of it, but even burning it wouldn't erase the twang of guilt she felt every time she thought about it. She'd read it a hundred times, witnessed his honor and his honesty, and wondered all over again if she'd been wrong about him, and if he would make June a good match after all. But then she'd remember she'd as good as heard from Clyde's own mouth that the only reason he wanted his brother to marry June was that he believed Uncle Lem was leaving her everything. And then Lindie's insides would twist up again—June into Jack into Diane into Artie into Clyde—and she'd see Casey tap his watch, and she'd let out a little groan and get on with her day.

As for Clyde, he'd apparently left town on business; somewhere south, Lindie'd heard. He'd left behind his Olds for Thomas to chauffeur Diane and Jack during the day (and, apparently, Jack out to Idlewyld at night, although Lindie had decided the less she knew about the details of that arrangement, the better). Eben didn't touch Clyde's coffee cake, so Lindie took it out to Idlewyld and Jack and June washed it down with mouthfuls of warm coffee from his thermos.

After the weekend, Eben announced he was going on a trip himself, down to Columbus. He'd be gone a few days. Of course Lindie thought of the lawyer he'd mentioned to Clyde. Lindie hoped her father knew what he was doing; she doubted Clyde would be pleased to hear of him digging into all that business. But she was just a child, so she watched Eben drive off without a word, then latched the windows and locked the doors until the small wooden house was tight as a bread box.

It was stormy that third week of June. Thunder and lightning sent the crew running for cover on more than one occasion and had Electric grumbling about safety issues. By Wednesday the fifteenth, they'd only gotten a day of shooting in for the week, and the crew was in a mood to match the weather; especially concerning was whether they'd be able to keep to their production schedule, which had the film slated to wrap on the thirtieth. Promises had been made to the crew back in early May that everyone would be home to their families the Saturday before Independence Day.

While the crew took cover in their slickers and rain boots, Ricky and Sam and the makeup girls debated whether the shoot was cursed, and listed the myriad setbacks that had dogged *Erie Canal* from the beginning: the food poisoning from a batch of bad shrimp while they were on the studio lot; losing the original location in upstate New York and waiting for a week in Los Angeles to get word on the new one; and an epic argument on the studio set between Diane and Jack that involved her beaning him with a prop head of cabbage. Lindie could tell the crew had plenty more to say about Diane, but Ricky made it clear he wouldn't bad-mouth a star to her set pet, so Lindie made an offering with an exaggerated rendition of Diane's line flubs, which had them all in stitches, and haunted Lindie the next day in the trailer, when Diane's face lit up at the sight of her and Diane told her she was her favorite person in the whole state of Ohio.

BEFORE LINDIE KNEW IT, it was Thursday the sixteenth. Eben was back from Columbus and had headed down to the Red Door Tavern for a night of cards. The rain had stopped but the clouds were still gathered over town like grazing sheep, making the midnight bike ride soggy and buggy. At Idlewyld, the bullfrogs and crickets were quiet compared to the whining thicket of mosquitoes. Lindie curled under a blanket on the damp mattress in the corner, struggling to keep her eyes open as Jack's and June's familiar voices lulled her to sleep. Their conversation had turned speculative; Lindie had hoped that, once they'd run out of facts to share, they'd get to the romance, but apparently she was wrong. Jack asked what June wanted more than anything in the world.

"To have a place and time to paint. I suppose I have that in my room, but not really. My mother's always there, ready to point out what I've done wrong. I know that sounds silly, since I'll never paint more than those stupid still lifes. And, anyway, I know I won't be painting much when, well, you know." Lindie was surprised to hear June refer to Artie, however obliquely; he'd never been mentioned inside these four walls. June's voice turned practical. "Soon I won't have time to paint. I'll have a family and a household."

"June." Jack's tone was sharp. "Tell me you aren't going to marry that man." But there was tenderness there, the kind men used with women when discussing love.

"You don't know him," June replied softly, after a minute.

"I know he isn't here."

"His work takes him—"

"I know he's a damn fool to leave you behind." Jack's voice tightened.

"He's . . ." Her voice trailed off.

Lindie inched up the mattress so she could watch them from a better angle. Now this, this was what she'd been hoping for: something unbridled. Jack was kneeling before June on the hard wooden floor. He had her hands in his. Their eyes were locked; there was nothing else in the world.

"Is he like this?" he asked.

A shy smile danced across June's face. "Like what?"

He lifted June's hand then, slowly, carefully, until it was an inch from his lips. He turned her arm, exposing her soft wrist. He rubbed his thumb there, his eyes closing at the softness of her skin. He opened them again, and met her gaze. Then bent to kiss her inner wrist. Once. Twice. Three times.

A dreamy bliss overtook June as Jack's lips pressed her flesh. She lost all composure; even her hair seemed to loosen. Lindie believed she could hear June's heart hammering until she realized it was her own.

Jack was the one who ended it. With visible restraint, he lowered

June's hand. "You're young," he said. "You think this might be what happens every time. But I promise you, this"—and his voice swelled with emotion—"this is extraordinary. To be such friends, already."

June withdrew her hands and folded them into her lap. The possibility dissipated the second she said, "I gave my word." Jack sat back onto his heels.

They watched each other for a long time, only their breath tangling. Jack wanted to touch June again, and she wanted it too, Lindie could see that. But June had an aggravating willpower beyond Lindie's understanding. Why not forget stupid old Artie when you had the most famous man in the world sitting before you, offering himself up?

But June told Jack it was best for them to stop meeting like this. "Don't you think so?" she asked, her voice masking a swell of tears. How could June say one thing and so obviously feel the opposite? Lindie wanted to fling herself up and insist, demand, that June stop lying to herself, that Jack not let her ruin everything. But nosing in would only make it worse, so Lindie lay there, listening, instead.

Jack begged June to come back the next night. He promised he'd respect her wishes and try to never speak like that again, to never touch her that way, even though it seemed impossible to promise such things when what he felt was so undeniable. June replied that it was time to wake Lindie.

On the bicycle, June reached her hands around Lindie's waist. The night had quieted with the promise of dawn. Jack stayed inside. Lindie called out good-bye. Then Jack was running toward them, his dark form desperate in the night.

"Please," he begged. Lindie could hardly bear the ache in his voice. "Please come back tomorrow."

"I shouldn't," June said. "You know it. I don't know what I was thinking, Jack." Her voice trembled as she said his name.

"Don't do this," he said.

"I'm doing what's right."

"Sunday, then. Come back Sunday. Promise? You won't regret it. I'll be good."

June's arms clutched around Lindie. She told Lindie to go.

"She'll be here," Lindie said. "I promise."

"He loves you," Lindie said, after a mile on the open road.

"Men only want one thing," June replied angrily. So that was it? She was afraid of how Jack had touched her? He hadn't even touched Lindie and she could feel his lips shimmering on her skin. Wasn't that the whole point of this—to feel that powerful urge?

Lindie braked. She turned to look at June. Her friend's features were murky in the thick night. "Artie's not a saint just because he doesn't seem to want it. And Jack's not the devil because he does. You want it. You want him. You want him so bad it hurts."

"And what would you know about it?" June sniffed. Lindie inhaled the damp, dewy sourness of June's armpits. The girl's lashes curved against the swell of her full cheeks. Her lips were bee-stung, her nose small and precious as a shell.

Lindie couldn't bring herself to answer. All she could manage was to pedal June into the last of the night.

CHAPTER THIRTY-THREE

———

UNE WAS DIFFERENT ON SUNDAY NIGHT, WHICH WAS MID-
night black and moonless. She clambered onto the back of Lindie's
Schwinn. She wore saddle shoes and a simple cotton dress; no
pretty frock. But it hadn't been very hard to convince her to come, even
if June hadn't been exactly friendly about it.

When they got to Idlewyld, lit up with its now-familiar kerosene
glow, June set her shoulders and took a long breath, stepping onto the
porch with her jaw tight.

As soon as they stepped inside, it was obvious that the place had been
transformed. First of all, it was clean—no clouds of dust to set them
coughing, no spiderwebs hanging from above. An Oriental rug lay on
the floor, and the broken windows had been covered with plywood so
the breeze no longer whistled in. But that was just the beginning. The
broken furniture had been replaced by a new armchair, a sturdy, wide
table, and a giant easel. And there were canvases and tubes of oil paint,
paintbrushes, watercolors, reams of paper, and colored pencils. And
books. Books stacked everywhere. Heavy, expensive, colorful art books.
Chagall and Picasso and Monet and van Gogh, and, of course, Pollock.

In the middle of it all stood Jack, grinning. June couldn't help
herself—she gasped in delighted wonder, then turned, slowly, through
the space, lifting each new object with her delicate fingers. She opened
the slim Pollock monograph, eyes drinking in the photographs of the
splattered paintings. Then closed it again as though she couldn't bear
its pull. She stepped back, one step, and said to Lindie, "Please wait
outside."

There was no point arguing. Lindie took one look at Jack before
slinking out. He offered a grim smile.

Of course she eavesdropped. Plywood could do its best to cover a window, but sound leaked out, and there were plenty of cracks to peek through around the edges. Lindie planted her Keds in the milkweed and peered in.

"How did you do all this so quickly?" June was asking.

"Think of me as Santy Claus." Jack was clearly pleased with himself, if careful as he spoke.

"No one can know about our meetings, Jack. I hope you haven't broken my confidence."

"I told you," he replied, "this time with you is sacred. I wouldn't endanger it for the world."

"I'm sure Diane would disagree." June crossed her arms. Was that jealousy?

"Diane is none of your concern."

"Isn't she? She sleeps in the house right beside yours, and sometimes in your bed."

"June, I assure you she's been nowhere near my bed since I met you."

"But she's been in your bed before."

Jack didn't reply.

"It doesn't matter," June said crisply, as though he was the one who'd brought Diane up. "It doesn't matter who you take to bed or who you love because I'm getting married in three weeks."

"He isn't even here," Jack replied impatiently. "But let's say he does come back. Do you really want to marry a man who'd abandon you until just before your wedding day? You don't have to marry me, but please marry someone who can't stand to be apart from you. Please marry a man who aches to hold you, who sees only your face when he closes his eyes."

"And you're that man?" June's voice was bold.

Jack was quiet for a moment. Then: "I'd like to be."

"It's impossible." June's jaw tightened. "It's impossible for you to do things like this." She gestured toward the room's transformation. "This is too much. It isn't even my house. Someone will discover it. We'll get found out."

"So let them find out." He had her now, hands on her shoulders. "Marry me, June. Marry me and come away and live the life you never imagined."

"It's too fast," June said, her voice suddenly thin. "It's too much. Don't you see? I'm not ready. I had everything worked out." She started to weep.

"Oh, June. June June June." She let him pull her in against his chest. He soothed her, and Lindie leaned her face against the house and imagined he was comforting her too, that she could feel his heartbeat through the warm fabric of his shirt.

June's tears abated. Jack took her face into his hands. "June June June," he cooed. "I forget how young you are. This place has been your whole world. It's not fair to assume you're ready to leave it, not yet." He kissed the tip of her nose. She blinked up at him as he pulled away. He seemed in control now, which Lindie liked. He'd speak reason. "I made it this way because you deserve to paint whatever you want. Not because I think you owe me something or even because I've grown to love you."

June gasped.

"Paint the sky. Paint the night. Paint yourself. Just paint, please. I can't bear to think of you stopping." Jack let her go then, and stepped back and away. His heavy step carried him across the room. At the door, he stopped. "Every artist has the right to her privacy. So I won't come back unless you invite me. But I won't say I'm sorry for getting in your way. Maybe someday you'll agree with me."

He opened the front door. Lindie darted away from her eavesdropping spot, toward the first oak that lined the drive. Soon, she heard the crunch of Jack's soles, the rocks skittering, and the sound of his voice, quiet: "She's a hard nut to crack, Rabbit Legs."

"I know," Lindie said, but she couldn't tell if he heard.

Lindie found June in the middle of the small room, arms crossed, brow furrowed.

"You're not going to give him a chance?" She couldn't help herself; she couldn't believe, that after all that, June was just going to let Jack go.

"I don't have to explain myself to you."

"He's a movie star, June. He wants to marry you. For all we know, Artie's lying in a ditch somewhere."

June's lip curled. "You can go."

"Don't end it like this. You love Jack. You should be with him."

"Don't tell me what to do." June was mad now, mad enough to sound mean, Lindie realized in a satisfying wave of fury.

"I'm only trying to help."

"Why do you care so much about helping me? I'm the only one who should care who I marry. It's my business, not yours."

"I care because you're my friend, June." Lindie was seized with regret. She didn't want to fight. She only wanted June to be happy.

"You care because you have no life." June's mouth had formed a cruel line. She held up her fist and ticked her fingers off, one by one. "No mother. One friend. You dress like a farmhand. And people are going to start calling you 'sir' if you keep this up."

Sticky tears bloomed in Lindie's eyes.

"Go ahead, cry," June said, coldly crossing her arms. "At least I have a future planned out. I don't even know what yours looks like."

Lindie tore her way outside, through the scratching branches. She found the cold metal of her Schwinn and pedaled off. June would have five lonely miles to walk before sunrise. She deserved it.

LINDIE HARDLY SLEPT those few remaining hours of darkness. When her alarm clock blurted its shrill instruction, she tried to ignore the heavy weight on her chest and completed her first morning ritual: checking Uncle Lem's from the window. She was surprised to discover Clyde Danvers's Chevrolet Bel Air—the car he drove himself—just pulling up out front.

In the blooming dawn, Lindie watched a tall man emerge from the passenger seat. He unfolded his arms and legs like one might an umbrella, then turned and took in the grand home. He removed his fedora at the sight just as Clyde clambered from behind the wheel. Clyde clapped the other man's shoulder and pressed him toward Uncle Lem's. The tall man dropped his head, like a captured prisoner in some western on the big screen at the Majestic.

Lindie's heart sank. Artie Danvers was back in town.

June 2015

CHAPTER THIRTY-FOUR

———

TWO OAKS HAD FORGOTTEN HOW PETTY AND SELFISH HU-
mans are. Perhaps the balm to its decrepitude was not as easy as
it had once believed, simply securing people to inhabit it. Under
Cassie's watch, a hole had broken through the roof, a hole that hadn't
been there before. Tate had damaged one of the master bedroom's door
hinges when she slammed it. And Hank's solvents had turned from efficient to offensive; Two Oaks didn't especially want to be rid of the layer
of grime on the dining room table, practically all that was left of June
and Lemon and Adelbert.

It wasn't that Two Oaks wanted them out. It only wanted the humans to care about the state of its need. The festering gash atop its roof
might be an opportunity. Perhaps it could utilize that emergency—and
others like it—to demonstrate its true state of crisis, and galvanize the
humans, and win repair.

Tate and Elda's vicious argument was met, then, with a jostling of
the termites from the base of Two Oaks's foundation. When Cassie
locked herself into the office with the stack of bills and forced herself,
finally, to look at them—thus releasing great swaths of anxiety into the
floor and walls and ceiling—the house responded with rusty water, un-
bidden, from the taps. And the phone call Tate received midafternoon,
which kept Nick shut into Tate's bedroom for hours as she wrung her
hands and begged him to fix it, resulted in an epic toilet backup that
even Hank's industrious plunging couldn't repair.

They reconvened for roasted salmon and asparagus, but ate at arm's
length at the mahogany table, barely making small talk from their sep-
arate corners. After dinner, Tate didn't give any of her father's boxes
a glance, instead calling Nick to her. Nick cast Cassie a disappointed
glance but followed Tate nonetheless. Cassie remembered how powerful
she'd felt in the upstairs hall, commanding them to do her bidding, and

wondered what had gone wrong in the intervening hours. Elda yawned theatrically. Hank started clearing.

The plumber came after dark. Cassie couldn't imagine what that cost; she was letting Tate pay. Tate and Elda hid in their respective rooms, but Cassie had the feeling that even had they been twirling through the foyer in ball gowns, the man wouldn't have noticed; he didn't seem a popular culture type. He emerged from the upstairs bathroom with a grim prognosis. "I fixed it best I could, but these are old pipes. You're going to need an overhaul." Hank paid him in cash. Cassie felt relieved Nick was locked in with Tate; she knew he'd remind her about the roof.

Cassie spent the evening with Elda and a bottle of Jack. The more she drank, the less she cared about being left out of Nick and Tate's confidence, and the question of Jack and June's affair, and the house falling to pieces around her. Elda had good stories and she sure knew how to pose. Cassie shot off two rolls of film even though the light was terrible, because she knew, from the way Elda lit up her tall tales, that her charisma would illuminate the pictures. There was that time Elda rode a white stallion into Studio 54. And that other time she and Jack had played a fabulous practical joke on Candice Bergen's family (it involved two pigs set loose at Bella Vista, the family compound; the pigs were painted with the numbers "one" and "three"). The time she'd gotten high in the bathroom of the Concorde and woken up wearing a clown costume in Istanbul, with no memory of how she'd gotten there. But when Cassie asked casually, from behind the lens, if Elda could remember anything about the summer Jack had spent in St. Jude, the older woman shrugged and equivocated, and the optimistic sheen that had spread over them, as darkness smudged the windows, dulled.

At the westernmost border of the eastern time zone, St. Jude stayed light until ten on a midsummer's night. Cassie waited until darkness to brush her teeth, feeling a dull headache throb into the spot where her buzz had so recently been. The moon was bright and a breeze tickled in the window as she tried to feel where, exactly, Nick was in the house at that moment, as though Two Oaks was an extension of her body, with nerve endings and cilia, and she could feel the weight and movement of him inside her. Then she did her best to pretend that wasn't what she was doing, because the thought of feeling him inside her—just the phrase of it—almost made her want to pass out in a desperate, embarrassing way.

She was shuffling back across the wide upper hallway toward her bedroom when, suddenly, Tate's door opened. "Can I talk to you?" Tate looked left and right like a spy; it was endearing to see how eager she was to get Cassie alone.

But once Cassie was inside Tate's inner sanctum, the woman busied herself in front of the marble sink. The number of serums and oils in tiny white bottles and jars was dizzying. Each had a specific and vital part to play in Tate's bedtime regimen. She was wearing white loungewear—cotton and silk, draped and billowing. Her hair, even after a long day, fell just so around her shoulders. Her toes were perfect little pebbles lined up on the wood floor, her wrists slender and long, her earlobes the size of a gentle peck on the cheek.

The movie star had been respectful of June's belongings. None of the old woman's knickknacks had been moved; the Jackson Pollock postcard—blank, Cassie'd checked—was still propped on the mantelpiece, beside a framed black-and-white photograph of a young June with a bundled baby—Cassie assumed it was her dad—in her arms. Next to that sat a snapshot of a six-year-old Cassie between her parents, all three of them grinning, which Cassie could hardly bear to look at. She allowed her eyes to skim over it now. Did her young father have Jack Montgomery's nose? His eyebrows? His mouth? All she could see was her dad, the dad she missed.

June's modest belongings had accommodated the much larger collection Tate had brought from home: two dozen framed snapshots of a French bulldog standing in front of international monuments, including the Lincoln Memorial, the Eiffel Tower, and an Egyptian pyramid. Cassie picked up one taken in front of the Taj Mahal, realizing the frame was, in fact, silver, instead of the silverish metal of the frames regular folks bought at T.J. Maxx.

"Not one of them is Photoshopped." Tate's clean finger tapped at the glass. "That's my Benny boy. I bring him everywhere."

"Not to St. Jude." Cassie settled the picture back into its spot, wondering if Tate really lugged these everywhere—that seemed more like Hank's handiwork.

"Well, we didn't exactly know we'd be staying so long. Anyway, he's safe with Daddy." Cassie watched Tate's eyes trail over the last picture atop the mantel, a snapshot of Benny the bulldog between Tate and Max in front of the Great Wall of China. The humans were wearing baseball caps and sweatshirts, trying to look like a normal couple, but the effect, with their perfect skin and glowing smiles, was that of gods playing at mortality.

Cassie pointed her chin toward Max. "What's he like?" She figured she deserved a bit of gossip, if only getting to see how Tate would react.

Tate considered the question evenly. "He works harder than anyone I know. You know, Aloysius started in his dad's garage in Burbank." She smiled brightly. "Oh! Funny story—did you know that was the name of Daddy's character in *Erie Canal*?"

Cassie shook her head.

"Well, Max didn't exactly name the band after him, I mean, Max loved what the name evoked—manliness, America—but I also happen to know the band wasn't officially called Aloysius until he met me." She beamed. "Anyway, Max came from practically nothing and worked his way up and now he's the lead singer of the most famous band in the world."

"Yes, but what's he like?"

Tate flopped down onto the bed. "Smart. Funny. Sexy. Kind." She hesitated over that last word, and sucked in a raggedy breath. Then her face melted into something real and sad. "When he wants to be, he is very, very kind."

Cassie thought she'd seen Tate cry on that first day she'd come to Two Oaks—really cry—but in the face of what was happening before her, she wasn't so sure. This was something else entirely. This was being ravaged by an onslaught of sobs, turning ugly, making sounds you wouldn't ever want another soul to hear. Watching immaculate Tate dissolve into this devastation was like witnessing a statue crack open to discover a slimy creature writhing inside. It wasn't that it felt satisfying, exactly, just that Cassie couldn't help but feel triumphant that she'd finally gotten to something true.

She found herself muttering unhelpful clichés: "It's okay. Just let it out." Tate's tangible sorrow didn't feel this honest in any of the movies in which people she supposedly loved had died of cancer or had left her on the tarmac and gone back to their wives, which meant she was a much better actor than even Cassie had known; she had, apparently, made up a palatable version of sorrow that seemed real and yet had nothing on this. This anguish, the actual kind, went fathoms deep.

Cassie had started to wonder if she should leave Tate alone when Tate rasped three words. She was huddled on the bed by then, and Cassie had to lean over her red, wet face to understand. Tate repeated the three words—"He left me"—and then dissolved again.

Cassie warmed a washcloth. How had it come to be that she, of all people in the whole entire world, was being confided in by Tate Montgomery, America's Sweetheart, about the end of her marriage? It was not a scenario Cassie would have believed even five days before, and, yet, here Tate was, letting Cassie mop her brow, drinking from the proffered glass of water, thanking Cassie once she'd gathered herself together. Cassie felt infinite in her own kindness, proud in the way she had on the day Tate had first wept—or seemed to weep—over the loss of her parents' love story.

"I'm sorry," Tate mumbled with her stringy mouth. She dabbed at her reddened eyes and pulled herself up against the headboard. "It's so embarrassing."

"It's not a big deal," Cassie said, spreading out across the bed. Tate tossed her a pillow. "I mean, it is a big deal, obviously. I'm so sorry to hear you and Max are separating. You can cry. You should cry."

Tate balled the tissue and nodded as her tears welled up. "I don't have anywhere to go. Isn't that stupid? He's in the house in Malibu so I can't go to L.A. The apartment in New York is under construction. And if I check into a hotel, the paparazzi will smell it all over me. Oh god, what am I going to do?"

Cassie let Tate sob again for a bit, then said, "You'll stay here."

Tate covered her face with her hands and shook her head vehemently; she was still wearing her giant diamond. "You're too nice."

"I'm not very nice."

This made Tate laugh and cry at the same time.

"Anyway, we're family, right?" Cassie said. "Hank might have to turn the volume down on the quinoa/yoga thing though."

"Oh god," Tate cackled. "She's the worst. Most of the time I want to wring her little neck."

Cassie felt momentary pity for Hank. But she also knew slamming the girl would bring Tate closer. "Doesn't it hurt her face to smile that much?"

"She smiles like that because I treat her like gold. She worked for some real bitches before she came to me. I said, 'You don't have to kiss my ass, honey, but it'll get you a raise.' Isn't that horrible? Most days I want to kick in her teeth, but if she wasn't so damn perky I'd fire her." Tate shook her head and muttered, "It's her job to pretend I shit rainbows, and I know it, and I still believe her when she says I do."

Cassie wondered if Hank was in her bedroom right next door, and how much their voices were carrying. Ah well, if Cassie knew her at all, she'd bet Hank would smile and say, "It's my job to take Tate's abuse!" And then she'd rah or cheer or something.

"Can I ask you a favor?" Tate asked.

"Tate, as far as I'm concerned, you can stay as long as you need."

"Oh, thanks," Tate said, as though they'd already gotten past that point. "Could you take my picture?"

"Sure," Cassie said, confused. She'd already taken Tate's picture a dozen times over the last few days. But then she realized what Tate was asking. "What, now?"

Tate smiled ruefully. "I know it sounds crazy. I just don't have any pictures of what he does to me. I want to remember, so that when he begs me to come back, I can look at this night and see how destroyed I am. Anyway, I trust you. I need to trust a photographer to give her something real."

Cassie obliged, because of course she couldn't resist capturing this golden goddess on film, at her most vulnerable, broken on a bed, tearstained and messy. She got her camera. Back behind Tate's closed door, she shot off a whole roll, easy. Then Tate thanked her in her imperial way and Cassie knew she was done. Out Tate's window, the clouds closed over the moon.

Tate's chin dipped, so she was looking up at Cassie with those liquid eyes. "You really mean I can stay?"

Cassie nodded. "Even after we do the DNA test. Whatever it shows."

Tate put her hand over her heart, like a prima ballerina moved by a standing ovation. "Thank you."

Cassie wanted to hug her but the urge felt a touch needy, and Tate wasn't making any move toward it, so she just said, "Good night," and made her way for the door.

"One more favor?" Tate asked, as Cassie's hand alighted on the door-knob.

"Sure."

"Try not to distract Nick?" Cassie made every effort not to betray emotion at the mention of his name. "I need him focused right now. I'm the one paying him. I know it's purely physical for you guys—he's made that clear to me—so if that's all you want, awesome; sex can really center a man. Just don't get too attached." Tate shrugged and offered an adorable smile. "Keep it up as long as it's fun!"

Cassie's limbs had grown numb, her mouth like cotton. Nick had told Tate their attraction was purely physical? And clearly that wasn't all he'd told her; he was sharing all sorts of intimate details. She felt betrayed, undone, but all she could muster was a chipper "Of course."

"Thanks, sweetie. I love how honest we can be with each other."

"Yeah," Cassie said, opening the door, "me too."

"And let me know how I can repay the favor," Tate said, her voice carrying out into the hallway. "Elda's such a bitch sometimes, and I know Hank's impossible. This is your home. If you want them gone, just say the word."

"No," Cassie said automatically, turning back to glimpse Tate on her grandmother's bed. "No, of course they should stay." She closed the door and listened for signs of life, but the rest of the house had bedded down.

CHAPTER THIRTY-FIVE

————

CASSIE BUMPED INTO HANK IN THE HALLWAY THE NEXT morning, or maybe it wasn't an accident after all. Hank was superperky, of course, and dressed like Fitness Barbie, and she just wanted to go over a list of improvements for Two Oaks.

"Improvements?" Cassie croaked.

"The plumbing, the oven, the ant infestation in the dining room." Her nose wrinkled. "And Nick said the roof needs repair."

Cassie felt a wave of exasperation. She'd hardly slept, going over and over her conversation with Tate the night before; she really didn't have much patience for Hank's OCD. She held out her hand for the list, which was sixteen items long. Hank had cross-referenced it, with multiple price quotes from different service providers. The damn thing was color-coded.

"I can take care of this," Cassie mumbled. It was too early in the morning to do anything but lie.

"Oh." Hank shook her head quickly, the way one might rattle a toaster on the fritz. "Oh. No—Tate asked me to do it. Then you don't have to worry! She'll pay! We don't want this to turn into a construction zone, but we do want to make it livable!"

"It's livable. I live here," Cassie growled, crumpling the list into her pajama pocket.

Hank offered a panicked smile, eyed Cassie's pocket, apparently decided it would be impossible to steal the list back, and darted toward the back hall.

Cassie harrumphed into the bathroom, ignoring the half-closed door until she discovered Nick flossing.

He was just about the last person she wanted to see. "You floss in the morning?" she asked grumpily, to hide the way her stomach lurched at the sight of how achingly cute he looked caught off guard; his hair was tousled, and he was wearing a plaid pajama set she couldn't help wondering if his mom had picked out.

"You don't floss in the morning?" he asked.

She sidled up beside him and squeezed toothpaste onto her toothbrush. "I don't floss. Period."

He raised his eyebrows in the mirror but didn't say anything.

"God," she said, "Hank's on a crazy rampage to get everything fixed."

He kept flossing.

"I mean, I get it, the place is a little funky, but it's a hundred-and-twenty-year-old house. There are going to be quirks."

Nick cleared his throat.

"What?"

He caught her expression in the mirror and shook his head.

"What?" she pressed.

"I'm concerned about that roof. A big rainstorm and you could have some serious water damage."

She started to brush her teeth with more vehemence than usual, but it felt good and it kept her from being mean. This was what drove her crazy about these people—thinking they knew better. From his expression, she knew he had no idea he was out of line.

She spat.

"Is something wrong?" he garbled, flossing at his molars, hands wedged up inside his mouth.

"I have to pee," she blurted.

"Sure." He went toward the door.

"And just because Max is leaving Tate, and she doesn't have any place to stay, doesn't mean I have to change everything for you people. This is still my house, you know."

He closed the bathroom door and whispered, "How do you know about Max and Tate?"

She narrowed her eyes. "She told me."

Then he was pacing, running his hands through his hair. "You can't tell anyone."

"Who am I going to tell?" she cried. Apparently he didn't care a lick about anything but Tate's marital crisis, because he just opened the door and started out.

"Where are you going?" Cassie was just getting started.

But he looked at her, and frowned. "You have to pee." And then he closed the door and left her alone.

So Cassie escaped. For one harebrained moment, she considered climbing out the bathroom window, onto the top of the overhang above the driveway, and down one of the columns that held it up. But she was a grown woman. And this was her house. This was her life, dammit, and she could go anywhere she wanted. She got dressed and made it out the front door without any of them noticing, which didn't exactly feel like the victory she'd expected it to. She didn't leave a note, but she did take a picture of her house from the outside, and decided to title it "Filled with Lunatics."

On her way past the house across the side lawn, she noticed her elderly neighbor peeking from between the blinds. Cassie lifted her camera and snapped away. Her stomach growled, but Illy's wouldn't be open until lunch. She rummaged in her canvas shoulder bag. She came up with half a squashed Snickers, which would have to do for now.

Cassie took the bridge over the sludgy canal that cut through Montgomery Square, then walked under the graffiti-covered rotunda where teenagers liked to smoke and outswear each other on the deadly slow St. Judian afternoons. Chip bags tossed like tumbleweed across the patchy grass. Cassie counted crumpled cans of beer to avoid thinking about the last time she'd been there, with Nick. She snapped shots of the old fire station and Memorial High, then doubled back through to the western edge of the square, having settled on a destination.

THE ELDERLY LIBRARIAN was seated alone behind a counter, her nose in a Kate Atkinson novel. Linoleum counters surrounded her on three sides, stacked with hardcovers swathed in those plastic sleeves Cassie knew would crinkle under her touch. The woman wore a blue cardigan, and with good reason—the AC was humming a Freon tune in time to the flicker of a fluorescent bulb.

She looked so shocked when she noticed Cassie standing there that she nearly fell off her seat. She clutched the keys hanging around her neck with her knobbed knuckles and declared, "You must be Cassandra Danvers."

"You recognize me?"

"You only look just like your grandmother June."

"You think?" The library was deserted, save for an old man making photocopies over by the drinking fountain; Cassie wanted to wave to him and shout, "She thinks I look just like my grandmother!" She was flushed with a sudden longing for June's physical self—for her cold, small hands, and the silver hair at her temples, for the dry rasp of her lips when she kissed you.

"I'm Betty." The woman's hand nestled gently into Cassie's like a little creature. "I hate that cancer. Your grandma was a real special lady."

Cassie felt proud and sad at once, and wondered why she'd been hiding out, which suddenly seemed an obvious thing to wonder about. Why hadn't she sought the company of a woman like this, who'd counted June as her friend? It seemed so much more humane than the isolation chamber she'd shut herself in for months. She felt as though she was breathing again, painful as it was to notice the empty spot June had left behind.

"Last time I saw your grandma was last summer, just before she was set to visit you in New York. She picked up a couple extra travel guides: for Southeast Asia, Taipei, Shanghai." Betty watched Cassie carefully as she mentioned those three places, as if Cassie might betray some fabulous secret.

"She did?"

The woman offered an energetic grin. "Well, I've got my theories."

"Please, illuminate me," Cassie said. "You have no idea how badly I want to hear your theories."

Betty's head tick-tocked as she put her thoughts in order. "Your grandma sure could keep a confidence. But I got some Frangelico into her a few years ago and she told me about these frescoes she'd seen a few months back in a Florentine monastery, frescoes by the actual Fra Angelico, she just went on and on describing them to me, and I said, 'June,' I said, 'you were in Italy a few months back?' and she looked shocked and set down the drink and excused herself right then."

"You think she'd really been in Italy?" June had never, not once, mentioned Italy to Cassie, especially not in the past few years. Maybe she'd been losing it.

"Well, why not?" Betty said. "She was gone so much, and she always said she was visiting you in New York City . . ." She leaned forward. "Only she wasn't always in New York, was she? Seemed like an awful lot of visits to me."

Cassie felt, suddenly, like crying. She shook her head, which was what she could manage.

"Oh, honey, I didn't mean to make you blue. I only wanted to say I admired her. She was a role model, living on her own like that in that big old house, traveling places, taking care of you." She reached for Cassie's hand, and Cassie tried to focus on the friendly squeeze she offered. "You were her pride and joy, you know that? She was so impressed that you followed your dreams. I think if she'd lived in a different time, maybe she would have pursued art like you."

This woman was really going to make Cassie lose it.

"Oh, I've gone and made you sad. I've been looking forward to seeing you for so long, and now I've gone and made you sad."

"You've been looking forward to seeing me?"

Betty looked torn, as though she wanted to say something important but didn't quite know how. "It's only—my husband, Bob, he was the first responder for your accident." Cassie couldn't keep the lump in her throat any longer. She felt a sob choke up through her. She felt tears stream down her cheeks. She was messy and unhinged, and reminded of why she wasn't allowed to leave the house. "Oh, please don't cry," Betty tutted. "I only mentioned it because I wanted you to know how dear you are to us. We think of you as a little bit ours, even though I know that sounds funny. Like you're a miracle we got to witness."

"Well, jeez, Betty," Cassie said, wiping at her face with her sleeve, "this is not what I expected at the library."

Betty laughed lightly. The old man gathered up his stack of pink copies and tucked them under his bare, liver-spotted arm. He waved good-bye, and the glass door coughed shut behind him.

"And what exactly were you expecting at the library?" Betty asked in her best librarian voice.

Cassie explained about *Erie Canal,* and June 1955. "Do you remember it?" she asked.

Betty pulled the cord of keys off her neck and pressed the warm brass into Cassie's palm. "I'm afraid not. I didn't live here yet—I hadn't met Bob. But Bob's father fancied himself something of a photographer! I'll bet you'd be interested in his shots. Only trouble is they're in a storage unit up in Lima. I'll see if I can get Bob to dig them up, and we'll have you over for tuna casserole. In the meantime"— she shifted her attention from Cassie to the far corner of the library, where a glassed-in room was locked and dark; the door had ARCHIVES painted across it in golden letters—"you should try in there. Lock is a little sticky."

"Okay if I take your picture first?" Cassie asked. It was.

THE THREE HOURS Cassie spent in the St. Jude archives gave her a great appreciation for Mr. Abernathy's diligence, curiosity, and detective work. With Betty's help she got the microfiche up and running. Hunched over the machine, scanning the archives of the *St. Jude Caller* and the *Columbus Dispatch* for the months of May, June, and July 1955, Cassie gaped at the St. Jude she found—a veritable boomtown. The photos were crowded with people trooping up Main Street and playing in Montgomery Square on a daily basis (which was called, yes, Center Square back in those days). She even found a picture of Two Oaks, which she spent a solid ten minutes examining; though she couldn't place her finger on why, the house looked proud, and she wondered if she shouldn't take Tate up on her offer to pay for repairs.

As for any pictures of Jack and June together, well, that was a pipe dream, but there were plenty of shots of the handsome man himself, surrounded by onlookers and costumed extras. There was always the chance that June was in those crowd shots. But, even with a magnifier, Cassie couldn't pick out her grandmother from the hundreds of tiny smudged faces. Anyway, it wouldn't prove anything to find June there— apparently everyone in town had shown up to watch.

The headlines were ecstatic: HOLLYWOOD COMES TO OHIO! JACK MONTGOMERY—WHAT A GENT! and ROMANCE BLOOMS IN ST.

JUDE, accompanying a picture of Jack Montgomery and tall, leggy "up-and-comer Diane DeSoto."

"Betty?" Cassie poked her head out of the archive room and nearly killed the old woman for the second time that day. She certainly hadn't shouted, and there was no one else in the place, but Betty clambered down from her chair, lifted the gate separating librarians from the rest of the world, and shuffled across the pile carpet in her sensible brown shoes until she was two steps away.

"Yes?" she whispered.

"Do you have Internet?" Cassie made sure to lower her voice.

"Of course!" Betty looked a little insulted.

"I don't," Cassie confided, to make Betty feel better.

"Well, the library is the perfect place to binge when you're on an information diet," Betty declared. Cassie followed her to the back wall, where they found three PCs banked on a high desk. Betty turned one on, and together they watched it boot up. "They've cut our funding, so we keep these off unless they're being used." Betty leaned forward and lowered her already whispering voice. "Not to mention that someone was using them for pornography."

"Who would look at pornography on your watch?"

"A damn fool is who," Betty pronounced, and Cassie snapped another picture.

Cassie made sure Betty was out of sight before typing "Diane DeSoto Jack Montgomery" into the search engine. Hundreds of hits came up, pictures of the couple at black-tie affairs throughout the fifties and sixties. Cassie scanned the list of links, clicking on the first that caught her eye, a post about Jack Montgomery on a website cataloging the children of movie stars:

> *Esmerelda "Elda" Domenica Montgomery b. March 9, 1951, mother Conchita Hernandez*
> *Tate Michaels Montgomery b. April 24, 1967, mother Diane DeSoto*
> *Dennis Adelbert Montgomery, stillborn, June 6, 1971, mother Diane DeSoto*

Cassie sat back in her seat. A dead baby; that was hard. A dead baby with her father's name as his middle name. She remembered Nick telling her that Jack's real name had been Adelbert, and clicked on Jack Montgomery's Wikipedia page, which had come up in her original search.

Jack had been born Adelbert Alan Michaels in Little Rock, Arkansas, to a janitor and his wife. Upon setting out for Las Vegas to seek his fortune, he'd ditched his given name for the one his manager dreamed up to match his good looks. Cassie skimmed the description of Montgomery's hasty marriage—and subsequent divorce—to Elda's mother, a dark-eyed Vegas showgirl named Conchita. Next came a series of girlfriends, a veritable laundry list of famous movie stars from the forties and fifties, capped with the mention of Diane DeSoto: "Although sources indicate DeSoto and Montgomery became involved before the summer of 1955, their affair reportedly intensified while on the set of the critical and commercial failure *Erie Canal,* half of which was filmed in the small town of St. Jude, Ohio, in June 1955. On November 18, 1955, Montgomery proposed to DeSoto in his Hollywood Hills home, and their wedding on March 12, 1956, was the event of the spring, attended by such luminaries as Dean Martin and Marlon Brando. Daughter Tate Montgomery was born on April 24, 1967, followed by a stillborn son, Dennis, delivered at Cedars-Sinai on June 6, 1971. After Dennis's death, Ms. DeSoto reportedly slipped into a depression that spiraled as she turned to drugs and alcohol. She was found dead in her bathtub on January 20, 1977, reportedly by a nine-year-old Tate Montgomery, the daughter she and Jack Montgomery shared. Rumors of suicide have surrounded Ms. DeSoto's death ever since, but no autopsy was performed."

Cassie felt terribly sad for Tate. That she had discovered her mother's body explained so much. Screw Elda for referring to that horrible event, even in the heat of the moment. Cassie could hardly bear to think of the agony little Tate must have endured, finding her mother's body.

She opened a new tab and typed in "Tate Montgomery assistant Margaret," more for the element of distraction than anything else, when she felt a particular itch at the back of the neck; someone was behind her. She turned to find Hank standing quietly at her elbow.

"Well, there you are!" Hank said with a smile just shy of bared teeth. "We looked everywhere!"

"I'm sorry," Cassie said, closing the Internet window, wondering how much Hank had seen. "I should have left a note."

"No worries." Hank laid her hand on Cassie's shoulder. "I'm great at sniffing people out."

CHAPTER THIRTY-SIX

———

THEY CLIMBED THE CRACKED CONCRETE STAIRS UP TO MAIN Street, with its empty storefronts and taped windows and tarps flapping in the breeze. Even Weight Watchers had moved out. The video store Cassie had begged her grandmother to take her to on summer vacations was gone too, as were the antiques emporium and the Red Door Tavern, which had been in operation since the 1890s, until it closed in early 2002. Up close, the strip didn't seem quite as quaint as it had through Nick's windshield.

But Illy's was still there. The food was terrible and the service was worse, but at least it still existed, and, if Hank wanted to stay outside, well, that was just fine. But she remained at Cassie's heels as they stepped into the squat, hot room.

The restaurant was exactly as it had always been: thick paper napkins rolled around the stainless-steel utensils; those big glass shakers of sugar that made you want to let loose a pile of white upon the red-lacquered tabletops; and, hanging over the register, that signed black-and-white photograph of the leading man Cassie had never recognized until now. What had June thought of Jack, up there on the wall, watching them from under his handsome brow? Maybe that picture was why she'd always resisted coming here for the little bit of civilization St. Jude offered; if it had been up to Cassie, they'd have eaten every meal here.

With its fried chicken and mashed potatoes, Illy's had always been a second home for widowers; Cassie and Hank were the youngest patrons by a good fifty years, and the only women save the waitress.

Cassie didn't need to look at the menu. When the waitress came, she ordered a cheeseburger with extra special sauce, fries with a side of Russian dressing, and a black-and-white milk shake. The fifty-year-old nodded her approval as she scribbled on her pad.

Hank greeted the waitress and tried to remind her that she'd been in a few days before and wasn't it funny about the egg-white omelets? Needless to say, the waitress did not think it was funny, not at all. The whole thing was so awkward that Cassie actually liked Hank for a second, but then Hank wrinkled her nose and shrugged her shoulders and turned on her baby voice, asking for a spinach and cucumber salad with lemon juice on the side.

The waitress stared at her longer than was necessary, then deadpanned, "Sure, honey." An old man dropped his spoon on the floor, which she apparently took as her cue to head back toward the kitchen, patting her spit-curled hairdo as she went.

Across the booth, Hank's hands were neatly folded on the Formica. Her blond hair was parted just so.

"Your first fried salad!" Cassie said.

Hank looked like she'd been electrocuted. "It'll be fried?"

Cassie waved off Hank's concern. "It's a phrase my dad came up with for any salad you order around here. Iceberg lettuce with cheddar, bacon, and croutons on top, slathered in a cup of ranch dressing."

"Disgusting."

Cassie tore a roll in half. "I love ranch dressing." She unwrapped a pat of butter from its gold foil and spread it on the roll, relishing Hank's look of alarm. Then she shoved it into her mouth. She reached for the other half of the roll, spread another pat of butter on it, and held it out to Hank.

Hank shook her head.

"I get it. Kale good. Gluten bad. But don't you ever just want comfort food?"

"I can't."

"Oh, stop it with the Hollywood diet."

"I'm allergic."

"No you are not."

Hank's mouth formed a thin line. "I have celiac disease."

Cassie shrugged and gobbled up the rest of the roll herself, even though she didn't want it. She was buoyed by the memory of Tate badmouthing Hank the previous night. "I knew plenty of emaciated women in New York who said they had celiac when what they really had was a case of the an-o-rexia."

Hank opened her mouth, then closed it.

"What?"

"Can I have my list back?"

"What list?" Cassie knew perfectly well what list. She wondered why she was being so mean. June, she knew, would be horrified.

"Why won't you just let me help you?" Hank said, eyes burning feverishly as she pounded her fists on the table. "I know exactly who to call and exactly what to ask for and you don't know any of it. You will screw it up."

"Chillax, sister," Cassie said, wondering, herself, where that loathsome word had come from, and why she'd chosen to sound so smug.

Hank's eyes brimmed with tears.

The bread suddenly felt terribly dry in Cassie's throat. "You can have the list," she said. "It's still in my pajamas, though, so you'll have to wait until we get home."

Hank crumpled back into the booth. Tears were now streaming down her cheeks.

"I shouldn't have taken it, okay?" Cassie mumbled, reaching her hand across the table. "I'm sorry."

Hank grabbed a stack of napkins from the dispenser and dabbed at her eyes. "It's not about the list," she offered up unhelpfully, inside a choked sob.

The waitress approached with the dewy metal milk shake container in one hand, and two glasses in the other. She set them in front of Cassie, glanced at Hank, who had covered her face with napkins, and shuffled away.

"Please don't cry," Cassie said, trying to sound soothing. She poured two half glasses of the black-and-white, and pushed one of them toward Hank. A few of the old men were looking her way, and they did not appear pleased. Cassie glanced back at Hank and tried to figure out what was going on. "Why are you crying?"

But Hank wouldn't answer.

"Do you ever get a vacation? Tate"—Cassie caught herself, adopting the paranoia of her houseguests and changing to a neutral pronoun—"she has you doing everything. You've got a lot of weight on your shoulders." She paused, then added, "I only took the list because I wanted to help you out," which wasn't exactly the truth, but Cassie figured it wouldn't hurt to try to spin it.

Hank emerged from her napkin shield to blow her nose. The sound was gratifyingly disgusting. "Everybody works hard."

"I don't."

Hank didn't disagree. Instead, she surprised Cassie by saying, "You are so lucky."

"Lucky?" Cassie almost started laughing.

Hank rolled her eyes. "You have any idea what it took to get where I am? I work my butt off every day—"

"No one's disputing that."

"—because without my job, I have nothing. Without her, I'm nothing."

"I mean, you're really pretty," Cassie said, trying to figure out the right thing to say. "And you cook well, and you can teach yoga and—"

"No offense, Cassie, but without her, you've still got that big fancy house." Were they talking about Cassie? Cassie was confused. "Plus, worst-case scenario, you've got a million bucks for doing nothing. I'd kill to be in your shoes."

Cassie felt her jaw drop. "You think I want this? My life is miserable. I'm an orphan living in a house that's about to fall down around me."

"Oh lord," Hank groaned, "the orphan thing."

"Wow," Cassie said.

Hank blinked at her, and then, as though she'd pressed her own reset button, seemed to alter entirely. Cassie watched as she took a deep breath, bringing her shoulders up to her ears, then releasing them. She rocked her head side to side and closed her eyes. Then Hank shook her head and perked her whole face up and said, "I'm sorry. That comment was uncalled for."

"Yeah," Cassie replied, not exactly sure what had just gone down. Was Hank mad at her? Was she a little crazy—crazier than Cassie'd thought?

"It's just with everything going on, you know?" Hank said now, leaning forward on the table as though they were besties. "It's a lot, you know?"

Did she mean Tate and Max? Or Jack's inheritance? Or something else entirely? Cassie nodded, to keep it neutral.

"It's just so . . . intense. There in that house? All together?"

Cassie could agree on that. She took a chug of her milk shake and nodded. Were they friends now? Had they had a fight? Had they made up?

"And honestly, with her sister there, it's just . . ."

"Yeah," Cassie agreed, "they don't seem to get along."

"First her dad dies! Then he leaves everything to you."

Cassie was glad they'd found some common ground. "Yeah, and then Elda—I mean, her sister—comes and attacks her, and we're all stuck in that house together—"

"Oh my god yes, and the stuff with Margaret and Max and the infidelity rumors." As soon as the words were out of Hank's mouth, she clapped her hands over it. Her eyes grew wide.

Cassie forced herself to be very interested in the milk shake. She took a careful sip, allowing the cold lump to slide down into her gullet as Hank started to cry all over again. Cassie then asked, as casually as possible, "What infidelity rumors?"

Hank's hands were over her face as she shook her head. She was making this hmmmming sound that Cassie supposed was her version of a low sob.

"Maybe it'll make you feel better," Cassie said, trying not to sound hopeful, "if you tell someone."

Hank squeaked a lengthy reply that Cassie couldn't make out.

"Huh?"

Hank dabbed at her face with more of those leafy white napkins, then emerged to say, "Nondisclosure agreement."

These people were obsessed with their secrets. "Who am I going to tell? Anyway they're pretty much my family now, so it's totally my business."

Hank balled the soggy napkins into her fist, resting them on her lap. Her nose and cheeks were flushed and her eyes bright, as though crying had improved her. She checked behind herself and leaned forward with a low voice. "I don't exactly know what happened. I wasn't full-time yet. But supposedly"—and she checked around again in the most obvious way; had Cassie been looking to eavesdrop on anyone in the state of Ohio, she would have picked Hank—"supposedly something happened."

Cassie crossed her arms at the lack of information. "Like what?"

"Like. You know. Cheating."

"With Margaret?"

Hank nodded triumphantly.

Of course. That was why Tate had fired Margaret. That was why Nick always bristled at the mention of Margaret's name. "Margaret had been her assistant for a long time, right?"

"Forever," Hank mouthed, looking much more gleeful than she had only moments before. But then she caught herself, and glanced down mournfully at the milk shake.

"You know you want it," Cassie said.

"I really shouldn't have told you." Hank was doing her best impression of a basset hound.

Cassie crossed her heart. "Your secret's safe." A year before, such gossip would have slipped from her lips into the ears of the Pyke gallery girls she worked with—preceded, of course, by "Don't tell anyone, but"—but really, truly, she had no one to tell. Even if she did, who'd believe she had the inside scoop on the most famous couple in the world?

Hank lifted the glass to her blue eyes and examined it like it was poison. Her eyes squeezed shut. Right before she put the cold glass to her bubble-gum lips and chugged, she growled, "Bottoms up."

June 1955

CHAPTER THIRTY-SEVEN

———

INDIE CROUCHED IN THE AZALEA BELOW TWO OAKS'S FRONT parlor window and watched June smile at Artie like a china doll. Slim and sallow, he sat beside June on the buttercup yellow couch, his long, limp hand resting between them like an ailing greyhound. Clyde and Cheryl Ann toasted the happy couple with goblets full of something brown and sticky, even though it was barely breakfast time. Cheryl Ann remarked how glad she was that they'd kept the church booked and gone ahead with planning the reception. Cheryl Ann and Artie had never felt like they belonged to Lindie, but Clyde and June certainly had, and the sight, first of Clyde laying a thick stack of bills into Cheryl Ann's hand, and then of June pretending amusement at a quiet remark made by Artie, her laughter a thin, sad line carrying out through the screen, sent Lindie sprinting toward set, chest heaving with desperate sobs.

"He's back," she whispered to Jack later that day, in front of the Congregational church. They'd both been too busy to discuss June any earlier; with the looming deadline of the wrap just on the horizon, there were no more idle moments. But for now, the camera operator was setting up a tricky shot, and Diane was taking her beauty rest. "Artie," Lindie clarified. "June's fiancé."

Jack squinted off toward the throng gathered in Center Square.

"She's going to marry him." Was he dumb?

"That's her decision," Jack finally said. Lindie fought the urge to pick up the stone at her foot and pitch it at his head as he sauntered off.

So it was up to Lindie, then. She needed to talk sense to June; it was simple as that. They'd been unkind, but they'd mend their fences. She pushed away the memory of June's fingers counting off her deficits; after all, she'd also been cruel, keeping Artie's letter from June. And perhaps June was right, perhaps the letter was the perfect example of what June had been saying: Lindie thinking she knew best when really it was June's life. Lindie took the letter from the cigar box under her bed, where she'd kept it hidden alongside a note her mother had once left on the kitchen table asking Eben to buy a loaf of bread, and the blue meany marble she'd won off Bobby Prange, and the buffalo nickels and silver dollars she'd collected over the years. Perhaps the time had come to lay the letter humbly at June's feet, to show June she'd learned, and was changing.

Eben made a rare, proper dinner that night—pork chops and crosspatch potatoes. Lindie washed the dishes and dried and put them away, all the while keeping her eye on June's darkened window. But then Eben took up with his earmarked Chicago book in the squealing rocking chair on the front porch. Lindie was exhausted, but instead of letting her limbs sink into the humid sheets, she lay awake, mind tumbling. She waited Eben out and tasted victory when, past midnight, she finally heard him mount the stairs. When his snore began, she crept out her window and scrambled down to their meager lawn, then across the road and onto the Two Oaks property.

Lindie had done this dozens of times: across the side lawn, up the column, onto the roof of the porte cochere, and into June's window. She could do it with her eyes closed, without cracking a branch. Her ascent started out the same as all the others. But one instant, she had a foot perched on the rough-edged stone upon which the column rested, and the next, she found herself unexpectedly bathed in blinding light.

"Linda Sue." It was Cheryl Ann's voice, just beyond the source of that light.

Lindie put her hands up like a fugitive, shielding her eyes.

"June is tired," Cheryl Ann said.

"Yes, ma'am."

"Tired of you disturbing her beauty sleep."

June had turned Lindie in! The realization stung. June was probably at her window, watching Lindie right then, with gleeful revenge in her heart. Lindie remembered June's cruelty, the way she'd spat out the word *sir*, and felt nauseated by sorrow. "Yes, ma'am." She turned toward home.

"If you come back again like this, Linda Sue, I'll see to it you're properly punished. Your father may not be concerned about your nighttime excursions, but the police arrest prowlers."

Lindie hung her head in surrender and loped back across the lawn. Cheryl Ann kept the light on Lindie's back until Lindie set foot on her own porch. Lindie gingerly turned the doorknob and tiptoed inside, but she was a fool if she believed Eben wouldn't be hearing about this tomorrow.

ON SET THE next morning, Lindie spotted Thomas. She'd had little time to gather herself, but she knew one thing: she wasn't going to give up on June. She'd seen the way June wrestled with herself when she told Jack things were over. June could be as mad as she wanted, but Lindie was going to fight for her happiness, even if June wasn't.

Thomas was the one who'd been driving Jack out to meet them at Idlewyld, and Lindie felt sure he must have some bit of useful information. She watched him climb out of the Olds, then stride across Center Square toward the cast trailers. She called his name, but he didn't stop. She sprinted to catch up, a stack of fake election signs weighing down her arms.

She noticed the envelope immediately, with the initials "J.M." written across the front, in what she could have sworn was June's hand. A bit of luck. "What's that?"

Thomas kept walking. "Mind your own business, Linda Sue."

"Who's it for?"

Thomas shared Apatha's unnerving talent of rarely betraying what he was feeling. It was a quality Lindie found inconvenient in old women and downright dangerous in any kind of man, especially one who was privy to the secrets she was also keeping. "Oh, come on, be a pal."

"Run and play." His eyes darted around. Lindie felt a flash of victory; he was afraid of trouble, and the quick flit of his eyes gave that away.

She decided to let him go; at least she'd gotten something. Maybe she could use it; all she had to do was find out the trouble he was avoiding, and why. "If you don't tell me where you're taking it, I'll just watch you," she called after him.

"Watch me, then." He strode off without looking back, knocking on Jack's trailer door and disappearing inside without a backward glance.

IF THOMAS SAW her hiding in the bay laurel beside Jack's car at the end of the day, he didn't let on. He smoked his pipe atop the hood until Jack arrived, then popped down to open the door for him. Lindie took her chance, jumping up and rapping the other rear window. Jack didn't look all that surprised to see her, nor, for that matter, did Thomas, who slipped into the driver's seat and started up the engine. Lindie made a frantic gesture for Jack to unroll the window. He obliged with a tolerant smile.

"Was that a letter from June?" she asked. She knew she seemed desperate to these men, but they were running out of time; the wedding was less than two weeks away.

"Last I heard, what a man reads in a letter addressed to him is his affair."

"But this is an emergency!" She howled. "Don't you understand? She is going to marry that horrible tree trunk of a man!"

"Should I go?" Thomas asked Jack, flashing Lindie a dirty look in the rearview mirror.

Lindie grabbed the top of the window with both hands; they'd have to drive off with her. "You don't know her like I do, Jack. She will marry him. Sure, you'll be done filming next week. You'll go back to your fancy house and your steak dinners and kissing Diane DeSoto, but we will still be here. June will still be here. And there will be no one left to stop her from making the biggest mistake of her life."

Jack's eyes flashed for a split second; she knew she'd hooked him. But what he said was heavy with resignation: "I can't change what she wants, and neither can you, Rabbit Legs."

That nickname was getting on her nerves. She shook her head, even as she wondered if she'd lost her mind. Why did June's destiny, her heart, seem more important than Lindie's own? It might be love, but it was something else too, wasn't it? Something June had put her finger on. Something more selfish than that.

But Lindie didn't let that revelation stop her. "What did her letter say?" she begged.

Jack watched her a moment, then sighed. Pulled it from inside his jacket. Held it out:

Dear Jack—

I can't see you anymore. Please understand it's nothing to do with you. I'm certain your heart will heal more quickly than mine. It's no use trying to change my fate. Thank you for the paints. Thank you for giving me back a little hope. You'll never know how much it means to me.

Yours,

J.

" 'Yours,' " Jack said, tapping at the simple word and shaking his head as the car idled.

"She can still be yours," Lindie said softly. "You just have to try harder. You're a champ at getting out of sticky situations, right? You said it yourself. So get her out of this. Please."

Lindie let go of the car. Jack rolled up his window. Thomas drove off, a filmy dust rising from behind the tires to leave the girl, coughing, in its cloud.

CHAPTER THIRTY-EIGHT

———

THAT NIGHT, IN BED, LINDIE HEARD IT AGAIN: THE SCREEN door opening, followed by the sound of Eben's "Hello." She was dead asleep, but the possibility of a visitor jolted her into full, alert consciousness. The night sky spilled with a smattering of stars, like salt across a tabletop.

"I get you anything?" she heard her father ask. She hoped he wasn't speaking to Clyde.

But it wasn't a man's voice that replied. Lindie had a hard time grabbing hold of who the voice belonged to; its alto pitch was soft, but not girlish. She crept down to the bottom of her bed to be closer to the vent.

"Make yourself at home," Eben replied. Then his footsteps disappeared under Lindie and into the kitchen, where he took out a pot and set it on the stove. She couldn't imagine anyone coming over in the middle of the night to ask for soup, but that was all her mind's eye could see: her father's hands prying open a can of Campbell's tomato while some strange lady sat in their rocking chair.

While he was in the kitchen, the woman said nothing. Lindie churned with possibilities: it was Diane DeSoto, come to hire Lindie to work on every film set with her; it was a secret liaison; it was Cheryl Ann, demanding punishment for Lindie's trespassing. But Diane would have driven up in a car and Lindie had heard no motor; and no man—not even Eben—would leave a woman he loved unattended (and who could imagine her father in love with anyone?); and Cheryl Ann would have had no qualms about marching over in the middle of the day. The puzzle of the visitor's identity teased at her, the suspense excruciating, and she nearly traipsed down the stairs, feigning thirst, just so she could get a glimpse.

But then Eben came back into the dining room and said, "Ready," and Lindie heard the shuffle of someone else's feet as this unknown woman came to meet him at the table.

"Mmmmmm," the woman said, after a moment. She had tasted it. Lindie wished for superhuman smelling powers.

"More vanilla?" he asked. "Honey?" and, in a flash, Lindie knew exactly who it was. Those years when Two Oaks had been hers, Apatha had made her cups of steamed milk with vanilla and honey if she couldn't sleep, or burned with a fever, or had skinned her knee. Lindie could still feel the weight of Apatha's dry hands atop hers on the kitchen table.

"Cheryl Ann caught Lindie last night," Apatha said.

"You don't think I heard?"

"How she supposes I'll be able to keep that feral child in line is beyond me."

Eben chuckled. "I'm sorry for your trouble. I could nail her window shut, but then that girl would just saw a hole in my damn roof." Apatha laughed too. Lindie's pride purpled as she blushed in the dark.

"At least she's scared now. She walked by today and she"—Lindie imagined Apatha freezing in a mocking pose, moving her eyes back and forth as though Lindie had actually looked anything like that. Really, she'd just moved on, because Apatha was sweeping the porch, and the way she'd lifted the broom at the sight of Lindie didn't exactly say warm reception. But Eben guffawed as if he didn't know Apatha was exaggerating.

"I appreciate your coming," he said, as their cheer faded.

"Anything for you, Eben. You know that." So there was a reason he'd invited her; Lindie was ready for them to move on.

Eben cleared his throat, ready to talk business. "I'm hoping you can shed some light on something I've been . . . well, not investigating, that's not the right word . . ."

Apatha was patient as he searched for the one he wanted. She was always happy to let someone finish his own sentence.

"I've discovered an inconsistency," Eben declared at last. Did he sound a little nervous? "You know that development Clyde has up over on the other side of town? He's calling it Three Oaks."

Apatha's laugh was dry.

"The estate's name isn't the only thing he stole," Eben said. "He took

Mr. Neely's land, Apatha. A good portion of the land he built on isn't his. I can't believe I didn't catch it. I guess I thought no man—not even Clyde—could be that proud. Course, he claims it was an innocent mistake. But you know as well as I do that he knew it all along."

If Apatha was shocked, she didn't let on.

"Naturally," he continued, "I want to protect Mr. Neely's interests, especially because Clyde just about came right out and said he doesn't care it's Neely's land. He says once June marries his brother, Artie, it'll as good as belong to him." He whistled. "So's I get to thinking—Clyde doesn't know for sure who Neely's giving all his money and land to once he dies. I don't know either, and I'm Mr. Neely's accountant! So last week, I go down to Mr. Neely's lawyer in Columbus. I decide I'm going to find out if Clyde's scheme will turn out as planned after all."

"And?" Apatha asked.

"And—the lawyer says he can't help me, because Neely doesn't own any of it by himself. The lawyer says there's another person who shares every cent with him. Says that person's the only one besides him and Neely who knows this, and, if that person survives him, she'll be inheriting every cent." He took a breath so deep that Lindie could hear it through the floorboards. "And, Apatha, he says that person's you."

The silence that followed this last statement was not uncomfortable or cold. It was firm, like Apatha. Temperate. It carried up through the vent and over Lindie, as she tried to understand what her father and the lawyer and Apatha and Mr. Neely all knew. Apatha said nothing, as though she was waiting to see if Eben would drop the matter. But Eben Shaw was damn fine at cards, and he'd be glad to sit there all night.

"After Lem lost Mae," Apatha finally said, in her careful drawl, "you know, he saw how people get around death and money. He didn't want any of that nonsense mucking up his life. He loved Mae. But he felt it was private, that love. He must have told me a thousand times that the biggest mistake of his life was building that big old house just to fill it with his children. Called it his 'monument to hubris.' He felt he cursed Mae with that house. Cursed their love. Swore he wouldn't put his heart on show ever again."

"Are you saying what I think you're saying?" Eben asked in an astonished voice. Wait—what was she saying? Lindie was behind.

"October tenth, 1939," Apatha said. "That's the day I became Mrs. Lemon Gray Neely."

Eben gasped. Lindie had never heard him make that sound before.

"We met in Baton Rouge in the twenties, when Lemon was living down there, overseeing his oil fields. You can imagine what it's like down in Louisiana, a black woman, a white man. Not so different from up here in plenty of ways you don't see, Eben. But even if I'd been white, Lemon would have wanted it to be just the two of us. I didn't mind either way; all I wanted was him. And I got him." Her voice warmed. "I still have him." She answered the questions bubbling up inside Lindie before Eben could ask. "We came up to Columbus to be married. You were here that first Christmas, remember?"

Sure he did; Lindie had heard the story a dozen times. Eben had brought red-haired Lorraine up from Columbus for the winter break. It was a cold winter, and Eben's parents, Loftus and Ellen, old and gnarled in the way of those who'd spent their lives in service, had been caring for Two Oaks in Lemon's absence, ever since he'd fled south—to Louisiana, Oklahoma, Texas—escaping the great home in which his young wife, Mae, had died of influenza. Two Oaks was lit up like one of Ellen's porcelain houses set atop the upright piano. Inside Two Oaks, the fireplaces and overheads flickered with Lemon's preferred natural gas. A twelve-foot Christmas tree stood in the parlor window, and a wreath the size of a Great Dane hung on the front door. There was new furniture, too: a davenport of lemon-colored velvet stretched across an oak frame; a great floral chair set before the roaring fire in the front parlor. A maid named Apatha offered a tray of nog and cookies, and Lemon himself stood in a red vest in the middle of the grand foyer, sealing Lindie's father's fate with a handshake: Eben would come home once he'd graduated to be Lemon's personal accountant, wouldn't he? Lemon had decided to move back to St. Jude for good.

But now that bit of family lore was proving itself to be not quite so true.

"I suppose Lemon believed we'd show up married and people would leave us alone. He thought St. Jude would be more accepting. But, you know, we moved in and everyone just assumed I was his maid. Your family too, Eben. Your mother was so happy to have another woman to teach how to keep up the place. And we realized it would be nearly impossible to explain to all you people all the ways that I wasn't the maid. Not to mention it would make us stick out everywhere we went—even more than Lemon already did because of his moncy."

She stopped then, and the ticking of the clock on Lindie's bedside table was a loud metronome before Apatha spoke again. "We just wanted to be alone. To enjoy each other. We'd started out together so late in life. We didn't have time to dawdle. Anyway, we didn't mind what anyone else thought, because we knew what we felt, and that was all that mattered."

It was more words strung together than Lindie had heard Apatha say in a whole year. Lindie lay there dumbstruck as she realized anew that Apatha and Lemon were secretly married.

"Does Cheryl Ann know?" Eben asked.

Apatha laughed then, truly, as though she'd never heard anything so funny in her life. "Poor thing! Doesn't have the imagination for it!"

Eben joined her, guffawing at Cheryl Ann's blindness.

"But how can you stand it?" he interjected. "She treats you terribly."

"She's just sad, Eben. Whenever my blood boils, I just think about what the poor woman's been through. How alone she was made to feel. I know Marvin was your friend, but he took her whole life away. And, I think, Lemon would want me to help her feel a little less alone."

"By washing up after her? Cooking for her? Apatha, you should have someone else doing all that."

"It's my house. If I didn't do things my way, she'd do them hers. And you know I couldn't abide that."

Eben sighed. Apatha was not to be convinced of anything. "Oh, poor June," he muttered then, and Lindie realized what June's marriage really meant. Clyde was wrong—June would inherit nothing when Lemon died, because Apatha would. For the first time, Lindie had incontrovertible proof that June was being married off in vain.

"But you know, Eben," Apatha said, "it's up to June whether she marries Arthur. I've told her more than once that Lemon will make sure to take care of her if she says no." Lindie wondered why June had never mentioned this offer to her.

Eben was quiet for a bit, mulling it all over.

"But why take them in, Apatha? These are your last years with Lemon. You certainly don't owe Cheryl Ann a thing."

"They're family."

"Not by blood. Mae was Marvin's aunt. And neither Mae nor Marvin is on this earth anymore."

"Mae was Lemon's love, so I love her too." Apatha's voice was just this side of impatient. "Cheryl Ann can't help what her husband did. She needed family, and I'll be that for her, even if she doesn't know that's what I'm being."

"So be it," Eben said, although Lindie could hear his aggravation; the secret lady of the house had been willingly taking Cheryl Ann's abuse out of the kindness of her heart. Lindie could tick off hundreds of times she'd heard Cheryl Ann speak sharply to Apatha, ordering her to bring the lemonade immediately, chastising her for overcooking the roast. Lindie's face grew hot as she realized she'd been an accomplice. They all had.

"This was delicious," Apatha said. Lindie heard the gentle tap of the mug upon the tabletop. She thought Apatha would say her good night, but instead she said, "All this business with Clyde—none of it has to do with Lorraine?"

Lindie didn't expect to hear her mother's name in the air, and strained to hear Eben's soft response. "Of course not, Apatha."

"He was wrong to pursue her, Eben, you and I both know that. But we also know she'd have left you anyway. No, I'm sorry, but it must be said. She was miserable, Eben, and it's no one's fault, but it's not Clyde's either."

"It's not about that," Eben said sharply. Lindie marveled at this revelation. Had Clyde loved her mother? Had her mother loved him back?

"Good," Apatha said. "Because I'm not interested in revenge plots." Her voice carried an indulgence that warmed Lindie's heart. She heard the old woman's chair squeak across the floor as she pushed herself back from the table. "And I'm not one to pick a fight"—her voice turned steely—"but I don't like what Clyde's done any more than you do, and I agree, he should be stopped. I suppose if he thinks he can steal our land from right under our noses, he's capable of worse. Do what you think is necessary. Whatever money you need. But . . ."

"You don't want Lemon's name anywhere near it."

"He's going to be gone soon, Eben." And the way Apatha's voice turned soft, Lindie knew she meant Lem, not Clyde. She loved that man dearly; Lindie could hear it. How had they mistaken love for loyalty all these years? "I don't want him mixed up in ugliness."

Lindie heard Eben rise. "Your secret's safe," he said, although she wondered if even he could keep a secret like this. Could Lindie? For it was hers now too.

Apatha stepped out onto the porch. Lindie tiptoed to the window. It was a dark night, the moon just a crescent of a crescent. Could she make out Apatha heading back across the lawn? Was that movement up by June's window? Was that June Lindie saw, creeping down the column she herself had clambered up so many times?

Lindie couldn't know for sure. She didn't know much of anything, it seemed.

CHAPTER THIRTY-NINE

———

T HE TWO OAKS DOORBELL RANG BRIGHT AND EARLY THE
next day. June had been up since yesterday; she wondered if staying up so many nights in a row had turned her nocturnal for good.
She saw the Olds pull up in front of the house, then watched Thomas
rush out of the car to open the back door, as if neither of the passengers'
hands worked. What she felt was irritated; why couldn't everyone just
leave her alone? It was a selfish thought, she knew, especially as the man
and woman disappeared from view as they came onto the porch. She
withdrew her gaze, casting her eyes accidentally over Lindie's house, and
guilt swirled inside her.

This was what she'd meant by "too fast." She didn't like who she
became when people wanted her to make decisions. She felt skittish. She
felt mean. The doorbell rang, and she tiptoed down the upstairs hallway, making her way to just above the servant stairs. She was relieved
to see no sign of her mother or Apatha, who frowned upon eavesdropping. She heard Apatha open the front door, then the sound of Jack's
low greeting and Diane's enthusiastic "Well hello there!" June hated this
jealousy, hated wondering if she looked right, hated that she ached to see
him, hated knowing that seeing him with another woman, here in her
home, would be a horror.

"You sure you have the right house?" Apatha said in her dry, usual
tone, which made even June smile; Apatha wasn't impressed that famous movie stars were standing at the front door.

They came in then, and June could hear them better. Jack was Mr.
Salesman; it turned her stomach to hear him using that bombastic voice,
already pitching when only one step inside. Apparently he'd had a harebrained idea and needed to talk to the household, could they trouble the
powers that be for just a moment? At Idlewyld, he'd cooed like a warm
ember, a purring kitten, a rushing brook, but there was none of that

softness here. Apatha asked them to wait in the front parlor, and June heard her make her way up the main staircase.

June leaned her head back into the hall and listened. Cheryl Ann was waiting in the upstairs hall; she squealed in delight when Apatha told her who'd arrived. Then she groaned in horror—"I don't have my face on!"—and June heard the door slam to what Cheryl Ann insisted on calling her boudoir, really just the master bedroom, which she'd taken over when she decided Lemon needed to be moved to the back bedroom near Apatha's servant quarters.

Then June heard Apatha making her way back to the servant stairs, but the only way not to get caught was to go downstairs herself, and June couldn't face Jack. She cringed when Apatha spotted her.

But all Apatha said was "What do you suppose they drink in the morning? Sanka?"

"I don't think they came to drink anything," June whispered, as Apatha headed past her and down the stairs.

"Stop hiding up there," Apatha replied sharply. "They sit on the toilet, same as you and me." And then she was gone, into the kitchen.

But of course June wasn't hiding because they were famous. She was hiding because Jack was here, in June's home, in the place she knew inside and out in detestable and precious ways—the squeak of the branch against the front parlor window, the groan of the pipes as the water turned warm. By the end of this month, Jack would know nearly every detail of June's whole world, and she would know nothing of his. She could imagine that some girls would love that mystery, but it set her on edge. Not to mention the fact that he'd brought his known lover into her home. She heard Diane say something just then—not the words themselves, but the curl of them in the air—and that was, apparently, enough to send her rushing down the stairs, into the foyer and into the parlor, dreading the sight of Jack and Diane together.

"Good morning to you!" Jack boomed at the sight of her. June lost her tongue. She'd forgotten how gorgeous Diane was, and Jack's beauty, angry as she was at him, was undeniable.

Diane smiled her plastic smile. June wondered if she knew. But there was no chance to discover more because just then Cheryl Ann burst down the stairs, flapping her hands with shock and delight, filling both parlors with her feigned deference, fawning over Jack, fanning herself, kissing Diane's cheek with her sweaty lips. The small spit of skin between Diane's eyes wrinkled in concern. Then came Apatha with a tray of biscuits that they all knew none of them would touch.

"We want to host a party," Jack announced.

Diane leaned one shoulder into her smile. "We'd like to do it here."

"On Saturday, I'm afraid." Mr. Salesman smiled in false concern, and June resisted the urge to kick him in the shin.

Cheryl Ann clapped her hands together and wheezed. It was like a vaudeville act.

Before Apatha could open her mouth to object, Jack said, "I'll pay for everything." Diane shot him a significant look, and he corrected himself. "We'll pay. You won't lift a finger."

Diane clearly felt he was taking the wrong tack. "You see, we want to show St. Jude how much we appreciate everything you've done to welcome us. And we can't think of a better place to hold the celebration. Why not choose the most magnificent building in town?"

Cheryl Ann looked as if she might explode.

"And since we'll be wrapping up the shoot next Thursday," Jack added, "we'll be going back to Los Angeles by the holiday weekend." June felt his eyes skim over her as he mentioned leaving. Then he held out his hands as if he'd done a magic trick. "I'm afraid the only option is to have the festivities in a few short days."

One look at Apatha told June the old woman believed there were, in fact, many other options. But Apatha listened patiently as Jack and Diane detailed their plans of musical acts and tents for the yards. It seemed a banquet caterer had already been contacted, and waitstaff would be brought in from elsewhere.

Jack fingered his gray felt hat. It was hard not to notice the way Diane's gaze drank him in and swatted him away at the same time. June felt sick at the thought of a party here, hosted by them. She could hardly believe that this very man, right here in this room, had knelt before her only three days ago and told her he wanted her. She had said as good as no, and it had been the right choice—had it not?—because here he was with another woman. How quickly he had moved on.

"It's settled then," Cheryl Ann said, without consulting Apatha or

June on the matter, and there were handshakes all around, which June made sure to avoid by picking up a biscuit. Artie, she thought (and the thought was like a breath of fresh air), Artie is uncomplicated and he would never do this to me, and the idea warmed her as she watched Apatha let them out.

ON SET BY NINE, Jack winked at Lindie. He was still in his street clothes. "I made her jealous." He cocked his head and pulled a cigarette from behind his ear. "That should do the trick."

CHAPTER FORTY

———

A S SOON AS THE *ST. JUDE CALLER* ANNOUNCED THE PARTY
the next morning—YOUR INVITATION, the headline read in
scripted letters, TO THE NIGHT OF A THOUSAND STARS—it
was the talk of the town. The St. Judians had only three days to dust
off their proverbial ball gowns (none of them had actual ones), polish
their shoes, and set their hair. No surprise that the movie stars who'd
transformed their humble town into a Hollywood set had been able to
convince crusty, crazy old Lemon Gray Neely to open his doors.

That morning, Jack had a cleaning crew up from Columbus. If
Lindie hadn't been P.A.'ing, she'd have volunteered herself, for the
chance to see June. When they wrapped for the day, she raced home,
eager to glimpse what was reportedly a grand operation in the last bit of
waning light—gardeners, a phalanx of maids, and a dozen men pitching
a tent the size of the gymnasium in the side yard. Cheryl Ann was pacing the property like an officer would his fort, Two Oaks lit up behind
her. Lindie leaned back on her front porch, hands behind her head, and
beamed her best smile; there was no law against sitting out, enjoying a
beautiful evening.

Did June see Lindie? Did she watch her from her window? What was
she thinking and feeling in there, about Jack, about the party? Had Jack
successfully made her jealous? What would making her jealous actually
accomplish? And was it just Lindie's imagination, or was her Schwinn
parked in a slightly different spot—front wheel askew—from where
she'd left it the day before? Could it be that June was sneaking out to
Idlewyld—or elsewhere—alone? These questions were Lindie's torment
and reality. Despite all this turmoil, she could admit that, in one respect, June's distance was good: it made the secret of Apatha's marriage
to Uncle Lem easy to keep.

ON FRIDAY, they erected a second big tent, this one in the backyard. Lemon was spotted on his porch that afternoon, taking a lemonade in his wheelchair, and those who saw him agreed that he didn't look quite as close to death as they'd imagined him to be. That night, after another long day of shooting, Lindie watched June's window from her own, listening to an owl's lonely call from one of the branches somewhere on the Two Oaks lawn, until her eyelids cried to be given sleep.

She awoke Saturday at dawn to the clattering arrival of the trucks with the flowers, tables, and food. A crowd had already gathered to watch the preparations. The St. Judians were awed to witness this long-dormant home finally waking up, whipped into shape like something touched by the wand of Cinderella's fairy godmother.

But on set that morning, the mood was decidedly less jovial. There were only five budgeted days left; they'd have to breeze through every single scene in order to finish shooting in the time allotted. Nervous they wouldn't get back to Los Angeles by the holiday weekend, most of the crew blamed Diane. It was no secret, by now, that she couldn't memorize her way out of a paper bag. That wouldn't have really mattered as long as she'd been able to cry on command, or seduce the camera with a sultry gaze. Plus she wasn't especially friendly, and never said "thank you," or laughed at any of her (numerous) gaffes. Gone was any memory that the shoot had been delayed because they'd lost the original canal location; now the story had it all falling on Diane's shoulders. Unless she made serious changes, no one would want to work with her again, or at least that's what Ricky said.

They broke early for the party, which thrilled no one. Up until that week, Lindie hadn't heard one bad word about Jack. But by the time the director yelled the day's "Cut," she'd heard more than a few grumbles about Jack being a show-off, and the lunacy of throwing a party when there was so much work at hand, and that now that Jack was surely back in Diane's bed he cared more about getting laid than getting paid. Lindie wondered if he'd miscalculated. Whom was he trying to win over with this grand gesture? Quiet, private June? Lindie wasn't entirely convinced this would do it. But then, if he really was in Diane's bed again, maybe he didn't care about winning June at all.

At five, the town and crew slipped into their houses to gussy up. Lindie took a proper bath, scrubbing all the important bits, although she knew from experience that the soles of her feet would remain a permanent black. Back in her small bedroom, the heat bore down from the eaves, scalding the top of her head. She heard the first neighbors arrive. A small orchestra struck up a Strauss waltz from underneath the great white tent. Parched and exhausted, she stood before her closet and realized, with a growing sense of doom, that she'd outgrown nearly everything in it. But that wasn't really it, was it? Not entirely. Because even if she had a dozen dresses in her size, the prettiest, most stylish dresses available, they'd still be wrong. Most of the time, Lindie could get by in dungarees, but tonight's event was highlighting something she already knew but had been afraid to look straight in the eye: she couldn't get away with her current wardrobe much longer.

All the anger and disappointment she'd been carrying around seemed to rush into her at once: June's meanness, and June's wedding, and Apatha's secret, and the movie almost being over, and even, yes, having no mother with whom to talk about any of these things, and she looked down at her strange body and wept. She threw herself onto her bed and let the sobs overtake her.

On the bed, Lindie reasoned with herself—she could surely find some dress that would fit the bill. But as soon as she sat up, she was encircled again by doubt and fear. Even if she had a dress, could she bring herself to put it on? What was wrong with her? Because if she couldn't wear a dress, she couldn't go to the party of the century, which was happening just below her window. She was considering just flinging herself out that window once and for all, when she heard a knock.

She sat up and sniffed, wiping at her eyes. "Come in."

Eben opened the door. He held up a boy's suit on a hanger. The outfit was old-fashioned, with knickers instead of trousers, sewn from a shadowy velvet no boy would have worn anymore. "Uncle Lem had it made for me when I was about your age." He hung it on the doorknob.

Lindie cleared the gunk from her throat. "I should wear a dress."

"You should wear what feels right."

TWENTY MINUTES LATER, they stood in the Two Oaks foyer, side by side. Lindie's fingers fiddled at the fine gray-brown fabric on her thighs. The collar was tight around her neck, but not uncomfortable. She'd opted to go without a tie, and made sure to brush her ear-length hair, hoping that, if she was clean, no one would make fun of her for dressing like a boy. She wore a pair of her mother's shoes her father had dug up, simple, nondescript leather flats that most girls her age wouldn't have been caught dead in, but which she already treasured.

Around her whirled the party of her dreams—bow-tied waiters and paid musicians, St. Judians unrecognizable in their fancy getups, glasses of real champagne, tea cakes, tiny little sandwiches on tiny little plates. Every door, save the one leading into the kitchen, stood open. There was a bar in one corner of the living room. A feast of candied ham and cookies and cut-up pineapple, of meringues and mint patties and plenty of other foreign delicacies, was spread across the dining table. Lemon's office-cum-bedroom had been transformed into a sitting room for the oldest St. Judians, but people of all ages mingled across the front and back parlors, climbing the grand staircase and then ascending to the third floor, where she could make out Count Basie's orchestra swelling on the record player in the long-forgotten ballroom. Children darted in from the side yard. Football players snuck sips of liquor when they thought no one was looking. The movie people arrived: Ricky and Sam wore bow ties; the makeup girls had done themselves up to look like stars. Lindie admired the physics of the girdle as Cheryl Ann glided across the parlors toward Uncle Lem, who was propped up on the yellow tufted couch. Dressed in a brown cotton dress, Apatha stood at his shoulder, leaning down to whisper the names of the mayor and the police chief. Lindie felt Apatha's eyes pull at her. Lindie looked away, afraid the secret would be written all over her face.

But June—where was June? Where, for that matter, was Jack? Diane? Artie? Clyde? A new wave of guests arrived through the front door, and the crowd pushed Lindie and Eben apart. Eben rode the wave farther into the back parlor, where Fred Ripvogle and Alan Shields clapped him on the shoulder and ordered a round of whiskey. Lindie was drawn toward the spine of the building, that intricately carved staircase she'd once thought of as hers. She ran her hand along the smooth banister and decided to simply knock on June's door. She'd apologize. She couldn't stand this silence.

The Two Oaks stairway had been built for a party like this. Plaster garlands adorned the top bit of the ceiling, mirroring the wreaths that decorated the waxed, quarter-hewn oak baseboard railings. Lindie joined the stream of traffic to the second floor, avoiding jabbing elbows and bare heels and short strides. On the eighth step, she passed Gretchen Beck and Ginny Sherman. They snickered as they traveled past, but it didn't occur to Lindie that she was the object of their derision until she was nearly on the landing.

But those stupid girls didn't matter. Not as she forged her way up through the tightly packed stairs, darting under arms and around canes. Evening light streamed in through the stained-glass fleurs-de-lis. She was about to make things right with June. And then she sensed it, above her—an ever-so-slight parting of the crowd. She lifted her eyes to the top of the stairs.

June. June looking as Lindie had never seen her before, but somehow distilled to her most essential self, head held proudly but without pretension, hands folded neatly at her front. Her hair was pinned up in an old-fashioned chignon. Her dress was virginal white cotton; simple, unadorned. Cheryl Ann had probably picked something much flashier and would be steamed. But June had the right instincts. She looked like something out of a storybook, and she was coming right toward Lindie.

But then, she was coming down toward everyone, and Lindie was not the only one to notice her. The stairway leading down into the foyer was like a stage, and June its ingenue. People just entering the foyer hushed to watch her descend. Those as far away as the back parlor quieted their conversations to eye her. The crowd on the stairs parted ever so slightly; as she passed, Lindie found herself tongue-tied, unable to say June's name or draw her attention. Instead, Lindie stepped out of June's line of sight and watched everyone watch June—Ricky and Sam, the makeup girls, Mr. and Mrs. Freewalt and their four little Freewalts, and, there, at the far end of the foyer, Diane DeSoto and Clyde Danvers.

As soon as June's foot touched the ground floor, the curtains swayed shut across the moment. The St. Judians went back to their conversations, to chasing after their hooligan sons, to finding refills of their gimlets. June turned toward the side door and out onto the side lawn, where the orchestra was now playing standards from the war. Lindie changed tacks, deciding to head back down the stairs to follow June, but, without the collective hush of June's presence, the river had turned back into sludge. Lindie found herself caught behind old Mr. and Mrs. Fishpaw; she had a bad knee, he took each stair with two careful feet, supporting her.

Diane's eyes followed June; once the girl was out of sight, Diane whipped back to Clyde, a sly smile raking her lips. He leaned into her and whispered something that produced from her a cool, wicked laugh. Her eyes flicked up to catch Lindie watching. Diane curled her finger in a gesture of enticement. Lindie didn't much want to see Clyde, but, by the time she reached Diane, he had disappeared into the crowd.

"What a handsome little monkey you are," Diane said, holding Lindie by one hand and insisting she twirl with the other. It didn't sound like a compliment.

"It was my father's."

"I'm going to take you shopping," Diane said. "Find you some proper clothes, little beast." It wasn't the first time she'd promised this, and Lindie thanked her politely, as she always did, without believing it meant anything real.

Then the crowd parted for the second time, this time at the front door, and a collective cheer went up, and Diane turned her swan-like neck toward the entry, and Lindie could tell, from the way her smile snaked its way across her lips, that Jack Montgomery had finally arrived.

CHAPTER FORTY-ONE

—

OUTSIDE, THE AIR WAS SWEET AND THE LIGHT WAS FAD-
ing. Crowded as it was inside Two Oaks, most of the St. Judians could be found seated at tables under the vast tent, or
dancing to a crooner who'd adopted all the best vocal tricks of Frank
Sinatra and Dean Martin. Lindie wended her way through the great
herd, eyes darting for a glimpse of June's ear, for her delicate hand or the
milky nape of her neck, but June had disappeared into thin air.

Lindie made her way slowly, steadily, around the tent at the side yard
and into the back, where a smaller tent had been pitched. She downed a
root beer poured by one of the imported soda jerks.

"What are you wearing?"

Lindie turned to find horrible Darlene Kipp and her henchmen,
Ginny Sherman and Gretchen Beck, giggling a few feet away.

"Is it made from drapes?" Gretchen added before Lindie could summon a witty retort.

"If you want my opinion, a girl shouldn't come to a party without
a party dress." Darlene's voice was all Miss Priss to match her golden
curls. Lindie called up the delicious memory of Ricky's pin stabbing her
ankle.

"Maybe she's not a girl." Ginny smirked coyly at Darlene.

Gretchen shrieked. She covered her mouth with her hand.

"Maybe she's finally grown a little man," Darlene whispered lustily.

"Well, hello there, ladies." They all looked up to discover Jack
Montgomery's arm falling familiarly across Lindie's shoulder. Darlene, Ginny, and Gretchen all gaped, but he played it cool. "Nice night
for it."

"Yessir," they mustered in unison.

"Linda Sue." Jack cut them off. "You're the only one I can trust."

He glanced at the other girls then, as if they were an afterthought. Furrowed his movie star brow. Deepened his voice to a grave bass note. "You mind giving us a minute? It's a private matter."

They blathered apologies, tripping over themselves as they kowtowed toward the house. Jack waited until they were gone, then winked.

"What is it?" Lindie asked.

"Top-secret message," he replied gravely.

Lindie leaned in to receive it.

Coyly, he put his hand up to shield the confidence, but all he said was: "Don't let the bastards get you down." His eyes twinkled as he picked up a whiskey sour from the bar. And then Diane found him.

"Darling," she said, as though Lindie wasn't there, "I'd love another vodka tonic." She held up her empty glass and shook it in his face. For a fleeting moment, she looked messy, unhinged. Then she straightened herself and narrowed her eyes.

Lindie watched a muscle in Jack's jaw clench, then release. He took the glass from Diane's hand, careful not to touch her, and headed for the back porch and into the house.

Diane watched him go, then swayed toward Lindie. "You know what I'd like to do?" She didn't wait for Lindie's reply. "I'd like to take you on a shopping trip, get you some proper clothes."

Apparently Diane had no idea she'd just mentioned this. How many drinks had she had? The party was only an hour old.

She reached out and brushed Lindie's cheek. "You are too, too pretty to waste your life in pants."

"Yes, ma'am," Lindie said, pretending to believe her.

It wasn't yet dark but the lanterns had been lit. The evening took on a boozy, raucous quality. Out on the side lawn, the band played "Cheek to Cheek," "I've Got a Crush on You," and then "As Time Goes By," which everyone recognized from *Casablanca*. Those who'd made it through the war clung together on the dance floor. Diane signed autographs; Lindie tried to slip away, but Diane kept her close. The party dazzled on as they awaited Jack's return.

But instead they heard a "Miss DeSoto?" and turned to find Cheryl Ann charging toward them. She waved a drink in the air. Her hair had come unpinned and she was slick with sweat, breath rasping as she pushed through the crowd.

Diane couldn't hide her disdain. Her lip curled and she tried to edge away, but everyone was watching and she couldn't exactly brush off her hostess. "Jack told me to bring you your martini!" Cheryl Ann explained, as Artie Danvers walked by balancing two drinks. Lindie slipped behind him, into the party, unnoticed.

Soon she found herself in the side yard. June was waiting at the edge of the dance floor under the vast white canopy. The orchestra was playing "It Had to Be You." June was turned away from Artie, and Lindie, swaying ever so slightly, watching a handful of married couples twirl together. Artie sidled up beside her and offered the drink. She turned to him with a wide, friendly smile, and Lindie ducked behind one of the tent poles so June wouldn't see her. She had to admit they looked genuinely happy as they talked and sipped. She thought again of Artie's letter; what had read, at first, like cowardice, now seemed as though it might have been the brave truth. What if he was a truly honorable man, the kind who'd stay away from the woman he loved in order to give her a choice? Maybe the choice, for June, wasn't simply between Jack or Artie; maybe it was based on a much more complex calculus than even Lindie could understand.

The orchestra began "I Get a Kick out of You." Artie tipped his head toward the dance floor. A blush brushed June's cheeks. He offered to take her drink, and she acquiesced. He set it down on the nearest table and held out his hand. She looked at it, then him, resting her palm on his and letting him lead her onto the dance floor. Lindie watched them swirl out into the music together, his right hand light against her lower back, his left hand gripping hers. They eyed each other. He looked grateful and pleased, and she looked as elegant as ever.

When the song finished, a bright sound tinkled across the tent: silverware rapping against crystal. It grew louder and more definitive as it became clear that Cheryl Ann, Jack, and Diane had gathered below the porte cochere, that damn porte cochere that Lindie had spent the past three years scrambling up.

Diane beamed at the crowd as it pressed in around them, appreciative silence falling over everyone. A flashbulb lit up the night. "On be-half of the cast and crew of *Erie Canal,*" she said, "Jack and I want to say thank you." The crowd clapped and murmured gleefully. Diane tilted her head like a queen might, overseeing her peasants.

Jack raised his glass too. "You've been the best hosts us thugs from the West Coast could hope for. We sure are going to miss you." Diane interrupted him then, apparently not yet done with her speech. He frowned, peeved.

As Diane interjected her thoughts about the perfect weather and the true meaning of hospitality, Lindie's attention was pulled toward the front of the house, from which two men had just emerged. A flash of silver at one of their waists drew her eye. Curious, she edged out of the crowd. By the time Lindie made it to the porch, the men had walked around the far side of it, toward the kitchen. She followed, dashing across the front of the house and then leaning into the rhododendron bush to hear better.

It was Uncle Clyde; the torchlight had caught the silver gun at his waist. The other man was Fred Ripvogle, and, though Lindie couldn't hear what that man was saying, she could see he was trying to calm Clyde down.

But Clyde was steamed. His voice carried across the night wind. "That's what I'm trying to tell you, old man. You go back into that office and you fight for the bid. 'No' isn't good enough. I thought you had this locked down."

Ripvogle was crisp and efficient in his long suit, and Lindie could tell that he wished to be anywhere but there. But his back was turned to Lindie, so she couldn't hear his response.

Clyde laughed hard at whatever Ripvogle said; it was clear he'd been drinking. He looked all around them then, to make sure no one was lis-tening; Lindie pressed herself between the bush and the house. Through the leaves, she watched Clyde lean toward Ripvogle, one hand shielding his mouth. "I shouldn't be telling you this, old man, but as soon as you-know-who dies, and this house is mine, well, let's just say I've got plans." Ripvogle didn't seem the slightest bit interested in hearing what these plans were, but Clyde plowed right through. "We both know a house like this is worthless, taking up all this space. Who wants to live like this anymore? We're talking three acres, right in the heart of a perfect little town on its way up in the world. I say, let's tear it down and build modern houses, modern amenities. With you winning the bid on the interstate—"

"I told you, Clyde," Ripvogle said, trying to extract himself, "none of that is going to happen."

But Clyde came around Ripvogle, blocking him. "What the hell is wrong with you? If you know what's good for you, you'll walk right into the governor's office and tell him you're back in."

Ripvogle was a gentleman, Lindie could see, but Clyde had tested him. "You're the big man, aren't you, Clyde. Full of ideas. But seems to me you've got no way to carry them out. Nice dream to think of turning this place into small lots, but how will you do it? Who holds the deed after he goes? How will you get it from them? You're small town, Clyde. I should have known better than to waste my time with small town."

Then Ripvogle stormed right past Clyde, and right past Lindie, down across the wide front lawn, Clyde nipping at his heels the whole way.

CHAPTER FORTY-TWO

———

INDIE TREMBLED BEHIND THE RHODODENDRON BUSH. SHE laid her hand against Two Oaks's cool brick and tried to keep from crying. It seemed so obvious now: all along, Uncle Clyde had had nothing but money on his mind. Thank goodness Apatha was Lemon's bride; Lindie told herself there'd be no way he could get at Two Oaks, because Apatha wouldn't allow it.

From the other side of the house came a great clattering of crystal against crystal, and the sound of the whole town hurrahing, then the orchestra striking up "So Long, It's Been Good to Know You."

Lindie made her way around the front of the house, pulling leaves from her hair. Under the tent, Diane was wearing a broad, genuine smile in Jack's arms; a smattering of applause dusted over them. Diane gazed up at Jack adoringly, but his face was a placid mask. Lindie wondered why Diane would want to hold so tightly to a man who didn't seem to like her very much.

"I'm so sorry."

Lindie turned to find June standing right beside her.

"I shouldn't have butted in," Lindie blurted, tears already springing to her eyes. She was flooded with forgiveness, and ready to forget June's cruelty.

But June shook her head. "Those were nasty things I said to you. I don't know what's come over me. Sometimes I feel as if I've become a monster, this wild, selfish beast who wants to eat everything in sight." Her hands twisted against each other. Lindie laid her own hand on them to calm June down.

"It's as though there are two parts of me," June explained, searching Lindie's eyes for an answer. "The part that wants to do what I'm supposed to—the part that wants to be a mother and have a hope chest and live here forever. And then there's this other, beastly part of me that I didn't even know was there before. It doesn't care what anyone thinks. It just wants to"—she paused, searching for a word—"eat Jack up." She turned red, realizing what she'd said. "Not like that."

"Sometimes like that," Lindie offered, then giggled, wondering if she'd gone too far.

June was the color of a beet, but a smile slunk across her lips. Lindie felt a wave of relief.

Cheryl Ann waved frantically from the side door, calling June's name. June sighed and tipped her head toward the house. "I'll find you?"

"Sure."

June's hand cupped Lindie's elbow and squeezed, and then she walked to meet her mother.

Lindie let the insults drift away, up into the purple night. The nearly quartered moon was finally in the right spot; the stars were scattered around it like thousands of its children. It was beautiful, this party, all the people she'd grown up with dressed as though they were part of a movie themselves, everyone laughing and dancing, Two Oaks spangled like a lady too. Torches twinkled. Lindie drifted into the backyard, then up the back porch and into the house, picking up bits of conversation and amusement, watching people flirt and compliment.

NEARLY AN HOUR LATER, belly full, head a bit fuzzy from some stolen gin, Lindie found herself back out on the side lawn. Children were being carried home, the middle-aged bidding their good-byes. The musicians were taking their final break, and she could hear the tinny sound of the record player playing Count Basie from the ballroom. She had just decided to fight her way back inside and up the humid staircase when her arm was suddenly clenched from behind, the rest of her held firmly in place by a hand that clamped her shoulder. Her body tensed as she strained to see who was holding her.

"Where's your fucking father?" Clyde's whiskey-stained fury sprayed her ear.

"Ouch," she cried, prying herself away from the talons embedded in her arm. Clyde's eyes were wild. Lindie cast around for help, but everyone was too drunk and distracted to notice his hands on her.

"You scared?" he growled.

"Uncle Clyde," she said, trying to win him with reason, "what's the matter?"

"You should be scared. No one crosses me and gets away with it." And with that last, spitting sentence, he let her go. Lindie ran across the lawn and into her house, mind blazing with his threat. Even in her fuzzy state, she understood that the conversation she'd overheard between Ripvogle and Clyde had something to do with her father's "research" about Clyde's claim to Lemon's land. She had never seen Clyde like that, never felt frightened of him, or felt how her fright might fuel him.

The house lay quiet. She could hear the muffled party through the walls. Her heart was a bass drum. Her eyes stung. She tore through the dark rooms, begging for her father, but he was nowhere to be found. Clyde was right—she was scared. She changed into dungarees quick as she could and tried to think of a good place to spend the night. Idlewyld was the first that came to mind.

She was out in the garage, pushing the Schwinn toward the alleyway, when she heard the man's voice. She ducked back into the darkness. The voice was coming from the window that led onto the alley, and she edged her way against it, grabbing a hammer from Eben's tool bench as she went. She flattened herself against the inside wall.

Whoever it was was standing just out there, where the garage met a tangle of thornbushes.

"But don't you see," he was saying, "it's all for you. All the booze and the music, every dance, every laugh, I put it here for you. I wanted you to see it could be like this. We could have one of these every single day."

"And if I don't want this every single day?"

"We can live in a shack by the ocean for all I care. All I want is you."

It was them, of course: Jack and June.

June hesitated. "I do want to be with you."

"Oh, June." His voice opened with desire.

"But maybe it doesn't matter what I want. What we want. It's selfish to only do what one wants."

"So call us selfish then."

Lindie heard him kiss her. A small moan marinated in June's throat. The sound of that quiet glory made Lindie warm and wet.

"But I love them. Even, yes, Artie. Not anything like how I love you but—"

"You love me?"

June sighed. "And my mother. And even St. Jude, though I know you can't imagine it. This is home. It's too much to think of just walking away."

"If you love St. Jude so damn much, I'll build you a replica on the Santa Monica Pier." He was only kidding, but Lindie wondered if he was playing his part right. June's concerns were not to be taken lightly. A breeze rustled in through a crack in the wall, and she crouched down to find the chink. It offered her a partial view, dim in the light thrown off the back porch. Jack was pressed against June, her back flat against the garage on the other side of the alleyway. Her dress was halfway up her leg.

"But there's a perfectly lovely St. Jude right here." June had her hand against Jack's chest to keep him from burying his face in her neck.

"We can't stay here."

"But this is my home."

"June, June." He stepped back from her then, and took her face in his hands. "Do you want to bring them along? We'll bring them along." He kissed one of June's cheeks. "Your mother." He kissed the other one. "And that funny old man from the pharmacy." He bent his face to her neck and kissed her there. "And the boys who set off firecrackers in the mailboxes—"

"Don't tease. They're counting on me."

"We'll find a way." He rubbed her cheek. "Every promise is made to be broken."

She was silent then. Lindie thought June might weep, but instead she watched her look at Jack, really look at him. And then June's arms found their way around his neck, and her lips drew up to his. Lindie sighed at the kiss, at the sound of it, at the length of it, at the way June's breasts pressed up against Jack, and how he leaned into her with something like possession. He drew June's arms up above her head, pinning her wrists onto the wall. He kissed her deeply again, as if drinking from a well.

Then he drew June's skirt up and up and up. He gripped both her wrists together with one hand, passing his other one from her shoulder, down to her breast, then gently over her stomach and into the waistband of her underwear. June's eyes popped open, but he kissed her again, and soon any alarm June might have experienced was replaced with a dazzle of ecstasy. Lindie felt it too, like a bolt of lightning crackling through the wall that separated them. She placed her hands against it to catch her breath, but her eyes never left the sight of June and Jack together.

June writhed against Jack's fingers, head tipped back. He let her arms go, supporting her weight as she collapsed into him. Every bit of her seemed to have focused and melted into that one small spot between her legs, where Jack was stroking her.

June's breath grew rapid. Her eyes fluttered. She moaned, and then, at once, cried out. Jack pressed his hand over her mouth; she licked and bit it until she had quieted.

Afterward, she giggled. "On second thought, let's not bring my mother." Jack laughed too, then leaned forward to extinguish the laugh on her flushed cheek.

LATER, MUCH LATER, June found Lindie sitting on Lindie's porch. Eben was nowhere in sight, so Lindie'd dared him home by lighting a cigarette. It was long past midnight. The party was over, but St. Jude was resisting sleep like a reluctant child.

"You looked happy dancing with Artie," Lindie said, because she couldn't say, "You looked happy behind the garage with Jack." The night had only complicated matters, when all she'd wanted was to have them smoothed out.

But at least she'd made up with June. They sat together on the top step, and Lindie leaned her head on June's shoulder. They watched the orchestra pack their instruments, and the waiters box the glasses and fold the linens. In the morning the trucks would come to drive everything back to Columbus. The girls' hands looped around their knees. They were nearly invisible in the darkness.

Sometime after that, Diane DeSoto came tearing out from behind the far side of Two Oaks. Her heels were hooked on her fingertips. The blond helmet of her hair attracted the moonlight. June grabbed Lindie's wrist and pulled her onto the porch. They scrambled behind the safety of the porch's wall, where they could peek out at the street but stay hidden.

They were rewarded when Diane stopped only feet away, dropping her shoes onto the sidewalk and shuffling them on. She was sniffling, shivering, and a low hum was emanating from her that set Lindie's teeth on edge. Then, somehow, he was there too, behind her. June shivered at the sight of him—Jack, grabbing Diane by the wrist and drawing her to him in the same forceful gesture Lindie had seen on set that day early in the shoot, when they kissed in front of the camera more than a dozen times.

But the words out of Jack's mouth were not loving. His other hand clenched the base of Diane's throat. "Dare me," he snarled. "Just dare me to destroy you."

A sob seized Diane. The girls watched her break free to hobble down the sidewalk. Jack watched her too. Then, as the wind sighed through the oaks, he shook his head and went after her, as though he regretted what he had no choice in doing.

June 2015

CHAPTER FORTY-THREE

———

OME FROM ILLY'S, CASSIE WAS SURPRISED TO DISCOVER Tate and Elda seated side by side in the dining room, sifting through the three big boxes of Jack's papers. The sisters' pursed mouths were a matched set. Tate's diamond flashed an occasional beam of sunlight. Cassie leaned her head against the doorframe and watched them passing documents and pictures back and forth, laughing and nodding and mmm-hmmming in the secret language of family. She clicked off a picture before they noticed her.

"Well, hello, stranger," Elda said, tipping her reading glasses off her nose.

"We were worried," Tate added.

"We weren't that worried. Not like Nick was worried." Elda wriggled her eyebrows suggestively.

"All right, all right." Cassie's hands shushed her as she stepped into the room. "You need help? I could be a third set of eyes."

"Well of course you could," Elda said in an indulgent auntie voice, standing to clear the seat beside her of its papers.

The Vitamix started up in the kitchen—they hadn't been back five minutes and Hank was already prepping dinner. It seemed to Cassie that she and Hank had come to a détente; the milk shake had sealed it. Cassie was still unsure of whether they'd had a fight, and the orphan comment smarted a bit, but Cassie had a thick skin, and she felt for Hank, she really did. It was kind of gratifying to learn the girl was a wreck under that shiny façade.

Tate explained that they'd gone through half of Jack's personal papers and hadn't turned up a single mention of June. She'd even called Jack's biographer, author of *Jack Montgomery: A Man of Experience*, who'd interviewed Jack and Tate five years before. It was clear she adored the title, and the fact that her father had an authorized biographer, and the fact that she, herself, would someday have one too. Tate was kind of a nerd, an adorable side she never showed the public.

The biographer didn't have much to offer except that *Erie Canal* was a stepping-stone in Jack Montgomery's storied career, and was personally significant because it had fueled Jack and Diane's legendary romance. Diane had famously told the press, "If it weren't for that charming little town, I'd never have fallen for Prince Charming." Tate proudly read the quote back to them, enunciating every syllable.

"Let's not waste more time on chitchat." Elda was clearly annoyed.

"Nick's upstairs going through the papers Hank dug up on her search through the house," Tate added, "but he isn't finding much, not even in that huge stack of letters from that girl named Lindie. It was mostly a lot of 'How are things with you, how is married life, what exciting news about the baby?'" Tate said in a flat voice. Cassie could see she was pleased nothing was getting in the way of her parents' mythical love story.

"You sure you wouldn't rather go work with Nick, Cassie?" Elda asked.

"You don't want me?"

"Of course we want you. Not like Nick wants you, but . . ."

Cassie had learned it was best to let Elda's comments die. She picked a piece of paper off the top of the stack before her—it was a contract of some sort—and thumbed through it until Elda deemed her too boring to tease.

As the afternoon passed, they settled into a rhythmic symbiosis, like working with another photographer in the darkroom. Tate would lift a pile of papers from the open box, place them at the center of the wide table, and each of them would draw and discard, as though they were children playing with a giant deck of cards. No one spoke, but the smells of Hank's productivity in the next room buoyed them, as did the veggies and kombucha she brought in halfway through the afternoon. Cassie felt genuinely grateful, and Hank looked her right in the eye and smiled, which felt like something good.

They stretched, they drank espresso, they left for the bathroom but came right back. The soft summer light drifted across the dining room.

Cassie's eyes limned the brown tapestried walls and their Arcadian scenes, their goatherds and Roman ruins, and she thought of June, of what June would want her to do. The truth was, they weren't finding anything irregular at all; if her father was Jack's son, June and Jack had both done a very good job of hiding it. The possibility of the easy answer the DNA test would provide—yes or no—was starting to sound appealing, but Cassie didn't know if she could pull the plug on all this familying just yet. She liked it.

Nick poked his head in and confirmed he'd found nothing of note in the Two Oaks papers. He smiled at her, and she felt a flood of pleasure. No matter what happened, she didn't need to worry; what they shared wasn't going to disappear.

Dinner swept in precisely at seven, as though delivered by elves: amaranth and salmon and haricots verts. They slid the papers to one end of the table, and settled in at the other. There was a fantastic bottle of Barolo and then another and another. They lit tall pillars in a massive silver candelabra that Cassie had never seen polished before. Nick sat beside Cassie. She could feel his hand inches from hers along the shared sides of their plates. The tap of his foot resonated across the floorboard and up through her heel. Elda and Tate were easy on each other, talking not of Hollywood or their father but of Elda's four sons in Houston, where she spent most of the year, of their car dealerships and children and wives.

"You'll come for Thanksgiving," Elda said to Tate. "It's been too long since you came to Houston." She paused. "You and Max."

Private grief flickered over Tate's face before she hardened against it. "I loathe Thanksgiving." In the precise way she pronounced *loathe*, Cassie could tell that she was drunk.

"No one 'loathes' Thanksgiving," Elda replied, air-quoting with her fork and knife.

"I do." Hank had eaten her dinner quietly at the fringes, and now the rest of them looked at her in surprise. She wrinkled her nose. "I guess it's fun if your family isn't full of alcoholics."

Nick chuckled. "I kind of hate it too."

Elda groaned in exaggerated exasperation.

"I don't know," Nick said, "it was just my mom and me. We usually ended up ordering Chinese food."

Elda pointed her fork at Cassie. "And you?"

Cassie started laughing, knowing how her honest response would be received. "I mean, my parents died when I was eight. I'm not in love with any holiday or, as I like to call them, 'annual reminders of my orphanhood.'" She cracked a smile at Hank, who clearly appreciated her levity on the topic.

Elda's head dropped back as she cackled. "You are the saddest group of pathetic losers I have ever met!" Every one of them cracked up.

"Well, that settles it," she declared. "You're all coming to Thanksgiving this year. We'll get our hands on a copy of *Erie Canal* and watch it in the screening room. I don't want to hear one protest. Every single one of you is coming, for the turkey and the stuffing, and the pleasure of fourteen brats running around your feet and football blaring and the goddamn pumpkin pie."

Nick distributed the last bit of wine. He smiled shyly at Cassie. "That sounds lovely."

Hank started clearing.

"Let us help you," Cassie said, but Hank insisted she stay put, squeezing an arm around Cassie's shoulder. It was a quick gesture of intimacy, and Cassie could feel Tate's eyes on them, a jealous gaze that made Cassie tingle.

Once the table was cleared, Hank and Nick set to work on the dishes in the other room. Elda groaned as she stood. "Time for my beauty sleep."

Tate offered her cheek up to her sister, yawning. "I'm wiped too."

"I never knew you hated Thanksgiving."

Tate shrugged.

"'Loathe'"—Elda swayed above Tate—"has nothing to do with that horrible fight, though." Cassie could tell she smelled blood.

Tate crossed her arms. "I don't know what you're talking about."

"Oh, come off it. I was home from New York. You were, what, nine? It was the November before she—"

"I'd like to go to bed," Tate said, but she remained in her chair. Elda loomed over her.

"He comes home drunk. She's high as a kite. They get into a screaming match over who was supposed to feed you dinner. She comes at him with a crystal vase and he calls her a psychopath." Elda was clutching the back of Tate's chair. "Admit it! Admit they were horrible. Admit they were horrible to me, and, God, to you, too, honey. What was your nickname? The Tub. Who does that to a little girl?"

Tears brimmed in Tate's eyes. All Cassie could think of was how wrecked Tate had been the night before. Cassie didn't think either of them could survive that again. "It's been a long day," Cassie heard herself say. "Let's turn in."

Elda and Tate both startled at the sound of her voice. Their faces wore the same tired, resigned expression. Elda tilted her head, then sighed and flapped a good-bye before stumbling out into the foyer.

Cassie gripped the stem of her wineglass and gulped the last traces of the red. Tate leaned over the candle stumps and blew them out. The black wicks sent trails of smoke up to the ceiling.

CHAPTER FORTY-FOUR

———

THE RAIN STARTED AFTER TEN, ACCOMPANIED BY THE OC-
casional rumble of thunder. Cassie was on her bed, going through
the weekly letters June had sent her over the last four years. June
hadn't missed a week—except for when one of them was visiting the
other—and all the envelopes bore the postmark "St. Jude." Cassie re-
opened a few of them, trying not to be overwhelmed by the sadness her
grandmother's slanted script called forth. The letters were just as she
remembered: accounts of small-town life, of the garden, of the books
June had read. Cassie simply couldn't reconcile their content with Betty's supposition—or Mrs. Weaver's or Mrs. Deitz's—that June had spent
the last years of her life gallivanting around the world.

She heard a knock at the door and placed the letters aside. Nick
lifted a finger to his lips as he entered, wearing the same pajamas he'd
had on that morning, buttoned all the way up to his neck, despite the
heat. She felt herself blush; she hadn't expected him to be this forward,
especially as he shut the door behind himself. But then she saw that
he had something clasped in his right hand. He waved it at her triumphantly, but his voice lowered to a whisper. "I found something," he
declared, and he came to her on the bed and pressed the sixty-year-old
paper into her hand.

It was a letter, postmarked from Chicago, November 1955, addressed
to June Danvers. Cassie held it beside the bedside lamp as she slipped
the single piece of onionskin out of its envelope.

Dear June,

    *You said I shouldn't write about such matters. You said the past
will stay in the past. But I think that more likely to be a wish than
the truth. Please believe me when I say I've tried to forget. I know
you made me promise never to speak of it again, but no matter*

how long I live, I will never forget that horrible night, and what
you chose to give up for my freedom.

I cry for you. Every night, June. I miss you, that's part of it. But
I'm also crying for the life I made you choose. For your baby. For
the fact he'll never know the truth. You say there's no reason to ask
for forgiveness, but as long as I live, with every breath I take, I'll be
asking for it. You can burn this if you have to—I know how angry
it'll make you. But I had to tell you, June. I had to say I'm sorry.
Lindie

Thunder grumbled overhead as Cassie lifted her head from the page. "What does it mean?"

Nick's eyes were wide. He flicked at the postmark. "November 1955. That's not long after *Erie Canal*."

She sat on the bed and reread the letter, picking out phrases and wondering at their meaning. "Are there any others like this?"

He shook his head. "That's the strange part. There are dozens of letters from Lindie, starting a few months before this and lasting through the late sixties, all sent from this Chicago address. They're the kind of letters you'd write home from camp—'I saw this, I did this'—except for this one."

"This is the address I used when I wrote Lindie."

He nodded. "From the other letters it sounded like she moved there sometime in the summer of 1955."

"I wonder if she left St. Jude because of whatever she's talking about here." The thunder was rolling closer; lightning flashes heralded its cry. "What do you think they did? 'That horrible night.' Why is she crying for June's baby? What's the truth he won't know?"

Nick sat down beside her. "Maybe who his father is?"

He was much closer now. Cassie searched his eyes. "It really could have something to do with Jack."

"It could."

"Or it could just be, I don't know, girl stuff. They snuck out one night. They raided the liquor cabinet."

"'I will never forget that horrible night, and what you chose to give up for my freedom.'" Cassie found herself watching Nick's lips mouth the words. She couldn't shake the memory of the kisses they'd shared in the ballroom. So he had told Tate this attraction was purely physical; maybe that could be enough.

When he got to the end she said, "Thank you for sharing this with me."

He blushed, as though he'd finally realized they were sitting alone on her bed together.

"I won't tell Tate you're the one who found it."

He waved the offer off, but she could also sense his relief.

She cleared her throat and glanced toward the door. "And you should probably go." He looked startled, wounded, which surprised her. She elaborated. "So she doesn't catch you in here."

Lightning flashed open the darkness. A thunderbolt clapped. "I might not care if she does," he said. Lightning again. In the moment between when it flashed and the thunder rolled closer, a jolt of pleasure danced over Nick's face, as if he was seeing her for the first time. He put one hand up to Cassie's head, cradling her cheek and her ear and her skull. She could hear her own pulse whooshing, as if she was a seashell. And then they were leaning toward each other, his lips on her lips, his chest on hers. And then they were lying down, and the kissing—oh, the sweet kissing—was slow and soft, as though each of them had been made just for it.

What came next was easy and fun. Their bodies were warm against each other as they pulled off their clothing—her shirt, his pants—and they laughed and whispered as they grew fearless. Then she could see all of him. Lightning flashed. Thunder growled. He lifted himself above her. He looked down over the wash of her nakedness as if she was a wonder. He touched the skin of her arms and thighs and belly, his eyes drowsing hungrily as if he'd never felt anything so soft. And when he was inside her, a part of herself relaxed, a part she hadn't even known she'd been tensing.

Their clothes tangled on the floor and their limbs tangled in the bed. Cassie let herself laugh. She let herself kiss and laugh and hold him. She let herself be held.

CHAPTER FORTY-FIVE

————

THAT NIGHT, FOR THE FIRST TIME IN MONTHS, CASSIE SLEPT without dreams. Two Oaks didn't bother her; even if it had tried, she wasn't interested. She was too aware of Nick breathing behind her—his hand on her hip, his tangy breath in her ear, the warm lump of his sex against her lower back. Sometime in the night, he kissed her, and then she kissed him back and soon found herself astride him, and they moved and moaned together until they were both spent, and slipped back into sleep. His pulse and breath and hunger pinned her to reality, and the dream people didn't care to argue.

Cassie woke early. She was surprised to discover herself alone. The light was thin; drizzle pattered the windows. Her head was foggy, her teeth fuzzy, her lips bruised. She put her hand over her naked chest and felt the abundance of her heart. She remembered Nick, every square inch of him. She covered her face with her hands and felt her avid breath against her palms.

Where was he? She wouldn't let disappointment or regret set in, not just yet. He'd gotten up to take a shower. He'd snuck into his bedroom to protect her from Tate. He'd decided to show Tate the letter from Lindie after all.

She wanted to stay in bed until he came back, but practicality took over as she noticed the dark circle on her ceiling. It hadn't been there the day before. She could remember, now, the gentle sound of the rain pattering on the roof all night.

The roof. She sat up.

Out in the hall, the doors to Tate's and Hank's bedrooms were wide open. She should have made a house rule against exercise before 7:00 a.m., although how were you supposed to know to even make a rule like that? She strained to hear their downward dogs above her and considered just going up. But if she did, she'd feel compelled to open the closet above her bed, and she wasn't sure she wanted to face that reality just yet.

"Oh." Hank was standing at the far end of the upper hall, frozen at the sight of Cassie. Her expression was disturbingly, uncharacteristically solemn. She looked as if she hadn't slept a wink.

"I was going to join you guys. Can't get enough of that burn." Cassie flexed her bent arm.

But Hank was gaping. Cassie wondered if she had some kind of horrible sex remnant on her face. Or what if Nick had told them a tale of regret? What if he was downstairs right now, mocking her sex face and they were all laughing?

Hank's phone chirped with a text. She offered a murderous "shit," then jetted back the way she'd come and down the servant stairs without a second glance at Cassie.

Cassie took a quick trip to the bathroom—no sex remnants to be found anywhere but where they should be, thank goodness—and headed to the stairs. She couldn't see or hear any of them, but she could feel them. Their anxiety rose from the first floor like heat shimmering off a tarred highway.

They were, all four, in the front parlor. Only Elda, settled on the corner of the yellow couch with one of June's afghans tucked around her shoulders, glanced Cassie's way.

It was darker in the parlors than usual, darker even than on a regular rainy day. Then she noticed the sheets up over those windows that didn't have curtains or shades. Even the windows in the foyer and the glass in the front door were covered, and in the round office.

Nick was huddled over his laptop with his phone tucked under his ear. His smartphone sat in front of him. Cassie cleared her throat. But he didn't so much as glance in her direction. Hank paced behind him, tapping at her phone and cursing. Behind her, huddled into the ancient armchair where Cassie had settled the first day Nick had come into her house, Tate was folded into her duvet like a rag doll. Cassie could hardly believe this was the same flawless woman who'd been in her house for the last five days, not to mention the star who'd graced television and movie screens for decades. She looked haggard, wrecked. Even her hair was ruined.

"What happened?" Cassie asked.

Silence.

To no one in particular, Elda said, "She wants to know what happened."

Tate folded further into herself, eyes down, arms hugging her twiglike form. Hank glanced up briefly before dismissing Cassie again. Which left Nick. He eyed Cassie from his conversation—"Yes, I'll do that. Yes, of course I am. I know. I will. Good-bye"—and checked the screen before lifting his eyes to Cassie.

"Someone," he began coldly, "took it upon themselves to tell the press that Tate is here."

That's why windows were blocked out—of course. Cassie walked to the nearest one and lifted the sheet, and, sure enough, just on the other side of the property line, on the sidewalk, stood a line of paparazzi, too many to count, with too many cameras strapped to their bodies. It was raining. She thought, protectively, of her own camera, which she'd never subject to such a raw day. But she supposed these people didn't care. Their flashes lit up like diamonds at the movement in the window. She dropped the sheet.

She turned back to find her visitors watching her. "But why does it matter if Tate's in Ohio?"

Hank and Nick both ventured careful glances at Tate, who pointedly dropped her eyes.

"This someone," Nick went on, "also told the tabloids that Max and Tate are splitting up."

"I'm so sorry," Cassie said.

"See?" Hank said. "She's sorry."

It dawned on Cassie that she should qualify her apology. "I'm sorry someone went to the press. No one should be sharing your private life." She tried to catch Nick's eye, but he looked away.

"What's awful," Hank said, "is that Tate felt safe here, and now she—"

"Hold on. You don't think I had anything to do with it?" That was obviously what they all thought. Cassie felt Elda's eyes on her, and met them. "Elda, come on."

Elda held up her hands. "I'm Switzerland."

"Tate," Cassie said, approaching her—Hank stood aside, her hand on Tate's shoulder as though shoring her up—"you can't think I did this. You spoke to me in confidence, a confidence I respected. But even if I hadn't kept your secrets—which I did—I wouldn't know how to contact the press. I don't even know who I'd call or e-mail or whatever." She turned to Nick. "I don't even use my landline. You know that."

There was an icy silence.

Nick's jaw flexed. He leaned over his computer and typed in a URL, shaking his head at whatever appeared onscreen. She craned to see.

Her pictures—the ones she'd taken over the last few days. She recognized them instantly. Three, four rolls' worth—she couldn't get a precise count on the thumbnailed shots as Nick scrolled through. But she knew them at once. She'd made them: Tate sobbing on her bed. Dozens of these, shots of the disarranged, desperate movie star, weeping for the end of her marriage. Another series of Elda and Tate together: Elda looking pissed, Tate looking pissy. Elda posing in the front parlor with the bottle of Jack Daniel's. Another of Tate and Nick talking, his hand on her arm. Someone had commented on that one: "New lovah for Tate?"

"What the hell is this?" she asked.

Nick crossed his arms. "You tell me."

"You think this was me?"

"You took these pictures."

She prayed her voice wouldn't shake. "I didn't do this, Nick."

"Leave her alone." Tate's voice was a thirsty rasp. "You should have made her sign a nondisclosure."

Nick nodded. "It's on me, Tate. Margaret wouldn't have fucked this up."

"Oh my god," Cassie blurted. "Do they know about Margaret?"

It was the wrong thing to say.

"Do they know what about Margaret?"

Cassie tried to backtrack. "What Hank told me."

Hank's eyes grew wide.

"About . . . you know. The affair."

"I have no idea what she's talking about," Hank said quickly.

But Nick wasn't listening. He was tapping at his computer. Then he stepped back, arms spread wide, as though he'd won the jackpot. Cassie came toward him, trying to catch his eye, but he was looking everywhere but at her. She reached out to touch him, but he withdrew as if she was on fire. She wanted to howl then, deep from the growing, gnawing hollow inside herself. The women were watching her every move and he wouldn't even look at her.

She bent over the screen and read silently to herself, trying to ignore the trail of her own photographs that tiled the article above and below, and already had millions of shares.

June 18

EXCLUSIVE: TATE AND MAX ARE SPLITSVILLE!

After seven years of wedded bliss, "perfect" couple Tate Montgomery and Max Hall are calling it quits. Why? A source close to Montgomery points to Tate's recent firing of longtime assistant Margaret Philips. "Margaret was a source of jealousy between Max and Tate. She drove a wedge in their marriage. Is it possible there was cheating? Definitely."

It's been a rough few months for Tate. Back in April, she canned Ms. Philips, two days after a reportedly loud argument broke out after a dinner together at Sushi of the Valley in Van Nuys. Then, on June 10, her father—Hollywood icon Jack Montgomery—died, leaving his entire estate, the source confirms, to a previously unclaimed heir (the legal documents naming this heir were not available at press time). In a puzzling turn of events, Tate has retreated to the small Ohio town where her father and mother filmed the movie *Erie Canal* in 1955, a movie that began their legendary romance. Photographs released from an anonymous source within the camp show her looking distraught and unhinged and show her eccentric sister, Esmerelda "Elda" Hernandez, drinking directly from a bottle of Jack Daniel's.

"[Tate] was blindsided by her father's will," says the source. "Now that she's lost Margaret, her father, and Max, she's truly alone, and desperate to get back the only thing she can hold on to—her father's money."

Reached via telephone, Max Hall declined to comment, saying he's "focusing on Aloysius's latest album, which the band and I are thrilled to be recording at the legendary Abbey Road Studios."

Cassie couldn't read another word. "I can't believe you think I did this."

Nick looked momentarily regretful, but it passed. "Someone will give them Jack's will in a matter of hours," he said drily. "So congratulations—now they'll be digging up everything they can on you too."

"I have no idea how the pictures got out. But, as for the rest of it, couldn't Max be your leak?" Cassie asked.

Nick sighed as though she was an impudent child. "Max is the one they approached first—he was the one who gave us the heads-up this was about to break." He frowned. "He's less than pleased. Tate and he had an agreement to keep the separation under wraps."

"But the photographers will go away, right? I mean, eventually, they'll have to go away. They'll get bored. We'll stay inside. We'll wait them out."

Nick shook his head. "They won't leave until they've drawn blood. Plus, now that we backed out of our agreement with Max, he's under no obligation to hold up his end of the bargain. So he can speak to anyone he wants about anything."

"Wouldn't that maybe be a good thing?"

Even Elda looked at Cassie like she was speaking in tongues.

"You know, just to finally get the truth out there?" Cassie spoke to Tate. "Maybe you could turn this to your advantage. Wouldn't it feel better if you didn't have to hide anymore?" Tate looked blank. Cassie wanted to convince her. "You should give a press conference."

Tate stood. The comforter nearly swallowed her. "I need sleep." To Nick she said, "No calls."

"Tate," Cassie said, moving toward her, "I really didn't do this." What did it mean that someone had? Obviously the pictures had been leaked by someone with access to Cassie's film—and that meant Hank or Elda, or even Tate. She couldn't for a second suspect Nick—which galled her, because he, apparently, had no trouble suspecting her—because he was obviously miserable. What did it mean that it was preferable to imagine some stranger breaking into her home and stealing the rolls of film while they slept?

She'd been so naïve.

Cassie summoned her conviction and steadied her voice. She needed Tate to believe her. "I meant it when I said you could stay as long as you want. I care about you, Tate."

Tate scanned Cassie with a withering look. "Care about me?" She snorted. "Please." She shook her head in weary disbelief. "It'll be the sweetest moment of my life when I finally learn we aren't related." Before Cassie could process that comment, Tate turned to Nick and said, in a steely voice, "When I wake up, you'll have a plan to get me out of this hellhole." She took to the stairs.

Nick's phone rang; he moved into the dining room to answer. Hank retreated to the kitchen. Elda groaned as she rose from the couch. Cassie opened her mouth to appeal for solidarity, but Elda shook her head. "Switzerland," she repeated, and then she was gone too.

From the dining room, Nick's voice was muffled but angry. Cassie could hardly bear to think of him; she could hardly bear to think of any of it.

And then: that horrible sound again. The sound that had started everything: the doorbell.

The only way to end its wail was to answer the door, even though Cassie knew, from Nick's grimacing appearance in the foyer, that he didn't want her to. But this was her house—her hellhole—and the sound was a cruelty that she had to end. As the door swung into the foyer, she braced herself for the flash of a hundred photographers.

It was the mailman. She had known all along there was a mailman, but this was the first time she'd looked into his face. He was middle-aged, with a nicely tended mustache. He reminded Cassie a bit of Mr. McFeely from *Mister Rogers' Neighborhood,* and she felt herself sweeten.

Down on the sidewalk, a paparazzo started clicking away. Cassie tried to think what the sound of his shutter reminded her of, but she couldn't name it; it was a threatening sound, a clattering, so different from the friendly tick her camera made.

Then the herd swarmed onto the sidewalk, elbowing and angling for a better view of her, and the racket was amplified a thousand times. She noticed that a policeman had shown up, waving back the crowd with a confused expression. Neighbors had come out onto their porches. Her doorbell would be ringing a lot in the next few days.

"Return to sender," the mailman said, holding up an Express Mail package.

Cassie took the envelope, recognizing the address: it was the letter she'd addressed to "Lindie" in Chicago. She'd been crazy to think it would be so easy to locate someone with answers. The only answer lay in the secret code her cells held, planted there before she was even born.

"Thanks for bringing this back," she said, distracted by what she knew she had to do. Tate wanted to leave anyway. And Cassie couldn't bear the thought of Nick anywhere near her, not anymore.

The mailman handed over his bundle of envelopes, the stack he usually ka-thunked through the slot in the door. He tossed his head back toward the throng of reporters now shouting Cassie's name. "You kill someone or something?"

She felt a sad smile lift her lips. "Apparently."

Then she went into her great-uncle Lemon's office and tugged the pocket doors as close to closed as they'd go, scraping them along the hardwood floor to create some semblance of privacy.

If she had to make this phone call, she was going to do it alone.

June 1955

CHAPTER FORTY-SIX

———

A SHARP KNOCK AWOKE LINDIE. WHEN SHE WAS LITTLE, she would have wondered if such a knock, just before dawn, signaled her mother's return, but, as she turned down the stairs, Eben's snores sawing over her, she found she was too weary to play that guessing game.

She'd spent Sunday, the day after the party, with her father. But really she'd spent the day inside her head, mulling over all that had happened the night before, especially how angry Clyde had been, and the promises he'd made to Ripvogle about tearing down Two Oaks. He couldn't do that, could he? Especially if Apatha was inheriting it? The thought of Two Oaks destroyed made her sick to her stomach, and she'd had a fitful night of half dreams. Come Friday, Hollywood would snap back into its suitcase and leave forever. And, whomever June chose, she'd be leaving Lindie behind. The prospect of all that would soon change made Lindie's stomach roil. And now it was barely morning and she was due on set and someone was insistently knocking at the door.

It was Diane DeSoto. She didn't belong out there, on the creaking, unpainted porch, white gloves covering her dainty fingers, wearing the same black suit she'd had on the night she came to St. Jude. An ivory silk scarf was knotted around her throat. Her platinum hair was curled up and under; her lips were painted stark red. She stood only a few feet from where the girls had watched Jack take her by the neck two nights before. But she bore no traces of their argument. In fact, she smiled.

"Well, hello there, Linda Sue."

"Aren't you supposed to be on set?" Lindie's voice was croaky. She knew she must look a sight.

"I took the day off," said Diane. She was scheduled to film four scenes.

Diane laughed at Lindie's expression. "Well, get some shoes on. And run a comb through that hair."

"Ma'am?" Lindie noticed then that the Olds was idling at the curb, with Thomas at the wheel.

"I'm taking you on that shopping trip I promised. Now hurry up, we want to get to Columbus before lunch."

"But, ma'am . . ."

Diane leaned forward, narrowing her eyes. Lindie pulled back, thinking Diane's serene face might suddenly turn cruel. But instead she tapped Lindie's nose. "I've taken care of everything, little lamb. Casey said you've earned the break."

Lindie hesitated. There were so many reasons not to go: Clyde. June. Work. But here stood a beautiful movie star with an invitation to spend the day in the city. Lindie had been to Columbus a dozen times, but she had a feeling that that Columbus was markedly different from the one she would visit with Diane.

"Oh, c'mon, Linda Sue, where's your sense of adventure?"

Ten minutes later, Thomas gunned the engine as they left the Welcome to St. Jude sign in their dust.

Clyde's Olds—which might as well belong to the movie stars, even though it would stay in St. Jude once they were gone—sported hunter green leather seats with a dashboard and steering wheel to match. It sailed past the cornfields on the razor-straight, two-lane road. Lindie suddenly understood what it meant to leave your worries behind. Clyde and Eben would work out their differences, wouldn't they? June would find happiness, no matter who she chose. Ripvogle would work it out with the governor, and Cheryl Ann would come to accept Apatha and Lemon's union. Lindie was in a movie star's car because a movie star had picked her. She leaned her head back against the soft seat and let the Ohio countryside skip on by.

TEN MINUTES LATER, June stood at the top of the Two Oaks stairs listening to Jack sweet-talk Cheryl Ann. He'd had the gall to invite himself right in, and could Cheryl Ann please give his extra thanks to Uncle Lem when he was done with his nap, and also, oh yes, he'd almost forgotten, he and Diane had arranged, as a thank-you, for a surprise for June—would that be all right? Something special, since she was so dear to them. They'd have her home in time for bed.

On the landing, June's bare feet were warm against the floorboards. She heard her mother clap her hands in delight at the thought of two movie stars taking her daughter out on the town, never mind what the wagging tongues might say. Never mind that June didn't see any trace of Diane in that little red roadster in which Jack had just roared up. Never mind that June felt sick to her stomach whenever the memory of Jack's hand on Diane's throat flashed before her eyes, that moment when he'd shown himself to be something other than the man who'd moved his fingers up into her and made her feel infinite.

But June knew that hiding on the landing would only delay the inevitable. It was best to face Jack sooner than later. So she slipped into her shoes and pasted on a smile and stepped out the front door as Jack held it open, and waved to Cheryl Ann, who flapped a handkerchief from the wide porch.

Jack's right hand rested along the top of the white calfskin passenger seat as they raced over the town line.

"Where are you taking me?" she demanded.

But he whistled and winked and drummed on the wheel, red to match the exterior of the shiny new machine.

"Whose car is this?"

"Nice ride, ain't it? Thought we'd need a car for when we drive back across the country on Friday." So he believed he'd won her then. "Thought we could stop in Arkansas."

"Arkansas?" She balked.

He cleared his throat. "Meet my folks."

The immensity of what he was proposing slid, like an ice cube, down June's spine. She felt, briefly, that she might actually be sick all over this fancy new car.

"Aren't you supposed to be on set?" she asked.

"I'm not on the schedule today. And I'd rather not watch Diane flub her lines for ten hours."

"Does she know you're with me?"

He let the other woman's name slip out the unrolled window. He asked June to light him a cigarette. When it was clamped into the corner of his mouth, he grinned like a little boy with penny candy on his tongue. June couldn't bear to look at him. She pressed her face against her window and filled her eyes with the same green light off the cornfield that Lindie had sped past only twenty minutes before.

"I love having you all to myself." He leaned into her neck for a kiss.

"Keep your eyes on the road, Casanova."

He pulled back in surprise. But soon he forgot her concern. He smoked, and fiddled with the radio, and speculated on rumors that the Dodgers would soon be leaving Brooklyn for Los Angeles. June didn't know what surprised her more: how Jack could elbow and tease her without even noticing her anger, or how stupid she'd been to think of giving up her whole life for him.

CHAPTER FORTY-SEVEN

———

T HE OLDS WAS TEN MILES FROM COLUMBUS WHEN DIANE requested that Thomas turn off the road. They exited onto a country lane that ran perpendicular to the main road: the way to someone's farm, lined with trees and not much else. Thomas started to slow, but Diane instructed him to drive on. "I'd like privacy," she said, and that was when it really sank in that Lindie and Thomas, Jack's main accomplices in his quest to woo June, were now completely alone with the woman who believed Jack should be hers.

Thomas found a shady spot by a field of alfalfa. In the distance, Lindie could make out a silo and a barn and a throng of Holsteins. The smell of freshly cut grass whirlpooled with the tang of manure through the open windows. Diane gazed out at the day, as though taking in a beautiful view instead of a tangle of weeds and tree limbs. In the rear-view mirror, Thomas gave nothing to Lindie but a blink.

Diane turned her focus onto the buttery inside of the car. "I know Jack has made you both party to all sorts of shenanigans. Poor little June."

Thomas groaned, surprising both Lindie and Diane. "Leave me out of it."

"But you're in it already," Diane pushed back shrilly, "so very in it, Thomas, wouldn't you agree?" He didn't reply. Lindie's heart was already thrashing in the confines of her chest.

Diane cooled her tone. "I'm sure Jack made you believe that this is all very special, that he's never felt this way before. But you must understand: this is what he does. He is a philanderer." She pronounced the word delicately, and didn't stop to ask if Lindie knew what it meant. "It's not his fault women always love him back. But a good girl like June— none of us want to see her get into trouble."

Thomas and Lindie held their tongues.

"Good. I'm glad you're not denying it."

"Miss DeSoto," Lindie choked in a panicked voice, because she knew she should at least try to file a protest, but Diane silenced the girl with a raised hand.

"I've been lucky to find a friend in Clyde Danvers. You see, I have Jack's best interests at heart, and Mr. Danvers has June's, so it works out for all of us. Not to mention that Mr. Danvers seems to know all sorts of helpful things about the people in your town."

Worry knotted itself in Lindie's gut.

"Take you, Linda Sue. You're a good girl, aren't you?"

"Yes, ma'am," she said, although, as Diane went on, Lindie turned that answer over in her mind.

"But you haven't had much help, I'm afraid. Unnatural mother. And your father does his best, I'm sure, but no man can be expected to raise a girl alone."

Thomas shifted in the front seat. The air in the car seemed to thicken, as though it was no longer air but a heavier atomic compound, unstable and prone to explosion. Lindie found herself looking at the floor, kicking at a pebble that had made its way in.

"Now, your father is a man with a lot of power. He could choose to use that power for good. He could choose to keep the interests of the rest of St. Jude in mind. But instead he's been snooping into other people's business." Lindie'd guessed this was where this was leading, and she tried to think how to best defend Eben against Clyde's accusations. But Diane surprised her with: "Course, I don't care about all that. All I care about is getting Jack and me back to California in one piece." She leaned toward Lindie. "Look at me, Linda Sue." Lindie did—she had to. Diane untied her scarf. There, on her skin, sat the bruise Jack's fingers had left behind. Diane made sure Lindie got a good view. "What if I were to tell my producer, Alan Shields, and Clyde Danvers, and, oh, for good measure, the police chief, that your dear old daddy attacked me after the party on Saturday?"

"He didn't," Lindie yelped.

"I imagine the good, upstanding citizens of St. Jude would want to run an animal like that out of town."

"He didn't do that to you." Lindie's teeth were gritted now.

Diane tilted her head and narrowed her eyes, the way a cat might assess a delicious-looking birdie. "Do you have proof?"

"I saw Jack do it," Lindie replied.

If that threw Diane off, she gave no sign. Instead she fastened the scarf back in place and continued, "And you, Thomas." Thomas turned to look her in the eye, betraying nothing. "What do you think that same mob would do if they discovered that you are not Apatha's nephew at all? That you are, in fact, her son? And that your father is not just any ordinary man but likely Lemon Gray Neely?"

A slick of sweat broke out on Thomas's forehead. Lindie understood from his expression that the possibility of this paternity was not news to him, but that it was a secret he'd believed would never be found out.

Diane continued. "When Clyde first mentioned it, I couldn't believe him! And then—I tell you, Clyde knows so many interesting things!—he told me you're wanted for questioning in a case down in Louisiana? Seems a white girl has found herself with child? Must run in the family, I suppose."

Thomas's eyes had dropped. But Diane didn't let up. She seemed so different from the meek, unsure person she was on set; here, she was sharp, conniving, and organized. Lindie realized that, if she hadn't been on the receiving end of Diane's attacks, she might genuinely admire her. And then the gears started turning in Lindie's mind: if Clyde knew Thomas was Lemon and Apatha's son—which, as far as Lindie knew, even her father Eben didn't know—then what else did Clyde know? Did he know Apatha was going to inherit Two Oaks? Maybe he'd already figured out some way to get around that, to keep Apatha from getting any of what Lemon was leaving her. June would marry Artie for nothing, and Two Oaks would be torn down anyway. Lindie had to find a way to stop him. But it was impossible to think clearly because Diane was still talking.

"For what it's worth, I happen to believe that love is love no matter your color. But I'm not sure everyone in St. Jude agrees with me. The small-town mind doesn't differ much, no matter where you find it."

"You can't prove any of that," Thomas said weakly. Lindie wanted him to call Diane a liar, to put her out on the side of the road by the cow manure and leave her in his dust, but of course he did no such thing.

For her part, Diane was looking quite pleased with herself. "In fact I can. But I'm not even sure that's necessary. I imagine that the good people of St. Jude would only need an anonymous tip that they've been harboring a dangerous criminal to turn them against him." It almost sounded as though she'd memorized these sentences. If Lindie hadn't tried to help her learn lines, she'd have thought, for sure, that reciting a monologue was the way that Diane had gained such confidence and command.

Diane pouted as though she pitied Thomas. "If you haven't learned it already, there are two kinds of people in this world: those who think secrets can be kept, and those who seek to discover them. I'm the second kind, I've learned, and I believe I've found a kindred spirit in Mr. Danvers. The good news is, once I've gathered up secrets, I like to keep them. You can see, for example, that these tidbits were desperate to be used today. But, on the whole, I prefer to keep my collections to myself." She winked at Lindie.

"What you said about my father isn't a secret," Lindie said. "It's a lie."

Diane sighed, as though Lindie was just incorrigible. "Simply tell me where Jack and June's happy little clubhouse is. Tell me and I'll keep all this"—her hand gestured to the muck of their conversation—"to my grave."

"No deal." Lindie crossed her arms. She would have gotten out of the car herself, but they were miles from home. She had to give Diane credit; she'd planned this well.

Thomas cleared his throat and turned back to Lindie. "Think of your father," he said gently, as if Diane wasn't there.

"I won't agree to be blackmailed over something that isn't even true!" Lindie cried.

He sighed. "June's always looking out for number one, isn't she?"
Lindie rolled her eyes.

"Maybe you should do the same."

"Just where they've been meeting. That's it," Diane nudged.

Thomas told her. Lindie didn't stop him.

CHAPTER FORTY-EIGHT

———

ACK PULLED THE ROADSTER UP ON BROAD STREET. JUNE knew exactly where they were. Her father had once driven her to this exact same spot in the burgundy Plymouth he'd adored. The sand-colored art museum boasted three two-story arches across its front; on its wings, spread out east to west, were friezes of robed men. Artists, thinkers.

"It's Monday," she said crisply, as Jack pulled the key from the lock. "Why are you mad?"

"The museum will be closed."

He took her chin and turned her head toward his. That same hand had gripped Diane's throat. She was sick of Diane, sick of him with Diane, sick of all of it. She pulled away.

His eyes danced all over her, worried. "What'd I do?"

She held back her tears, but they wanted out. "I saw you on Saturday. After the garage. With Diane."

"I didn't touch her."

She realized he thought she meant romantically. "You hurt her."

He pulled his hand away quickly and lowered it into his lap. He groaned in resignation. "My temper flared."

"You should never touch a woman like that." She hated how shrill her voice sounded. "I don't care what she did."

He looked pathetic now, slumped behind the wheel, a little boy caught kicking a puppy. Then he looked back at her, his eyes great sink-wells of sorrow. "She spoke ill of you. She's obsessed with me. You're in her way. I can't stand by and let her threaten you."

"But that's just it, Jack. I never asked you to protect me. I don't need protecting."

"Believe me"—he chortled—"Diane is different from any girl you've ever met."

"I'll bet she fits right in in Hollywood."

"Not everyone is like her out there."

But the words were dazzlingly true now that they'd escaped her. "You keep saying you want me to come with you, but, Jack, be serious."

"I am serious." His hand was on his door handle. "Let me show you." He got out of the car. She waited, watching the traffic pass, and then he was at her door, opening it as if she was his queen.

ON THE DAY June's father had taken her to the Columbus Museum of Art, they'd gone in through the center arch, directly into a marble lobby and up a set of steps that matched the sandy outside of the building. But, today, Jack led her around the left wing of the building and toward a small, dark door on the ground floor marked STAFF ONLY. He took her hand in his. She almost withdrew—she was still angry and it was broad daylight—but then his grip loosened and she decided to keep her palm pressed against his just for the risk of it, and because she couldn't ignore that fluttering in her chest at the touch of him, or the warm bud of desire between her legs.

He knocked a playful tattoo on the door, raising his eyebrows to ape for her. She let herself smile, but only for an instant. Then the door pushed open and, peering up at them stood an older woman with glasses tipped onto the end of her nose. She wore a cardigan and a wool skirt. June withdrew her hand from Jack's.

"Mrs. Scott?" Jack asked.

"Mr. Montgomery." Mrs. Scott looked amused at the sight of them.

"This is my friend June Watters," he said.

June was surprised to find her hand enveloped in the other woman's grasp. Her paper-thin skin was soft and cool. "Pleased to meet you," Mrs. Scott said, shaking hands like a gentleman. Jack held the door ajar and ushered them inside.

It was cool and dark on the ground floor. The place smelled of the parched earth after a good rain. Every footfall and whisper ricocheted. Mrs. Scott wasted no time, briskly leading them toward a wide staircase and up to the main floor. "I must say, I've had some unusual requests in my time," she remarked, as they passed galleries hung with landscapes, "but this takes the cake."

June caught a glimpse of Jack lifting his finger to his lips. Mrs. Scott locked up her mouth and threw away the invisible key. June was surprised at the old woman's deftness. In St. Jude, women like Mrs. Scott ran the library or sewing circle, but she was in charge of Picassos.

Up the stairs they went, footsteps echoing, until they came to the museum's entrance. June hesitated, glancing at the ticket booth where her father had opened his billfold. Jack took her hand, gently leading her behind Mrs. Scott up the final set of wide stone stairs and onto the main floor of the museum.

Down the hall, June knew, there hung a Cézanne of a man sitting in a chair with his hands folded, and a John Singer Sargent of a girl with a red ribbon in her hair called *Carmela Bertagna,* and a Picasso composed of brown squares and pieces of fruit with the word *Journal* emblazoned across a small black panel at its center. Her father had laughed in front of that painting, shaking his head in delight as if he and Picasso were in on some joke, and she'd flung her arms around him, which had only made him laugh harder.

But they weren't going down the long hallways into the other galleries. Instead, Mrs. Scott was leading them straight ahead, into the central, covered hall at the heart of the building. The vast room was fancier than a simple banquet hall; red velvet curtains hung all about its edges, which were carved with a series of grand archways on either side. Mrs. Scott pulled one of the curtains aside, and June thought this must be what Italy was like. Jack bowed, letting go of her hand.

Mrs. Scott flipped on the lights.

There, leaning against the eastern wall, stood a Jackson Pollock.

It was bigger than June had guessed it would be. Vibrant. Alive. It contained every color she knew, but it somehow achieved that with mostly black and white. She moved toward it, realizing it was twice her height and three times as long. If you looked at one spot long enough, it revealed the other colors hidden below: greens and browns, golds and beiges. The trick reminded her of what she had once read about zebras, how they were camouflaged in relationship not to their environment but to each other. It was as if color itself was camouflaged inside the paint-ing. Part of the giant piece looked smooth like marble. Part of it looked violent, filling her with the urge to run and jump as she had as a girl. And part of it looked wet, as though it had just been made. And part of it looked like what Lake St. Jude looked like when you skipped a rock across its still surface. There was no way to have known a painting could take up this much air.

June felt as though she was being reunited with an old friend she'd never known before. She felt very worldly and very wise. Mrs. Scott and Jack and the museum and the memory of her father fell away as she drank the canvas in, top to bottom, left to right, back again, up and down. Why couldn't she contain all of it at once?

She could feel Jack's eyes on her.

"You did this for me?" She turned toward him.

"This is what it would be like." His hand waved toward the painting. "Every day would be like this."

Just like the party. June realized this would always be their problem; he would never stop gilding the world for her. He couldn't understand that what makes a rare thing wonderful is just that: it is rare. June's heart surged at his simple blindness. She curled a hand around the back of his neck and nestled her fingers into his short hair. She kissed him. Right there, right in front of Mrs. Scott, never mind Artie or Diane. Jack Montgomery was kind and dumb and proud of himself, and he had to be kissed.

CHAPTER FORTY-NINE

———

N THE CHINTZ ROOM, ON THE TOP FLOOR OF LAZARUS, LINDIE ordered the Little Red Hen—creamed chicken in a mashed potato nest. The dress she wore flourished with yellow roses; lemony rickrack ticked its way along the neckline. Under the table, her white patent leather Mary Janes capped cotton kneesocks. She did her best to keep from kicking the table legs, because Diane pursed her lips every time she did. The lunching ladies were doing a fine job of pretending this was an ordinary Monday afternoon. They chewed and whispered, forks scratching china, but it didn't escape Lindie that what they were really doing was watching Diane DeSoto's every move.

Meanwhile, Diane was watching Lindie like she was her own little pet pony. She looked so pleased. Lindie tried to ignore the brassiere digging into her rib cage and pulling at her shoulders, the crinoline scratching her waist and rasping down along her legs. Never had she felt so far from herself as when the woman at the store escorted her to the full-length mirror, hands hiding her eyes. The woman had peekabooed them open, revealing Lindie to herself as though she was the bride and her reflection, the groom.

Lindie had never understood what the word *faint* meant, not from the inside, before that moment. She'd believed it was weak to swoon at the sight of something awful, that swooning was something only prissy girls did. But in front of that mirror in the Lazarus dressing room, she felt her head grow light as a balloon, and her arms prickle, and her chest tremble, and she understood that fainting was a very wise reaction to seeing the worst of what life had to offer.

She wasn't herself anymore. Not dressed like this. She saw the truth now. Saw that it wasn't simply a matter of having the right dress or a mother who could show her how to wear it—she couldn't wear a dress, not ever again. The problem of this revelation sickened and thrilled her at once. She didn't know how she'd be able to grow up to become a woman if she couldn't wear a dress, even though her body was turning into a woman's body. And yet she felt a tingle of conviction run up her torso every time she let her mind trip over the discovery anew. What she felt was not hopeless or angry, but curious and proud.

Of course she wanted to rip the horrible yellow confection off immediately, but that challenge was simply a question of mind over matter. Clyde and Diane were in cahoots. Thomas was not brave. Her father was in peril. It was up to her, Lindie, to get them out of this mess. So what if Diane had forced Lindie and Thomas into telling her about Idlewyld? There was plenty to be done with the information Diane had revealed as well. Diane had underestimated her, thinking her just a dumb small-town girl. Let her keep believing it. Let Diane believe she'd bested Lindie; Lindie would keep her close, observe and calculate and gather, and, along the way, figure out how to exact revenge. Besides, the dress had an oddly powerful appeal; feeling estranged from oneself, Lindie learned, made it possible to distill one's focus, keep one's eye on the revenge to come.

Diane tried to pay the check, and the waitress tittered nervously that lunch was on the house. Diane feigned surprise, putting a hand on her chest and gasping, "Well, aren't you just adorable." She loved being treated like royalty.

They made their way back down through the department store. News of their presence had spread, and groups of starstruck Ohioans clapped and gaped along the parade route. There, at the front door, the saleswoman waited with a cart hung with garment bags and piled with hatboxes and shoes. Diane had spent hundreds of dollars on Lindie, and already Lindie knew she wouldn't wear a stitch of it. But she turned with Diane to wave at the crowd. She was very good at this game of pretend.

The press had been called. They were outside, between the entrance and the car. Diane placed her hand on Lindie's shoulder, instructing her to stand up straight and smile. The shutters clicked, the bulbs flashed. To the reporters, Diane spoke in generalities, about her love for the good people of Ohio, and how much she'd miss the tuna casserole. They asked who Lindie was. Diane drew Lindie closer and said she was a sweet little friend from St. Jude. "I dream of someday playing dress-up with my own daughter."

"Has Jack proposed yet?" another reporter shouted.

Diane fluttered her eyelashes and offered up a perfect crimson blush before slipping through the car door that Thomas held ajar.

As they pulled off, Diane retrieved a gold pocket watch from her handbag. "Six o'clock, you said?" she asked.

"I don't know anything," Thomas mumbled, pulling away from the curb.

"But you made the reservation. So you know something."

Thomas shrugged grudgingly. Lindie guessed this meant they were going out for dinner together before heading back to St. Jude. Maybe she would order a Shirley Temple.

"We have plenty of time for Marshall Field's," Diane said.

"Marshall Field's?" Lindie whined, dropping her mask for a moment.

"You don't think we're done shopping just yet? We have to find you play clothes. And, besides, we're meeting the mayor's wife for tea." Diane reached over to brush Lindie's cheek with her delicate fingers. And, remembering that she was not herself, Lindie leaned in to the touch.

CHAPTER FIFTY

———

JACK DROVE THEM TO THE GREAT NORTHERN HOTEL, WHICH shared a vast fireproof building with the Northern Opera House. June watched the valet dash toward the car. "You don't think I'm checking in with you?" she asked.

Jack laughed. "I'm here for dinner. Though if you're game to get a room afterward, you'll get no objection from me." He was playing with her. His eyes skittered over her breasts, and she knew he was desperate to undress her. She was desperate too, which was dangerous; they were walking into a hotel together in a city that was not their own.

The steak house was on the first floor. They entered at the restaurant instead of through the lobby; whatever happened tonight, there could be no mistaking their good intentions. A table was waiting at the back, behind a plaster column and a cloud of smoke. The tall man who seated them didn't bat an eye, but June supposed men like this were paid not to bat an eye. He handed them their menus over an arm draped with a white cloth. June took the menu as if this was the way she ordered every meal.

"Rib eye," Jack said, waving off a menu. "Medium-rare. Whiskey, neat. Baked potato and creamed spinach."

"And for the lady?"

Just when Jack made you feel at the center of his world, he reminded you that there wasn't much room. "I'll need to look first," she said.

Jack seemed surprised. "Hold my order till she makes hers. Except for the whiskey. Bring that now."

"Drink?" Jack asked her before the waiter was dismissed.

June shook her head. She thought of Persephone's pomegranate seeds. How many meals like this would June be able to eat before she had to join Jack's world? How many Jackson Pollocks would she be offered before she believed she had a right to own one?

She glanced around the hazy dining room. White tablecloths, candles flickering. The few businessmen eating early dinners didn't notice them as anything but a good-looking couple out on the town. June had never been anywhere so fancy. But she could see it was nothing to Jack.

"Order me a filet mignon," she said, handing Jack her menu.

"You all right?"

"Just need to powder my nose." But the truth was she'd never ordered a filet mignon and her hands were shaking. She needed a moment, or maybe a few of them.

She followed the sign for the restroom out into the lobby, which was a marble wonder. Three stories above her, a crystal chandelier sparkled. She supposed that, too, would be small potatoes in Jack's eyes. Her blood coursed at how willingly he could take this place for granted. How easily he might take her virginity here. How gladly she would give it to him. The ladies' room was across the great hall, but she climbed the stairs instead, up to the second floor. She needed to stretch her legs. She needed to think, carefully, before she went back down and ate that steak.

THOMAS PULLED THE Olds up to the curb. Diane was quick, not giving the valet the chance to open her door. She grabbed Lindie by the wrist and pulled her from the car and across the sidewalk. Lindie was so shocked that she obediently followed.

Just inside the restaurant, they were met by a tall man in a suit, but Diane didn't want to be seated and she didn't want his help. She was smiling now, but it wasn't a smile at all. A few tables in the front were occupied, but whomever Diane was looking for wasn't seated there. Smoke hung in the air, stinging Lindie's eyes. Diane muttered to herself, something about knowing he had a reservation, voice lowering into a snarling lament. If anyone recognized her, they didn't let on. And, all the while, her hand was clamped hard around Lindie's wrist.

They paced toward the back of the restaurant. Suddenly the tall man was in their path again. "Miss DeSoto, we're so pleased to have you

here." His voice was loud now, unnaturally so, as though warning someone of their arrival.

Diane smelled blood. She charged right through.

There, at the back of the restaurant, tucked in beside a column, sat
Jack Montgomery with a glass of whiskey. If he was surprised to see
them, he didn't show it.

"There you are!" Diane said, much too loudly for the room. "Thomas
told us we'd find you here!"

Jack glanced at Lindie perfunctorily, but when his eyes reached her
face, he showed genuine surprise. "Is that you in there, Rabbit Legs?"
Lindie blushed, not in pleasure, looking down to take in the awful rickrack at her neck, the yellow rosebuds spread tight across her bumpy
chest. They both knew she looked awful.

"Expecting someone else?" Diane asked. She hovered over Jack now,
taking stock of the two sets of silverware on the table.

He held up the single menu. "Just me. Needed to get out of town.
Aren't you supposed to be on set?"

"No," said Diane.

Over Diane's shoulder, Lindie noticed the tall man slip into the hotel
lobby. It occurred to her, only then, that Jack really might not be dining
alone.

He frowned. "You're not helping your case, you know."

"What are they going to do, reshoot all my scenes? The movie is
made, Jack." Diane's voice was pitching toward something frantic. "A
girl is entitled to a break every now and then." She wobbled a little on
her heels.

Jack offered his hand. She released Lindie's wrist to take it. Blood
tingled back into the girl's fingertips.

"You look exhausted," Jack said in an even, lowered voice.

"Well I am!" Diane was practically yelling now, voice churning
with emotion. Her back was slumped, her posture ruined. Her hair
had shaken loose on one side. Her face glistened with sweat, and
Jack rose to hold her up. "In fact, I suddenly find myself so terribly
tired. I need to go home, Jack. I need you to take me home. Have
you had too much to drink? I need to be alone with you. Tell me you

haven't had too much. We'll go in your car and I'll send her home with Thomas."

Jack flagged down another waiter, short and squat, for the tall man was still out in the lobby somewhere.

"Yes, sir."

Diane's body weight was now fully supported by Jack. It was hard to imagine that this was the same woman who'd blackmailed Thomas and Lindie on the drive south. She was fragile, pale, her thin ankles barely keeping her upright.

"I'll take the steak in a doggie bag," Jack said.

The waiter cleared his throat, eyeing Diane. His voice came out high. "The rib eye or the filet?"

Diane's eyes cut toward Jack. But he was smooth as silk. He grinned widely at her. "Couldn't pick. So I got both!"

The waiter bowed and dashed for the kitchen.

Diane swayed before Jack now, inches from his face. "You are alone, aren't you?" Each word quivered.

Jack pulled out his billfold and threw a fifty down on the table, then hitched his arm under Diane's. "Did you take your pills today?"

Fury passed across her face, but then sorrow rose over it like a great tidal wave. She began to sob.

"You've got to take them every day, honey," he said gently and, without another look at Lindie, led Diane—practically carried her—out the front door toward the valet.

Lindie stood in their wake, in the haze of the restaurant, wondering what to do. Just go get in the car with Thomas?

And then Jack bounded back toward her. He grabbed the fedora he'd left at the table, and tipped it to her. "Tell June I'm sorry," he said gravely, but, before she could ask what to do next, he was gone.

She wandered toward the waiter who'd helped with the steaks, and asked if there'd been a girl with Jack. He pressed his lips together primly. She said, "I'm her friend and she needs my help." Had June actually come with Jack to a hotel? What was she thinking?

The waiter conferred with another well-dressed man at the back of the restaurant, then led Lindie into the lobby, toward a dark corner where June sat huddled in an armchair. She looked stricken. At the sight of Lindie in her costume, she cried, "What happened to you?"

Thomas drove them back to St. Jude. Lindie watched the headlights beam out into the night, gamboling with the insects who then gamely splattered themselves across the windshield.

June wept.

June 2015

CHAPTER FIFTY-ONE

———

I T RAINED ALL DAY, COLD DROPS DOWSING THE GREEN WORLD. The DNA lady left, having duly swabbed those who needed swabbing. Tate and company started packing. Cassie shut herself in her room with a box of hemp crackers and a bag of grapes, the closest she could get to junk food under Hank's regime, and watched the dark, wet circle on her ceiling grow.

She ignored the knocks at her door. She didn't want to see anyone, especially Nick. Hank and Tate were equally loathsome, and Elda wasn't Switzerland in Cassie's eyes.

Eventually it got dark. Eventually she slept. The dreams she had were drenched with humiliation, of the girl version of June weeping in the very bed in which Cassie was now dreaming of her. Inside the dream, it finally occurred to Cassie that this girl might be June, and what she felt was a quivering, sorrowful longing for her grandmother as she had never known her, in full bloom.

By morning, Cassie was ravenous. The circle on her ceiling had grown. The light of day sharpened her intentions. She wanted her visitors to leave. As soon as they did, she would call someone to come look at the roof. Today was going to be different.

The women were downstairs. The house was still shut up; the paparazzi had made soggy camp out on the sidewalk. Boxes and suitcases lined the foyer. Hank and Elda eyed her carefully, as though she might break.

Tate was her fabulous self again. She came toward Cassie with arms outstretched, enveloping Cassie's stiff form in a cashmere embrace.

"Can I talk to you?" Her voice was a mix of pity and forgiveness.

"You've heard back from the lab already?" Cassie tried to disguise any feeling in her voice. The woman from the Columbus DNA lab, whose name was Madison or McKenzie or something like that, had promised to "fast-track" their samples; Cassie was guessing the ten thousand dollars Nick had offered her to expedite things would grease any sticky wheels. She braced herself for the news.

Tate shook her head with a disappointed frown.

Nick strode into the foyer from the dining room, hands thrust into his pockets. "Can I talk to you?" He spoke directly to Cassie, as though none of what had happened the day before mattered, as though Tate wasn't there.

"No thank you," Cassie replied, making her voice cold. She could feel his eyes on her as Tate led her up the stairs.

MOST OF TATE'S belongings had been placed in the boxes along the edge of the master bedroom. But the pictures of her dog's goofy face still dominated June's mantelpiece; Cassie was angry at herself for having given the place over so freely.

Tate patted the bed next to her. Cassie did not obey.

"I'm sorry," Tate said, "if you felt accused."

"I didn't feel accused; I was accused."

Tate held up her hands. "It's an unfortunate situation. Don't punish Nick; he's on your side. He argued your case all night."

"Don't tell me what to do."

"Cassie!" Tate looked genuinely shocked that Cassie had such little tolerance for this. "Give me a chance."

Cassie crossed her arms. She felt like a teenager, sullen and gruff in a way her grandmother had never tolerated for long.

"I know I can seem . . . cold," Tate said. She was choosing her words carefully. Cassie saw that she wanted them to mean something. "That was my problem at the beginning. 'The Ice Queen.' You're too young to remember it, but that's how they billed me. I was too much like my mother, they said, too bitchy, too particular." Tate grimaced. "I was headed for a career of guest spots and supporting roles. Because no one would be honest with me. No one would say it to my face. Pedigree can work for or against you. I knew it was a question of changing myself into something more appealing. But I had no idea how."

The rain had stopped, Cassie realized. Now it was just the sound of the water spattering off leaves. She resisted the urge to lift the blind to check on the photographers.

"I had just hired my first real assistant," Tate reminisced. "One night, I'd gotten a particularly nasty casting rejection, and I asked her what I should do. How could I change myself into what they wanted? She said I didn't need to change so much as find the part of Daddy that everyone loved, the part of him that lives inside of me. That I needed to learn to lead with that. She said Mommy had made me strong, but Daddy would make me a star. I knew, right away, that she was right. I couldn't believe I hadn't thought of it myself." Her face lit up at the memory. "I worked on my smile, my walk, my clothes. Did practice interviews so I'd come off better, had plastic surgery to play up my best features, did exercise that would take me from severe to strong. I studied Daddy's movies, watched how he won over an audience; you couldn't take your eyes off him. And of course I took any opportunity to step out on his arm. So much of it was about brand recognition. Jack Montgomery, the man everyone wants to either be or marry. And I was the heir to the throne."

"Was your dad pleased?"

Tate waved her hand as if the question didn't matter, and, in that gesture, Cassie saw that, in fact, it had mattered a great deal and that, no, he hadn't been. "He was busy. But he supported me. No matter what Elda says, he supported both of us. He wanted us to be happy; I truly know that in my heart. And the last few years—well, we didn't see as much of each other as we both would have liked—but he seemed . . . lighter. He made sure I knew how much he enjoyed my company. I'll be forever grateful we had that time."

"Okay," Cassie said impatiently.

"Anyway, that was Margaret."

Cassie waited for more of an explanation; when it didn't come, she said, "I'm not sure I follow."

Tate looked flummoxed; the logic was perfectly obvious to her. "You see what a mess my family is. Elda hates me. Mommy chose to slit her wrists on a Thursday, the one day she knew I'd be home to find her. And Daddy, well, he tried. He tried."

"But Margaret."

"Yes, Margaret. She was the assistant. She believed in me. She cared about me from the beginning, when I was nothing, just the Ice Queen. Before the money, before Max and Aloysius and my Emmys and my Oscar nomination. Before I was famous on my own terms."

Fascinating that Tate Montgomery still lived in a fantasy world in which she'd started out as "nothing." Cassie tensed as she predicted how this would go: Tate would recount how Max had cheated on her with Margaret. She'd weep in Cassie's arms about the greatest betrayal of her life. Cassie would be expected to comfort her, and Tate would believe they'd made amends. At least she'd be gone by sundown.

But instead Tate said: "I fell for her." She gasped at her own declaration. "Not right away. At first we were boss and employee, and then friends and then . . ." Tate stilled her hands. "I fell for her. That's the only way to describe it, Cassie. I'd never been attracted to women, or whatever, but Margaret wasn't just some woman, she was Margaret. We'd been working so hard to get me what I wanted. But by then Max and I were married, and I loved him too, as much as he'll let anyone love him. We were the It couple. The roles came pouring in. He won Grammies, I won Emmys. I finally had everything I'd ever wanted." She sounded dazed.

Was Tate Montgomery actually telling Cassie that she'd cheated on Max Hall with a woman? Was that what the infidelity rumors had really been? Cassie had just assumed Hank meant Max and Margaret. But it was really Margaret and Tate?

"So what happened?"

"Margaret asked me to leave Max. Said if I truly loved her, I'd do it. Said I was America's Sweetheart now, and they'd love me no matter who I was sleeping with. But you and I both know that's a damn lie."

"I don't care who you sleep with."

Tate fixed Cassie squarely in her gaze. "If you read in some tabloid that I cheated on the hottest man alive with my overweight, middle-aged dykey assistant, it wouldn't change how you feel about me?"

Cassie swallowed. Tate nodded triumphantly.

"Anyway, it didn't matter. Margaret quit. Then Max found out. I don't know how. For all I know, she told him. He said a lot of very nasty things. Made a lot of very nasty threats. Margaret completely cut me off. Won't so much as answer a phone call. At least they can agree on hating me."

"So why would Max agree to keep the circumstances of your divorce a secret? He comes out of this looking fine."

"'The Sexiest Man Alive Turns His Wife Gay'?" Tate laughed at the implausibility of the tabloid headline. "No way."

Cassie's eyes skimmed the pictures of that ridiculous dog in front of all those fancy places. How many frequent flier miles had that poor canine logged? "Why are you telling me this?" she asked. She felt bored and exhausted. She didn't know why she was supposed to care.

"I thought a lot about what you had to say. About how it's going to come out eventually. And you're right, I'd rather control it. That's how you have to handle these things." Tate looked Cassie keenly in the eye. "I'd like for you to leak it to your source."

Cassie stared at Tate for a long time. "My source?"

"I don't blame you for releasing the pictures—they're very arty. The online optics are much more positive than we would have thought. As for the divorce stuff, well, I'm not thrilled it's out there, but the truth is, hon, you didn't know any better. Nick messed up; you were too much of a distraction, and well, he . . ." She shrugged. "Anyway, we can use it to our advantage now, even if Nick's being a wet rag about the whole thing. Better to rip off the Band-Aid, that's what Daddy always said."

Cassie couldn't believe what she was hearing. "I didn't give the press those pictures. I didn't tell anyone about your divorce. And I'm certainly not going to tell a soul about your affair with Margaret."

"Would money be a motivator? I'm sure we can come to terms."

Cassie had to get out of there.

"You seem upset."

"Damn right I'm upset. I can't believe—"

There was a sharp knock at the door, and Nick's head popped in. "Sorry to break this up"—he wasn't at all, Cassie could tell—"but I've got the lab on the phone."

Tate held out her hand impatiently.

"Downstairs," he said sharply, clutching said phone to his chest. He turned back toward the master staircase without waiting to see if they were coming too.

CHAPTER FIFTY-TWO

———

W E'RE ALL HERE," NICK HALF SHOUTED INTO THE LITTLE black box. Nick, Cassie, and Tate were crouched over the smartphone on the yellow couch in the front parlor, like freezing people around a fire.

"Hey, everyone," the DNA girl, Madison McKenzie, said. She was about Cassie's age. Her stylish black glasses had made her look like a sexy scientist out of central casting, although Cassie had simply called the first number for a DNA lab offered by information. Nick had picked Madison McKenzie up behind the old video store, where he'd made her leave her car, in a cloak-and-dagger arrangement he'd insisted upon as soon as Cassie made the appointment and handed him the phone.

"Cut to the chase." Tate was done with niceties, apparently, although she'd buttered up Madison McKenzie before and after her cheek swabs, as though the girl would be able to change the outcome of the test if it wasn't in Tate's favor. Tate had been supremely displeased that the DNA test wasn't being done on her terms, with her doctor, but Cassie had made it clear this was the only way she'd submit to it; she'd told Tate she'd consider taking another test for the state of California if it came to legalities, although now she wasn't so sure.

Of course, Tate couldn't resist running the show from the moment the girl walked in. The story Tate told was about her movie star parents' love affair and the people in the way of it—"people" presumably being Cassie and June. Poor Madison McKenzie had driven all the way up from Columbus at a moment's notice, against the policy of her lab (ten thousand dollars cash was nothing to sneeze at, even if she did mention more than once that she was afraid she could be fired), agreed to be picked up by a strange man and to sign a confidentiality agreement on his dashboard, submitted to being driven to a house surrounded by photographers, and walked in to discover the biggest movie star in the world yammering her ear off about destiny and true love.

"This is seriously against policy," Madison McKenzie reiterated over the phone. She'd said that a lot since Cassie had called her.

"We know." Cassie raised her voice so the woman would be sure to hear her on speaker. "That's why Tate's going to pay you another ten thousand dollars once you've given us the news."

Tate glared, but Nick jumped in. "Cash," he agreed.

Elda offered up an amused grin from the armchair. She looked like the cat who'd eaten the canary.

"I'm not supposed to tell you any of this information over the phone," Madison McKenzie said.

"And you're not supposed to come to our house to swab us," Tate reminded her, "but you did. Honey, you opted in when you took my money yesterday."

Out of the corner of Cassie's eye, she could see Hank edging into the hallway from the kitchen. She'd been banished there by Nick as soon as Tate and Cassie had descended. Cassie knew it was killing her to miss this.

"Okay." Madison McKenzie's tinny voice quavered. "You're right. I guess I should just ask for verbal confirmation that you're all, you know, there and okay with me sharing your private medical information with the group."

"Whatever you need," Tate replied in a clipped voice.

They confirmed that, yes, they were Tate Montgomery and Cassandra Danvers, and that they were both okay with sharing their private medical information with the people present.

"Just so you know," Madison McKenzie said, "I've run the results a couple of times. What I'm finding is consistent. To remind you, I took multiple swabs from both of you. Just to be sure there were plenty of samples to crosscheck."

This was interesting; Madison McKenzie was covering her ass.

She cleared her throat. "From these tests, there's a zero percent chance that Tate Montgomery and Cassandra Danvers are related."

Disappointment. Relief? Maybe, but mostly disappointment. The triumphant look on Tate's face wasn't helping matters.

Nick was all business. "So you're saying," he confirmed, "that Cassie is not Jack's granddaughter."

"Well"—Cassie tasted a note of excitement in the woman's voice— "you'll remember that I also took a swab from Esmerelda Hernandez. Just to be sure to determine paternity with Jack Montgomery, since Ms. Montgomery and Mrs. Hernandez are his daughters, and you didn't have a sample of Mr. Montgomery's DNA."

Tate frowned and shook her head. She was not interested in this line of inquiry. Obviously, they'd already gotten what they needed.

"Mrs. Hernandez, do I have your permission to share the results of your DNA test with this group?"

Elda's grin had come back, and it was bigger than ever. She sat forward, joining the huddle over the phone. "Abso-fucking-lutely."

"Well then, as I've said," Madison McKenzie said, "I've run this test a number of times." She held a juicy, dramatic pause. "And every time, it indicates there is a zero percent chance that Ms. Montgomery and Mrs. Hernandez are related."

Tate cackled, loud and mean and triumphant.

But Madison McKenzie wasn't done. "Here's where it gets interesting. There is a ninety-one point nine percent chance—the highest percentage you could hope for in an avuncular test between an aunt and a niece—that Mrs. Hernandez and Ms. Danvers are. Related, that is."

There was a silence then, a horrible, chilling silence, ended only by Tate's question: "What does that mean?"

Madison McKenzie cleared her voice. "I'm not supposed to interpret the data," she said meekly.

"What does it mean?" Tate cried, her voice violent with need.

"In layman's terms," the girl's voice replied after a sharp intake of breath, "Mrs. Esmerelda Hernandez is Ms. Cassandra Danvers's aunt, and Ms. Tate Montgomery isn't."

It roared up again, that sudden, shocking sensation as Two Oaks flustered to life around them, just as it had on the day Nick first arrived. Only this time—Cassie could tell—Nick felt it too; his eyes widened, his hands gripped the corners of his chair. The air inside the parlors and the foyer suddenly thickened with everyone who had come before, everyone who had cared about and thought of and wandered into and polished and hammered and shined and worried about Two Oaks for all the many years it had stood, long before Cassie and Nick had come here, long before they were even twinkles in their fathers' eyes. The experience of all those beings together, so close—and yet unseen—reminded Cassie of a room filling with natural gas, the burner unlit, tightening toward a dangerous ignition point.

Tate was standing over the telephone, voice shaking, eyes wild. "Did you just fucking tell me I'm not Jack Montgomery's child? He fathered Elda, and he fathered fucking Adelbert, but I'm the bastard?"

"I can run the tests again," the poor woman said. "And I encourage you to get a second opinion."

Tate picked up Nick's phone and flung it as hard as she could against the far wall. It smashed into a million pieces, scattering all over the floor of the back parlor. Then Tate strode across the foyer and up the stairs, snapping her fingers at Hank and Nick to follow, but only Hank obliged.

"Well holy shit and hallelujah," Elda purred.

Could Elda not feel the house alive and breathing around her? In contrast, Nick was a send-up of a man in a state of shock—mouth open, eyes darting to the same spots where Cassie could hear the whispers and scuttlings and speculation that seemed to fill the space—and Elda was cool as a cucumber.

The sensation of all the dream people filling the house ratcheted up, tighter and tighter. The whispers grew louder, the heat of curiosity and judgment and blame became more intense—and Cassie tried to wade through the ruckus to understand what had just been revealed:

Cassie's father, Adelbert, had been Jack's son.

But Tate was not Jack's daughter.

Cassie was going to inherit Jack's money, his houses, his fortune.

And all that Tate had built her life upon was a lie.

"It's going to be okay," Cassie mumbled, although the house was making her sick. She felt dizzy, nauseated. She finally knew, for sure, that June had slept with Jack. That Elda was her aunt. And Tate was . . . what? Poor Tate, poor Tate. Cassie kept coming around to Tate, bereft of everything that mattered to her.

Just then, from above, came a startling, deafening crash. Next Nick and Cassie and Elda ran up the stairs, which had filled with dust and a damp, moldy smell that Cassie couldn't name. As Cassie took the steps two at a time—was it a gun? Had Tate thrown something?—she heard Tate sobbing, and the sound of Hank's shriek, a lament that quaked over them—over the dream people too; they were parting for her, and, as they parted, dissipating, as though suddenly disinterested.

But Cassie didn't have time to consider the dream people's whereabouts or intentions, not as she mounted the last stair and launched into the upstairs hall and discovered what she thought was white smoke pouring from her bedroom. A fire? An explosion? Behind her, Nick and Elda gathered. In front of her, Tate was sobbing, moaning, and Hank looked terrified. Cassie peeked into her bedroom. The place where her bed had once been was now a dusty mess of floorboards and plaster, roofing and beams.

"What the fuck?" Tate was screaming now. "What the fuck?" She was raging, untamable, her hands bare and aggressive. Hank tried to get her arms around her, but the girl was like a toothpick caught in a hurricane.

"Ceiling collapsed," Elda noted placidly. Cassie realized that, yes, that was exactly what had happened—she felt a surge of gratitude that Elda had put a name to it—but Elda's sanctimony only churned Tate up. It was hard to understand what she was saying, although Tate was actually now startlingly close to her, alarmingly, unnaturally close. Cassie's ears rang from the high decibels of Tate's cries.

Nick put himself between them, shielding Cassie from Tate's fists, which had started to pound Cassie's shoulders and chest.

"No," Nick said sternly. "No." But there was something gentle about the way he treated Tate, something Cassie admired, a firm kindness that effectively managed Tate almost at once, that soothed her fury. Nick pushed back against her, leading her into the master bedroom, where he shut the door behind them. Cassie stepped into what was left of her bedroom and looked up through the hole in her house. She saw sky.

CHAPTER FIFTY-THREE

―――

S ITTING ON THE FLOOR OF LEMON GRAY NEELY'S OFFICE, surrounded by unread mail, Cassie listened for the sound of the cameras; she knew they'd snap to life as soon as Tate stepped out the door to leave St. Jude for good. The lace curtains furrowed in the grass-bitten breeze. Light flirted across the ceiling. Any minute. Cassie counted to ten, and then she counted to ten again.

A knock.

She watched as Nick's hand squeezed between the rounded pocket doors. He did his best to push one open—enough, at least, to squeeze through and still give some semblance of privacy. He looked a wreck. "I have to go."

"So go."

"I'm sorry." His voice was raspy, real.

"She didn't hurt me."

He tugged at the door he'd come through, trying to close it behind him. Then he looked up at the ceiling with a nervous grimace. "Should you be in here?" She'd left her bedroom, directly above, just as it was, covered in all the pieces of the house that had fallen down. But she couldn't imagine that everything that was up there would fall another floor; that seemed an indignity even Two Oaks wouldn't muster. She shrugged.

"And I don't mean I'm sorry about Tate," he said. "Obviously, that insanity was inexcusable. But I mean about us."

She waited for more, but it didn't come.

She sat up. "Hank stole my pictures."

Nick shifted uneasily.

"Hank leaked the story."

He offered a weak smile. "I suppose anything's possible."

"So you're not sorry, then. Not enough to believe I didn't do it. Hank did it, I know she did."

"How do you know?"

"Because I know." And she did—not because she had proof, but because she could feel it in her bones. It didn't make logical sense; who would sabotage their dream boss? And yet, at Illy's, she should have seen the truth: Hank was a woman who would do anything to win. "You should believe me."

He cleared his throat.

"What?"

"Tate—wanted me to ask you something."

Cassie crossed her arms and looked up at him defiantly. "Well?" He cleared his throat again. She wanted to scratch out his eyes. "Spit it out," she said.

From behind his back, he pulled a silver frame she recognized immediately—it must have been tucked into his waistband. It had been the frame that held the picture of Benny the dog, and Tate and Max, in front of the Great Wall of China, the one Tate had kept on June's mantel. But it was empty now.

Nick cast his head down, as though he already knew what he was asking was wrong. It reminded her of how he'd looked the day they met, and she cringed even as she felt a part of herself harden into anger in anticipation of his question: "Do you know where the picture is?"

"Fuck. You."

"It's my job to ask," he said, voice drenched in apology. "It's my job to protect Tate. To believe the most likely scenario and do my best to protect her."

"Well, you have a terrible job."

"I've worked hard to get where I am."

"Newsflash: where you are is working for a lunatic. A spoiled tyrant. She'll only protect you as far as your next mistake."

"I'm sorry, Cassie, but I like my job. Yes, it's a job. Yes, that means I have to sometimes do unpleasant things. But that's what a job is."

"I know what a job is, Mr. Responsible."

"Oh, I'm sorry," Nick sniped, no longer so neutral, "I didn't know

it was a crime to act like an adult. You want some kind of prize for letting your house fall down around you? Apologies for not thinking that's
heroic."

She could see it out of the corner of her eye—his hand on the edge
of that door. So let him go. Just let him go and she could bury him with
the rest of her skeletons, and get along with the business of dreaming in
her haunted house.

But then she saw the uncertain shuffling of his feet, and knew those
same feet would soon lead him right out her door. The pain of his sus-
picion overwhelmed and shocked her; she felt it like a stab wound in
her gut. How could he believe she would have leaked those pictures?
How could he have touched her with such respect and now just as easily
disdain her?

"I don't understand," she said, as he was about to go. "How could
you think I'd want those pictures out in the world for everyone to see? I
made them. They're personal. They were mine." And she knew she was
crying, and she hated those tears, hated that he could see them, but they
wouldn't stop.

"I don't know," he replied. "I guess I just figured . . . it seemed like
maybe . . . like it was your pattern or something."

"My what?" The question came out angry. He shifted his weight. "If
you clear your throat again, I'm going to kill you," she snarled, cutting
him off at the pass.

"I just mean, like your show," he said. "That show was raw. It was
personal—intimate, even. The *Times* loved that about it, loved that you
re-created every inch of the crash that killed your parents, the way only
you remembered it—from the installation you made of the sounds you
heard in there, trapped in the darkness, to the real car that people could
climb inside with that little mannequin who looked like you in the
backseat. The leaking bottle of Jack Daniel's on the floor, which didn't
show up in the police report but which you, in your spoken word piece
that played over the exhibit, remembered being there. You put your family's biggest secrets right out there. I guess I just thought that was how
you do things."

"Well, you're wrong." But he'd laid the truth bare. That was exactly what she'd done, exactly what she'd made, and it had broken her grandmother's heart. She'd had nothing to do with selling Tate's secrets to the tabloids, but what she'd done to June was much worse.

They stayed there, each in their solitary sorrow. Then Hank called: "Nick?"

"Coming," he yelled, without a second's hesitation. But he stood there watching Cassie instead.

"Go."

"Can I ask you a question?"

"Go."

"Did you feel it too? The house, clenching in around us? That's what it was like on the day I first came, wasn't it? All those people . . ."

And she had, and she wanted to go to him, to thank him for feeling it too, for knowing her—by knowing, yes, how strange her house was—as no one had known her. But he didn't deserve that.

He stood there for three counts to ten. She didn't look at him and she didn't get up. Eventually, he pried open the pocket doors and left her.

The sound of the paparazzi rushing toward the car was like that of a hungry wave on a stormy night, chewing up a beach. But no, not quite—that was the feeling of the sound, the urge of it, but the actual sound of it was different. It was brisker than that, and more immediately frightening, the clattering of all those camera shutters, threatening and untamed. As Cassie heard Tate's engine curl off onto the wind, and listened while the photographers got their shots, she located the name, the idea, the sound, of their cameras clattering together: it was like rattlesnakes.

CHAPTER FIFTY-FOUR

I T WAS PAST MIDDAY AND THE SNAKES HAD STOPPED RATTLING.
Food, then. Cassie pushed her way through the jammed pocket doors,
scraping her knee, and went into the kitchen, jumping when her eye
caught movement.

"Cheers!" Elda sat at the shaky wooden table, the bottle of Jack before her.

"I thought you got a ride on Tate's plane."

"I opted out." Behind Elda, the windows flashed with another vibrant summer afternoon; soon, Cassie would forget to feel guilty about
not making the most of it. Soon she'd be able to spend every moment in
the dark, cool caves of this giant house.

"Let's drink before my cab comes." Elda held up the bottle in one
hand and two glasses in the other. So she'd been waiting. Cassie couldn't
see any reason to say no. As she neared the table, Elda rose. Then she
nodded toward the only other object on the table—Cassie's camera.
"Out back."

"Are the paparazzi gone?" Cassie reluctantly picked up her camera
and followed Elda through the pantry door, shuttling through the dark,
tight pantry and then through the second swinging door into the dining room. The leaded glass of the back door cast rainbows across the
room as Elda pulled it open. The compact back porch gleamed white in
the sun.

Elda marched down the rickety steps and across the meadowy lawn,
and plopped herself down right beside a flower bed. Sure enough, the
dwindling swarm of photographers spotted them from the other side of
the road. Cassie would never forget the unlikely sound of a dozen tele-
photo lenses snapping away from that sidewalk. Rattlesnakes—she was
pleased with having named them. At least half the horde had followed

Tate to the airport. The police had been nice about it; the neighbors midwestern enough to keep to themselves.

"Sit." Elda poured.

"They're shooting us." It occurred to Cassie that her image would start appearing in tabloids now too. She'd have to begin thinking about her hair and her outfits and watching what she said, unless she decided not to care what America thought of her. She'd have to decide once the news broke about her having gotten Jack's money. Which was probably any day now.

"This is my time to shine." Elda held up a glass to toast the throng. "I'm aces at bringing the crazy." The photographers hooted her name. "They've tasted Tate's blood, but I'll be the one to feed them."

"So you figure you can get away with anything, now that they're going after Tate?" Cassie took a swig and coughed.

"I figure she could use my help. I distract them with tarot cards and day drinking, maybe they're not so hard on her."

Cassie leaned back on her hands. "I don't get you."

"Elda!" one of the photographers called out. "Turn toward us!"

Elda lifted her middle finger. The rattlesnakes went wild. Then she picked up Cassie's camera and rounded off a dozen pictures of the paparazzi—which they loved—and of Cassie too. Cassie felt shy, but that didn't stop Elda from shooting her, rapid-fire.

"You act like you hate Tate," Cassie said. "You taunt her. You say awful things. And then, when you find out for sure she isn't your sister, that's when you want to help her out?"

"Weird." Elda sat back. "I don't know why. Maybe now that she's not so perfect it's easier to be nice?" She took a long slug of whiskey and stared up at the house. "I sure am going to miss this place."

"Really?"

"The dreams, at least. I keep dreaming about your grandma."

"Yeah," Cassie said, because if anyone would, it was Elda.

Elda patted Cassie's ankle. "You going to be okay, kid?"

Cassie shielded her eyes and surveyed her grandmother's land. She felt bereft, as though a door leading into her had been torn off its hinges. So June and Jack had screwed. That's all she knew now, for sure. According to Tate, Jack was a saint; according to Elda, he was a jerk. But who was he, really? How had he felt about her grandmother, and how had she felt about him? Had June been married when she slept with him? If not, why had she married Arthur anyway? Just like Mr. Abernathy had said, she'd never get to know these things. What had really happened between Jack and June had been reduced to money and blood.

Her grandmother's words from the night of her art opening danced through her mind: "What have you done, Cassandra? That was for us. That was our business, and not for the world to know." Wasn't that what she'd say about all this too?

"Hey, take a picture of me," Elda said, breaking into Cassie's thoughts.

"Why?" Cassie asked, but she was already calculating the aperture and focus and angle.

Elda grinned. "Because I want you to be able to remember the moment I told you something that knocked your socks off."

Cassie took the picture, not because she believed Elda—it was the kind of thing Elda said all the time—but to move things along.

"I remember your father," Elda said. She said it so smoothly that it took a moment to register.

"Wait—what?" Cassie dropped the camera into her lap.

"I met him. Adelbert. When we were little."

"You met my father?"

"He was two. I was seven. Your grandmother drove him out to Los Angeles. I didn't know it was them for sure until I saw that picture on Tate's mantel."

Cassie was crouched forward now, desperate to know everything. "Why didn't you say something sooner?"

Elda topped off their glasses. "You weren't ready to hear it. And Tate—you know Tate. She would have stolen it for herself, and then it wouldn't have been ours anymore. She can't help that, by the way. It's just how she is." She patted Cassie. "I knew I'd have a chance to tell you."

"That's why you came to St. Jude, isn't it?"

Elda smiled triumphantly.

"So tell me!"

"I don't remember much; I was only a kid, after all. I just remember that it was my weekend with Dad. Diane was somewhere else. She was usually somewhere else; they didn't like each other even then. Anyway, Dad said he wanted me to meet a couple special friends." She smiled wryly. "Wildly inappropriate, of course, but that was him at his best. We drove out to the Santa Monica Pier. June and your father were waiting on the beach. Dad swung him up into the air and carried him on his hip to the boardwalk. I remember being jealous. Your father had these big, fat cheeks—I pinched one until he cried, because he was adorable and, well, because I was jealous." The memory cracked her up. "We went on the rides. A photographer grabbed a couple pictures of the four of us together, and Dad yelled at him first, then paid him for the roll of film. It was a lot easier in those days to keep what you wanted out of the press."

She was looking off into the middle distance, toward the Victorian with the nosy neighbor. It was a beautiful profile. Cassie snapped the picture.

"We watched the sunset from the beach. Your father fell asleep in Dad's arms, and I remember thinking I was in the way, keeping Dad and this woman who was his friend from saying what they wanted to say. But maybe that's why he brought me along."

They sat in silence. The rattlesnakes had died down, nothing new to see. The sun was a press of hope upon Cassie's back. "How did you know he was your brother?"

"The way Dad looked at him." Elda's voice dripped with envy. "He called him 'my boy.' Your grandmother shushed him. Also, he had my father's secret name, the one he'd given up before he became my father. I remember thinking you only name a kid Adelbert if that's what they call his daddy." She chuckled then, and Cassie had to laugh too.

Elda looked up at Two Oaks and whistled. "For an empty house, sure is full of a lot of people."

The thought of Elda getting on an airplane made Cassie pour another drink. The edges of the day had softened, but they'd still be there tomorrow, sharp as ever, waiting for her alone.

June 1955

CHAPTER FIFTY-FIVE

———

INDIE HARDLY SLEPT AFTER RETURNING FROM COLUMBUS, but she was due on set at first light. In the darkness of the kitchen, she fumbled for the sugar bowl. In an instant, she sensed a form, a man, standing just on the other side of the cabinets. She screamed. She switched on the light. It was only her father.

"We're moving," he said.

"Good one," Lindie cracked. Heart still pounding, she opened the icebox, searching for leftover rice.

"Chicago sounds good, don't you think?" The sorrow in Eben's voice made her check him again. He was unshaven, unsteady on his feet. He moved his head from the shadows. There was a bruise around his eye, and a cut above it.

"Daddy, what happened?" Lindie's heart sank at the sight of him. Without the particulars, she already knew—Clyde.

She reached for a cloth to wet, but Eben brushed it aside. There was a wild look in his eye that she hadn't seen there since the days after Lorraine left. Lindie had forgotten all about this hollowness. Now that it was back in the room, she wanted to wrap her arms around her daddy, but he grabbed her wrists instead. "I promised we'd be gone by the holiday. Gives us five days to pack the house."

She wrested her arms back. "Daddy, you're scaring me."

"He says he'll let us go with no trouble."

"Who, Daddy?"

"Ripvogle's out." Eben slurred the contractor's name. So he was a little drunk, an encouraging revelation. Maybe their lot would improve with the light of day. "Clyde lost money. A lot of money. He blames me. Says I went to the governor and tattled. Says he's going to kill me unless we leave."

"Daddy, Uncle Clyde's your best friend."

"He's not your uncle anymore."

Lindie's mind was a tangle of everything she knew: Clyde's anger, his threats, how he'd grabbed her at the party, how he'd told Ripvogle he was planning to tear down Two Oaks, what he knew about Thomas's parents. He was capable of such destruction.

Her voice trembled as she asked, "But you didn't go to the governor, did you, Daddy? You didn't tell on Clyde?" Clyde Danvers held nothing so high as his reputation; she hoped her father hadn't dared to tarnish that.

But questions made Eben angry. "Go pack your room." He swayed against the kitchen cabinets. Maybe Apatha had been right; maybe it was a more personal reason—Lorraine—that two grown men were fighting like little boys. Lindie couldn't bring herself to ask.

"I have to work today, Daddy."

"No more sneaking out," he boomed. "We pack this house now."

"Okay," she said, placating him. "Okay, Daddy." She started to grasp what he was proposing: leaving everything they knew. Fleeing like criminals. Making a new life in an enormous city full of strangers. The thought of it fluttered inside her like a robin with a broken wing.

"We have until Sunday, when he burns this whole thing to the ground," he mumbled. Was he speaking literally? Lindie took him under one arm and helped him into the dining room. There, on the table, sat her father's ledgers, which were usually locked up in Lemon's safe in the office at Two Oaks. She was surprised to see them splayed open in the daylight; Eben usually kept such careful track of them. He wobbled against her. She supported him into their small front room, depositing him in the rocking chair. She covered him with the ratty blanket that had been there forever. Everything in the room seemed wrong, as though she was seeing it through a pane of mottled glass. Even her father had been transformed. She rubbed his head as if he was a pet dog; he was snoring in five minutes flat.

THEY WERE FILMING on a bridge over the canal, north of town. Lindie raced toward set on her bicycle. Her stomach growled. They were already setting up a shot. She dumped the Schwinn at the side of the road and ran toward the encampment of trailers and the crew, brightly lit by the sun. The sky was open and blue; it would be a beautiful day. But she already knew something was wrong, just by the awkward way Ricky looked at her, then away.

Casey stepped into her path.

"Sorry I'm late." She ducked her head and kicked her foot in an "aw shucks" gesture that usually worked.

But Casey wasn't biting. "You're done," he said, in his superior voice.

"I'm late, I know, but—"

He shook his head one definitive time. "You're fired."

Lindie had seen plenty of other folks show up late to set, and she was about to argue just that when he said, "For future reference, this is what happens when you don't come to work."

"I'm here," she shouted impudently.

His lip curled. "Yesterday."

"But yesterday, Diane—I mean, Miss DeSoto—she spoke to you." Lindie was sputtering. "You told her I could take the day off work."

He came as close to laughing as he ever would. "She did no such thing. In fact"—and here he stepped forward so that only Lindie could hear him—"she shared some concerns about you this morning. She fears you've grown . . . attached."

Fury filled Lindie as she understood how well Diane had played her. "That's a lie. She's a liar."

Casey dismissed her with a grimace. "You have ten minutes before I call the police."

LINDIE LOPED TO her Schwinn. She could feel the eyes of Ricky and who knew how many other crew members on the back of her neck as they observed her humiliating retreat. She restrained herself from a backward glance; although she wanted, more than anything, to soak in the last of that glorious experience, she had her pride.

Almost back to town, she heard a motor purr up behind her. She waved it around, but it stayed right there, on her tail. Irritated, she pulled into the mass of clover and crabgrass at the edge of the road to let it by, but Thomas pulled the Olds up beside her. It was empty, save for him.

"You remember those secrets?" he asked, eyes darting to make sure they were alone in that large, flat country. "About my mother? And maybe who my daddy might be? About me and Louisiana?" She nodded solemnly.

His hands were jumpy on the wheel. "Clyde came to Two Oaks last night. He told Apatha he knows every bit of what we're hiding, and if he doesn't get what he rightly deserves, he's going to ruin us."

She'd underestimated Clyde. It didn't matter that Apatha was Lemon's wife; Clyde would make sure no one in town cared about that. Eben's laws, Eben's rules, Eben's ledgers, none of them would matter if Clyde had scared Apatha off. Once Lemon died, Clyde would find a way to get what he wanted, no matter what he had to do to get it.

"What do you plan to do about it?"

"I plan to run," he answered, just as plainly.

She couldn't blame him, though she'd try to get him to stay. "Is Apatha really your mama?"

"By birth I guess," he said, as if there was any other way. "My auntie raised me. I don't suppose anyone but Apatha knows who my daddy is. She knew Lemon back then but they weren't married yet. Then she headed up here for a life of luxury. My auntie only told me the truth when that girl down in Louisiana started telling people I'd been with her." He raised his hands in innocence. "I never touched that girl, I swear. But it doesn't matter. I had to get out. I came north. Asked Apatha to take me in. You would have thought I was a stray dog, not someone who'd grown inside her."

Lindie knew what that felt like, how cold Apatha could be when you didn't fit through the doorway she'd opened for you. "But why do you think she left you?"

"I don't know and I don't care." His scowl told her otherwise. "All I know is I'm leaving."

"If you run, they'll send the police after you. They'll send you back to Louisiana." Clyde had to be stopped, and she wasn't sure she could do it alone. "Please," she begged. "Just till the end of the week. We'll work this out—I know we will. Think of Apatha."

"I don't owe her anything."

"Just your life."

"She's living like a queen and she couldn't share it?" Thomas's agony filled the car, then spilled out over the clear morning. Lindie didn't have an answer for why they'd left him in Louisiana, so she told him her mother had left too, in case it made him feel better. He sighed then, and shook his head, and told her he'd give her until Friday morning, but if anything happened before then, he was gone. He pulled a U-ie and headed back to set.

She biked the long way around to Elm Grove Cemetery. It was cool and quiet down there. A person could think. Lindie weeded graves and studied the baby headstones with morbid fascination: OUR DAUGHTER, LAMB OF GOD, BABY BOY LARSH. At least when someone died, you got a place to visit.

Round about lunchtime, she strolled down to Lemon's personal mausoleum, built of yellow brick to match his mansion, with its own stained-glass window to boot. Through the intricate iron gate, she could see that the shelf that held Mae's coffin had room for him on it too. She wondered if Apatha would get a spot.

Her stomach churned; she hadn't eaten since the night before. Soon, she told herself, June would arrive. Any minute now, she'd be rounding the drive. She'd be carrying a basket full of Apatha's biscuits. She'd sit beside Lindie and Lindie would tell her everything. June would have answers. They'd solve it, all of it, together: first do this, then that, on and on until everyone got to be happy.

It was a nice story. Lindie told it to herself for hours.

CHAPTER FIFTY-SIX

———

INDIE TOOK WHAT DIANE HAD TAUGHT HER—THE BEST WAY to break the rules is to look like you're following them—and used it. Eben was serious about Chicago; she'd learned that the second she sulked in at sundown, when he threatened to throw her possessions in the trash. "We're going, Linda Sue, with or without your things." He'd already boxed up half the china cabinet. So fine, good, she could make it seem as if she planned to go. Into a cardboard box went the crumbling pinch pot she'd made for one of her mother's birthdays. She balled up her collection of shoelaces and sorted out the clothes that no longer fit. It was strange, taking stock of her little St. Jude life. Had she done so only a few weeks prior, she would have turned up plenty of treasure. But even the cigar box under her bed seemed as though it belonged to someone else.

Meanwhile, she schemed. It came down to one thing: Clyde could be bought, which was lucky, since not everyone could. In fact, Lindie was now sure that the language of money was the only one Clyde spoke fluently. The downside was that she, personally, didn't have any money to speak of, but her father held the purse strings of the richest man in town. If she couldn't do something with that, she might as well burn her house down herself.

BY SUNSET ON Wednesday the twenty-ninth, Eben and Lindie had hardly spoken. But when he knocked on her door, she could see that fear was no longer his fuel. He looked like himself again.

It was hot in her room, the sun pressing like an iron through the roof above. Lindie was pulling pictures down from the wall above her bed; some she'd drawn, some were from movie magazines, from the days before she knew what movie stars were like in real life. Eben sat beside her on the crazy quilt Apatha had sewn. He handed her a cup of water. His hands were dry and cut up and he smelled of newspaper dust. "I want a better life for you," he said, after she gulped the water down.

"I have a great life."

"Hear me out." His hand on her leg was gentle. "I saw how they talked to you at the party. Darlene and Gretchen and Ginny."

Lindie filled with shame at the memory of those girls talking about her so meanly. She knew now that her tomboyishness would extend beyond this era of her life, that it was something essential, and not just a habit, but that didn't erase how awful it felt to hear how much people hated her because of it. She thought of the horror at the department store, with Diane and the ladies oohing and aahing.

"Here, in St. Jude, I'll never be anything but the son of Lemon's handyman," Eben said. "I'll always be the man Lorraine left. And you'll always be the girl who doesn't act like a girl."

"I'm sorry, Daddy."

"No," he said sharply. "You're not understanding. The point is, this is who you are." He sounded proud. "I don't want you to change. I don't want you to waste another minute of your life on those cruel children. Don't you see, Linda Sue, in a city, it'll be different. No one will know us. No one will know about Lemon Gray Neely or Clyde Danvers or care that your mother left. We'll just be us. Together."

Put that way, it didn't sound so bad. But she knew it wouldn't be so simple.

"What about Apatha?" she asked.

"We have telephones. I'll help her, you know that. But we also know Lemon's not long for this world. She's told me she'll make her life elsewhere once he's gone. Might as well get a head start."

Lindie nodded, because that's what he needed from her. He needed to believe she agreed with him. She looked right on the outside, but inside, her mind was busy, carving, sanding, detailing her plan. "Does it have to be so soon?" That was what she was supposed to say.

He patted her knee. "Say your good-byes."

The only way to win the war was to seem to lose the battle.

CHAPTER FIFTY-SEVEN

———

INDIE BIKED OUT TO THE THREE OAKS ESTATES LATE THAT
night, before the last day of shooting. The air was muggy in her
lungs. A halo ringed the moon. She didn't care a whit if that old
Diane DeSoto caught her; Eben and she were already as good as run out
of town on a rail. She chucked rocks at Jack's bedroom window, until
he bumbled out the back door in a T-shirt and pajama bottoms, his jet-
black hair no longer coiffed but ruffled. He rubbed his eyes like a baby
and let her into the kitchen. A fluorescent bulb buzzed above. The vinyl
chair, one of dozens someone had purchased for the homes of the movie
folks, stuck to the backs of Lindie's weary legs.

Jack was grim at the mention of June. No, he hadn't seen her. He'd
tried to send word through Thomas, but Thomas had said he wasn't in
that game anymore. And where the heck had Lindie been?

She told him Casey had fired her.

"Casey's under a lot of pressure," Jack said. "That disappearing trick
Diane pulled on Monday set us even further back than we were. They've
been slashing and rewriting left and right. The crew's about to mutiny."

"Don't you want to say good-bye to June?" she snapped.

He really considered the question. "I want her to come to Hollywood," he replied. "I want her to be my wife."

"So why'd you leave her in that restaurant and drive back home with
Diane?" It took all she had not to slap the back of his head.

He dropped that big old head into his hands. Was he crying? His
breath was jagged. She gave him a few minutes, tipping the open box
of Rice Krispies into her hand and crunching it dry. Leaning back onto
the rear legs of the kitchen chair, Lindie realized that she might even be
enjoying herself. There was a strange sweetness to standing on the brink
of disaster.

Then Jack spoke. "I got Diane into . . . trouble. A couple months back."

Lindie had heard Apatha say this word, *trouble,* in this same way once, when Apatha didn't think she was paying attention. Apatha had been talking about a girl in the next town who'd gotten pregnant out of wedlock.

So that was why Diane was such a wreck.

"She decided not to have the baby," he said. "I wanted her to." His voice didn't swell with conviction, so Lindie assumed this was one of those things you only claim to have wanted in retrospect. "She wanted to be a star. Couldn't let something real get in the way of . . ." He looked up then and saw Lindie, remembering that she was just a child. He swallowed his words. He poured himself a whiskey. He leaned back against the kitchen counter. "It tore her up."

Grief washed over his face, but he drank it down. "I have to get her to California. When she's back on solid ground, I'll cut her loose."

Was he really expecting to step onto an airplane with Diane on one arm and June on the other? Lindie could hardly stand to be in that tight little box of a room with him anymore. "Is there a party tomorrow night, after you wrap?"

"If we wrap," he mused. "If."

"Fine." His self-pity was not her concern. "If you wrap. Will there be a party?"

He turned the glass in his hands, watching the tawny liquid spread up around the inside of the glass.

"Make sure there is," she instructed. "Make sure Diane is entertained, or she'll follow you. She knows about Idlewyld, Jack. Find your way out to us. June and I will be there."

SHE WAITED UNTIL the next morning to ring the Two Oaks doorbell. June's curtains had been drawn since the night they returned from Columbus. June didn't even know Lindie was moving. She certainly didn't know that Clyde had threatened Eben, or that Lindie had been fired from the film set. Plus, June was supposed to marry Artie on Sunday. As

Lindie mounted the steps to the Two Oaks porch, she realized that, if Clyde had his way, this might be the last time she ever stood there.

If Apatha was surprised to see Lindie on the porch like a regular guest, she didn't show it. She smiled wide and quick, and Lindie felt blindsided by affection.

"You've been growing."

Lindie tried not to feel proud. She'd put on a pair of her father's old pants that had turned up in the packing, and found a belt to hold up the waistband. She knew she didn't look like much, but Apatha's face told her she looked like something.

"June here?" She already knew the answer.

"Come on in."

"Who's that at the door?" Cheryl Ann bellowed down the stairs.

Lindie ran past Apatha, pecking her sweet old cheek, and thrilling at the expression on Cheryl Ann's face from the landing.

"Isn't she getting married on Sunday?" Lindie asked as she passed Cheryl Ann. "Seems you'd want her out of bed."

Cheryl Ann sputtered and gaped, but she let Lindie by.

Lindie knocked once on June's door, out of duty, but she knew June wouldn't answer. She turned the doorknob and went on in. It was darker than a tomb in there, but she could just make out the lump of June at the center of her bed.

Lindie said June's name. June moved, but barely.

"You can't let him leave without saying good-bye." It was hot in the room; the windows were closed.

"I don't want to."

"But you have to." Lindie softened herself. "I'll be waiting at eleven."

If June thought she was crazy, she didn't say so, which was good, since Lindie needed her. This was no longer about June and Jack. This was the only solution Lindie had.

CHAPTER FIFTY-EIGHT

———

J ust before midnight, june's bottom pane flashed in the moonlight. Her dark, nimble form descended to the newly cut lawn, which was sweet and wet and filled with the thrush of crickets. When June was close enough to touch, Lindie saw that she was like a baby bird thrown from its nest—scared, needy, excitable, breath jumping. Lindie's pack was heavy, straps digging into her shoulders. When June clambered aboard the Schwinn, Lindie missed feeling the length of June's front against her back, but, then, she missed so much about June. She wouldn't speak of Chicago. She wouldn't mention being fired, or her conversation in the kitchen with Jack. No talk of Diane's pregnancy. Just Lindie and June and the night.

They biked out into country. June's hands were warm. No matter what happened next, it would be their last night like this, out alone, two girls in the darkness. Lindie knew the plain truth, that June was only wrapped around her because Lindie was of use to her, and that was how their friendship would always work: Lindie pulling, June coming along. But that was okay with Lindie, because Lindie loved June. She closed her eyes and biked them down the center of the road, feeling June's arms around her and loving the other girl's impossibilities and cruelties, loving her strange, small self, which would not, could not, let herself have what she wanted, not without Lindie's help, encouragement, and drive.

They turned down the gravel road that led to the lakefront. Lindie ditched the Schwinn against the wide oak trunk. The night skittered with crickets and bullfrogs. Leaves scuttled. Their feet crunched the small rocks.

A light glowed ahead. June led the way. They both knew Lindie would wait outside, although June didn't know what Lindie had planned. At the house, near the spot where she usually eavesdropped, Lindie found her tree and leaned against it. She watched June slip past the little building and to the front of Idlewyld, and heard the door yawn open as June stepped inside.

Out on the road, the nearly full moon had cast the world into an eerie almost-day, the same as it had on the night Lindie had first taken June out to Clyde's development. But, at the lake, the clouds were quick moving, like hands across a face, obscuring one minute and gone the next. Those clouds were running for something, something out of sight.

Thomas waited a few moments before whispering Lindie's name.

"It's me."

Then he stepped out from behind the trees. "Do you have them?"

Indeed. The straps from her bag had dug deeply into her shoulders. She let the pack thump to the ground as Thomas drew close. They were near the house; she figured once June and Jack were finished, she and Thomas could approach Jack with business of their own. Jack had to help them; whether Jack and June were saying good-bye forever or were spending their lives together didn't change the fact that Thomas and Lindie had sacrificed an awful lot to organize this love affair.

"How will he use them?" Thomas asked. He held up the bag, which contained the four heavy ledgers she'd swiped when Eben wasn't looking. These large leather books held everything there was to know about Lemon's money—his account numbers, the deeds to his land, how much money he was sitting on, what Apatha was due to inherit. Lindie knew Clyde couldn't just walk into a bank with one of those things, pretending to be Lemon Gray Neely, and steal his money outright. But she figured there was something in there that Clyde would want to know, and that was her bargaining chip. She wouldn't have to be the one to offer it to Clyde either, for presenting the ledgers would be Jack's final act of goodwill before he left town, even if Jack didn't know it yet. She'd even written Jack a speech to recite, but she was open to ad-libs: "Clyde, we must come to an agreement. In exchange for leaving Apatha, Mr. Neely, Thomas, June, Lindie, and her father, Eben, be, tonight I give you free and unfettered access to Mr. Neely's private financial documents. Do with them what you will, and, come tomorrow, you'll leave these good people alone. Handshake deal, that's how gentlemen do it."

It wasn't a perfect plan, and Lindie didn't love knowing what Clyde might do with all that information. But he was going to make their lives a living hell if she didn't do something, and this was her only bargaining chip.

"We have to hope Clyde goes for it," she said in a low voice, feeling the darkness at the edge of the water gather in around them.

"Go for what?"

In that moment, Lindie realized that she and Thomas were not alone. She recognized the voice—Clyde himself, and close at hand. He was behind them, mere feet away. The moon bathed his skin in ghostly white.

"Uncle Clyde!" she yelped, wondering if she should shout for Jack. But no, she could play this out herself. This was Clyde, after all; he'd never truly harm her.

"What's all this?" Clyde asked.

Beside her, Thomas's breath had grown rapid. "We don't want any trouble."

Clyde's teeth bared into an ugly grin. "Now why oh why would there be trouble?" Lindie didn't like the play in his voice. She didn't like how he was moving slowly toward them like a hungry animal, or that he had one hand on his belt, right where he holstered his pistol. It was time to play her hand.

"I brought Neely's ledgers," she said, opening the bag in the moonlight. "I thought we could come to an arrangement. You get to look at them tonight, learn anything you want about his money and accounts. In exchange, my father and Thomas and I stay in St. Jude. You leave Apatha and Lemon in peace, and June doesn't marry Artie."

"Well look at you!" Clyde said, voice tinged with something like pride. He'd seen Lindie grow. He'd raised her up. "Making deals. Making plans."

"I just want everyone to be happy," she replied, which was the truth.

"There's only one problem," Clyde replied, and Lindie discovered that what she'd heard as pride was actually disgust. "I'm not interested in those fancy ledgers."

"Everything you want to know about every acre of Mr. Neely's land is in here," she said, making her voice shiny with hope. "What he buys, what he trades, what he owns. Think what you could do with that."

"I don't care," Clyde said, and she heard, in that last word, *care,* that he'd been drinking. The wicked smell of whiskey belched out of him, and Lindie felt afraid.

"Lindie," Thomas said beside her. "Best we get home."

"And leave just as the party's started?" Clyde asked.

"There's no party, Uncle Clyde."

"Well, I want to call it a party." The moon flashed back over him, and Thomas and Lindie saw it at the same time—the small silver gun in Clyde's hand.

He pointed it toward Lindie. Terror enveloped her in its cold, slippery shell. The tang of urine filled her nostrils, and her legs flushed hot. Only after her bladder was empty did she realize she'd pissed herself.

"Go on," Clyde said, tipping his head toward the lakeside front of the house. "You two get out that direction so we can see each other." Good, Lindie thought, we can make noise. June and Jack will come out and help. She gripped the bag of ledgers tightly as she felt the cold lip of the gun press into her side. Thomas led the way. Lindie followed with Clyde's salty breath at her neck. Was he really pointing a gun at her?

Lindie's mind flashed with escape plans as her footsteps crackled the undergrowth. Her legs were wobbling. It was all she could do not to drop the ledgers. Her chance to cry out had passed. Though they were mere inches from the building where Jack and June were probably kissing, they seemed to be across the universe. The whole world was breath—Thomas's, Clyde's, Lindie's—and the thump of her heart.

They'd nearly reached the front of the house, when she remembered the rock. That first night Jack had been waiting for them, June had tripped. There were sizable rocks all along that path, big enough for a girl to stumble over, and maybe—she hoped—small enough to lift. She kicked her feet wide, hoping to feel one blocking her path. She had to find one soon; in a few steps, they'd be at the lakefront, where the land was clear.

Her right leg swung wide and her toes slammed into something hard. There it was. She deliberately bashed her shin against the rock, hurtling herself over it and onto the ground. The ledgers thumped as she let them go. Clyde cursed. He pulled at her. He moved the gun to the back of her skull and pressed hard. She thought for sure that she was going to die, but her fingers knew their work, and, all the while, as he pressed that metal against her, they were scrabbling over the loosening stone, edging, lifting, desperately trying to pry it from the ground.

Clyde cursed again. She looked up to see Thomas's feet flashing off into the forest. Had he run for help? Or had he just run off? The ammonia smell of her piss washed up into her nostrils as she felt her luck turn. The rock was bigger than both hands, but she could lift it. The moon was going behind a cloud. If she could make it to her feet, she might have the advantage.

"Get up," he hissed.

"Please, Uncle Clyde."

"Don't call me that. You're nothing to me. You're the worthless product of a whore and the fool who thought he could tame her."

The next thing Lindie knew, the rock was leading her hands in a beautiful arc through the air. That gun was nothing compared to her rock. The sky was dark, and Clyde was in love with his ugly words, so in love that he didn't see the rock at his temple until it was already crunching there.

The first hit surprised him. He cursed and fell to Lindie's left, toward the house. It felt good to watch him fall. It felt good to hear the wind knocked out of him, to see how easily he faltered. It was self-defense, that blow, saving herself from Clyde's gun and drunken logic. Leveling the playing field.

The second hit was glorious. With his left hand, Clyde tried to block her, but the rock was already landing on his skull. That hit was for how he'd scared her. He collapsed on the ground.

The third hit was the end. Back came Lindie's arm. She adjusted herself over him, crouching low. She could just see him in the last bit of moonlight. He was gurgling now, trying to speak as he writhed in the grasses below her. But she didn't stop herself. She was tired and angry and she wanted him dead. Why hadn't she seen this was the real solution? It was so easy now that it was in front of her; there was no need to negotiate. All she had to do was drop a rock on his head.

And that's exactly what she did.

CHAPTER FIFTY-NINE

———

WHEN JUNE ENTERED IDLEWYLD, SHE FOUND JACK—AS she knew she would—standing in front of her self-portrait. It was the best thing she'd ever painted. It wasn't pretty, no. It wasn't something she thought anyone would want to hang on a wall— she certainly hoped Jack wouldn't—but she'd known, as she worked the canvas on the nights she snuck Lindie's bike out of the garage, that the painting was just plain good. Not because it was perfect, but because it was honest and flawed. The blemish on her chin. The wrinkles at the corners of her mouth that looked just like her mother's. A bit of hair tangling against her long cheek, her narrow eyebrows, the funny turn of her ears where they slipped into the lobes. Looking at the painting was like looking in a mirror, if a mirror could show your insides, too, everything you loved and feared at once.

He turned at the sight of her, and ran his hand from his mouth down over his chin. "It's tremendous," he said. His voice quavered. She saw that he was moved, maybe even amazed. It struck her then. Despite it all, he knew her. He'd known that giving her this place to paint would bring her to herself the way nothing else could. That it would electrify and make her reckless. He was a cheater, probably, and a liar too, and he had already brought her toward the self she feared becoming, and he was standing there before her, waiting to be hers. She was supposed to marry another man in only three days' time, and finally, at last, she didn't care anymore. She pushed everyone else out of her mind—Artie, Lindie, her mother, Clyde, Diane—just pushed them all out and went to Jack.

His hands received her delicately. His lips were warm, sweet. Even out behind the garage she'd been holding something back, but here, at Idlewyld, she was as honest as her painting. She wanted him. She would have him. Simple as that.

He kissed her back, gently at first, then hard to match her frenzy. His hands trailed from her head down her spine and across the small of her back. She found the buttons at his chest and started to undo them. He pulled back and held her face in his hands. His eyes asked the question and she answered with another kiss.

She heard something then: the cry of her name? Was it Lindie calling? She wondered, but forgot to care in the next breath when Jack, who had been fiddling open the buttons of her blouse, grazed his thumb across her bare nipple.

It happened quickly after that. Shirt, blouse, pants, skirt, everything off, and he was hard under the only bit of cotton cloth between them, and she was wet for him, wetter than she knew was possible, and his fingers were dispensing with the last bit of modesty.

They made a kiss-drenched exodus to the mattress at the corner of the room. He laid her down and stayed above her, his eyes everywhere. She could hardly believe how bold she felt, arching her back, putting her nipple into his mouth, opening her legs and then closing them, so he could see her unfolding. She laughed. She drew him down. His face grew solemn, and he kissed her once, sweetly, a question of a kiss, and she loved the feeling of his skin all along her skin, the heat of him, his want, and she answered his kiss, a yes of a kiss back, and then Jack's warmth was slipping into her, and it felt at once that he was through and around her, a sharp tightness that gave way to something warm and aching. She couldn't believe this feeling of him, as though he was everywhere at once. She savored the taste of him on her lips, treasured his concern and his longing, realized she had so much to learn about this strange and mostly enjoyable matter, which she now knew was what every married couple did in their bed, together.

Afterward, he rested his fingers on the notch at her neck and grinned.

"I'm coming with you to Los Angeles," she whispered.

He kissed her deeply, and she felt him harden against her all over again. But she needed to say what she needed to say.

She put her hand on his chest. "I'm your only girl. From now on, Jack, I'm the only one for you."

"Adelbert," he said.

"What?"

"Call me Adelbert. That's my name." His real, honest name—not pretty, just him.

She kissed him and laughed and he frowned and then they laughed together. Was this really her life? Lying naked with this movie star with a secret name? Was he really going to be hers? But she had to make him promise, before she got carried away. "Adelbert, then. I mean it. No more Diane."

He lifted his hand in a scout's honor. Then he lowered himself over her and entered her again. This time, she understood better how the act itself could be a pleasure beyond compare.

They lay together for a good while after that. "I can't wait to show you this country," he said. "We'll drive across the whole thing, and I'll make love to you in every state of the union."

"I'm excited about airplanes too."

He kissed her. "We'll take airplanes everywhere—Paris, Cairo, Florence."

"All right then," she said, "but first I suppose we've got to get out of St. Jude."

They played like that for a while, until they were both tired out and June supposed Lindie, spying through the window, now knew all the gory details of the marriage bed. June wanted to stay here forever, but there were bags to pack, and good-byes to say, and only a few hours left in the night.

"Eight a.m.," Jack concurred, reluctantly drawing on his pants. "In front of Two Oaks. If I'm taking you away, I want your mother to hear it from the horse's mouth. We're doing this right, June."

A dull gnawing came at the mention of her mother, but June's conviction was strong. She was going to go with this man who made her feel like no one had. She was going to leave this small world behind.

He dressed. He kissed her. He had to pack. Could he drive her? No, Lindie was waiting; June wanted to break the news to her herself. He wrapped his arms around her and kissed her again. He made for the door, then came back, grinning, and kissed her. He forgot his hat, and came back and got it, and kissed her, and it fell on the bed and he left it there, until he made for the door again and then had to come back and kiss her all over again. It went on like that until she pushed him away, reminding him she'd be his, in his car, in only a few hours' time. His eyes trailed around the little Idlewyld room, and she knew he had loved that humble place for bringing them together, and that endeared him to her even more. Back at the door, he gestured toward the painting. "Can I?" he asked. And she nodded and giggled, embarrassed, emboldened, amazed to still be naked on the bed and feel a movie star's eyes all over her. He went to the painting and lifted it, and came back and kissed her, and went out into the night.

June heard Jack's footsteps across the porch, the jaunt of his gait, his pleasure, and she felt the warmth that was still between her legs and laughed to herself in the swoony light.

Ah well, to home then. She had a suitcase to pack. Now that she had decided to go it seemed so obvious. She supposed she should tell Artie to his face, but a letter would have to suffice. He was a kind man, small in his ambitions, but good enough to make a life with; she hoped she wouldn't be his only chance.

And then there were footsteps again, back across the porch. Jack's? Lindie's? She felt guilty for making Lindie wait outside for so long, and for the fact that she was abandoning her. Oh well, June supposed everyone had to grow up sometime, and this would begin a whole new chapter; Lindie would visit her in Los Angeles. There were adventures to be had.

The door opened. June turned with a bawdy smile, ready to tease Jack for wanting more again so soon. Oh, to be that irresistible. She supposed she'd have to get used to it.

But it was Diane DeSoto.

CHAPTER SIXTY

———

G ET DRESSED."

Outside, Lindie was crouched over Clyde's lifeless body, but inside Idlewyld, only a few feet away, a thin line of disgust had formed between Diane's eyebrows. She stepped into the little shack, but just that—only a step. Her eyes skimmed over every surface touched by the kerosene glow. Her mouth formed a knot as June pulled the sheet around herself, skin scarlet, stricken with disgrace.

"It's quite simple," Diane began, as though they were midconversation. "Jack will arrive to pick you up tomorrow morning, and you will not come downstairs. When he rings, you will tell your mother you are ill. You will draw your curtains and stay in bed. He will wait outside for you but you will not come down. Eventually, he will leave. He will find his way back to Los Angeles and you will not stop him."

At the first sight of Diane, June had let herself believe the woman had no idea Jack had just been there, couldn't possibly know what he'd been doing with, and to, June. Of course, now June knew that was folly; Diane had likely heard—and maybe even seen—every moment of the most private thing June had ever done. Politely playing along would not stand. June opened her mouth to protest, moving toward the movie star, but Diane cut her off.

"Oh I see!" Diane sounded delighted. "You were too distracted just now to notice any of what happened outside." She leaned forward with a sharp, conspiratorial smile, as though they were confidantes. "It can be difficult to keep one's eyes and ears open when a man is inside of you. But let me give you a piece of advice: I've learned it's one of the best times to pay attention. One discovers all sorts of wonderful tidbits." She hooked her finger and wiggled it to draw June closer.

June stood her ground.

Diane tutted. "Don't you want to see? It certainly does change just about everything." She sounded practically delighted. June gripped the sheet tighter across her chest as she watched Diane hold the door open to the night. A white moth flapped into the room.

June didn't want to follow Diane, not at all, but a part of her believed that if she acquiesced, Diane would leave her be. All she wanted was to relish the feeling she'd had with Jack. The future remained delicious. If she did what Diane wanted, she'd be rid of her. So June followed the movie star out into the night, which was surprisingly alive. Frogs and crickets, and something splashing giddily in the lake. Only a few moments before, June had forgotten there was a world beyond these four walls.

Diane led her around to the side of the house. It was bright when they first stepped out, but the moon was quickly obscured as they made their way into the brush beside the small building. June became aware of someone else's breath, ragged and just below her. Diane was somewhere to her left and fiddling with a zipper. Then a small circle of light, pointed at the ground, revealed two people—one lying, the other crouched over him. The flashlight showed Lindie to June.

JUNE NEVER TOLD Lindie about the moment when she realized Lindie was the one making that animal sound, and that the person lying below her was missing a large bit of his head. June recognized the parts of Clyde that weren't his face: his pressed shirt, his meaty hands, and the pistol clutched in one of them. By the time she got Lindie into the shack, and she could see that the girl was covered in blood, that she smelled of piss and had brains on her hands, that she was shaking and nearly catatonic, June knew that Clyde Danvers was really, truly dead, and that Lindie had killed him.

"Don't let her touch anything," their guide instructed. Diane was a pale vision, out of place in that messy, warm room. But the girls needed her; she was the adult. It didn't occur to them until much later that Diane had watched Clyde attack Lindie, then seen Lindie murder him, all the while spying on Jack and June together, thrilling with her good fortune as she honed a plan to use it all to her own advantage.

June wrapped the top sheet around Lindie. She checked her face for injuries, pressed her limbs for broken bones.

"Girls," Diane said, "we haven't much time before daylight."

June put her arm around Lindie. They turned to Diane like flowers toward the sun.

"We have two choices," Diane said calmly. "The first has me taking you both out for a midnight drive. We've grown close over the course of *Erie Canal*'s filming. You wanted to take me back to all my favorite spots, for old times' sake. We lost track of time, I took you home, you snuck up through your windows, and that's that." She dusted off her hands. "That's the story I will tell the police when this body is discovered. I'll call the sheriff myself and say how dreadfully sorry I am to hear this horrible news, and tell him all about my lovely night with both of you. So sad how even the most perfect evening can be marred by tragedy."

June pursed her lips as though the story was ridiculous. "Why wouldn't we just say we were asleep in our beds?"

"Because you'll need an alibi." Diane's words turned vituperative. "Your parents know you sneak out. You need something airtight, a reason you snuck out tonight. I'm airtight. They'll believe anything I say."

"Who's 'they'?" June asked.

"The police, dear girl. The police, who will be very interested to discover Clyde Danvers lying dead only ten feet from this little love nest you've made for yourself." She took stock of it, inch by inch, with her steady gaze. "We'll need to put this back the way you found it." But the girls stayed frozen in their spots. "Because if we don't, dear girls, what do you think will happen?" She paused, but not long enough for them to answer. "I will go to the police and tell them I saw her"—and here she pointed toward Lindie with a shaking finger—"take a rock to that man's head in cold blood. That is the truth. I like to tell the truth."

Lindie was making a terrible sound. June shushed her with her hot breath. One of them was crying.

June turned to Diane. "What do we have to do?"

"Why, exactly what I said at the beginning! You let Jack go. You just let him go. You never tell him why. You never see him again."

Lindie wanted to tell June she shouldn't agree. Lindie hadn't worked so hard to just see it all dismantled by Diane. But Lindie hardly knew how to say her own name, so she stood there helplessly inside her humming, numb mind.

They set her in the corner. June dressed under the carapace of the sheet, while Diane piled Jack's gifts to June on one side of the room. They filled milk crates with art supplies and then the books. Diane went back into the night and returned, twenty minutes later, with the car that Thomas had hidden somewhere off the road. How she knew where to find it, how the keys were waiting inside, was a question that puzzled them. But they accepted their luck because they needed it.

They loaded up the car and tied Lindie's Schwinn on top. Diane disappeared around the house, toward where Clyde's body lay. When she returned, her face was red and her breath fast, but she said nothing. She had the bag of ledgers and Clyde's gun. They got into the car and backed up the gravel drive to the main road. The girls kept their eyes on dark, lonely Idlewyld until it vanished into the night.

The drive back to St. Jude seemed to last forever. They stopped once so that Diane could go into the woods and toss the gun off into the night. The moon had set. Morning stirred.

Diane pulled the car up a few blocks away from Two Oaks's property, in front of the Fishpaws', because they were old and deaf and sure to be asleep. She turned to look at the girls in the backseat. She instructed them to go to bed. "Take your bicycle and your bag, Lindie. I'll get rid of everything else." A grateful warmth spread in Lindie's stomach; she just wanted someone to tell her what to do. She was so far away from herself that the bag hardly weighed anything at all.

Diane turned to June. "If you go to Jack, I'll see to it that Lindie is arrested for Clyde's murder."

"I know that."

"So we have a deal?"

June put one hand on Lindie's arm and opened the door into what remained of the night, pulling Lindie out behind her.

"Do we have a deal?" Diane whispered after them.

Out of the car, the near dawn was cool. The whole world seemed to be sleeping. June untied Lindie's Schwinn and lowered it to the sidewalk; the tires bumped as it found the ground.

"I killed him," Lindie mumbled. Her mind was coming back.

"Shh," June said. She placed her arm over Lindie's shoulder and drew her in.

"I killed him, June." It felt horrible to say.

June was safe and warm. She was Lindie's best friend and Lindie loved her more than the world. And she was talking just for Lindie now. "We'll never speak about it, you understand? It didn't happen."

"But—"

"It's nothing to do with us."

Diane whispered June's name desperately. They were all on edge.

But June held up her hand to the woman; she wasn't done with Lindie. June pressed her forehead against the younger girl's. "You'll wake up tomorrow like it never happened."

"But you love Jack," Lindie said. "You can't give Jack up, not for me."

June's hands on Lindie's shoulders were firm, her resolve contagious, her voice calm. "All this time, Little Bear," June whispered, "you've tried to make sure I can leave St. Jude. But I can be happy here. If I leave with Jack . . ." She shook her head. "I can't do that to you."

"But I can't stay in St. Jude with you," Lindie whispered. "Not after what I've done."

"All this time," June said. "All this time. We thought I was the one who had to leave. But I think it's you."

And with that, June lifted her head from Lindie's, dropped her hands, and looked Diane square in the eye. "Deal," she said. And she walked off toward Two Oaks without a backward glance.

Summer and Autumn
2015

CHAPTER SIXTY-ONE

———

THE PHONE RANG AND RANG. LIFE INSIDE TWO OAKS WAS almost as it had been: she did not answer the doorbell and she did not open her mail, which piled through the slot in the door into a great mound of disappointment. But the house had stopped dreaming.

Elda had insisted on hiring roof repairmen, so they came and went from the side door, the footprints from their work boots muddying the brown paper they'd taped to the master stairs. Cassie slept in the maid's room on the air mattress, which she had to inflate every night before bed, and which had her lying flat on the floor by morning. She kept to the back of the house: kitchen, dining room, servant stairs, which felt right somehow, new, and punishing. But still no dreams.

Soon, the photographers figured out that Tate was gone for good. Cassie supposed they'd follow the trail of Jack's money back to St. Jude eventually. But when would the millions find their way to her? It was a fun guessing game; she supposed other, more responsible adults would seek out the solution to it. She very much considered getting a lawyer, especially when she lay in bed and watched the moonlight fill the small pine box of a room. She'd probably have to pay a lot of taxes. So, then, also an accountant? Or one of those money managers or something? She meant to call the bank, really, she did. But it was so much easier to stay in bed. The executors and financial advisers and attorneys and accountants could come to her. Maybe if she stayed in bed long enough, Two Oaks would swallow her again in its velvety dreams.

She didn't know many, or any, people anymore, so she didn't have to suffer advice. She didn't talk to anyone for weeks, except for Elda, who left her with a cell phone and insisted Cassie pick up when she called, which happened every night between the hours of ten and one. Elda mostly blathered on about her grandsons' swimming lessons and helping her twin granddaughters prepare for college in the fall, lulling Cassie into a false sense of security until she'd interject—"are you eating?" or "have you taken any pictures?" or "did you go outside today?"—and Cassie would resolve not to pick up the cell phone the next night, and then, the next night, the cell phone would ring, and she would, of course, pick up.

The truth was, Cassie did eat well, at least for the first few weeks, since Hank had left truckloads of food behind. But then Hank's groceries dwindled to a small bag of French lentils and a single block of frozen spinach, and even Cassie couldn't justify gumming frozen vegetables for dinner. Before, she'd enjoyed the walk to the Pantry Pride, but it felt like an epic journey now—her little old lady cart, the patch of town without a sidewalk, and, worst of all, the stares and whispers as she passed her neighbors' homes. They held up their cell phones and took her picture. Soon, whenever the money came, she'd be able to buy herself a car and she wouldn't feel so on display. Soon, she'd open her mail and she'd start answering the landline; maybe today was the day.

They watched her in the grocery store—a round old woman picking up a birthday cake with fluorescent rosettes from the bakery counter, a teenage girl who snapped a picture in the cracker aisle—but at least they didn't talk to her. Cassie supposed she should care what she looked like, since pictures were probably making their way onto the Internet, linked as she now was to Tate and Elda, but she found she didn't much mind sullying the family name. And then she remembered that Tate wasn't actually in the family, and that she, herself, was, and she felt guilty (three frozen pizzas) and mad at herself for feeling guilty (okay, fine, some zucchini).

When she got up to checkout, all three tabloids above the conveyor belt featured Tate. TATE'S TANTRUM! TATE'S SCANDALOUS SEX TAPE! MAX MOVES OUT! Tate looked an absolute wreck in the pictures, even with her sunglasses on—her cheeks were gaunt, her mouth severe. Apparently she'd gotten into a drunken screaming match at someone's party? And she'd fired Hank? And Nick was threatening to quit after a blowout over his paycheck? Cassie felt a stirring of sympathy, a tingle of curiosity. She grabbed a Twix and finished it before she got to the register. The girl pointed to the corner of her own mouth, and Cassie wiped away the chocolate with her sleeve. At least she'd made it past the magazines.

It was July. Hot and quiet, every door swollen in its frame. Even the dogs weren't barking in the middle of the day. Cassie felt like a vampire. It was too much to put everything but the perishables away, too much even to shower, or to do anything but go to bed. She was alone. She longed for the dream people. Sleep in the maid's room was dark and impermeable, nothing more than heavy-limbed slumber.

SUMMER PUSHED ON. Some days, Cassie awoke crisp and rational. She'd be seized with the desire to sort the mail and answer the phone and do crunches and eat kale salads. Those days, she could see the whole pathetic tangle from a polite distance: Why are you depressed, Cassie? Is it because your grandmother died? Are you sad because you left Jim? Or because Nick left you? Was either of them really ever "with" you to begin with? You didn't really want Tate to stay, did you? You know she's a sociopath, right? Get up get up get up. Everyone loses their grandmother. Plenty of people lose their parents. You didn't even know about Tate and Elda and Jack a month ago, and now they have you cowering in bed? You sad little freak. You're going to die alone.

Occasionally, original thoughts cleared the brambles. Such as: she was disappointed in her grandmother. Since finding out about Jack, Cassie'd had this hope that he and June had shared some great eternal love. But maybe Tate hadn't been so off the mark when she'd called June a townie—maybe June had only been some slutty girl who'd done a movie star. And maybe Jack had only left everything to Cassie in order to screw over his daughters. Daughter—she kept forgetting it was singular now. She wondered if Jack had always known Tate wasn't his. Maybe leaving everything to Cassie had been an elaborate way to make sure Tate found out her mother wasn't as saintly as she'd believed.

It was better in bed. Even without the dream people, who'd definitely abandoned her, it was better.

But then, toward the end of July, she had a Saturday of clarity. The landline was ringing again and she answered it, like that, on a whim. It wasn't the first time she'd done this—it was a fun game, like fishing for sport, because you could always hang up without saying a word. But this was the only time the person on the other end asked not for Cassandra, or Cassandra Danvers, but for Cassie.

"Yes?" Cassie realized she hadn't spoken in a couple of days. The word leapt out of her, as if it had been waiting for its chance.

"Oh hello!" The woman on the other end of the line sounded pleased. "I've been trying you but haven't had any luck."

"I've been sick," Cassie lied. Or maybe it wasn't a lie, but "heartsick" sounded ridiculous, and, anyway, she didn't know if that's what she was.

"I'm sorry to hear that."

"Who is this?"

"I apologize! This is Betty, Betty Prange, from the library? I was hoping to have you over for that tuna casserole Bob and I promised."

From the darkest corners of Cassie's mind, she pulled a memory of the lovely older librarian who'd said Cassie looked just like June. "Bob was up in Lima last week," Betty explained, "at our storage unit. I asked him to see if he could turn up any of his father's pictures—the ones I mentioned, of that party they had at Two Oaks—and, well, he has. I think you'll want to see what he found."

So tuna casserole it was. And how about tonight? Cassie had no reason to refuse, though it did take her a couple of hours to make herself fit for human companionship. Turned out Bob and Betty lived only a few streets over. She walked toward town in the evening light, admiring the sunny haze that had settled over St. Jude, sticking her tongue out at the old woman spying from the little wooden house across the side lawn as Cassie passed by.

CHAPTER SIXTY-TWO

———

OB WAS BETTY'S PERFECT MATCH. HE WAVED FROM THE
center of the front walk, a pink lump of white oxford shirt and
shiny forehead and red, bulbous nose; Cassie guessed he liked
his cocktails. She remembered what Betty had said about him being
the first responder at the accident, and, as she neared him, she searched
his face for any recognition she might feel. She remembered so many
strange shards from that awful night, but not his face, even though, she
could tell from the grandfatherly way he drank in the sight of her, that
he and Betty really did think of her as "our miracle." He made sure she
smelled each and every one of Betty's roses as they ambled to the front
door: citrus, musk, honey.

Dinner started at 5:30 on the dot. The sun was harsh through the
dining room windows of the small, old house. The casserole was accompanied by boxed mashed potatoes topped with Kraft macaroni and
cheese, and a side salad of raw broccoli swathed in thick, milky mayon-
naise. The women drank Smirnoff Ice screwdrivers, and Bob drank a
Bud Light.

Cassie felt, at once, at home. June's tastes had run a bit more
bohemian—the art books, the Chopin—but Bob and Betty's house
bore many of the same relaxed, practical touches as the Columbus home
in which she'd been raised: twinned tray tables, thick mauve curtains,
and, on the kitchen counter, a large ceramic cookie jar. Why, then, did
Cassie feel so nervous? Her gut churned uncomfortably, and she answered their questions with the sense that something big was about to
burst out of her, even if she didn't know quite what it was.

They wondered how she was doing all alone in that big old house.
What exactly did she do all day? Had the roofers finished yet? Looked
like a big job. She guessed, from the fact that they didn't ask about the

movie stars, that they knew all about the Montgomery situation but had decided not to bring it up.

Betty went to prepare dessert, and Cassie found herself alone at the table with Bob. It was easy, once she saw what her own question was—easy and terrible. "You were at my accident, weren't you?" she asked, although that was not the hard question. She endured the sadness he showed and smiled as he praised her survival—"not a scratch on you," he said, with tears in his eyes—then pushed on to the real question.

"I remember parts of that night," she said. "I'd been at my grandparents' for the weekend, and my parents had come to pick me up." Bob wanted to interject, Cassie could see it, but she held up her hand and he kept his silence. "I remember my grandmother begging my father not to drive, not in the state he was in. I didn't know what that meant. I remember her standing on the Two Oaks porch wringing her hands as we drove away. And then, I remember being a way out of town, and watching my father swig from a bottle of Jack Daniel's. He had one hand on the wheel and one hand on the bottle, and he passed the bottle to my mother and she drank too." Bob was looking uncomfortable now, but, to his credit, he wasn't stopping her. "But when I looked at the police report, there was no mention of a bottle of whiskey or of my father's blood alcohol level."

"He was dead at the scene," Bob said defensively. "No reason to test him."

"Okay," Cassie said evenly. "But the bottle. What happened to the bottle?"

Bob paled. The sounds from the kitchen had grown quiet; Cassie supposed Betty was listening.

"It's okay," Cassie said. "I won't be angry. I just want to know what happened."

Bob fiddled with his dessert spoon. "I was the first one there. Your dad was behind the wheel. Your mom had been flung through the windshield." The spoon again, twisting through his fingers. "You sure you want to hear this?"

She could have told him that the scene had obsessed her every waking moment for the two preceding years, leading up to her show last summer, as she painstakingly re-created every aspect of the accident that she could remember. She could have told him that nothing could faze her, not the hole where her mother had been, not the blood pouring from the back of her father's head, not the horrible sound of the panicked adults on the outside of the car when they'd heard her call for help, adults, she now knew, who had included Bob.

Instead, she put her hand on the spoon, on his hands, and stilled him.

"I was the first one to get there. I knew it was your dad's car right away. I called it in. I could see there'd be fatalities. I had no idea you were in there too—we didn't know until the ambulance arrived." She could tell it was costing him a lot to repeat this, and she squeezed his hand. "I saw it there, on the floor, the whiskey. You have to understand—I'd known your grandma a long time. She wasn't what I would have called a friend, but this is a small town, and she was a real special lady. So was your grandpa Arthur. They helped everyone, buying groceries for the families who couldn't afford it, tutoring kids who deserved a chance at college. I saw the whiskey, and I knew, if anyone else found it, it would have to go in the official report. That would have destroyed them both. So I reached in and got it, and I threw it into the cornfield, and I didn't tell anyone about it until just this second."

"But she knew," Cassie said, remembering June's words to her at the art show—"That was our business."

"Maybe she did," Bob said. "But what I mean is it would have been just awful to see her walk around this town with that gossip hanging around her. People already called Adelbert a party animal, said he was out of control—I'm sorry to tell you that, but it was the truth. And June and Artie were mild-mannered, good people. Better, I thought, for everyone to think it was a plain old tragedy than something worse." He frowned. "It might not have been the right thing to do, but I'm glad I did it."

Cassie nodded, finally understanding June's pain at the sight of that Jack Daniel's bottle in Cassie's installation. How that bottle must have confirmed her suspicions, and filled her with guilt and sorrow. Cassie wanted to climb into bed for a week, reliving that moment when she'd followed June outside, onto the Manhattan street, and June had turned back to her with a wild unknowing in her eye, as though Cassie was not to be recognized. That look was a black hole.

Betty reemerged from the kitchen. Her eyes were wet, but she'd put on a smile, and she bore red Jell-O, which quaked in the shape of a Bundt pan and was topped with Cool Whip. She served it in silence, then plopped herself down and said, "We've got those pictures to show you," urging the night along.

CHAPTER SIXTY-THREE

——

FTER THE JELL-O, BOB ROSE. HE RETURNED WITH A SHOE box. Betty cleared a spot on the lace tablecloth, but instead of leaving the room for a round of dishes, the older woman stayed, elbows perched on the table as though she was an excited little girl.

"My dad liked to take pictures," Bob began, groaning as he sat down—his knees must hurt him. "He had one of those old-fashioned cameras. He'd snap anything that caught his eye. You know there was a party up there at Two Oaks when they were shooting *Erie Canal*? Well, he took some pictures that night." He opened the box and took out a stack of brittle square photographs, white-framed and rippled along the edges in an old-fashioned way. Cassie felt a rush of pleasure just glimpsing them. How alive they were, how real, those captured moments—even though they'd taken place a full sixty years before. They brought to mind the picture of Elda she'd taken in profile out in the backyard, and familiar concerns surged through her: Would that shot be any good? Would she have to burn and dodge the grass in the lower right corner? She felt alive for a moment, truly alive; hungry to make, to see the world through her lens. Her hands ached for her camera, and, pleased and surprised, she smiled.

Bob handed a picture to her, just then, in the wake of her smile.

Cassie gasped. Not just because the image brought to life a Two Oaks Cassie had only imagined—a big white tent filling the side yard; a small band playing inside, brass instruments gleaming in the light from the stringed lanterns—but because she recognized the people in it. They were dressed to the nines, hair done, lipsticked and heeled, but their faces were unmistakable. She had seen them before.

The dream people. That woman with the mole on her chin, and the teenage sisters whose features were too small for their faces, those three old men sitting in the round office, that couple dancing cheek to cheek.

She couldn't say anything about it, of course. She knew what sensible people like Bob and Betty would make of her dreams.

Once the initial recognition faded and she picked out face after face, what Cassie felt was not so much shock as inexorability. She'd known all along that St. Judians were clogging up her home, hadn't she? It was fitting to see them gathered around the mansion in these photographs, the mansion that had held their attention even after they were no longer physically in its shadow. She tapped their faces as though they were her classmates suspended in elementary school pictures—people she knew but whose particulars she couldn't quite recall.

Bob beamed at her enthusiasm. "I wish I remembered more. I was a kid, you know? Spent most of the night trying to steal a bottle of booze." He chuckled. "And then Walter and I set off a firecracker in Mrs. Dowty's mailbox."

"Bob!" Betty elbowed him.

"Should have heard her scream." He was laughing outright now. Betty met Cassie's eye and pulled a "he's hopeless" face, but his laughter was contagious and they all giggled until he wiped his eyes.

"Show her," Betty urged.

"That's what I'm doing."

"The picture," Betty pressed. "The special one."

He didn't look too pleased, but Cassie saw Betty would win this, and every, tug-of-war. Bob pawed down through the box, finding what he was looking for at its very bottom. He examined it inside the box, out of sight, as though he didn't want Cassie to see it just yet. Cassie leaned forward. Betty told him to show her, Bob, show her, and then he lifted the picture into Cassie's hands.

Another snapshot, just like the rest. Only this one showed June Watters and Jack Montgomery, side by side. They were dressed up. He wore a dark suit with his hair slicked back; a cigarette was tucked into the corner of his mouth. His eyes twinkled with amusement; his broad chest filled his suit coat perfectly. June was just a whisper past a girl—womanly, but dewy—her hair twisted up and dress fastened just over the tops of her breasts.

Jack and June were not touching. It did not even look as though they had been standing together. But when Cassie saw the picture, she saw what she had been looking for since the beginning. There it was, what she had wanted since the day Nick had shown up on her doorstep and told her Jack had left her everything.

There was no word for what she saw, but it was tangible, the current between these two people who were now dead and buried. The proof was there in June's hand, splayed up into the space between her body and Jack's. It was there in Jack's warm gaze, landing directly onto the side of June's lovely, smooth face. They were gorgeously young. And, whether or not they had known it, it was obvious to Cassie's eye that they were in love.

"He's my grandfather," she said softly. Bob and Betty shared a look. Cassie couldn't take her eyes off her grandmother's calm, bright expression. Something unhitched inside her; she felt deliciously calm.

"Do you know," Bob said gently, "June and I shared a good friend. Linda Sue. People called her Lindie. She might be able to help you."

"I tried writing her." Cassie laid the photograph down. "In Chicago. The letter came back return to sender. Do you have her address? A number?"

Bob looked confused. "I thought you knew her. She says you're friendly."

"Friendly?" Cassie searched for any memory of an old woman who'd call her "friendly" and she came up blank. Betty looked as confused as Cassie felt.

"Mrs. Shaw," Bob explained to Betty.

It was Betty's turn to gasp. She sat back in her chair, mouth agape and touched, on its edges, with a warm smile. "Why, Cassie," she said in a delighted voice, "she lives across the street from you. In that funny old wooden house on the other side of your side lawn."

"It's the house she grew up in," Bob explained. "Came up for sale a few years ago, and she moved back from Chicago after she retired. It's a good, strong house, Betty."

Which was how Cassie found Lindie at last.

CHAPTER SIXTY-FOUR

——

I T'S AN UNUSUAL THING, TO BE OLD AND STILL CLUTCHING THE
secrets of your childhood. Moving back to St. Jude, living, once again,
in the shadow of Two Oaks, Lindie found herself returning to a mind-
set she'd all but abandoned sixty years before. She waited for the end of
the day with bated breath, for the light to enter the master staircase, and
when darkness came, for the shadow of someone in the window she still
thought of as June's. And also, yes, she found herself reliving that awful
night—and all that had come because of it—more times than she could
count.

It was because of June that she'd moved back. Lindie had an official list of reasons for her colleagues at the university, and for the many
friends she and Isabel had shared before Isabel lost the fight to breast
cancer. "I love the quiet of a St. Jude evening," she told them as they
frowned at her across dinner tables, wondering why on earth this lauded
activist and professor emeritus would move back to the small Ohio town
where she'd been born. Or: "my family's house came up for sale and I
couldn't resist." But the real truth was that June, having finally raised
Cassandra and seen her off to a life in New York, had asked Lindie to
come back and help her. Whether moving back was an act of love, or a
way to repay a lifelong debt didn't much matter to Lindie, because she
got to live near June again.

Of course, June ended up not being around much in that small window they had before her brain cancer was diagnosed; only five years and
change, and much of that time June was not in residence. After a lifetime of begging June to devise ways Lindie might pay her debt, Lindie
very much appreciated the fact that her friend had finally come up with
something concrete. It was a relief to know Lindie was giving up her
beloved South Side house for June's freedom—just as June had done for
her so many years before.

Lindie respected June's privacy. It was no one's business what an old woman wanted to do with her twilight years, and, lord knew, June had cut her teeth on secrets—which was largely Lindie's fault—so Lindie understood that secrecy had become her way. Once Lindie was settled back into the wooden house of her youth—she claimed her father's bedroom, but, otherwise, things went back to almost exactly as they'd been—she received her instructions with a respectful nod, and she kept her opinions to herself:

"Cassie is not to know. You will send her one letter for every week that I am gone, on Tuesdays; here is the stack of letters—you will see they are dated and stamped. You will check my answering machine on a regular basis, and, when she calls, you'll call me immediately—here is my private mobile number—and tell me at once so I can get back to her myself. Above all, no one is to know where I am, or what I am doing." And Lindie nodded solemnly and saluted and tried not to look so delighted that June was finally getting what she'd been denied for decades, and tried not to notice how shabby Two Oaks was looking these days, or ask who'd be taking care of it in June's absence.

But the fact that Lindie respected June's way of doing things didn't mean she agreed with them. Cassie, for instance—poor Cassie. Would it really scandalize a twenty-first-century college student to discover that her grandmother had a life? And then, once June was diagnosed, why not just tell the poor girl she was sick? Why wait until it was too late for irrevocable wrongs to be righted? Why insist Lindie stay away from the girl, even after June was gone? Were the secrets June had kept truly that poisonous, even in the face of death?

Lindie had watched Cassie arrive in the frigid heart of December. She'd considered cutting her way across the snowy lawn at once, knocking on the door, and inviting the poor girl for Christmas dinner. But by then it was already too late. That was the problem with secrets, wasn't it? They festered and grew until they infected everything around them. Lindie couldn't just go to Cassie and pretend she didn't know June, or that she'd simply known her casually; June was Lindie's best friend, her first love, the person with whom she had covered up a murder. Lindie wasn't a good liar; she knew the truth would be written all over her, and what would come next would only further ravage Cassie, who was justifiably angry with her grandmother for seeming so cold and distant. Lindie knew Cassie would only see June's private dealings as further proof that June had not loved or trusted her.

But Lindie hadn't counted on Jack. That old devil. He'd promised June he'd keep everything hush-hush, understanding, as Lindie did, that hush-hush was June's way, and it was June's way or the highway. But Lindie supposed he figured that, once June was dead, and he was gone as well, giving his granddaughter what he wished he could have given his son, and his son's mother—a lifetime of happiness, or, in lieu of happiness, a vast sum of money—was his business, not June's.

June was rolling over in her grave.

Meanwhile, Lindie had been watching Cassie, spying on her with those movie stars—Jack's daughters—and with that boy Cassie liked. Watching how she seemed to finally blossom in their company, which was a relief, because before they showed up, Lindie had fretted about whether the girl was on suicide watch. And then the photographers arrived, and, though Lindie wasn't an Internet wiz, she was no Luddite, and she surmised that the lid had been blown off everything—that June and Jack's secret, which she had, for so long, been the only one to keep—was finally out of the bag.

Once the movie stars left, once the photographers found their next mark, Lindie supposed it was inevitable that Cassie would come for her. Lindie had kept June's secrets for decades, and that had been right; it had been June's way. But it was not Lindie's way; when Cassie asked her for the truth, she knew she was going to tell her. Every night before she went to bed, she could taste the bitterness of that truth on her tongue.

Betty called after the tuna casserole, filling Lindie in in euphemistic St. Judian terms. "Poor thing seems to want to know if you know anything about her grandmother's romantic life? But I just don't know if she'll get up the nerve to ask. And I told her I'm sure you don't know a thing."

Lindie's confession was upon her.

Finally, on a Sunday afternoon, Cassie knocked. Lindie waited just inside the front door and counted to ten. She didn't want to appear too eager; she knew what kind of effect that can have on the young. Of course she'd seen the girl grow, in June's pictures and stories, and, yes, she'd been spying ever since Cassie moved into Two Oaks, but, when Lindie opened the door, she was surprised at how fresh the girl looked. New. She was expert at a scowl, and she'd dressed herself like a sulky, half-baked version of herself—dirty hair, filthy T-shirt. Her nails were bitten down to the stumps of her fingertips. But Lindie could see the real Cassandra under all that camouflage.

"Hello, Cassie." Lindie had spent her early life pretending to be something she wasn't; not anymore. "I expect you want some lemonade."

CHAPTER SIXTY-FIVE

———

INDIE CARRIED THE TRAY OUT TO THE PORCH AND SET IT down in the small space where her father had once kept his rocking chair. The view hadn't changed since she was a girl; you can't say that about most places. Lawns, white porches as far as the eye could see, Two Oaks looming to their right, although the lawn could have done with a good mowing, but Lindie wasn't about to start there.

"You knew my grandmother." It wasn't a question.

Lindie poured the sweet yellow drink and cracked open a wax paper tube of Ritz. "In fact, your grandmother was my very best friend in the whole world."

"How come I've never met you then?" More than a trace of surliness. "Or even heard of you."

Lindie didn't mention the weekend Cassie's father had driven Cassie up from Columbus and Lindie happened to be in from Chicago. Cassie was all pigtails and giggles, too busy with *One Fish Two Fish* to note that funny old woman in the corner who wore her clothes like a man. Nor did Lindie mention the dozens of nights she and June had sat together on the sagging Two Oaks porch, fretting about Cassie's apartment and the middle-aged artist she seemed to be falling for, the dark street she lived on, the challenges of being an artist in today's financial climate.

Instead Lindie said, "June was a private person."

Cassie huffed in annoyed confirmation. Her foot was jiggling the whole porch. Lindie wanted to place her hand on the girl's knee, but they weren't there yet. "I found your letters," Cassie said. But she handed Lindie only one.

What surprised Lindie about that letter, the one Nick had shown Cassie, wasn't that she'd been bold enough to write it all those decades ago, on a windy, fall Chicago night, or that Cassie had smoked it out, but that June had kept it. Lindie'd always assumed June had destroyed the only piece of paper on which either of them had ever written about the worst night of their lives. And yet, all these years, Lindie had also kept a letter from those days—Artie's letter—as a reminder to stick to her own business. Perhaps she shouldn't have been surprised June had done the same.

"So you know Jack Montgomery was your grandfather?" No reason to beat around the bush.

Cassie looked at Lindie then, really looked at her for the first time. "Tell me everything."

Lindie began where it had ended: "I killed someone." Cassie was not expecting that, or any of the story that followed.

Lindie thought about Clyde Danvers often. She understood why June feared the ghost of what they'd done, and didn't ever want to talk or think about it; once June had made her choice, she couldn't—wouldn't—look back. June never wanted to talk about that night; she hated whenever Lindie brought it up. June was private, yes, and superstitious, but, more than that, the ins and outs of her passion with and for Jack had become entangled with Clyde's murder in an irrevocable way.

Over the years, Clyde had become a different animal in Lindie's eyes. His sacrifice was a sin she carried with her, every second of every day, the reason she could never be truly intimate with anyone—not even beloved Isabel. It was why she had decided not to become a mother. She had murdered a man, a particular man, with her bare hands, and not a soul could know about it. Strangely, Clyde Danvers became—or the knowledge of what she'd done to him became—like an old friend, the familiar shadow Lindie would often meet on her long nights of the soul. There was something to be gained by committing your worst crime before you were old enough to drive; it put all your subsequent foibles in perspective.

Lindie looped her tale back to the beginning, glass sweating in her hand as she filled Cassie in on Clyde Danvers and Eben Shaw and Jack Montgomery and June Danvers and Diane DeSoto and Alan Shields and *Erie Canal* and Ripvogle and Thomas and Apatha and Lemon Gray Neely himself. It seemed quite pressing, after keeping the whole sordid tale bottled up all those years, to pour it into Cassie, every last drop.

Cassie gulped and sipped and repoured; the lemonade was Apatha's recipe. As Lindie wove her tale of woe and passion, betrayal, redemption, blackmail, and revenge, the girl placed the Ritz crackers on her tongue and closed her mouth onto them whole, crunching them down. Lindie was glad she'd thought of snacks. Once she started talking, nothing could stop her. She felt lighter, remembering herself as a child: her blind spots, daring, and love.

When Lindie got to the night of the murder, Cassie leaned forward in her seat, gripped by the shock of it, and Lindie tried not to smile; it was pleasing to know it was as good a tale as she'd always believed it to be. She told Cassie about June standing with her forehead against her own, as day broke over the morning when June would ignore Jack, and Lindie would go to sleep with Clyde's blood on her hands. That's when Lindie came back into her old self—her furrowed hands, wrinkled knees, and bony wrists. She realized the sun had moved and the air had turned humid, that her back ached, that her throat was raw.

"But they didn't catch you?" Cassie asked.

"They didn't believe he was murdered," Lindie said, just as bewildered now as she'd felt all those years before, when the act itself had slipped off her back. By and large, the St. Judians had believed what the police told them: Clyde had last been seen putting back a few at the Thursday night cast party. Presumably at some point he'd driven west, and parked near Mr. Neely's old camp. He'd wandered off the main road and gotten lost only a few steps from the lake. He'd tripped on a rock. Rotten luck to land facedown on a large boulder, rotten luck indeed, rotten luck to not be found until after the weekend, when a summer's rain had washed away most of the blood and what was left of him sent up a stink that poor fisherman who found him couldn't ignore.

(And if there were suspicious grumblings surrounding this trip-and-fall story, well, no one had any proof of it having happened any other way. Although it was mighty convenient that the movie folks were the last to have seen Clyde at their final wrap party out at the development, and that they had taken off for Los Angeles the very next day, out of St. Jude's jurisdiction. Given how Clyde played poker, well, it wasn't impossible to imagine he might have angered more than one of those rougher-looking grips, the men who looked like gamblers. And what about Thomas, the driver? He was last seen the same night as Clyde.

And he'd been driving Clyde's Olds for that whole month; he'd probably gotten tangled up in the same mess, whatever it was. Rumor had it
there was even a warrant out for his arrest in Louisiana. No, no, some
said, it went higher up. A conspiracy. Clyde had attacked Ripvogle at the
party at Two Oaks. Ripvogle was powerful. He wouldn't stand for any
threats. He'd surely exacted his revenge.)

"We moved the next week," Lindie said. "It didn't matter that
Clyde was gone; my father took his disappearance as an omen that our
planned departure was necessary. I missed June's wedding, which they
postponed when Clyde went missing. Once his body was found, well,
Arthur didn't think they should proceed, but June insisted. It was a
small family ceremony."

"But why did she marry Artie?" Cassie's scowl was gone. Her knees
were pulled up to her chin.

"Because she chose him."

"But she didn't!" Cassie cried. "She only stayed in St. Jude because
Diane was going to tell on you. And once they found Clyde's body and
the case was closed anyway, and you were in Chicago, June could have
done whatever she wanted. She could have followed Jack to Los Angeles.
She could have been with him."

Cassie's exasperation was as familiar as Lindie's own breath. She told
Cassie what she'd told herself a thousand times, knowing it would do
little good. "That wasn't June's nature."

Cassie narrowed her eyes.

"You don't think I blame myself?" The world blurred, but Lindie
ignored the mess her eyes were making. "She didn't resent me. She never
made me pay. She resigned herself to the life my actions forced on her."
Lindie lifted her hands in a gesture of resignation and nodded in agreement with Cassie's frustration. "That made it so much worse."

Cassie didn't believe Lindie's suffering, nor did she care for it. Lindie
felt the need to make the girl understand.

"June is the first person I loved." A rush of embarrassment overtook
her, the likes of which she hadn't felt in many years; lord knew, she'd
found her tribe and identity soon after she left St. Jude and realized
there were plenty of other people—women and men—like her. And yet
that ancient shame hadn't gone away, not after forty years of marriage to

another woman, not when Lindie went back in time to remember that dull ache in her gut, looking up at that bedroom which had once contained the object of her desire.

"Your grandma didn't love me back, not the way I loved her anyway. I suppose I always believed that, once she got married, she'd be done with me. She was older than I was, from a better family, so much more sophisticated. Given all that happened, and that I moved out of state, well, I just assumed she'd never want to see me again. But your grandmother . . ." A sob surprised her, but she forged on. "Your grandmother kept in touch. She never wanted to talk about what happened that night, but I could see she believed it had bound us together. All those decades we lived apart, not a month went by when I didn't hear from her."

Cassie opened her mouth to object, but Lindie kept going.

"She came to visit when your daddy was a little boy. She brought him along." Cassie winced at this mention of her father. Lindie made a mental note to tell her all the stories she'd been saving up, about the constellation of summer freckles across that little boy's nose, and the forehead cowlick that bloomed the front of his buzz cut in twenty different directions. How polite he'd been, his "thank you, ma'am"s, the warm breath tucked into Lindie's neck when she'd carried him home from the movie theater.

"We were older then. I was in college. June was a wife and a mother. And I'd met someone. The first girl who could love me back." Susan, black-eyed Susan, whose skin tasted of grass cuttings; Susan, with a starburst of moles across her downy back. "I knew I had to tell June I'd fallen in love. I had to tell her the person I loved was a woman. I remember I waited until twenty minutes before she had to leave for the bus home. I blurted it out." Lindie swallowed in the memory of her fear. "You know what she said?"

"No."

"She smiled her big, beautiful smile and said, 'Lindie, love who you love.' And then, oh, Cassie, I cried." And she cried as she recounted it.

Cassie stiffened, unsatisfied. "Well, that's just great that you got to love who you loved."

Lindie chose not to remind the girl that being a woman who dressed like a man and loved women in the nineteen fifties and beyond was not exactly a walk in the park. Instead, she said, "And what if I told you I think she did too?"

Cassie eyed her skeptically.

"It took me a long time to realize what I'm about to tell you. I expect it'll take you a long time to accept it, if you ever do. But I know she found her version of happiness, or true love, or whatever you want to call it."

"That's convenient."

Lindie liked the girl's doubt. "I mean your daddy, honey. You should have seen June with that boy. She loved Adelbert more than life itself. Once, we were out on the Two Oaks porch—he was riding his bike back and forth up that very sidewalk, Artie was out of town on business, and I said out loud how sorry I was. I was always apologizing in those days; I knew it drove her crazy, but I couldn't help myself. Well, she stood right up and her hands turned into angry fists and she said, 'Don't you dare think I've had any less of a life for putting my boy at its center.' She could get worked up, and her eyes were kind of flashing in that way she had. You remember." Cassie nodded knowingly, laughing at the part of June they shared.

"June said, 'If I'd raised him out in Hollywood, you think he'd be happy? I've seen that poor little Esmerelda, how they parade her around with ribbons and her sad smile. I don't want that for my boy. I want this.'" Lindie gestured to the same yards June had. "I'd never seen it that way. I'd never thought that maybe, in saying good-bye to Jack, June had actually gotten the life she wanted."

"But she didn't love Arthur!"

"Of course she loved Arthur. Love doesn't work like that, one or the other. Don't you know that yet? She loved Arthur because Arthur was her husband. Because he was a good man who loved her back. She and Jack were two fires burning toward each other, consuming everything in sight. They'd have burned each other up if they'd tried to make a life together."

Cassie considered that. "And you knew my dad was Jack's son?"

"I could always see it in him, even when he was a little baby. Probably Arthur knew it too, but he never treated that boy any different. Arthur was a very good man." Lindie left out how awful she'd been to him. Time enough for that.

CHAPTER SIXTY-SIX

———

THEY WERE QUIET THEN, FOR A LONG SPACE OF TIME IN which one of the neighbors walked by with his spaniels, and they listened to the steady buzz of someone's lawn mower. It was getting toward evening now, and Lindie knew Cassie was hungry.

"Why didn't she tell me?" Cassie's question was steeped in anguish.

There was nothing to do but tell her the only part remaining. Maybe June would have seen it as a betrayal, but, as long as Lindie was being honest, she couldn't keep the last delicious bit—the best bit—to herself.

The bundle of postcards was waiting inside the top of Eben's secretary, back in the corner, where it belonged. Were June still alive, Lindie knew that she'd never, not in a million years, condone her showing these to Cassie. But Lindie wasn't in the business of keeping the secrets of the dead anymore.

Out on the porch, as the evening began its gentle slide toward darkness, Lindie handed the stack to a baffled Cassie. The girl flipped through the two dozen shiny postcards—depicting Caribbean waters, the Roman Colosseum, the Ponte Vecchio—before turning over the first in the stack, of the Eiffel Tower, and discovering June's familiar script filling the white space:

Dear Lindie—
    Would you believe we dined alone at the top of this beautiful landmark last night? I have no idea how J. arranged it, but there we were with steak frites and a bottle of the most delicious red wine I've ever tasted. Today we've got a tour of Versailles, then on to the Netherlands on Monday. He says I won't believe the tulips.
    Xx,
    J.

Cassie turned the card back over in her hand. Lindie smiled at her confusion, which she knew would soon turn to disbelief as Cassie read the next card, sent from Japan.

Dear Lindie—
We met the royal couple today. I felt dumb and tall, but J. looked dumber and taller. I kid. He says to tell you I ate raw octopus and that I even seemed to enjoy it. On to the countryside tomorrow! Thank you for watering my flowers, but truly, if they all die I'm not a bit concerned.
Xx,
J.

"But." Cassie flipped the postcard over, then checked the postage again. "I don't understand. This is from two years ago."

Lindie smiled.

"Wait," Cassie said, reading the next one. "You're saying my grandmother was in Tulum a year ago?" Incredulity had crept in.

Lindie didn't need to say anything, because Cassie kept reading, and, as she read, she began to understand. Shanghai, Turkey, St. Thomas. She dropped the cards onto her lap and slumped back into her chair. "She went with Jack?"

Lindie felt triumphant, as triumphant as if she'd gone too.

"But . . . how?"

"As far as I know, they only saw each other one time when Arthur was still alive. Arthur was down in Louisiana for the month, and June called and told me she'd told him she was going to visit me in Chicago. If he called, I should say she was sick with the flu and couldn't come to the phone. I didn't find out where she'd gone until afterward. She'd driven your father out west in three days. They spent two nights in a little hotel. She met Jack in Santa Monica for an evening at the beach, then turned around and drove on home."

"Elda told me about this," Cassie mumbled, nodding in dreamy recognition. "Why only once, though? Why take Dad to meet Jack, but never see him again until they were old?"

"You know men. Even though Jack was married to Diane, he apparently thought June coming all the way across the country meant she was considering leaving Arthur. According to June, he was ready to leave Diane right then, to move June in that very day. June realized she'd sent the wrong message. She'd just wanted to give him the chance to meet his son, but Jack wasn't like her. Most of us aren't. He couldn't put what he felt into a box, couldn't pretend he loved someone else, even if he'd married her." Nothing nasty needed to be said about Diane; that woman had had her share of heartbreak. "So June made the decision not to see Jack again, not as long as their spouses were alive. Well, Diane died not so soon after that, and Jack never remarried, but he respected June's wishes. He kept his distance, even from his own son. When Arthur started slowing down, I think June thought her chance with Jack might come soon, but then your parents had their accident. I can only imagine how heartbroken Jack was losing the chance to know his son. But if he blamed June, I never heard about it."

"And then, instead of getting to be with him, she was stuck with me," Cassie said.

"Is that what you think?" Lindie took Cassie's chin in her hand; it was the first time they'd touched, and their lonely bodies felt a gentle charge. Lindie turned Cassie's solemn face to her. "She adored you. Losing your father was the biggest heartbreak of her life, but the gift of it was getting to raise you."

Cassie frowned.

"I know. Believe me, I know. June was a tough customer. But she loved you. She wanted you to have what your father had—a normal life."

"She deserved more than that."

"Your grandmother was a patient woman. She believed if she and Jack were meant to have time together on this earth, then they would get it."

Cassie mused on this. Lindie knew the depths of her frustration, because she'd felt it too, too many times to count. "The week after you went to college, after she was back in Two Oaks, she called me up. She said, 'Oh, Lindie, it's just so empty.' I told her she should call Jack. Say he was on her mind. She acted like I'd lost my marbles."

They laughed together at that vision of June.

"But before she could even get up the nerve, he called her, asked her out on a date. I suppose I might have had something to do with that. And I suppose time had changed him in the right ways. He was not a gentle man when we knew him, Cassie. He was angry. Impulsive. But in his old age, Jack Montgomery was no longer so quick to pick a fight. All those years waiting for June had taught him how to be right for her." Lindie looked over at Cassie, hunched in the flaking wicker. She knew the poor girl was sad. She reached out and took her hand. "She got to live her life. Finally, after all those years, she got to live it." She shrugged. "So she didn't want to tell you about it. That's too bad. But maybe that's the only way she could enjoy it. Maybe it wasn't about you or me or any of the rest of us. Maybe it was finally about her."

Then each of their minds turned to the thought of those two lovely old faces smiling at each other over steak frites at the top of the Eiffel Tower. Lindie pushed away her regret. Cassie put off her self-pity. The girl and the old woman forgot themselves, just for the moment. They thought of Jack and June together, up there on that tower, looking out across the warm night, and it made them glad.

CHAPTER SIXTY-SEVEN

———

CASSIE DREAMED THAT NIGHT, A LUSCIOUS TWO OAKS dream, the kind she'd had before Tate arrived. The colors were bright, the sounds crisp, the touch of the house under her hands almost electric. Even as she was dreaming, she knew this would be the last dream of its kind, the last offering of this sort that Two Oaks—which was grateful for its healed roof, and eager to feel the joy Cassie had felt in the arms of that man who'd left and had not come back—would give her. When she collapsed into bed and sleep closed over her, the sadness rafting off of her was oceanic in its scope; it threatened to drown her. But when the house understood the source of her doubt, it knew how to cure what ailed her.

The blaze of a dream began with Cassie lifting out of her bed with a familiar rush of anticipation; the house was once again full of the St. Judians she'd come to know so well. They lined the hallway and the stairs. From the main floor rose a double helix of laughter. As before, the dream people slid apart to accommodate her passing.

She stepped down the stairs and the bodies parted. The stained-glass windows were lit up, speckling her in color as she found her way down. Every inch of her felt fully alive, as alive as she'd felt with Nick's body against hers.

It was a bright day in the dream, but the foyer was dark as usual. Cassie had thought that might be where the delighted laughter was coming from, but no, the front door stood open, and she knew, now, that the porch was the origin of that luscious, irresistible sound.

A child, his giggle burbling back into the house, and a mother's laugh too.

Cassie darted through the foyer now. She needed to see with her own eyes. The dream people pressed out of her way. At the lip of the door, she saw them, hundreds of them, St. Judians filling the sidewalk and the street, the cross street, the porches. All of them turned her direction, but not to see her. No, they were delighting in the sight of what Cassie could only hear. And so she stepped out onto the bright porch too, only it was the porch as it had once been—tiled and tidy—and there, to her right, at the center of it, she found them:

June and little Adelbert, a tangle of limbs. The boy's head tipped back in the sunlight, thrashing with wild glee in his mother's arms as her lips and hands tickled his small, perfect self. He laughed. Her laugh answered. If they knew anyone was watching them, they didn't let on.

LINDIE AWOKE TO banging on her door. She moved through the house the way she had as a girl, forgetting herself in the dark. She half expected to open the door and see Diane DeSoto standing there.

But it was Cassie. Over her shoulder, Lindie could make out the first line of dawn. The girl was dressed haphazardly; tears were streaming down her face. At the sight of Lindie, she clasped her arms around the old woman; her musky breath filled the room.

"I dreamed about them," she wept. It was hard to tell whether it was anguish or euphoria she felt. The room was dark, her mouth twisted. "You were right," she said. "It was what she wanted. To have Adelbert, for herself." At her own words, she began to cry harder. Lindie urged her to sit, but Cassie held her back at arm's length; she had her own confession.

"My art show—in New York." The words raced out of her. Lindie already knew all about the art show; she'd heard it from June's perspective—how shocked June had been to see the death of her son— the worst event of her life (worse, even, than giving up Jack, worse than discovering Lindie had killed Clyde)—laid bare on the walls of that New York gallery. Strangers leered over every inch of it, dissecting the trajectory her daughter-in-law had taken through the windshield, the sound of the Jaws of Life blasting through overhead speakers, and, worst of all, worst of everything, not just her son's—her dear Adelbert's— lifeless form slumped over the steering wheel, but the bottle of whiskey at his feet. June had been angry then, had had to fight for breath. She couldn't imagine that Cassandra could make such an ugly thing. She had to get out of there, and she'd pushed through the gawkers out onto the street, just to get air. But then Cassandra was upon her, and she was angry too, desperate for June's approval, blind in the way of the young.

"And then I said the most terrible things to her," June had told Lindie, hands shaking. "I suppose they were true because of what I was feeling at the time, but I could tell they stung her. And now she won't return my phone calls, Lindie, and I'm feeling so tired lately, so dizzy; I fear we'll never work it out."

But Lindie didn't tell any of that to Cassie, now weeping in her arms, lurching with her version of the story. A gurgle of agony rose through her when she recounted June's striding out to the sidewalk, and of following her there. Lindie thought of a glass of water, a chair, a cool washcloth against the girl's brow. But the best she could give her was herself.

"All I could think of was that it was my accident," Cassie cried. "That I was the survivor. And it's good to be honest, right? That's what an artist does. I'd worked so hard, and people liked it. But she hated it. I knew she was going to hate it and I was right. She walked from piece to piece and she . . ." Cassie shook her head, renewed in her heartbreak. "It was the last time I really saw her, Lindie. Why didn't she tell me she was sick?"

Lindie didn't have an answer for that, not one that would satisfy the girl—"she was afraid" was never going to be a salve. Instead, she held Cassie as she sobbed, then tucked her into the bed in Eben's room, a cup of warm milk on the bedside table.

Cassie mumbled as Lindie tiptoed from the room: "In my dream, she was happy. It was just her and her baby and it was the happiest I've ever seen her. The rest of us were watching, but she didn't care. It was exactly the same thing as at the gallery, wasn't it? She wasn't like us. She didn't need anyone else to witness how she felt. She only needed to feel it."

As THE MUGGY August passed, Cassie wanted to hear Lindie's whole story again, right from the beginning. She had follow-up questions: What had Lindie done with her life in the intervening sixty years? (Professor of Gender Studies, Activist, Adventurer.) What had happened to Apatha, really? (Upon Lemon's death, she'd taken her inheritance—every cent Lemon had made—and moved home to Louisiana, leaving Two Oaks to June and Arthur's care, living out her days in the quiet luxury she deserved.) What had become of Thomas? (Lindie didn't know; she'd never heard another word about, or from, him since the night he ran.)

It was some days later that Lindie finally asked about Nick. They'd taken to meeting out on the Two Oaks porch in the mornings and sitting together through the day, sifting and resifting through every grain of truth, but he had not been mentioned.

Cassie stammered at the mention of his name. "What about Nick?"

"Are you going to call him?"

"No." She scowled again like that girl who'd shown up on Lindie's porch. "No. No." But they both knew she couldn't deny the way he'd lit up her skin, how he'd made her feel as alive as her father's laugh had in that sweet dream. Cassie's mind returned to something elemental, to the vision of Nick approaching her on that first day on that very porch, the delicate turn of her name in his mouth, the sun lighting him up, the brief relief on his face at the sight of her. Maybe that did matter more than how things had ended.

It was not quite Labor Day, the summer fat and lazy, but soon to hunker down in hibernation. They moved from lemonade to whiskey sours. They ate dinner together, which improved their respective lots somewhat; between Lindie's popcorn and Cassie's frozen pizzas, they had complete meals. Lindie nudged Cassie with elderly concern. When was she getting that furnace repaired? Why not just hire those nice young men who mowed the rest of the lawns on the block? Why not find herself a lawyer, and have him make some inquiries to the executor of Jack's estate?

Cassie didn't bristle as Lindie had feared she might. In fact, she listened to the old woman quite sensibly and, more often than not, did as she suggested. She started showering regularly. She hired a handyman. The mail was another matter; it had piled so high inside the Two Oaks front door that they took to coming in the side entrance.

Come September, the tabloids howled anew: HANK TELLS ALL! TATE'S ASSISTANT TURNED REALITY STAR? TATE BETRAYED AGAIN! Lindie picked them up at the checkout and brought them home; the two women pored over the news of Hank's tell-all interview, in which she spilled about Tate's unknown paternity and Tate and Max's divorce, alleging that Tate had been the one to sleep with Margaret. None of it could be proven, of course, but it only confirmed what Cassie had suspected: that Hank had sold Cassie's film to the tabloids, not to mention stolen that stupid picture of the dog to frame her.

"Isn't that crazy?" Cassie said. "Why would she do that?"

"Because she was jealous."

Cassie looked at her with mouth agape. "No way." She held out her hands to take in her surroundings. "I'm an orphan who lives alone in the middle of nowhere. She is a chef yogini goddess who was the right hand of a movie star."

"Exactly—she worked for Tate. But Tate and Nick and Elda love you."

Cassie snorted derisively.

"And that's why you should call him."

"He should call me."

"He probably has."

No use arguing that point; Lindie had made Cassie unplug the landline if she wasn't going to answer it anyway.

"I'll bet he wrote you," Lindie said, after they finished the popcorn.

"Oh? And how do you bet that?"

"Because Nick knows you aren't a phone girl. And you don't have e-mail. Short of carrier pigeon, a letter's his only option."

Cassie sniffed. She picked up the empty bowl of popcorn and took it inside. But when Lindie came by the next day, the pile that had accumulated in the foyer was gone.

Most of it was crap Cassie didn't want. She piled the bills and legal-looking bits to one side, promising herself she'd tackle them the next day. The catalogs and junk mail went straight into the recycling bin. The personal mail, which was paltry indeed, consisted of two letters, both from Nick, written a few weeks apart. The first one had obviously been written long before Hank's tell-all:

Cassie,

I've called a couple times. I'm not surprised you haven't answered. I've been thinking of you; it sounds flat like that, small, but it's a truth that's so much bigger.

I wanted you to know T. found the picture of Benny in Hank's things. You were absolutely right to suspect her of stealing it and more—once T. confronted her, Hank confessed to everything. She's the one who leaked your pictures. She framed you. Needless to say, T. fired her. I've asked T. to be in touch with you herself, but will it surprise you that I suspect she won't?

I doubt it'll amount to much, but I hope you know how sorry I am. Please, if you want, please write or call—I'd love to hear your voice.

Nick

The second one was dated mid-August.

Cassie,

I keep thinking about what you said that first day we hung out in Montgomery Square. About if I ever felt like I was doing someone else's dirty work. If I wanted my own life. Well, I do. So I quit. Suffice it to say things have gotten crazy, even crazier than they were when we were there. The day I quit, T. told me you think she should start telling the truth about herself to the world. I think she believed that suggestion would so horrify me, I'd beg to keep working. Instead, I realized you might be one of the wisest people I know, and I might be one of the dumbest. Call? Write?

Nick

Cassie read it aloud to Lindie in a hesitant tremolo, hand fluttering up against her throat. The light was orange across the front parlor as Lindie watched Cassie from Apatha's yellow velvet couch. She recognized that gesture from the night she'd climbed to June's window and told her Jack was waiting. Some things can be denied, but this was genetic imperative.

CHAPTER SIXTY-EIGHT

———

THEY'D PLANNED ON A SMALL HOLIDAY, JUST THE THREE OF them. Nick thought it would be a riot to use the old silver, so they'd polished for a week—candelabras and platters, pitchers and utensils. Cassie just wanted to get a rotisserie chicken, but Nick and Lindie insisted on the turkey and the stuffing, the mashed potatoes two different ways (with and without skins), the green bean casserole with those crunchy onions on top. Lindie and Nick wanted split pants and leftovers for weeks. Cassie tolerated their desires because they were something like family now, and because Nick ran to her in the doorway and lifted her up and swathed her neck in a million kisses and begged for a proper feast until she relented, eyes flashing, cheeks aflame.

She was taking pictures of everything now, of the filigreed hinges on the doors, and Nick's eyelashes, and Lindie's hand upon the banister. And although Cassie knew it didn't make logical sense—there was no way a house could lean into a touch—it seemed as though Two Oaks was doing just that, like an old dog getting a scritch from the human who knew just where he needed it. The foyer was brighter these days, seemingly lit from within, the water once again running clear from the faucets, and the ants were gone.

In bed at night, after they made love, Nick and Cassie whispered about their plans for St. Jude. Already, some of Jack's money had come through. They'd start small, with the Two Oaks bedrooms. Then the empty buildings downtown. Artists, she whispered. Painters, musicians, writers. A place for them to come and make. A way to breathe life back into a town that believed it was dying.

"I told Elda I want to share Jack's money," Cassie said. "With her. And with Tate."

"You don't have to do that," Nick replied, pulling away.

She put her hand on his chest and felt his pulse return to normal. "I know," she said, kissing him. "But it's the right thing to do. What June would want. What I want."

And Two Oaks could hardly believe its luck. Lindie was back. She was startlingly old, yes, but absolutely recognizable in the sure and enthusiastic manner with which she invigorated the stairs with her lively step. Cassie and Nick filled the bedroom with their human hopes and pleasures, and watched movies together on the yellow couch, and even, sometimes, made love on the dining room table—something that had not occurred since the succulent, early days of Lemon and Apatha's marriage.

Did all this togetherness mean the sisters would return? When would the artists arrive? Would there be children? The house didn't want to be greedy, but it hoped the human joy it felt heralded the promise of so much more.

THANKSGIVING MORNING, they were in the kitchen when the doorbell rang. Cassie dropped the *Joy of Cooking* on the kitchen table with a relieved "I'll get it," and Nick and Lindie exchanged an exasperated look.

The doorbell rang again, a proper ring; she'd had that fixed as soon as the first bit of Jack's money arrived.

Before Cassie even opened the door, she sensed that a troop of people had gathered out there. She wondered, for a moment, if she was dreaming, especially as she opened the door and found Elda standing before her, a pumpkin pie in hand. But these people on her porch were loud and unruly as the dream people had never been. They swarmed her. Enfolded into Elda's bosom, she realized that they were Elda's people, her brood, her babies, and that they had brought Thanksgiving.

Boys scrambled up the porch railing, men and women air-kissed and high-fived and strode into the house. "Richie, get down from there pronto," Elda bellowed. She took Cassie in with a long, careful look. "Next year, you come to me."

They came inside, all of them. Twenty? Twenty-five? They didn't hold still long enough for Lindie to get a number. Little boys jumped on the furniture. Wives took over the kitchen. Elda's sons clapped Cassie on the back and called her "cuz." They'd flown into Columbus the night before. They'd rented a party bus. They'd hired a caterer who'd be here within the hour.

"I found us a copy of *Erie Canal*!" Elda told her, as one of the sons brought in a projector and a folding screen. "I know football isn't Nick's thing."

It was a good move, the sneak attack, a real feat to pull it off, and Nick and Lindie and Cassie appreciated the many sacrifices, small and large, that had been made in order to bring this unwieldy crew all the way to rural Ohio. Cassie accepted wine. She sat on the yellow couch. Two Oaks was finally like the Two Oaks of her dreams—bustling, alive, full.

Eventually, they sat. Adult table, children's table, food for miles. Elda offered an Apache blessing, and reminded the crew of the smallpox blankets, because, as much as she loved the holiday, it's important to remember our history. A Catholic prayer was uttered in Spanish. Cassie stood and tinked her glass and thanked them all for coming. She looked out over everyone gathered in that nut brown room with its chocolate tapestries, and thought: this is my family. Nick. Lindie. The grand Hernandez hurricane. She was filled, first, with gratitude, and then with sorrow. So many hadn't made it: Her mother. Her father. June. Jack. Arthur. Diane.

Tate. Yes, even Tate.

And then, before she could sit again, the doorbell.

They, all of them, lifted their heads. They watched her go, through the foyer, toward the light.

She opened the door.

Tate. Tate Montgomery herself, nervous and taut. She held a painting in her hand. The painting, Cassie saw, was of her grandmother. Impossibly young, flawed and true, looking out at them as though she could see them there, together, on her porch; as though she had been waiting for many years to witness this moment.

"Elda invited me." Tate's voice shook as her hand lifted the painting. "And this was in his things."

Cassie saw that Tate feared, even suspected, she might be turned away; she had risked that possibility by coming. But she had come.

Cassie took the painting. She held the door open with her strong and sturdy back. A rattling of leaves scuttled across the wide, old porch. One after the other, the women went inside.

ACKNOWLEDGMENTS

———

THERE WAS A REAL Lemon Gray Neely. He was my grandmother's great-uncle, a wildcatter who built a beautiful yellow brick mansion in the middle of small-town Ohio in 1895. But that's where he and the character I've named after him diverge. I'd like to thank Mr. Neely posthumously for allowing me to borrow his moniker, a few of the facts about him, and imagine everything else.

There is no St. Jude, but the town was inspired by a real place, the one in which my grandmother was born in 1906. On my research trip for this novel, my mother and I were welcomed with open arms by the infinitely kind Brenda and Craig McDermitt and their daughters, especially Malika and Marketa; they live in, and are in the process of restoring, Mr. Neely's home, which I tried to capture on paper as best I could. These lovely people seemed to think nothing of welcoming a stranger—armed with a tape measure and a camera—into their home for days on end; it goes without saying this book would never have been written without their immense generosity.

I received a great deal of historical insight into Auglaize County from my cousin Kathy Schwartz, who grew up very close to where I imagined St. Jude to be; local historian and font of knowledge George Neargarder, who welcomed me into his home to share his remarkable personal archives; the well-informed librarians at the St. Marys Community Public Library; and Kalvin Schanz, who spied me taking a picture of Mr. Neely's home in 2010, and subsequently welcomed my extended family for a daylong tour of the town, whetting my appetite to tell this story. Liz Silver was incredibly helpful with legal advice about inheritance in the state of California. Mark Wynns at TCM handed me *Raintree County* on a platter, which proved to be an apt production model for *Erie Canal*. Charlie Malloy at Fastest Labs of Columbus schemed DNA outcomes and percentages with me so I sounded like I knew what I was talking about. Any errors or embellishments in the spots where this work of fiction intersects with real life are mine alone.

Emily Raboteau is the best writing partner (and bosom friend) I could ask for; without our biweekly meetings—and her consistent, careful feedback—this book simply would not have been written. Jennifer Cayer read with her perennially keen, kind eye. Elisa Albert, Dan Blank, Julia Fierro, Tammy Greenwood, Brian Gresko, Nicole C. Kear, Victor LaValle, Caroline Leavitt, Kimberly McCreight, and Amy Shearn are just a few of the literary friends to whom I regularly turn for companionship and inspiration.

Anne Hawkins is an extraordinary, wise true north who has never steered me wrong. Christine Kopprasch has remained a steadfast booster of, and believer in, this project, even as she's gone on to sparkle elsewhere.

Lindsay Sagnette championed this book from the start; I'm proud to call such a powerful, smart editrix my partner. Rebecca Welbourn, Kayleigh George, and Rachel Rokicki raise the bar on a daily basis; they're a remarkable team who believes in my work more than I do. And I'm infinitely grateful to Maya Mavjee and Molly Stern for giving me a literary home.

Rose Fox and Hilary Teeman have proven themselves invaluable; this final draft would not have been achieved without them. The work of Susan Brown, Christine Tanigawa, and Heather Williamson is meticulous and vital. Lauren Dong and Elena Giavaldi have made this book more beautiful than I ever imagined. And the whole team at Crown, from foreign rights to the sales team—and everyone in between—has my deepest thanks and admiration.

Amy March opened her exquisite home and cared for my child for days on end. Those others who cared for him over the course of this writing—too many to name—are my heroes. As are the many friends I'm blessed to call family, who've helped in immeasurable ways (you know who you are).

The family I'm blessed to call family is, well, the best. Kai Beverly-Whittemore read and cheered and is ever my closest friend; thanks to her, I'm now lucky to call Rubidium Wu my kin. Robert D. Whittemore is a lodestar of support and belief. David Lobenstine is my rock and my companion. Quentin Lobenstine is my bright sun, who has taught me more about storytelling than I ever knew before. And I can't imagine writing a book without Elizabeth Beverly, who schemes, travels, measures, brainstorms, troubleshoots, researches, asks, drives, reads, listens, welcomes, houses, feeds, distracts, counsels, and believes like no other person I know. She's the one who said, "The name Lemon Gray Neely has always sounded, to me, like a character in a book." Well, thanks to you, now he is.

SOURCES

Bergen, Candice. *Knock Wood*. New York: Simon & Schuster, 1984.

Bosworth, Patricia. *Montgomery Clift*. New York: Harcourt Brace Jovanovich, Inc., 1978.

Cohan, Steven. *Masked Men: Masculinity and the Movies in the Fifties*. Bloomington: Indiana University Press, 1997.

Dmytryk, Edward. *It's a Hell of a Life but Not a Bad Living*. New York: Times Books, 1978.

Fisher, Carrie. *Postcards from the Edge*. New York: Simon & Schuster, 1987.

———. *Wishful Drinking*. New York: Simon & Schuster, 2008.

Gilberg, Robert. *The Last Road Rebel—and Other Lost Stories*. True Directions, 2015.

Halberstam, David. *The Fifties*. New York: Random House, 1993.

Harvey, James. *Movie Love in the Fifties*. New York: Da Capo Press, 2001.

———. *Watching Them Be*. London: Faber & Faber, Inc., 2014.

Howard, Robert. *The Life and Times of Memorial High School*. Self-published, 2012.

———, ed. *The St. Marys Anthology*. Self-published, 2013.

Lev, Peter. *The Fifties: Transforming the Screen 1950–1959*. Oakland: University of California Press, 2003.

McAlester, Virginia, and Lee McAlester. *A Field Guide to American Houses*. New York: Alfred A. Knopf, 1984.

Neargarder, George L. *Auglaize County Postcard Images*. Auglaize County Historical Society, 2008.

Parker, Sachi. *Lucky Me*. New York: Gotham Books, 2013.

Pomerance, Murray, ed. *American Cinema of the Fifties*. New Brunswick: Rutgers University Press, 2005.

Roberts' Illustrated Millwork Catalog. E.L. Roberts & Co., 1903; Mineola, N.Y.: Dover Publications, 1988.

Schatz, Thomas. *Boom and Bust: American Cinema in the 1940s.* Oakland: University of California Press, 1997.

Swift, Earl. *The Big Roads.* New York: Houghton Mifflin Harcourt, 2011.

Williamson, C. W. *History of Western Ohio and Auglaize County.* W. M. Linn & Sons, 1905.

ABOUT THE AUTHOR

———

MIRANDA BEVERLY-WHITTEMORE is the author of three other novels: *New York Times* bestseller *Bittersweet; Set Me Free,* which won the Janet Heidinger Kafka Prize, given annually for the best book of fiction by an American woman; and *The Effects of Light.* A recipient of the Crazyhorse Prize in Fiction, she lives and writes in Brooklyn.